Praise for the Page Murdock Novels

"An exciting Western loaded with intrigue, suspense, and clever plot twists. One of Estleman's best, a smart, tightly wrapped story."
*—Publishers Weekly* on *The Book of Murdock*

"Estleman is best known for his mysteries, but he's equally adept at Westerns, as he demonstrates again here. His novels—regardless of type—are peppered with humor, irony, and melancholy, and, as a narrator, Murdock delivers all three. A clever plot and a satisfying conclusion round out a very enjoyable read."
*—Booklist* on *The Book of Murdock*

"A vivid, fast-paced Western adventure brilliantly presented by a masterful storyteller."
*—Publishers Weekly* on *The Branch and the Scaffold*

"A rollicking tale with characters Mark Twain would be proud to call his own."
*—The Denver Post* on *The Undertaker's Wife*

"A historical Western in mirror-smooth mahogany prose . . . Louis L'Amour looks down with envy."
*—Kirkus Reviews* on *Port Hazard*

"A wildly entertaining read with great period atmosphere and dialogue." *—Booklist* on *Port Hazard*

## • BOOKS BY LOREN D. ESTLEMAN •

Kill Zone

Roses Are Dead

Any Man's Death

Motor City Blue

Angel Eyes

The Midnight Man

The Glass Highway

Sugartown

Every Brilliant Eye

Lady Yesterday

Downriver

Silent Thunder

Sweet Women Lie

Never Street

The Witchfinder

The Hours of the Virgin

A Smile on the Face of the
   Tiger

City of Widows*

The High Rocks*

Billy Gashade*

Stamping Ground*

Aces & Eights*

Journey of the Dead*

Jitterbug*

Thunder City*

The Rocky Mountain Moving
   Picture Association*

The Master Executioner*

Black Powder, White
   Smoke*

White Desert*

Sinister Heights

Something Borrowed,
   Something Black*

Port Hazard*

Poison Blonde*

Retro*

Little Black Dress*

Nicotine Kiss*

The Undertaker's Wife*

The Adventures of Johnny
   Vermillion*

American Detective*

Gas City*

Frames*

The Branch and the
   Scaffold*

Alone*

The Book of Murdock*

Roy & Lillie: A Love Story*

The Left-Handed Dollar*

Infernal Angels*

Burning Midnight*

Alive!*

The Confessions of Al
   Capone*

Don't Look for Me*

Ragtime Cowboys*

You Know Who Killed Me*

*A Forge Book

# MURDOCK'S LAW

AND

# CITY OF WIDOWS

· LOREN D. ESTLEMAN ·

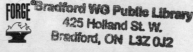
A TOM DOHERTY ASSOCIATES BOOK / NEW YORK

This is a work of fiction. All of the characters, organizations, and events portrayed in these novels are either products of the author's imagination or are used fictitiously.

MURDOCK'S LAW AND CITY OF WIDOWS

*Murdock's Law* copyright © 1982 by Loren D. Estleman

*City of Widows* copyright © 1994 by Loren D. Estleman

A Forge Book
Published by Tom Doherty Associates, LLC
175 Fifth Avenue
New York, NY 10010

www.tor-forge.com

Forge® is a registered trademark of Tom Doherty Associates, LLC.

ISBN 978-0-7653-8357-0

Our books may be purchased in bulk for promotional, educational, or business use. Please contact your local bookseller or the Macmillan Corporate and Premium Sales Department at 1-800-221-7945, extension 5442, or by e-mail at MacmillanSpecialMarkets@macmillan.com.

First Edition: February 2016

Printed in the United States of America

0  9  8  7  6  5  4  3  2  1

# CONTENTS

# MURDOCK'S LAW

# CHAPTER 1

The hearse was drawn by a pair of arrogant-looking matched blacks with coats that shone like stretched satin, plumed bridles, and the general appearance of never having been whipped up above a trot. Black bunting framed the casket between the side windows, an expensive affair of polished mahogany with gold-plated handles under a mound of lilies and hyacinth. The driver, a square, rough-handed Irishman whose nose glowed redder than the early spring chill dictated, looked bored and thirsty. The fellow beside him, rotund in a black cutaway, striped trousers, and a high silk hat screwed down to the eyes, looked inconsolable. I took him for the undertaker. The richer they get the sadder they look.

There was a respectable procession behind, led by a gray-whiskered preacher and a stout, middle-aged woman weeping behind a black veil, but before they reached my end of the street I stepped inside to avoid having to doff my hat. After living in it for four days I wasn't so sure my scalp wouldn't peel off with it.

A bell mounted overhead jangled when I closed the door. Racks of rifles and shotguns lined the walls of the shop, their straight black barrels glistening smugly in the light streaming in through the big front window. Standing out from the walls, wooden-framed glass cases containing more firearms in various stages of assembly formed a square within a square. The place smelled sharply of lubricating oil.

Behind the cases, at a bench littered with springs and rags and short screws and miscellaneous instruments, a scrawny old man was filing the rough edges off the inside of a rifle barrel clamped in a wooden vise. He said without turning that he'd be with me directly. His Swedish accent would sink a ferry.

"Who died?" I asked.

"Town marshal." The file rasped shrilly against the jagged steel.

"Shot?"

"Choked on a piece of steak."

I wondered if he was joking. He didn't strike me as the type. "That must have come as a surprise in this town. I hear folks around here raise some hell from time to time."

"From time to time."

"Not that I've seen any evidence of it."

He squatted to peer inside the barrel. His profile was clean but beginning to blur under the chin. He wore a massive blond moustache streaked with white that swept to the corners of his jaw and appeared to have sucked all the hair from the top of his bald head.

"What'd you expect, shooting?" he said then. "All day long, every day, like you read in the penny dreadfuls? There ain't that much lead in Montana." He blew through the barrel and scraped a thick finger around inside. Apparently satisfied, he straightened and turned to face me. His gray-blue eyes took me in swiftly from dusty crown to caked spurs. "What's your business?"

"Page Murdock. I wired you last week from Helena looking for a Deane-Adams. You said you had one."

"Hell of a long ride just for a gun."

"I was coming anyway."

His eyes narrowed. "You some kind of law?"

"Does it show?"

"You could be on one side or the other, from the look of you. In this business I see my share of both."

"Maybe you've seen Chris Shedwell lately," I said. "My boss got a report he's on his way here. He's wanted for a mail-train robbery near Wichita two years ago."

He shook his head. "Thought you boys favored those." He indicated the Army Colt in my holster. "Deane-Adams only shoots five."

"I know. I used to own one."

"You only got four if you keep the chamber under the hammer empty," he pointed out.

"I don't."

"Shoot your foot off someday." He drew a ring of keys from his pocket and bent to unlock a drawer in the bottom of the case between us. From its depths he lifted a skeletal piece and handed it to me.

It was a slim, lightweight .45 with an octagonal barrel, a smooth cylinder, and a skinny butt showing no more curve than a spinster's bodice. It looked exactly like the one I had lost the year before somewhere on the tracks between Fargo and Bismarck, except that this one had a mother-of-pearl grip.

"Who ruined it?" I asked.

"Tinhorn from Minnesota. He won it at stud and paid me to fit the new grip. Never picked it up. Miner caught him shaving the ace of clubs and carved him up with a pocketknife. They buried him in pieces."

"How soon can I have it refitted?"

"Tomorrow. Be twenty dollars for the gun and the work. Half in advance."

I gave him ten and got a receipt.

After the comparative silence of the shop, the noise on the street was terrific. Once a mining town, Breen had died when the vein east of the Smith River played out, only to be born again as the cattle industry stretched into the foothills between the Big and Little Belt Mountains. Merchants had swarmed in armed with canned goods and coal oil and curtain material and all the other paraphernalia of eastern culture, just as they had in countless other boomtowns across the Northwest in the eighteen-seventies, so that you couldn't tell Helena from Sutter's Mill, Bismarck from Dodge. I washed the taste of civilization out of my mouth in one of fourteen saloons that faced each other across a street as wide as a pasture and got directions to the marshal's office.

It was a solid affair built of logs, with weatherboard on the outside to give visitors the impression that it wasn't. A square of brown butcher paper was nailed to the door with GONE TO THE FUNERAL penciled across it in an educated hand. I waited.

After ten minutes or so a lean twist of hide in a frock coat and striped trousers strode down the boardwalk with a key in his hand. The face under a round-brimmed Spanish hat was leathern, cracked at the corners of the eyes and stretched taut across a very straight nose that came almost to a point. He wore a drooping black moustache and a gold star the size of a tea saucer attached by tiny gold chains to a nameplate on his vest. The nameplate was blank, but the words "City Marshal, Breen, M.T." were engraved on the star in the center of a lot of scrollwork.

I said, "You must be the new city marshal."

He stopped short, fingers dangling near the ivory butt of a Navy Colt on his right hip. I have that effect on people.

"You have the advantage." His voice was thin and tight, like everything else about him.

I gave him my name and got out the simple star that said DEPUTY U.S. MARSHAL, no chains or scrollwork. "It's not as nice as yours."

"You're the one wired Bram about Shedwell coming," he said.

"Bram?"

"Abraham Arno." He sounded like a schoolmaster prompting a slow pupil. "We just put him in a hole north of town."

"Did he really choke on a piece of steak?"

"That's what his widow says. I think she poisoned him, but that's only the opinion of a temporary marshal." He unlocked the door and went inside, leaving it open. I closed it behind me.

There was clapboard on the inside, whitewashed and broken up only by the stovepipe, a gun rack, a single barred window looking out on the dusty street, and a sheaf of wanted dodgers tacked to the wall behind the desk, brown and curling. A partition across the back partially screened a row of unoccupied cells beyond. Over everything hung a heavy odor of boiled coffee and cigars.

"You ride for Judge Blackthorne." He pegged his hat next to the door, passed through a gate in an oak railing, and took a seat in a wooden swivel behind the desk. He looked younger with his abundance of black hair exposed, somewhere in his late twenties. "I hear when folks in Helena get bored they stick him in a pit with a grizzly just to see fur fly."

"That's him. What about Shedwell?"

He slipped an ivory comb from the inside breast pocket of his coat and glided it through his pompadour. I watched him wipe bay rum off the teeth with a red silk handkerchief before putting it away and calculated the depth of my dislike for him.

"No sign of him yet," he said. "I think someone was having fun with your boss."

"That'll be the day. Are you as much law as they got around here?"

He lost his good nature. His eyes were murky pools of no color you could put a name to. "You ride a fast mouth for one man."

"They give you deputies?"

It took him a moment to answer. His eyes never moved. "Two full-time. And the geezer that watches the place when there are prisoners. Why?"

"They all been looking for Shedwell?"

"They're deputies, aren't they?"

"Do they even know what he looks like? Do you?" When he didn't answer, I pulled out the soggy reader I'd had plastered to my chest for fifty miles and peeled it open under his nose. It featured a fair likeness of the man I was after from his night-riding days, under a line offering a thousand dollars for his capture. The marshal studied it a moment, then leaned back, squeaking his chair.

"Haven't seen him."

"He was pretty fresh when this was done," I pressed. "He's aged some since."

He shook his head. His expression was condescending. I said, "What do they call you?"

"Yardlinger. Oren Yardlinger."

I blinked. "And you let them?"

"What the hell's that supposed to mean?" Pale slashes showed on his cheeks like healed-over scars.

I placed the paper on his blotter. "Tack it up. Have your men look at it and let me know if he shows. I'll be around."

"Why should he?" Something of his normal color had returned. "I hear he's selling his gun these days. There's no business for him here."

"How many men did you bury last month?"

"Six, but what's that got to do with anything?"

"How many of them died in bed?"

"One." He hesitated. "He held on for two weeks after a

crazy half-breed split his skull with an oak chair over at the Glory."

I tapped the bulletin I'd given him. "When you've got something you'll find me at the Freestone Inn. Room twelve."

I'd dropped my valise off at the hotel on my way into town. Returning, I got out my city clothes and a razor and went down to the bathhouse, where I spent a leisurely half hour scraping off the trail dust and the worst of my whiskers. Afterward I left my riding clothes to be laundered and mounted the stairs to my room, drowsiness spreading through me like the warmth from a shot of whiskey. But in the carpeted hallway outside I stopped.

You start to develop a sixth sense after you've been on the frontier a while. Camping in the desert, you know before you pull your boots on that there's a scorpion curled up in one of them. Riding along the trail, you feel a road agent waiting for you around the next bend. Those who didn't learn to detect the unseen signs of danger didn't last long enough to unpack their bags. That was how I was sure without opening the door that there was someone in my room.

And since whoever it was hadn't bothered to ask my leave, I could only assume that he felt it wouldn't matter much longer.

# CHAPTER 2

Once in Missoula I had waited outside a cabin for two and a half hours until the killer who was laying for me got impatient and tried to shoot his way out. I put three slugs in him sight unseen before he reached the door. I could have played it that way this time, except that I was too tired for stealth and too mad to give whoever it was the satisfaction. Instead I kicked the door open and dived in headfirst, sliding on my stomach with my Colt clasped in front of me in both hands. I interrupted a game of solitaire on the bed.

The player, seated on the edge of the mattress, was thin in a sickly sort of way, with pinched shoulders and a sunken chest and hollows in his cheeks that were accentuated by the curve of his reddish side-whiskers. Startled, he dropped the deck and swept aside the skirt of his Prince Albert to get at a small pistol stuck in his waistband.

"Call!" I shouted.

He froze with his hand on the curved butt. I could hear his labored breathing. Slowly he raised his hands to shoulder level.

There was another man standing next to the window, but his hands were empty and clear of his body. For what seemed a long time I lay motionless, the .44 cocked and commanding the middle ground between the two, before the thin man spoke. He had the kind of voice that made you want to clear your throat.

"You always come into a room like that, or is this a special occasion?"

"It varies with my mood." I got up, keeping them both covered. "Do you always break into other people's rooms just to play cards?"

"No one broke anything," he said. "The clerk let us in while you were bathing."

"Nice town. The merchants and the burglars work together. Who goes to jail, the marshal?"

"The responsibility is mine."

I studied the man at the window. He was small, not much larger than a twelve-year-old boy, but with a large head, and looked so dapper in spats, striped trousers, and a black coat with a pinched waist that I was reminded of a poster I had seen of General Tom Thumb in full uniform standing in the palm of a man's hand. His black hair was combed into a fussy lock on his forehead, which, together with his spadelike chin whiskers and moustache waxed into points, turned him into a junior-size Napoleon III. He had liquid brown eyes.

"I persuaded the clerk to allow us to wait for you in your quarters." His French accent was guttural. "It was unseemly for men of our reputation to be seen standing about a hotel lobby. We have tampered with none of your things."

I said, "Who are you? Just so I can introduce you to Marshal Yardlinger when we get to the jail."

The thin man chuckled dryly. I glared at him and he fell silent.

"I am Michel d'Oléron, Marquis de Périgueux," the little man replied, bowing his head slightly and exposing a bald spot like a monk's tonsure. "You may call me Périgueux if you wish."

"I'll think about it."

He turned his palm upward, indicating his partner. "The gentleman you found too slow with the firearm is Dick Mather, owner of the Six Bar Six, across which you doubtless rode on your way to Breen. We are both ranchers. As of last month, I control something over two million acres of grassland between Monsieur Mather's property and the Big Horn Mountains in Wyoming Territory."

"That's a bite to chew for someone from Europe," I said.

He smiled complacently without showing teeth. "It is larger than Corsica and Sardinia combined."

"Thanks. Now that I've had my geography lesson, I'd appreciate it if you and Dick would pile all your excess iron on the floor at the foot of the bed."

"But of course. Monsieur?"

Carefully, the emaciated one the Frenchman called

Mather drew the derringer from his waistband, got up to place it on the floral carpet, and backed away. I looked at Périgueux.

"I am unarmed, monsieur. *Voilà*." He unbuttoned and swung open his coat. His vest was yellow silk, with an ornament of red and gold dangling from one pocket.

"Nice fob," I said.

He fondled it. "It was presented to me by the late emperor. Unfortunately, military medals have no place in civil life, and so it must serve the purpose of assisting me in learning the time of day. It is all I have left to remind me of a glorious era."

"Show me the watch."

He raised his eyebrows. There were traces of gray in them, like dust in snuff. I explained.

"I cornered a rapist in Deer Lodge a couple of years ago who had a derringer attached to a fob like that one. I'm still carrying the ball."

With a continental shrug, he reached two fingers into the pocket and produced an ornate gold watch with a capital N engraved on the lid, encircled by oak leaves. I nodded. He replaced it.

"You and Louis Napoleon must have been pretty tight."

"I was a marshal of France."

"I didn't think the nobility got along with the Bonapartes."

"It is to them that I owe my title. It was bestowed upon me along with certain lands when I married into the family."

"Cozy."

"*Pardon?*"

I shook my head and put up the Colt to retrieve Mather's gun from the floor. Unloading it, I placed the cartridges on the writing desk next to the door and returned the piece to its owner. "Now, let's all have a seat and discuss why I shouldn't turn you over to the marshal."

"To begin with," growled Mather, "the marshal takes his orders from us."

I scaled my hat onto the bed and leaned back against the desk. Périgueux had claimed the room's only upholstered chair, while Mather had resumed his perch on the edge of the bed.

"Isn't that the city council's responsibility?" I asked.

"Indeed," responded the Frenchman. "In addition to the Six Bar Six, Monsieur Mather maintains controlling interest in two local saloons, which qualifies him for his elected position on the council. I hold no property in Breen. To do so would be just a formality in any case, since I am now the largest rancher in Montana and my word alone carries certain weight."

Mather was growing impatient. Two feverish spots of red the size of half-dollars showed high on his cheeks. Together with his otherwise sallow complexion and wasted frame, they branded him a consumptive. "Oh, get on with it, Mike!" He nailed me with glistening eyes. "We understand you're a United States marshal."

"Deputy," I corrected. "Yardlinger didn't waste any time spreading the word around, did he?"

"It was not he who told us," interjected Périgueux. "He mentioned it to one of his deputies, who got word to me at the Breen House, where I am staying on business. I decided to send a messenger for Monsieur Mather."

"All that for little me," I said.

"Yes." If the Frenchman had picked up on the sarcasm, he didn't respond to it. "Ever since Marshal Arno's death two days ago we have been discussing what steps we can take to alleviate the current situation, and it would appear that your arrival is most timely. To be succinct—"

"Too late."

Again he ignored my bad manners. "We wish to engage your services."

"We need a town marshal," Mather said.

"What's wrong with Yardlinger?"

"Monsieur Yardlinger," said the Frenchman, "is a boy. His experience—"

"There are no boys west of the Mississippi."

Périgueux looked patient. "Yes, we are familiar with your frontier slogans. The fact remains that his experience has not prepared him for the duties of a man in his position. This is not true in your case. Your reputation, Monsieur Murdock, precedes you."

I used a word I'd learned long ago in the cavalry. Even Périgueux was taken aback. "I do not understand."

"I don't know how to say it in French," I replied. "So far I haven't heard anything to change my mind about placing both of you under arrest. Why don't you start by telling me what's coming up that you'd rather I didn't know about until I'm pinned to that pretty gold badge."

"You see?" Mather told the Frenchman. "We should have come right out with it at the beginning, like I said."

The Marquis sighed. Why did I have the feeling I was watching a carefully rehearsed play?

"It is not really much of a revelation, since you have been inquiring around about it before this," he said. "You know that a certain man, a certain gunman, is expected here shortly."

"Shedwell."

"Yes. But you do not know why, and neither do we. For some weeks past, there have been difficulties here. Perhaps you have heard something of them in Helena."

"Range war," I acknowledged.

"Yes, but only a little one." He emphasized how little with his thumb and forefinger. "The small ranchers, they are jealous of the big ranchers and the grass and water we control. Until now the situation has been of small consequence—a fight with the fists between cowboys from different spreads, an occasional bullet through a window, aimed high so that no one is hurt. The presence of a hired killer, however, changes everything."

"Who's hiring him?"

He spread his delicate hands, hunching his shoulders at the same time in a Latin show of befuddlement. "Your guess is equal to mine, monsieur. Certainly not we. We have our suspicions, of course."

"I'll bet you do."

Mather said, "We can't have this kind of thing happening. If the small ranchers start hiring iron we'll have to retaliate, and then we've got a full-scale war on our hands. The next thing you know, the army will step in like they did in Lincoln County, and then everybody loses."

"What do you want me to do? I'm planning to arrest Shedwell anyway."

"That is precisely what we do not want," spoke up Périgueux. "These small fry, as I believe they are sometimes called, crave a lesson in competition. As a servant of the federal government, your duty is simply to take him into custody. As city marshal and keeper of the local peace, you would be expected to deliver a somewhat more stringent message to those who would endanger it."

I invested the better part of a minute picking apart his speech and turning the pieces over in my head before I grinned and said, "Mr. Marquis—"

"Please. Périgueux."

"That's got to be the politest way anyone ever tried to hire someone else to kill a man."

The mood in the room changed, grew lighter. The pair exchanged triumphant looks. Said the Frenchman: "Then may we assume that we have reached accord?"

"You may assume that if you aren't out of this room in two minutes I'll pump you both so full of lead you'll reach the lobby without using the stairs."

There was a very long pause. It might have gone even longer had not someone knocked at the door. I looked questioningly at Périgueux, who shook his head stiffly. His face had turned the color of old blood. I called out to the visitor to identify himself.

"Messenger, sir," came the muffled reply from the hall-way. "Telegram for Deputy Murdock."

Some more time went by. I was still looking at the Marquis. "If he has anything in his hand besides a telegram, you'll get the answer quicker than anything Western Union ever delivered."

I drew the Colt and sidled up to the door, opening it at arm's length with my back to the wall. A boy in worn overalls leaned in to stare at me around the jamb. He was holding an envelope and nothing else. I holstered the gun to accept it and gave him too much money to make up for feeling like a jackass.

"I had to make sure no accidents were arranged in case I turned you down," I told the ranchers, after the boy had gone. I tore open the envelope. The wire was brief, the way the Judge liked them.

HAVE BEEN NOTIFIED DEATH MARSHAL ARNO
STOP YOU WILL PERFORM DUTIES HIS OFFICE
UNTIL PERMANENT REPLACEMENT SELECTED
                    HARLAN BLACKTHORNE

I met Périgueux's gaze above the margin. He read the gist of the message in my expression.

"We took the liberty of wiring your superior before coming here," he explained. "We had no idea at the time that you would react so strongly to our little proposition. You will disregard the directive, of course." He got up and retrieved a malacca stick from the corner next to the window. "Monsieur Mather?"

"Just a minute," I said. "Where do I go to get sworn in?"

Mather's narrow face grew blotchy again. Périgueux studied me closely, his disproportionately large head tilted back to peer up at me.

"Your jest goes unappreciated." He forgot to say "monsieur."

"The gentle folk call me a maverick," I explained. "It's a polite way of saying I don't know who my father is. Rules are not something I pay a great deal of attention to. But I'm not thickheaded enough to ignore a direct order, especially not when it's in writing." I rattled the paper.

Mather called me a name I'd heard before. The Frenchman fingered the head of his stick.

"We shall of course take steps to have the order rescinded."

"Dandy. When it is, you'll find me down at the jailhouse." I opened the door for him.

His expression was hard to read. "May I remind you that you are no longer in the territorial capital and that out here the people have learned to make do with their own version of the law."

"Long live the republic," I said. Neither of my guests seemed impressed on their way out.

# CHAPTER 3

**A**fter they left, I gazed longingly at the bed for a few seconds, then retrieved my hat and followed them out. I had three hours of daylight left and too much to do to spend them between sheets, even if they were the first sheets I'd seen in days.

Yardlinger was poking a fresh chunk of maple into the

stove when I entered the marshal's office. A heavy-shouldered farm boy in overalls and a burlap-brown suit coat was reading a yellowback novel in a chair behind the railing. He marked his place with a dirty forefinger and studied me through suspicious blue eyes. His hair was corn-yellow, and a sparse sprouting of the same color glittered along his upper lip. He wore a plain star pinned to one overall strap.

"No Shedwell yet," announced the other, swinging shut the stove lid with a squeal of rusted hinges.

"I'm replacing you as marshal."

Some kinds of news are best sprung right away, with no waltzing. This wasn't one of them, but I was tired and didn't have a lot of time. Some of the murkiness had gone out of his gaze as he turned it on me.

"Who says?"

"Western Union." I extended the telegram. He hesitated before accepting it, as if that meant surrender. It struck me, as he read, that his paperwork had doubled since I had come to town. He went through it again, more slowly the second time, then refolded it and put it in his inside breast pocket.

"I'll have to confirm this."

"I thought you would," I said.

"You want him out of here, Oren?"

We both looked at the towheaded deputy, who had risen from his seat and slipped a hamlike hand into the right side pocket of his threadbare coat. He was two inches taller than I and a dozen pounds heavier, which didn't concern me. The lump in his coat pocket did.

"All right, you've stood by your boss," I said. "Now put the gun down on the railing and let the grown-ups finish their business."

"You talk tall for a dead man." He was quivering all over.

"So do you."

His brow knitted, and then he looked at my right hand. I had the Colt pressed to my hip and pointing at his navel.

"How the hell—"

"Experience. Empty that pocket or I'll paint you all over the wall."

"Do what he says, Earl," Yardlinger counseled.

The gun was a Smith & Wesson pocket model .38, good enough for indoor shooting, which was the kind lawmen usually had to deal with. When it was on the railing and he had moved beyond reach of it, Earl looked even younger, nineteen at the outside.

"Go home and get some sleep," the erstwhile marshal told him. "You'll be needed tonight when those rannies from the Six Bar Six start showing up."

"You ain't going to just let him take over!"

"Go *home*, Earl!" Yardlinger's voice was higher and thinner than usual. The deputy reddened around the ears and banged through the gate, trailing muttered barnyard expletives into the street.

I holstered the Colt. It hadn't been fired except for practice since I'd bought it to replace the lost Deane-Adams, but all this leathering and unleathering was going to wear it out. "Did you tell him about me?" I asked Yardlinger.

"Why?" He produced a long cheroot from the pocket containing the telegram I'd given him and struck a match on the stove, just to give himself something to do. He had quick, nervous fingers, lean like the rest of him and callused.

"One of your deputies told Périgueux I was in town." I told him about our meeting.

The former marshal finished lighting the cheroot and held up the match, watching the flame burn down to within an eighth of an inch of his thumb and forefinger before he blew it out. It seemed to calm him.

"They were all here when I brought up the subject," he said. "I told them to keep an eye on you. That was when I was still employed." He started to undo the splendid badge.

"Hold onto it. You'll just have to put it back on when Périgueux gets through wiring my boss about what a menace I am to the community."

"I never keep anything no one wants me to have." The scrap of metal clattered onto the desk.

"Pin on a regular star then. I need deputies."

He hesitated. "I didn't think you liked me. Besides, you don't wear one."

"They put holes in your shirt, most of them from bullets. And I haven't met anyone I liked since I came to this town."

I watched him lean across the desk and open a drawer from which he plucked an unmarked six-pointer like the one Earl wore. He wiped it off on his sleeve and put it on.

"I wouldn't be doing this except that I don't ever want to smell another cow close up," he explained.

I'd handled cattle too before turning to the law. I was beginning to like him in spite of myself. Brusquely I said, "This thing about deputies carrying tales bothers me. Did any of them leave the office within a half hour after you told them I was in town?"

"I couldn't say. I left right after to grab a bite. I put Randy Cross in charge. He's my—your other full-time deputy. You just met Earl Trotter. That leaves Major Brody, the old-timer who fills in as jailer when the rest of us are busy. He just stopped by to kill some time. Any one of them could have done it."

"Who would you suspect?"

"None." He smoked and brooded. "At least we know it wasn't Earl. You saw how much he thinks of your taking my place."

"I saw what he wanted me to see. That puts him at the top of my list."

"Well, you'll meet them all soon enough. That's your worry now. I don't suppose you want to tell me why it's so important for Périgueux and Mather to have a spy in this office, or why they're so het up to have you here."

"Were," I corrected. "I told you, they're worried about Chris Shedwell. They didn't hire him, so they figure the other ranchers did. They looked at my background and thought I'd be a good one to fire the last shot Shedwell ever hears. Sort of a noisy object lesson."

Yardlinger's cheeks paled slightly, a dangerous sign. "So here you are," he said. "A hired killer who carries a badge."

"I didn't say I took them up on the offer. You've got the reason I'm here in your pocket. They like me even less than you do right now."

He continued to stare at me. After a long time he nodded jerkily. "I'll believe that. Right up until you kill Shedwell or he kills you. Either way you die."

"I think your fire's gone out."

I indicated the stove. The cheery glow had faded from the space where the hinged lid didn't quite fit the opening. Clamping the half-smoked cheroot between his teeth, he yanked open the lid, worked the damper, and blew and stirred the embers until a flame appeared.

"What's the problem with the men from the Six Bar Six?" I asked.

"Hm?" He was watching the blaze creep along the edge of the split maple. It burned blue in the center.

"You told Earl you'd need him when those rannies from the Six Bar Six showed up. That's Dick Mather's spread, isn't it?"

He nodded, closing the lid. "He's got a lot of hotheads slapping his brand this year. A bunch from Bob Terwilliger's ranch east of here is staying in town and there might be trouble." He snorted. "There *will* be trouble. Mather's been accusing Terwilliger of cutting out Six Bar Six strays for months."

"Has he been rustling them?"

"Hell, you know these cowboys. Of course he has. But no one ever paid much attention to it. Until now."

"Is it just Terwilliger?"

"Probably not. He's kind of the unofficial head of the small ranchers around the territory, and none of them has enough respect for the big runners to fill a busted bushel basket, especially not for the Marquis. Folks around here generally tolerate foreigners until they start swallowing land like it's sugar-coated."

"Doesn't sound like you admire him much yourself."

His smoke didn't taste so good any more. He made a face and opened the stove to dispose of the stub. "Let's just say I don't have much use for rich people safe in Europe getting hold of the water rights over here and using them to control a hundred times more pasture than they own."

"I've seen it before," I said. "The rustling's an excuse for Périgueux and Mather to run the small fry out and claim their spreads. I take it there's been trouble already."

"Night riders. Grown men with pillowcases over their heads who gallop in and kidnap ranchers out of their beds and dump them out on the prairie to walk back ten miles naked. Last week they caught one of Terwilliger's hired hands on his way back to the bunkhouse and made out like they were going to lynch him to a dead oak."

He had been watching the fire. Now he twisted shut the damper and replaced the lid with more clang than was necessary.

"How'd you like to be set on your horse in the dark with your hands trussed behind you and a rope around your neck so tight you can't swallow, one slap away from a slow strangle? Yeah, they had a high old time that night. So high that when they finally untied him and let him go he just kept on riding until Terwilliger's son caught up with him to ask why he was stealing one of his father's horses, and the hand blurted out the story. He was so scared he'd soiled himself."

"You favor Terwilliger."

"I favor a man's right to do his job without having to hunch up every time he hears hoofbeats. Terwilliger's contributed his share to that feeling. He's offering a bonus to the first hand that brings back an ear belonging to a Six Bar Six man. Along about midnight, when every cowboy in town's had his fill of liquor, someone's going to try and collect that bounty. And that's why I told Earl he'd be needed."

"I hope you told the others the same thing. Those loaded?" I nodded at the rifles and shotguns in the rack behind the desk, chained together like convicts on a work detail.

"Every last one of them. Think we'll need them tonight?"

"Maybe not for shooting, but five men in badges standing around with long guns don't do much for a cowhand's fighting spirit. I'll need a key."

"Take mine." He pulled a ring out of his hip pocket.

"Keep it. They have a habit of getting lost just when you need them most. Did Arno have a separate key?"

"Up at the Breen House. He lived there the past year or so to get away from his wife. Room seven."

I'd seen the Breen on my way in. Four stories, with a restaurant on the ground floor and colored glass out front. I whistled. "What do you folks pay your marshals?"

"Forty a month and ten cents for every stray dog he shoots in the city limits."

"He must have shot a lot of dogs to afford a room in that hotel. Or that fancy box they planted him in."

When he scowled, the tips of his black moustache almost

touched beneath his lower lip. "It helps to claim a cut of the profits of every game in town."

"I figured as much. His stuff still in the room?"

"Most of it. I packed up his clothes and sent them over to his widow. The rest is going to take some time. He was long on taking and short on giving away."

"I'll fetch the key. Get word to all the deputies I want to see them here in half an hour." I started for the door.

"All of them?" he called after me. "Even the Major? Hell, he's just—"

"All of them." The door swung shut on the end of it.

The Breen's lobby was carpeted in green plush with petit-pointed leaves and lit by a crystal chandelier whose journey around the Horn had me beat by twelve thousand miles. I'd seen bigger places, but they didn't have walls around them. The desk clerk wore a waxed moustache and parted his hair in the middle. He didn't want to give me the key to Room 7 even after I'd showed him my badge. He changed his mind after I grabbed a handful of his cravat and prepared to pin it to his tonsils. I left him repairing his haberdashery and mounted a broad, curving staircase clothed in more leafy green.

The room was three times the size of the one I was staying in at the Freestone. It too was carpeted, and ringed with marble-topped tables and chests of drawers covered in brocade and supporting most of the doodads a nineteenth-century gentleman required to survive socially. The bed was shiny brass and required a stepping stool to get into it from either side. A pair of double doors on my right suggested a closet. I had just started my search for the key to the gun rack when the room swelled with a tremendous explosion and I went down hard.

# CHAPTER 4

The noise whistled in my ears for a time after I flattened out on my stomach, a position I was beginning to get used to. Pistols are noisy things outdoors; inside they're skull-rattlers. The air was hazy blue and stank of rotten eggs. I felt something on my back and knew that it was a litter of shattered glass from the mirror of the dressing table. An inch and a half to the right and I wouldn't have been feeling much of anything.

It may have been that my hearing was still affected or that my assailant was lighter on his feet than a prairie antelope, but I lay without moving for what seemed a long time before a shard of glass crunched not four feet back of my left ear. There was another long silence, and then I heard an almost inaudible rustle, as of clothing brushing against furniture. I heard it again a moment later, nearer, much nearer. Then silence again.

My heart was bounding between my ribs and the floor. I hoped whoever was in the room with me couldn't hear it. I kept my eyes open, concentrating my vision on a bit of gray lint on the carpet two inches in front of me to give them that glazed, motionless look. They burned in their sockets. I was working so hard on not blinking that I wasn't sure when the shadowy shape crept into the extreme corner of my range. Half a heartbeat later a shoe appeared beside me.

A woman's shoe.

It was expensive footwear, with a black patent-leather toe and an ivory top fastened with matching buttons. Above that was a trim ankle in a black stocking and six or seven petticoats under a gray taffeta skirt, gathered up to keep them from scuffing the floor. It was as tempting a target as had been presented to me since the day Judge Black-thorne entered his chambers wearing a brand new beaver hat as tall as a riding boot. I snatched the ankle in one hand and yanked.

She went down in an explosion of petticoats. More glass shook loose from the dressing-table mirror. Something tipped off the marble top, struck me between the shoulder blades and rolled off. I ignored it. Still grasping her ankle, I threw myself up onto my knees and forward, sprawling on top of her. I'll try to report the rest in order.

She tried to bring a knee up into my crotch but missed, the blow glancing off my left hip. Something flashed in her right hand and I grabbed for it, but I misjudged and the something banged the back of my skull. My hat had slipped to cushion the blow, and her aim was off anyway; still, I had to fight back nausea and unconsciousness to get my hands around her flailing wrist. She raked my cheek with the nails of her free hand. I cursed through my teeth and concentrated on gaining possession of the gun. She bit my hand, took aim at my groin again with her knee, and connected this time. The bottom dropped out of my stomach, but before the real pain started I threw a left hook at her jaw and she went limp.

By this time my insides were roiling. I started to climb off her and noticed for the first time that we had attracted an audience. A group of people whom I took to be guests were standing in the open doorway behind the prissy clerk, who had tucked his cravat and collar back into place and was staring down at us the way I suppose desk clerks everywhere stare down at men and women locked in mortal combat on hotel room floors. I drew my Colt.

"Get the hell out of here."

I don't know if it was the gun, or the look on my face, or the authoritative croak in which the command was delivered, but it worked. He backed out, herding everyone with him, and pulled the door shut.

My opponent was still out. When the first wave of nausea had passed I stashed the Colt, scooped her gun out of her hand—it was a Smith pocket .32, smaller in caliber and more streamlined than the S&W carried by Yardlinger's young deputy—and stuck it in my belt. I got up and spent a few minutes with my hands on my knees, breathing deeply and waiting for the agony to move up and out. When it had, I attended to the other pains.

There was a knot the size of a quarter on the back of my skull. It was tender but the skin wasn't broken. With the scratches I wasn't so fortunate; I touched the stinging cheek and my fingers came back bloody. My handkerchief was soaked by the time the leaking stopped. By contrast my sparring partner, whom I had to all intents and purposes vanquished, had only a purple-black smear on the side of her jaw to show for our introduction. It hardly seemed fair.

Aside from that, it was an attractive face, if you liked them unconscious. She had a high white brow and eyes with long lashes, set a little too far apart, but from there down I couldn't fault it. The nose was unremarkable, the jawline delicate-looking but strong (I'd confirmed that), and she had the broad mouth then out of fashion but more suited to her than the popular Cupid's pout. Her hair was auburn and a litter of pins around her head said that she usually wore it up. She had a decent shape if you could trust first impressions in those days of whalebone and wire.

The struggle had disarranged her skirt and petticoats, exposing three inches of creamy thigh over the top of her right stocking.

One of the closet doors stood open and a woman's handbag lay on the floor inside. I picked it up. Inside I found the usual feminine accessories, among them a lace handkerchief embroidered with the initials C.B. in silver thread and a milliner's receipt for fifteen dollars made out to Colleen Bower. A stiff leather holster, decidedly unfeminine, was stitched to the bag's lining. I tried the Smith & Wesson in the holster. Perfect fit. I left it there and put the purse on a lamp table next to the closet.

The woman on the floor moaned and began to stir, showing more flesh above the stocking. As luck would have it, she came to just as I was covering it.

"I guess you don't like them moving," she said.

She had opened her eyes without any of the preliminaries and sat up, catching me in the act. They were nice eyes, pale blue with gold flecks in them. At the moment they were accusing.

"I only beat women," I rejoined. "I don't ravish them."

She flushed from hairline to bodice. "You'll excuse me if I don't take you at your word." Savagely she readjusted the skirt, concealing everything to the tops of her shoes. Then she put a hand to her bruised jaw.

"I don't usually hit ladies unless they try to kill me first." I tossed her the federal star. She caught it in one hand—surprising me for the third time since we'd met—glanced at it, and flipped it back. I had to clap it against my chest with both hands. This round was hers.

"Does a name go with it?"

"Sometimes," I said. "Not always. It's the kind of information bushwhackers have to earn. You can start by telling me what you've got against me breathing."

"If I'd wanted to kill you, we wouldn't be talking. I'm a fair shot with a pocket pistol." She glanced around for it halfheartedly, then gave up. "When I heard the key in the door I thought you were the desk clerk or Yardlinger come to take away some more of Bram's things, so I hid in the closet. I opened the door a crack, saw you searching the room, and thought you were one of those ghouls that read the obituary column and then rob dead men the day of their funerals. I wanted to put a scare in you. Only you don't scare." She rubbed her jaw. "Did you have to hit so hard?"

"Probably not, but it felt good. You're Colleen Bower?"

Her eyes widened slightly, then shifted to the floor of the closet and wandered until they found her handbag on the lamp table. Her smile was rueful. "You're law, all right. Yes."

"How'd you get in?"

She reached inside her bodice and produced a key identical to the one I'd extorted from the clerk. "Bram gave it to me. Marshal Arno."

"I'm beginning to understand," I said.

"Bright fellow."

"What were you doing here?"

"I came to get something. May I stand?"

I nodded. She wobbled to her feet, found her balance, then brushed the dust and pieces of glass off her skirt and crossed unsteadily to a tall chest of drawers next to the bed. From the top drawer she took an ornate wooden jewelry box and opened it for my inspection. Its contents sparkled in the sunlight slanting in through the window overlooking the main drag.

"Pretty," I said.

"Bram sent all the way to New York for them. Of course, I couldn't wear them anywhere but in this room or there'd be talk. So we kept them here."

"That's like owning a fancy buggy and never taking it out of the stable."

"You're not telling me anything I don't know. But they're mine and I'm taking them with me."

"Guess again. How do I know he bought those baubles for you? Maybe they belong to his widow."

"That witch!" she spat. "They didn't even live together.

He only went home to eat, which is why he's dead. If she didn't poison him, I didn't graduate at the head of my class from Miss Jessup's School for Genteel Young Ladies. Anyway, what business is it of yours who takes them? What federal law am I violating?"

"None that I know of. But as of an hour and a half ago I'm Marshal Arno's replacement." I told her my name. Her lips curled mockingly.

"Page Murdock. It sounds chivalric, like Childe Harold. Do you rescue damsels from dragons?"

"No, I generally knock them cold and have my way with them. The box." I held out my hand. She hesitated, then snapped shut the lid of the fancy case and surrendered it.

"If your story checks out I'll give it back," I said.

"It won't. The jewelry wasn't in my name and no one knew about them but Bram and me."

"That simplifies things. I'll hold onto them, and if no one asks about them, I'll know you're telling the truth."

"How do I know you won't just keep them?"

"Because I'm telling you I won't." I tucked the box under one arm. "Now I have to ask myself what I'll do with you. So far I've only your word that an arrangement existed between you and the late lamented peace officer of Breen. I know from experience that getting a key to this room is no problem."

"Ask around." Her smile remained mocking. "Don't confuse discretion with secrecy. Out here everyone knows everyone else's business. We just didn't parade it around or we would both have been run out of town on a rail. I've come close to that in other towns and it's not pleasant. Ask anyone how it was between us. Ask them."

While she was speaking, the door flew open and Oren Yardlinger spilled in, accompanied by the hotel clerk and three armed men. One was Earl, holding the scaled-down

.38 I'd made him give up earlier. He glared at me with adolescent hatred.

"That's him, Marshall!" cried the clerk, pointing a nail-bitten finger at me from behind one of the deputies.

Earl was quaking worse than the last time. "Didn't I say he was a bad one, Oren? Look at them scratches on his face. You remember the last time we brung one in like that? The Judge hung him once for rape and once for murder."

Yardlinger's muddy eyes regarded me, lingering on the scratches, my disheveled clothes, the dust on my knees. Then he looked at the woman.

"What about it, Miss Bower? You want to prefer charges?"

"The lady tried to put a hole in me," I said. "Ask the clerk. He heard the shot."

"That's true," he acknowledged uncertainly.

"Trying to defend herself!" Earl was wound tight.

Yardlinger kept his eyes and his Navy Colt on me. "Miss Bower?"

I looked at Colleen Bower and read nothing in her expression. Tension grew in the silence.

"Randy, take his gun." The former marshal's voice was taut.

One of the armed men stepped forward. Tall and raw-boned in a hide jacket, he had wind-burned features and eyes that were bright points of light set in sharp creases, like nailheads driven deep into old wood. His weapon was a double-barreled shotgun cut down to pistol size.

They had me six ways to Wednesday, but I wasn't going to give up my gun in the face of twelve feet of hemp and a short drop to hell. I grasped the butt, ready to pull.

"Wait, Oren," said the woman.

# CHAPTER 5

"If you have something to say, you'd better say it damn quick, begging your pardon, ma'am," Yardlinger advised her.

He was standing where he had been when the door opened, sideways astraddle the threshold with his right arm extended and the Navy aimed at my head. Behind him and to his right stood the fourth armed man, a slack-skinned gaffer with gray stubble on his chin, bloodhound eyes, and a Colt Peacemaker nearly as long as a carbine held at chest level in both hands.

"I did take a shot at him," said the woman. "He knocked me down in self-defense."

The deposed marshal took his eyes from me for the first time in a while and it felt as if an anvil had been lifted from my neck. He studied her.

"No offense, but you don't appear to be someone a man would need much defending from."

She fetched her handbag and took out the .32, holding it by its butt between thumb and forefinger, the way my mother used to remove a dead rat from a trap by its tail. She hadn't held it like that twenty minutes earlier.

"Don't you men have a saying about these things being the great equalizers?"

"They say that about the Colt. Different gun. But you made your point." He held his stance. "If it's not too much trouble, maybe you'd care to explain why you shot at a federal officer."

"I caught him searching Bram's room and thought he was a burglar. I'm afraid I panicked. I was about to shoot again and would have if he hadn't hit me."

The lawman played statue a moment longer, eyes dancing from the woman to me and back again. Then he crooked his arm and let down the hammer on the Colt. "Something about it stinks," he said. "But I'm just the joker in this hand."

"Why don't we haul him in anyhow?" Earl hadn't lowered his weapon. "Could be he's wanted somewhere."

Yardlinger holstered his gun. "Earl, if we locked up everyone in this town who could be wanted somewhere, we wouldn't have cell space for those that are. Put up that toy pistol before you put a hole in United States property. Randy? Major?"

The rawboned deputy lowered the shotgun, followed by the old man, who replaced the Peacemaker's hammer and thrust the gun into his belt. Earl was last to comply. I kept my hand on the Army Colt until Colleen Bower had returned the little Smith to her bag and drawn the string. A disappointed sigh swept through the crowd in the hallway. Yardlinger ordered them to disperse. They obeyed reluctantly and he stepped the rest of the way inside and kicked the door shut.

"Anything else?" he asked the woman.

She shook her head. "Marshal Murdock was about to return some property to me when you came in. I'll just take it and be on my way." She held out her hand for the jewelry case.

"If that's a box full of pretties, we'll hold onto it for now," said Yardlinger.

"You knew about them?" She took an involuntary step backward.

"I found them in that chest of drawers when I came to pick up Bram's clothes for Mrs. Arno. Murdock?"

I gave him the box. "If there's a safe in the office, lock them up. We'll hold them for ten days. If no one claims them in that time we'll return them to the lady."

"Who the hell are you to give orders?" demanded Earl.

I stepped to the door and opened it. "Miss Bower?"

She tilted her chin haughtily, picked up her skirts, and swept out into the now-deserted hallway. Men keep making and buying better firearms, but women have all the weapons. When she was clear of the threshold I closed the door and in the same movement swung around and belted Earl on the chin with the fist I'd used to silence the woman earlier.

He was husky so I put everything I had into it. It wasn't enough. He stumbled backward, slamming into the dressing table and knocking the last of the glass out of the devastated mirror. Then he shook his head and came at me headfirst. He tripped over Yardlinger's outthrust leg and pitched forward his full length to the floor at my feet. The room shook.

"What the hell did you do that for?" Cross barked.

"For this." The former marshal pushed a telegraph form under the weathered deputy's nose. "Blackthorne's confirmation," he said to me. "I was reading it when the clerk came to complain that some rough-looking road agent posing as a deputy marshal was tearing his hotel apart." To Cross, "Murdock's the law in this town until someone in authority says different."

"Not my law he ain't." He started to take off his badge.

"Leave it alone," I said.

He paused, staring down the muzzle of my hip gun.

Earl had started to push himself to his feet. He held his crouch, glaring up at me from under pale brows.

I said, "I've been appointed to keep the peace in Breen, and until I'm off the hook that's what I aim to do. That means I'll need every man in this room. I may hang for it later, but I'll blast a hole a yard wide in whoever reaches for that doorknob."

"He's bluffing," said Earl.

"Raise or call," I countered.

There was a short silence.

"Hell," said a voice, "that's too rich for my blood. I'm in."

I'd almost forgotten the old man, seated now on the edge of the stepping stool next to the bed. His rheumy eyes glistened under his floppy hat as he placed a fresh cut of chewing tobacco skewered on the end of a wicked knife into his mouth. He spoke with a high Ozark twang dragged over Mississippi gravel.

"I like you, mister. You remind me of this here Yankee lieutenant a bunch of us boys cornered in a pigsty by Ox Ford. Sergeant Maddox shot him in the hand when he went for his side arm. He grabbed for it with his other hand and Maddox smashed that one too. Then he threw out his stumps and charged. The Yank warn't three feet off when ole Mad opened a hole in his chest you could drive a four-horse team through. He went down, but you know what? He crawled the rest of the way and bit ole Mad on the leg!"

His cackling turned to a hideous, racking cough and he bubbled off into silent convulsions that ended only when he stuffed a pink-mottled handkerchief into his mouth. He was a saintly old fellow.

"What about it, Randy?" Yardlinger asked the man with the shotgun. "I can handle Murdock's threats. In or out?"

Cross chewed on his ragged moustache. His bullet-like eyes surveyed me without affection. "I don't know," he said. "I ain't ever run from a fight yet, but I can't watch my front and my back at the same time. How do we know he's what he says he is?"

I laughed harshly. "I can't blame you for being suspicious. I bet they're beating down your door to be made lawmen in this town."

He ruminated on that for a moment. "I still don't know. How about you, Oren?"

"I never had any choice in it, you know that."

"Well, if it's good enough for you." I wouldn't have bet a Confederate dollar on the conviction in Cross's voice.

"It ain't good enough for me."

I looked down at Earl, who hadn't moved from his starting position on the floor. "Who said I wanted you? Hit the street and leave the star here."

"He's a good man," Yardlinger cautioned.

"He whines too much and he hides his gun. People who don't want you to know they're armed are looking for a chance to squirt one at your back. Besides, I think he's our spy."

"What makes you think so?"

"I don't like him."

The young deputy rose. Upright, he turned the tables and looked down at me as if from a great height. I had known a scalp hunter in the Bitterroots who could have palmed his head in one hand, but in that room he was formidable enough. I wasn't sure I could knock him down a second time even with a bullet.

"I'm as good a man as anyone here." He'd bitten through his lip when struck and the swelling slurred his speech. "Better than some."

"What's this about a spy?" pressed Cross.

Yardlinger filled him in. The old man guffawed.

"Hell, if I knowed someone'd pay for it I'd tell a story or two myself."

"If Earl wants in, I'll vouch for him," said the former marshal.

I stifled a yawn—from fatigue, not insolence. "Who'll vouch for you?"

"Son of a bitch," Cross muttered.

Yardlinger was unmoved. "You've probably been too busy playing the put-upon outsider to notice, but the likelihood of your being elected to Congress in this city hasn't improved since you came. Without me, you don't have deputies, and without deputies—"

"I'm sold. Introduce me."

"You they know." He nodded at each in turn. "That's Randy Cross with the scattergun. He's good with it. Couple of years ago he used one like it to blow the lock off a Wells, Fargo strongbox headed for Deadwood. Pinkertons tracked him down in Canada and he got twenty to life, but he was released for helping put down a riot in territorial prison. He put in time as a railroad detective with James Hill before Bram swore him in here. Earl Trotter's a Breen native and a hell of a fine pistol shot.

"And then there's Leroy Cooperstown Brody."

"*Major* Leroy Cooperstown Brody." The old man squirted a yellow-brown stream at a brass cuspidor six feet away. He hit it square.

"Major Brody commanded a cavalry unit in Virginia during the late hostilities, though I imagine he'd have a hard time recognizing the country in broad daylight."

"Night riders," I said.

Brody made a soggy snapping sound with the plug in his mouth. "The First Virginia Volunteers. Our flag was bonny blue, not black."

"I'm sure that was a source of comfort to the people you murdered," Yardlinger replied. "Anyway, when there's shooting to be done the Major doesn't back off, which is why Bram made him jailer. He doesn't have a badge because I don't want him to go around thinking he's a deputy. That's what you have to work with."

"I've worked with worse."

Yardlinger looked at Earl. "What about it? You've had plenty of time to make up your mind."

The hulking deputy squeezed his torn lower lip between two fingers. "I get to walk out when I don't like it, right?"

"Wrong," I said. "In now, in to the end."

"I got to take orders from him?" Looking at Yardlinger, he jerked his chin at me.

"There's room for only one marshal in any outfit," nodded the other.

"Come on, Earl-boy," twanged the Major. "What you going to do, you don't throw in with us? Go back home and haul plow for your old man?"

"*No!*" The violence of the retort made even the old reprobate jump. "Not for him. I reckon I'm in."

Brody chuckled nastily and took another pass at the cuspidor. This time he barely hit the rim.

"What now?" Yardlinger was watching me.

I considered. "When do you expect the hands from the Six Bar Six?"

"Sundown."

"Unless cowhands have changed, the trouble will start about two minutes after the first one has his belly full of whiskey."

"They haven't changed."

"I counted fourteen saloons. Any more?" He shook his head. I glanced out the window, at the sun straddling the false front of the livery across the street. "We'd best get started. Any temperance folks in town?"

"A few," replied Yardlinger, bewildered.

"Place like this, I don't imagine they have much to sing about."

"Of course not. But what the hell has that—"

"Well, they'll be singing tonight." I began rummaging through drawers. "Help me find the key to that gun rack."

# CHAPTER 6

Closing saloons is a shotgun job. At the jail, I used the late lawman's key to unlock the chain securing the long guns, handed an American Arms 12-gauge to Yardlinger and divided a pair of cut-down 10-gauge Remingtons between Earl and the Major. Randy Cross seemed content with his cut-down 12. For myself I selected a Winchester .44 carbine, as no one had yet balanced a scattergun to my satisfaction. Finally I pocketed a handful of cartridges from one of several boxes in the drawer under the rack.

"Take what you need," I said, fitting the padlock back on the chain. "If we're lucky we won't use what's in the chambers, but there's one thickheaded drunk in every saloon."

Yardlinger filled the side pocket of his frock coat with shells for his 12-gauge. "I don't much like this plan. Why don't we just set up a barricade at the end of the street and disarm the hands as they come in?"

"I heard of a Ranger who tried that down in Amarillo," I said. "They never did find enough of him to bury. A cowboy will kill to keep his gun, but not to drink."

"I've seen men kill for less."

"On the range. Not in a town full of witnesses, unless they've already been drinking."

"I guess you know how much faith I put in that," he said dryly.

"That's why the shotguns."

Outside, the sun was draining into the horizon in a wallow of orange and purple. A stiff breeze stirred the dust in the street and laid its cold hand against our faces. On the boardwalk in front of the jail I gestured with the Winchester. "Earl and Randy, take the east side. Start at the other end and work your way back up here. We'll come the same way along the west walk. Don't be afraid to make noise if anyone gives you trouble. One more thing."

The group had started to break up. Everyone looked at me.

"If anyone comes back with liquor on his breath I'll have him stuffed and stood up in the middle of town as a monument to the evils of drink."

Cross and Earl left with a dual snort. I'd impressed the daylights out of them.

Our first stop was the Pick Handle, a shack with canvas tacked over the spaces where boards were missing and one opaque window a foot square. A coal-oil lantern swung from a nail in a rafter, oozing greasy light over a plank laid across two beer kegs that served as the bar. Two men were leaning on it and a short man with a barrel body and a matted tangle of black beard was pouring red whiskey into a glass on the other side. He stopped when he saw our guns.

"Evening, Oren, Major," he said cautiously. "What'll you have?"

I said, "Nothing tonight. These fellows paid for their drinks?" I jerked my head toward the pair watching us from the bar.

The bartender considered the question, then shook his head. His eyes wandered left and down to where a sawed-off shotgun lay across a packing crate.

I tossed a coin onto the plank. It bounced and would have rolled off the edge if he hadn't slapped a meaty hand down on top of it. "They're on me," I announced. "Drain your glasses, gents. It's closing time."

"What the hell!" The bartender grabbed for the shotgun. I cracked the barrel of the Winchester across the back of his wrist. Howling, he yanked it back.

"Don't," snapped Yardlinger, covering the two customers, one of whom had grasped the handle of a revolver in his belt.

"It's just for tonight," I told the bartender, who was busy testing his injured wrist for breaks. "You don't want to lose the use of that arm over a few dollars." To Yardlinger, indicating the customers: "Either of these Terwilliger's?"

"No."

I held out my hand to the one with the gun. At length he drew it gingerly and placed it in my palm. It was a prewar piece, much in need of cleaning. I stuck it in my belt. "You're lucky you didn't get a chance to pull the trigger and blow your hand off. You can pick it up at the jail later. Get going, both of you." They slunk out. I returned my attention to the man behind the bar. "Lock up."

"How?" He was still rubbing the wrist. "Got no key. The place ain't been closed since it was built."

"Got a hammer and nails and a board?"

He said he did. Yardlinger went with him into the back room and they came out a moment later, the bartender carrying a hammer and a small sack in one hand and a weathered plank four feet long under his other arm. As we accompanied him to the front door his eyes sought Major Brody's.

"Who is this guy?" He gestured at me with the board.

The old man shrugged a thin shoulder. "Anyhow, what's it matter? He's got a weapon and you ain't."

Yardlinger leaned his shotgun beyond the bartender's reach outside and helped him nail the board across the entrance. "That won't keep nobody out," predicted the bartender.

"It won't have to," I said. "Tomorrow you can yank it down and throw it away." We watched while he retreated down the street toward home, carrying his tools. Then we moved on.

We encountered little resistance at the Sunset and French Sam's, establishments similar to the Pick Handle and just about as deserted. The sight of the Major's ravaged face above the 10-gauge, his tobacco plug bulging one cheek, calmed a sodden range cook who had staggered out of his seat to challenge our authority at Sam's. In each location the occupants were driven out and the front door locked from the outside. At the Glory we paused for a consultation before entering.

It was a big building with leaded-glass windows and mineral-oil lamps inside spilling rich yellow light out onto the boardwalk, a far cry from the stark simplicity of the places we'd visited previously. Yardlinger came back from peering over the batwing doors, shaking his head.

"There are six Terwilliger men in there that I can see. And one of the customers we ran out of French Sam's, drinking at the bar. Maybe a dozen others scattered around the room. They'll be ready for us."

"Is there a back way?" I asked.

"Side door off the alley."

As quietly as possible I racked a fresh shell into the Winchester's chamber, ejecting the one that was in there, picked it up and poked it into the magazine. I did it partly out of nervous habit and partly because I never trust a cartridge that hasn't moved in a while. "Who goes in through the front?"

"The Major," said Yardlinger, without hesitation. "No one takes him seriously."

"Should we?" I looked at the old man.

He grinned, showing a black crescent where his teeth should have been. Either molars were all he had left or he gummed his chew. "I ain't used up yet."

I nodded. "Start counting. Give us twenty to reach the side door. No one leaves till I'm finished talking, no one flashes iron. But try not to blow holes in too many of Breen's upstanding citizens."

"Hell, that's no restriction. They ain't none."

"Just don't forget this isn't Virginia and it isn't eighteen sixty-three," I cautioned. "I'm just getting used to having you around and I wouldn't want to see you stretching a rope."

I reminded him to count to twenty and struck off down the narrow alley with the other deputy. The sun was almost below the horizon, and except for a thin yellow L outlining the door we were surrounded by darkness. We hesitated before going in.

"Where are the cowhands?" My breath curled out in wisps of vapor.

"Two at the bar when I looked," said Yardlinger. "Three more sharing a table west of the front door opposite. Last one playing poker next to the bar with three other customers, one of them the guy we chased out of Sam's. You want to watch the Terwilliger man playing cards. Name's Pardee. It was his brother the vigilantes almost lynched. He'll be smoking a cigar. Never leaves his mouth."

"I'll take the bar side. You cover the three at the table. And watch out for everyone else. The man who gets the last shot is always the last one you suspect. Let's go."

I pushed the door open noiselessly and we crossed through a dim storeroom stacked with kegs and barrels and reeking of old beer and new vomit, the one thing all saloons have in common, to an open door through which bar sounds were leaking. As we approached, the buzz of voices in the outer room died. Major Brody had entered.

All eyes were on him as we stepped inside. A frumpy figure in a stained coat and trousers that bagged at the knees, he was standing at the end of an aisle that ran between the tables and a bar of glossy dark wood trimmed with brass. The huge twin barrels of his truncated Remington were trained on the room at large. His sagging hat brim masked his eyes and his tobacco cud raised a hard knot beneath his right ear.

"Who the hell are you supposed to be, Major?" The bartender, heavy-muscled in a calico shirt and tight silk vest, kept his hands hidden behind the bar. He had blunt features like an Indian and an upper lip that curled back and flattened under his nose when he smiled, exposing long, slightly discolored teeth. I figured him for an opium smoker and wondered if there were any Chinese in town.

"Who don't matter," explained Brody in a dead voice. "It's what you'll be if you don't get them hands in plain sight, Alf. Which is dead."

"I thought you guerrilla fellows generally went in for back shooting."

"So do lawmen," I said. "When it's convenient."

Alf jerked around, seeing Yardlinger and me for the first time. His left arm moved spasmodically. I shouted at him to hold it and came around the end of the bar, keeping the carbine pointed at his thick hard belly. There was a row of beer pulls behind the bar to his left, including one that didn't match the others. I grasped it and tugged a Schofield revolver out of a greased socket.

"For shame," I said, and backhanded him across his flat face, laying the revolver's long barrel along his right cheekbone. He clapped a hand to the cheek and staggered back against the shelves behind the bar. Bottles clattered. He took his hand away and looked at his fingers. There was no blood, but a reddish welt had risen under his eye.

Major Brody chuckled. Yardlinger stared at me in surprise, then remembered himself and swung his shotgun to take in his side of the room.

While the Major covered the bar side I rested the Winchester in the crook of my arm, unloaded the Schofield, and dropped it and the cartridges into a bucket of dirty mop water at my feet. The splash and clunk was loud in the silence of the room.

"That ain't no way to treat a good gun."

I looked at the speaker, a round-faced man, clean-shaven, with a long cigar screwed into the center of his mouth, calmly dealing cards at a table next to the bar. His fine blond hair was parted just above his left ear and combed across his scalp to make up for what he'd lost on top. In his town suit he looked as much like a cowhand as I looked like Eddie Foy. I recognized one of the three silent men seated with him as a lounger I had driven from French Sam's.

I said, "Who says the Schofield's a good gun?"

"Jesse James, for one."

"That explains how he blew the raid on Northfield. You're Pardee?"

He threw away two cards and slid two more from the deck. "You're Murdock."

"Now that we're on a last-name basis, let's talk. You know some men are on their way here from Dick Mather's spread."

"I heard something on that order. In for two." He tossed a pair of chips into the center of the table.

"Talk is you think it was Mather's boys almost strung up your brother."

"See it and raise you five." The man from Sam's sweetened the pot. The man at his right folded. The fourth man equaled the bet.

"Raise ten." More chips left Pardee's stack.

"Trying to buy the pot," grumbled the fourth player.

"It'll cost him." The man from Sam's saw the raise.

I leaned across the bar and brought the barrel of the Winchester smashing down atop the table. Chips and cards flew.

"Goddamn!" Pardee reached for his hip.

A roar shook the room. The cigar smoker's hand sprang away empty. In the loud silence that followed, everyone in the room gaped at the Major, standing in a cloud of swirling blue smoke, his shotgun pointed at the ceiling and a litter of plaster around his feet. He chewed casually.

"Hey!" The bartender was first to shake off the spell. "Who's going to pay for that?"

Brody drew his lips tight against his gums and shot a stream at the nearest cuspidor. "I reckon Pardee's the man you should talk to about that. It was him startled me into yanking this here trigger, going to scratch that there itch on his hip so sudden."

"The idea was to get your attention," I told Pardee. "Why do you think Six Bar Six riders are responsible for what happened to your brother?"

The cowhand took the cigar from his mouth, spat out bits of tobacco, and crushed it out in a crystal ashtray full of chewed brown butts on the table. In the excitement he had bitten through it. He lit another. Puffing it into life: "Six Bar Six, Périgueux, what difference does it make? They was trying to scare me into quitting as foreman. They know I don't rabbit when it's just my hide, so they tried to get at me through Dale. If I leave, Terwilliger goes under. He can't get no one else to ramrod with things like they are."

"So what's going to happen tonight?"

"I reckon that's between me and that consumptive bastard."

"I reckon not. The law's here now. We'll take care of Mather, if Mather's behind the raids."

"How?" He snapped the still-burning match into the mounded tray. "You going to throw the old bushwhacker in front of Dick's horse and trip it up?"

Mild laughter bubbled around the room. The Major went on chewing as if he hadn't heard. His shoulders and the crown of his hat were white from the plaster dust that was still dribbling from the gaping hole in the ceiling.

"Whose idea was it to bring in Chris Shedwell?" I asked Pardee. "Yours or Terwilliger's?"

He restacked his chips. "Wouldn't make much sense, would it? Us hiring him and then me coming here to square things myself."

He had a point.

"You're a gambling man," I said. "I'll make you a bet." Tucking the Winchester under my arm, I came around the bar and gathered up the scattered cards with my free hand. When the deck was intact I shuffled and dealt us each five. Then I peeled a five-dollar bill off the roll in my pocket and laid it on the table. "If I don't arrest the men who hoorawed your brother in a week, you can even things up your own way, short of killing."

Pardee pursed his lips around the cigar, drumming his fingers on the cards I'd dealt him face down. At length he picked up a chip and somersaulted it expertly across his knuckles and back, turning it over in the cracks between.

"And if you arrest them?"

"Call off the feud. Consider yourself square with Mather and Périgueux. For my part, I'll see that the night riders stand trial for abduction and malicious mischief. But I'll do it my way, which includes shutting down this saloon tonight."

He frowned at the chip as he manipulated it faster and faster, back and forth across his hand. Then he snapped it off his thumb. It rolled over in the air several times and landed flat atop my five dollars. "Pick up your cards."

I did, arranging them and placing them face up on the

table. I had a pair of jacks. He glanced at them, nodded, and turned his over. Three sixes and two kings stared up at me impassively.

"Full house," he announced. "Sure hope you're not on a sour streak, Marshal."

# CHAPTER 7

The Terwilliger crew left, some reluctantly but not inclined to argue with their foreman, and soon we heard their hoofbeats receding in the direction of the ranch. With them gone, the bartender at the Glory saw little point in stopping us from closing the place even if he had wanted to, which evidently he didn't any more. He helped us roust out the more stubborn customers, turned out the lamps, and locked up, grasping his dripping revolver uselessly in one hand. I sent him off with a reminder to send the bill for the damaged ceiling to the marshal's office and a warning not to jack up the amount.

We found the last two saloons on our side of the street dark, the doors already locked. Our fame was spreading. As we turned away from the final stop, Yardlinger said, "Why bother anyway? With Pardee and his boys out of town we've got nothing to worry about. Why not let Mather's hands drink up and go?"

"Two reasons. First, if we let them get a snootful in the mood they'll be in, they might decide to go hunting for Terwilliger men or take out their frustration on some other target." I paused while he set fire to a cheroot.

"Second?" He squirted smoke through his nostrils and watched the flame on his match creep close to his fingers. It was dark out, the only illumination a ghostly glow from the fogged windows of the hotels and late-closing shops.

"Second, a lawman has to finish what he starts, or folks get to thinking he's soft. If he keeps changing his mind, they'll wonder if anything he says is worth much."

"That why you pistol-whipped Alf back at the Glory?"

I sighed. "I was wondering when you'd get around to that."

"You didn't have to hit him. You had his gun."

"I didn't do it for him. I did it for the others in the room who were watching. The Major understands. He fired his scattergun through the roof for the same reason."

The old guerrilla shifted his plug from one cheek to the other. "You said not to be afeared of making noise."

"So the bartender puts steak on his eye and the ceiling gets a patch," I said. "Beats the cost of burial."

"I don't think that's the reason you hit him," insisted the former marshal. "I think it was because you liked it."

For a moment we stood watching each other in the gloom. Smoke drifted straight up from the glowing end of his cheroot in the motionless air before it was caught and blown ragged by the wind above brim level. Then there was a noise in the street and all three of us spun in that direction, long guns ready. Randy Cross and Earl Trotter mounted the boardwalk.

"Next time announce yourself," I snarled in my relief. "Another second and you'd have been breathing out your belly."

Cross ignored the comment. "Well, they're shut down on our side. If there's a drop of alcohol to be got in town, it's horse liniment."

"Any trouble?"

"Couple of prospectors tried to jump Randy in the House of Mirrors," said Earl. "I asked them not to."

The other deputy snorted. "He kicked one in the belly

and clubbed the other across the knees with his shotgun. You should of heard him howl. First one's still heaving, I reckon."

"That's the way I used to make Pa's horses behave," shrugged the younger man.

I turned to Yardlinger. "How many cathouses in town?"

"Just one, Martha's, over on Arapaho. But she serves claret. A man'd be all night getting drunk enough to start anything."

"Just so we know where they'll be if they decide to stick."

"That's them now," said Cross.

Rumbling hoofbeats swelled as a dozen riders swung into the north end of the street, trailing a fog of horses' breath. I pointed at the open doors of the livery stable, each of which sported a burning lantern hanging on a nail. "Confiscate those and bring them along."

Earl obeyed, ignoring the protests of the old Negro in charge, and hurried to catch up with us. As we approached the riders, the thunder of hoofs faltered and died. The darkness on the street had alerted the newcomers. Steel slid from leather, hammers rolled back with a racheting sound.

When the lanterns arrived I took one and held it up as I walked across in front of the line of horse-men.

Dick Mather regarded me in hostile silence, a sick man slumped in a linen duster and gripping the pommel of his saddle in both hands as if to keep from toppling off. The man to his immediate right had a broken nose and one thick black eyebrow that went straight across both eyes, giving him a primitive look that was completed by his close-cropped black beard. The gun in his left hand was a Smith & Wesson American .44. The other riders were ten years younger, but their faces were as hard as the weapons they brandished.

I finished my inspection and returned to Yardlinger's

side. The five of us were strung out across the street, forming a human barricade with guns in hand.

"That's Abel Turk next to Mather, the bearded one," the chief deputy informed me. "Foreman at the Six Bar Six. He hasn't seen many backs hereabouts since his reputation got around."

"What's going on, Murdock?" demanded the rancher in his phlegmy baritone. "Whole town in mourning for Marshal Arno?"

"Not until his replacement dried up the watering holes," I replied. "You're welcome to stay as long as you like, boys, but there'll be no drinking tonight."

"What gives you that right?" The man Yardlinger had identified as Abel Turk spoke quietly, with no threat in his deep voice. Never trust a man who's slow to anger. I looked him over again, then returned to Mather.

"Don't you tell your hands anything?"

"He told me some hot iron who calls himself Murdock is playing lawman," Turk said. "That still don't give you leave to refuse a thirsty cowman a drink."

"Maybe it doesn't. But this does." I patted the carbine.

"We aren't breaking any laws," huffed Mather.

"You're flashing a lot of steel for law-abiding citizens." He let that go. "You running us out of town?"

"Not at all. Like you said, you haven't broken any laws. But if you try to get into one of the saloons, I'll arrest you all for breaking and entering. I understand there's an open door on Arapaho Street."

"No thanks." The rancher gathered his reins. His shaggy gray tossed its head and whinnied softly, clouds of steam billowing from its nostrils. "I never did take to keeping all my chickens in one henhouse when there's a skunk loose."

I grinned. "There's an insult in there somewhere, but you're forgiven. Any word from Helena?"

"I sent your boss a wire asking him to relieve you as city

marshal. I haven't heard anything yet. He must keep banker's hours. What are you smirking about?"

"Life in general," I replied. Blackthorne had been in his office at least once since we'd parted, to confirm Yardlinger's query about my appointment. Ignoring Mather's request meant he wanted me to stay on as marshal. I didn't know why. His contrariness had been known to cause strokes among his superiors in Washington City.

The rancher's fever-sunken eyes darted to Yardlinger. "You in on this?"

"I do what I'm told." The former marshal's tone was noncommittal.

"What about the rest of you?"

Cross and Earl kept silent, letting their shotguns say it all. Major Brody spat tobacco at the gray's left forefoot, missing the hoof by less than an inch. The animal shied and blew out its nostrils.

Mather's breath whistled in his throat. Without a word he backed his horse out of line, wheeled, and spurred north. It took his men a moment to grasp that he was leaving, and then Turk replaced the hammer on the big American and rammed it into its holster. I caught the glitter of his eyes as he raked them over me, burning my face and figure into his memory. Then they were all gone in a cloud of dust.

"Twenty dollars says we'll see them again," I said, lowering the Winchester.

Yardlinger laid both his hammers carefully against the caps in the 12-gauge. "No bet."

"I'm thirsty," announced the Major.

I wasn't, but I needed a drink. "Is there a bottle in the office?"

"If you don't mind a dead man's liquor," the chief deputy nodded. "It belonged to Marshal Arno."

No one objected. Once the lamp was lit in the office, I

replaced four of the long guns in the rack along with the extra ammunition while Yardlinger excavated the bottle and Major Brody mopped out the bore of his Remington with oil and a rod. Earl, who had lagged behind to return the borrowed lanterns to the livery, entered just as the cork was pulled.

"That isn't store whiskey," I commented, looking at the crystal-clear liquid in the bottle.

"That's pure-oldie Masie-Dixie sippin' shine," whistled the Major. "Hunnert and ten proof."

"Longer it sits the stronger it gets," Yardlinger warned. "Bram wasn't much of a drinking man. He took it for evidence from a runner he arrested for introducing to the Cheyennes more than a year ago. I guess the marshal forgot he had it. The fellow hanged himself in his cell."

I said, "Don't talk, pour."

"Only one glass." He held up an amber-tinted container not much bigger than a thimble.

"Who needs it?" The Major seized the bottle.

So we sat around in chairs and on the oak railing, passing the vessel back and forth like kids in a barn, while Major Brody regaled us with progressively gorier war stories. The liquor was harsh and tasted of cork. After Earl's first pull and a fit of prolonged coughing, he left, and then the drinking got serious.

Somewhere a clock struck nine and Cross weaved out, mumbling something about dinner, a wife, and the imminence of violent death. Half an hour later the Major's monologue dropped to a growl and then silence. When he failed to respond the next time the bottle came around I made an effort to get out of my chair, then gave up and leaned forward, bracing my right arm with my left hand to tug open his eyelids.

"Well, he isn't dead."

"How can you tell?" said Yardlinger, and started

giggling. Someone else was laughing, high and quick like an idiot. I wondered who it was.

"I was just thinking—" He choked and went back to giggling.

I felt the laughter bubbling back up and tried to put it down with another swallow. Some of the whiskey got in my mouth. "What?"

"I was thinking," he said again, and gasped for air.

"Thinking what?"

"That we had about seven chances of getting killed tonight, and that if we did the city council would have been faced with the problem of appointing their third marshal in two days."

I was in the middle of another pull. I choked and he leaned across the desk to slap me mightily on the back, nearly falling over when he missed. I laughed then, so clearly and loudly I can hear it to this day. It was the funniest thing anyone had ever said. He laughed too. It went on like that for the better part of a minute, and when it died we looked at each other and started in again. Finally we were played out. I pushed the bottle across to him. There was a quarter inch left in the bottom.

"Who's Colleen Bower?"

"Who?" He was leaning as far back in the swivel chair as he could without going over, his head resting on the back and his eyes closed. His profile was limned in pale yellow from the low-burning lamp.

I repeated the name and tried to trace the outline of a female figure in the air with my hands. The result was closer to a bull fiddle, but I got my meaning across.

"No one knows for sure." The stove had gone out and his breath curled when he spoke. "She claims to have been a schoolteacher in Arkansas, but I don't credit it. For a while she called herself Poker Annie and dealt faro in and around the Nations. We got a reader on her a year ago, which was about the time she came to Breen. Couple of half-breeds got themselves shot up over her in Yankton. She cleared out right after and the U.S. marshal wanted to know what happened to a thousand dollars in gold one of the breeds lifted from the express office in Bismarck. Bram arrested her at the Glory where she was dealing and wired Yankton to come get her. Turned out they didn't want her any more. They'd found the gold in the Bismarck express clerk's closet."

"Arresting someone's a strange way to begin a courtship. You going to finish what's in that bottle or not?"

He opened his eyes and lifted it from the desk, missing the first time he reached for it. The contents drained, he replaced it carefully, using both hands. It fell over, rolled to the edge, and quivered there like a baby bird getting ready for its first flight.

"I think the rest of it was her idea," he said, watching the bottle. "Gamblers who expect to die in bed have two rules: don't get caught cheating and try to stay on the sunny side of the local law. That last part's easy when you wear petticoats."

"Where's she staying?" I could barely hear myself. I was warm from the alcohol and pleasantly drowsy.

"She's got a room at Martha's. What makes you so interested?"

"She's a double portion of woman."

He tried to focus on me, then gave up and returned his attention to the teetering vessel. "I might believe that's your reason if I didn't know you had black powder for blood."

"You wrong me cruelly."

"Sabers at dawn," he suggested, and flicked a finger at the bottle. It thudded to the floor without breaking and rolled to a rest against a leg of my chair. Then he got up, clawing at the edge of the desk for support.

Stumbling over to where the Major slumped snoring in a broken chair with his toothless mouth wide open, Yardlinger bumped into furniture a couple of times and placed a finger to his lips, shushing himself. Carefully he plucked the shotgun from the old man's grasp and returned it to the rack. When the chain was secure he curled up in the middle of a colorful Indian rug on the floor behind the desk and went to sleep with his hands under his head. I remember resenting him for taking the best spot in the room, after which I don't remember much of anything.

I felt fine the next morning until I opened my eyes.

# CHAPTER 8

Light showed pink through my eyelids. When I finally got them unstuck, slow pain opened in my skull like a dirty blossom and found the spot where the Bower woman had tried to split it open with her gun. I closed my eyes and waited for merciful sleep to overtake me again. When it didn't I opened them more carefully, shielding them with a hand from daylight as I levered myself out of the chair. Every muscle in my body had something to say about it.

Major Brody remained as we had left him, dragging air through a mouth gaped wide enough to tempt bats. I glanced toward the rug but Yardlinger was gone. At that moment he came in through the opening in the partition holding a wet washrag on the back of his neck. His face was puffy and unshaven.

When he saw me he snarled something about a basin in back. I thumped off in that direction, wondering if I looked as bad as he did. The wavy mirror over the basin said I looked worse.

He had thrown out his wash water, but the pitcher under the stand was half full. I poured some of its contents into the bowl and stuck my head in as far as it would go. It wasn't far enough. I toweled off and returned to the office. The Major's chair was empty.

"Went home," Yardlinger explained from his seat at the desk. "Chipper as a goddamn squirrel. He said the closest he ever came to dissipation was the time a Kansas jayhawker broke a Springfield rifle stock over his head. I told him that didn't qualify."

I placed my hat gingerly on my head. "Watch the office. If you've got a razor here you might do something to make yourself presentable. You look like a mile and a half of collapsed tunnel."

"You don't look like Edwin Booth in *Hamlet*."

My riding clothes were waiting for me at the Freestone, freshly cleaned and brushed. I put them on after a bath and a careful shave (the scratches from my Breen House adventure had scabbed over nicely) and gave my wrinkled city trappings to the attendant for the same treatment. In the restaurant next door I forced myself to eat a hearty breakfast, ignoring the curious looks of nearby diners as I scribbled with a pencil stub on a linen napkin. Word of last night's adventure had gotten around.

Next I presented myself at the office of the Breen *Democrat* on Mandan Street, where a chest-high counter separated me from a wainscoted chamber in which a man in shirtsleeves rolled up past his elbows and a greasy leather apron was screwing down a huge flatbed press. Nearby, a boy not much older than fourteen selected pieces of lead type from a flat case and slid them into a composing stick in his left hand. Stacks of brown newsprint and bound papers left only narrow aisles to walk through, and black ink was smeared over everything, including the man at the press.

I waited five minutes and then rapped my knuckles on the counter top. The press man glanced up irritably.

"Keep your drawers on. Newspapers don't run themselves."

Some more time passed, and then he climbed down from a step plate built onto the machine, set aside an oilcan he had been using to lubricate the big screw, and crabwalked between dangerously leaning piles of paper to the counter, stopping once to light a charred black pipe taken from his hip pocket. He was small and lean, in his late fifties, and had a shock of unkempt brown hair that looked black because of the ink in it.

"How soon can I have a hundred of these printed up?" I unfolded the napkin I'd borrowed from the restaurant and spread it out on the counter. He took a pair of wire-rimmed spectacles from a shirt pocket and hooked them on one ear at a time to read what I'd written.

" 'Reward,' " he read tonelessly. " 'One hundred dollars for information leading to the arrest and conviction of one or all of the culprits responsible for illegal harassment of employees at the Terwilliger ranch. See P. Murdock, acting city marshal.' " He peeled aside the spectacles. "You P. Murdock?"

The boy at the typecase turned to stare at me.

I admitted I was Murdock. The man said, "Maybe this will interest you," and left me to skin a broadsheet off the bed of the press. Holding it by the corners he returned to the counter and draped it over the top. "Ink's wet," he warned.

Half of the center two columns was claimed by a line drawing of a jowly old jasper with sad eyes and a great white handlebar moustache, encircled by a black wreath. The caption read:

ABRAHAM SHELLEY ARNO
1828–1879
Friend and Champion

"Folks around here hold the late marshal in high regard, do they?" I asked.

The newspaperman made an impolite noise around the stem of his pipe. "The old bastard. Last week I ran an editorial calling for his dismissal on the grounds of early senility. But that isn't what I wanted you to see. Third column, at the end of all that horse dung about Arno's years of service."

It was headed NEW MARSHAL IMPOSES PROHIBITON:

Page Murdock, Breen City Marshal by no other authority than the whim of United States Judge Harlan A. Blackthorne, spent his first hours in office yesterday evening closing down every drinking establishment on Pawnee Street. "Strong drink is at the bottom of man's baser passions," sources close to the peace officer have quoted him as saying. "Remove it, and you remove the need for law enforcement itself." Owners and patrons of the establishments visited by Murdock and his deputies found their protestations met with guns.

Our question is this: Does Marshal Murdock really yearn so strongly for unemployment, and if he does, is it not our duty as citizens to do everything in our power to fulfill that yearning?

I met the newspaperman's impassive gaze. "Who are the 'sources close to the peace officer,' or did you make them up?"

"If you want to refute the story, write us a letter to the editor. I acknowledge no arguments beyond the columns of the *Democrat*."

"If you knew what my head feels like this morning, you wouldn't accuse me of teetotaling."

"I thought your eyes looked a little bloodshot."

I tapped the napkin with my scrawl on it. "Are you going to print my handbills or do I have to do them myself in longhand?"

"Five dollars."

"Bill me at the office."

"In advance." He held out an inkstained palm.

I gave it to him. "You know what they call a man who doesn't trust anyone."

"A newspaperman."

He said the handbills would be ready that afternoon and gave me a receipt, after which I dropped by the gunsmith's to learn that the Swede was fitting the Deane-Adams' new grip. I said I'd check back later. Returning to the office, I found Yardlinger at the desk adding new wanted posters to a dog-eared folder nearly full of them. He still looked like someone who had had too much to drink the night before, but at least he had shaved.

"Telegram came for you." He indicated an envelope on the corner of the desk.

I tore it open. It was signed by Blackthorne.


SWAMPED WITH PROTESTS STOP CITIZENRY
CALLING YOU CONDEMNED TEMPERANCE WOMAN
STOP WHAT THE DEUCE HAPPENING


"Condemned" was Western Union's prim substitute for "damned." I wondered about "deuce" for a moment, decided it wasn't important anyway, and disposed of the litter in the stove. "Anything else?"

He smirked. "Poker Annie didn't come around asking for you, if that's what you mean."

I didn't acknowledge. I had hoped he'd forget that part

of last night's alcoholic conversation. "I'll spell you at noon." I turned back toward the door.

"Where are you going now?"

"Martha's."

He raised his eyebrows. "In broad daylight?"

"Business," I said.

"Yours or hers?"

I told him to go to hell and left.

The den of ill fame was a pleasant-looking white-washed frame building two stories high, set back from the street with a freshly winnowed lawn between it and the boardwalk. Tulips were budding in boxes attached to the ground-floor windows, promising better things later in the season. As I turned into the short walk I was passed by a hatchet-faced woman in a dull charcoal dress who picked up her skirts and her pace with a loud "Hmph!"

The brass door knocker made a genteel sound, followed by a short silence and then a slight shifting of floorboards as footsteps approached. Colleen Bower opened the door.

She was wearing chocolate brown today, relieved only by a dash of ivory-colored lace at her neck. Her hair was up and a dust of powder effectively concealed the discoloration on her jaw. She recognized me and tried to take an impression of my face with my side of the door. I leaned my shoulder against it.

"Why so testy? I thought we'd made up."

"That was before I found out I couldn't eat solid food." She spoke through her teeth.

I touched my scratches. "At least you don't have to shave."

"You can live without shaving. Liquid diets are for geraniums."

"Is it any worse than what they serve in jail?"

She glared. The gold flecks in her eyes seemed to spin and give off their own light. "So you checked up on me.

Did they tell you about the time I was almost hanged in New Mexico?"

"That story hasn't reached here yet. What did you do?"

"Took cattle in trade. Some of them turned out to be stolen. Now that you know more than you did coming in, I'm sure you'll excuse me. There's a draft." She tried again to push the door shut, but my body was still in the way.

"I'm on official business," I explained. "Is Martha in?"

"I'm in."

The voice was mannish, like its owner. When Colleen turned her head I saw Martha standing before a beaded curtain in a doorway opposite, tall and square-shouldered in a severe black dress closed at the neck with an emerald brooch. She had a firm jaw, and the bones of her face protruded sharply from the frame of her hair, brushed back into a black halo like Japanese women wore in the indelicate prints butchers sold in the back room, and pinned in place. She nodded slightly at Colleen, who opened the door wider and stepped aside. I entered and the door was closed.

"Martha Foster." The older woman gave me her hand. It was warm but dry and nearly as large as mine. "I'm sorry, Marshal, but the maid is out and we can't offer you the hospitality we're famous for."

Colleen executed a cold curtsy and rustled out, leaving me alone in a room full of too much furniture with a woman as tall as I was. Martha Foster had a faint moustache and one milky eye from a cataract, but she held her head like a grand lady. She looked amused.

"I think Colleen likes you."

I laid my hat on a pedestal table covered with a lace shawl. "Last time she saw me she tried to part my scalp with a bullet. Just now she made a spirited effort to rearrange my features with your front door. I'd hate to have her fall in love with me."

"That's just her way. But you haven't come to ask me for her hand."

"Not if her nails go with it," I said. "I suppose you know about my agreement with Pardee."

"Very little happens in Breen that I don't know about, Marshal. Men tell things to women in my line. Which is why you're here, I would guess."

"You're a very canny woman, Mrs. Foster."

"Please. Martha," she said, smiling tightly.

# CHAPTER 9

She offered me a chintz-covered armchair but I declined, inviting as it looked. My muscles were still complaining from the ride from Helena and last night's excesses, and there was no guarantee I'd be able to get out of it when the time came.

"I'll only be a minute," I explained. "What I'm after is a drunken boast, a chance comment overheard by one of your girls that might lead me to whoever's been terrorizing Terwilliger's waddies. It's a kid thing. Chances are it'll never come to trial, but an honest effort on my part with some kind of result might head off a range war. That kind of thing is bad business for everybody."

"Everybody but us," she corrected. "Range wars bring guns and men to operate them. The only thing I have to worry about in this business is a shortage of men."

"I expect they'll start getting short soon enough. Does that mean you won't help?"

"I can't. There are no secrets here. If anything important had passed about those raids, I'd have heard. I haven't."

I breathed some air. "I was afraid of that. From what

I've seen of Périgueux and Mather, they're not the type to hire flapjaws. If they're behind it. What about the Frenchman? Is he a customer?"

She shook her head. The milk-eye refused to glitter like its mate in the sunlight sifting through the door fan. "He has a wife with whom he appears to be content." There was the least suggestion of disrespect in her pronunciation of the word "wife."

"Dick Mather?"

"Mather is married too, and I'm told he's very sick. I doubt that he's thought of a woman in months."

Next time, I told myself, I'd make my wagers with the cards face up. "I suppose all the cowhands come here."

"Most of them."

"I'd appreciate it if you'd ask the girls to keep their ears open. If they hear anything, I'd take it as a personal favor if you'd pass it along."

She smiled, keeping her lips pressed tight. I'd noticed that when she spoke she held her hand in front of her mouth. Bad teeth were one of the lesser evils of her profession. "Don't misunderstand me, Marshal. I have nothing against casting my bread upon the waters, as long as I can expect something more than soggy crusts in return. To be coarse, what's in it for me?"

"Breen must have a fire ordinance," I said, "and if it doesn't, it will. I doubt that all this furniture cluttering the escape route would fit its guidelines. It might become my duty to close you down until the proper adjustments were made. The decision to allow you to reopen would also be mine, based on a thorough inspection."

"Your predecessor proposed something of the sort." She was still smiling. "It had to do with a fee for protection from damage and robbery. He didn't get it. We entertain some influential people."

"I don't answer to local authority."

"So I heard. Unlike the situation with the saloons, however, there are men willing to defend our right to dispense our services, with guns. It could be very untidy. But there is a way we can agree."

"I'm listening."

Her head was turned slightly to bring her good eye square on my face. "You may have noticed that this building bunts up against the harness shop next door. The structures share a common wall. I'd like to buy the shop, cut an arch into it, and expand my operation before the railroad comes. But this town has strict deadlining ordinances and the good ladies of Breen have bullied the council into denying me access. If someone were to persuade them to reconsider, I'd be willing to take your request under advisement."

"That's a lot to pay for information that may never come."

"Those are my terms."

I picked up my hat. "You'll be hearing from me."

"Our door is always open, Marshal." She walked me to it.

I went from there to the telegraph office, where I killed an hour drafting a full report of my activities up to that point for the Judge and sent it collect. Then I hastened out before the answer came.

The Swede was perched on a high stool behind the glass counter, eating lunch from a greasy bag when I entered the gunsmith's shop. I could smell his hardboiled egg sandwich from the doorway. He set aside the half he was eating and climbed down chewing to transfer the English revolver from the workbench to the counter. My fingers curled around the walnut grip like a woman embracing her lover after a long separation. It felt good. The sight was true, and when I freed the cylinder it spun without a catch.

"You're a true artist," I said, thrusting the gun under one arm while I dug out a ten, the balance of the price.

"Been told that." The Swede held the bill up to the light and popped it, then folded it in quarters, and poked it into a pocket of his vest. "Compliments don't buy doodly."

I bought a box of .45 cartridges in a brand that fit the Deane-Adams and left him sitting on his stool, picking up where he'd left off on his odorous sandwich. Back at the hotel I dismantled the new gun, laying the parts out carefully on the bedspread, and wiped each part with an oily rag from the kit I carried in a cigar box. I used a clean rag to remove the excess and put the whole thing back together. It hadn't needed cleaning; that was just my way of getting acquainted.

Finally I unbuckled the belt and holster I was wearing and put on the one I'd brought with me from the capital, designed for the gun I'd lost in Dakota. The rig seemed light even after I'd loaded the five-shot. I walked up and down the length of the room to get the feel of it before going back out.

"You're five minutes late," observed Yardlinger, putting away his watch and reaching for his hat. "I hope she was worth it."

It took me a moment to realize he was referring to my stop at Martha's. "Don't be disrespectful. Have Earl spell me at two. I've got an errand to run this afternoon."

"I'll tell him five minutes after."

After he left I wasted some time with my feet on the desk and my hat tilted forward over my eyes the way lawmen did in the *New York Detective Library*, and when I tired of that I went through the drawers, found the yellowback novel Earl had been reading the day before, and began reading. My study was uninterrupted by shooting in the street or window-smashing barroom brawls or runaway horse teams towing the banker's screaming daughter. Next to a cell, the marshal's office in a western town was the dullest place this side of Commodore Vanderbilt's drawing room. It got so I looked forward to the occasional trips from the woodbox to the stove.

Earl came in just as I was finishing the book. I tucked the loose pages into place the way you straighten up a deck of cards, dropped it back into its drawer, and rose, my backside feeling as if it had been slapping a saddle all day.

"How do I get to Périgueux's ranch?" I adjusted my hat.

He checked the stove, decided it didn't need stoking, and pushed the lid shut. "Ride due east from anywhere in the world and you can't miss it. Why?"

"I've got poker fever. Think I'll offer the Marquis a piece of Pardee's action."

"Huh?"

"Mind the store."

I was riding a white-faced roan stallion that year, with one walleye and a disposition like a trodden snake. The old Negro who looked after the livery stable appeared glad to see me and rolled back a checked cotton sleeve to show me two semicircular bruises on his forearm where he'd been bitten while strapping on the feedbag. I paid him for the horse's care to that point and tipped him handsomely. He couldn't write, so I scribbled the transaction on the back of Blackthorne's last telegram and got his mark.

The roan made a halfhearted attempt to reach back and nip me as I was mounting, but I ignored it and he didn't follow through. He remembered the first time he'd tried that and the taste of blood on his tongue when I kicked him in the teeth. We understood each other.

It was shaping up to be a fine spring day as I cleared the city limits and swung east. The air was crisp—my breath was a quick gray jet that vanished as soon as it left my mouth—but the sun was pasted alone on a construction-paper sky and hills of dead grass described wavy lines of fuzzy yellow crayon between the mountain ranges to east and west. The scenery looked like a child's drawing.

The sun was an hour down when a solitary rider crested a rise a couple of miles ahead, moving fast across country. He dropped out of sight behind the next hill, reappearing closer a few minutes later as he came to the top of that one, then vanishing again. By the time he came over the fourth swell I could see that he had a rifle crossed behind his saddle horn. I loosened the Deane-Adams in its holster and kept riding, cursing myself for leaving behind the Winchester.

He pulled up four hundred yards short and sat waiting. He had a buttermilk horse with a white mane like you see in the Wild West shows, that lashed its head up and down on a long neck, shaking it with a wobbling motion.

The road swung right past him. When the distance closed to a hundred and fifty yards the rider brought his rifle upright, bracing it on his pelvis. I slowed up after another fifty and stopped. My roan shied toward the road edge and the new grass beginning to poke through the surface. I reined its head back to face the other rider. His horse pawed the ground and looked bored. He didn't.

"This here's Périgueux land," he announced in a high, clear voice that rang like a new penny on a polished counter.

He was even younger than Earl, about eighteen. His yellow hair was long as a girl's and he wore rimless spectacles that flashed white in the sun. His Stetson was the color of dried sweat and dust and his jeans had faded to match the hide of his fleece-lined jacket. The only thing bright about him was a red bandana knotted loosely at his throat. His rifle was one I hadn't seen before, which for me was going some. A single-shot from the look of it, it had a long barrel and a lever shaped like a question mark, and looked about as native as his employer's accent.

For all I knew it could fire out both ends and never need cleaning.

"I'm Murdock, here to see Périgueux," I explained. "Likely he's mentioned me."

He chewed on that for a space. He had thick lips that slacked open and a gap between his front teeth. "Let's see something."

Keeping my right hand hidden, I dug the first two fingers of my left into my shirt pocket and flipped the star over his head like a coin. He lost it in the sun for a moment, then spotted it on the way down and snatched at it with his free hand. It sprang out of his reach with a twang that was swallowed by the accompanying report. The echo growled in the distant mountains and died hissing.

His reflexes were fast. He swung the rifle down between the shot and the echo, but I recocked the Deane-Adams and he froze with his finger on the trigger.

He said, "That ain't necessary. That there's a double-action, it don't need recocking. I seen it in Thorson's shop."

"I didn't want to chance your not knowing that. The rifle." I held out my empty hand.

He stalled as long as you're supposed to in his situation, then extended the weapon butt first shamefacedly, like a boy handing over his slingshot to a sharp-eyed schoolmaster.

"Nice," I said, balancing it on top of my wrist. "What is it?"

"English. The Marquis gave it to me."

I looked it over and lowered it to the throat of my saddle. "I know you're doing your job, but I don't like rifles pointing at me from horseback. You never know when the animal might jar your finger on the trigger. Let's go talk to your boss." I holstered the revolver.

He swung the yellow horse around and started walking. I left the road to follow. At length I spied my badge gleaming in the grass and leaned down to pick it up. There was a dent between two of the points where my bullet had glanced off, not its first.

# CHAPTER 10

"**Y**ou need those glasses?"

We had been riding side by side for half an hour. The scenery hadn't changed and the silence, together with the constant hammocking between the rolling hills, was stultifying. I'd about given up on getting an answer when he said, "Beats walking into doors."

"Don't they get in the way of the little holes?"

He turned that over and studied it from both sides before responding. "Holes?"

"The ones you cut in the pillowcase to see through while you're wearing it. It's a mystery to me how you can see to sling a rope over a branch. Or are you the one that holds the horse?"

Our mounts' fetlocks swished through the grass, the only sound for miles. He was either slow or cautious. I had my money on the latter. "You been talking to Pardee."

I shook my head. "His mind is made up it's Mather's men doing the harassing. I think it's spread around a little more than that."

"Don't believe I'll say anything more."

"About time, chatterbox."

Two hours out of Breen we topped a rise higher than most and the framework of a huge building sprang into view atop a graded hill on the horizon. It was taller than it was wide, towering forty feet over the ranch house sprawled an acre away. The outbuildings in between looked like children's scattered blocks. Here and there across the rippled vastness that separated the Big and Little Belt Mountains, cattle grazed alone and in clumps. Squinting, I could just make out men crawling over the half-finished roof of the skeletal structure like termites.

"That's some barn your boss is building," I commented.

"Barn, hell." For once he spoke without hesitation. "That's his new headquarters."

"What's he need a castle for way out here?"

"He calls it a chateau." It came out "shat-oo."

A couple of lanky cowhands were leaning on the corral fence, smoking and watching as a third sidled up to a black mare in the enclosure with a coil of rope in hand, making kissing noises to calm the skittish animal. The pair turned their heads to follow our progress to the ranch house. They were young, but their faces were brown and cracked at the corners of their eyes and mouths from months of squinting against harsh sunlight.

As we neared the long front porch, a maple block of a man came out and rested the barrel of a Remington rolling-block rifle on the porch railing. He was dressed in colorless jeans and a red-and-white plaid shirt that had bled pink from too many scrubbings.

"Who we got, Arnie?" His pleasant baritone didn't go with the steel in his eyes. Hatless, he was bald to the crown, but the blond handlebar that swung below his cheeks more than made up for the dearth of hair topside. He looked forty and was probably closer to thirty.

"Who's got who is open to question." I held up Arnie's English rifle. "Just for the record, though, the name's Murdock."

He studied me. "I heard you was mean-looking. You don't look like such a much to me."

"That's what a good night's sleep will do for you. Is he in?"

"To you maybe. Not to all that iron."

I thrust the foreign rifle into Arnie's hands. He flushed beneath the older man's angry gaze.

"Sorry, Uncle Ed."

There was a brief silence, and then the other's face clouded suddenly and he clomped off the porch carrying the Remington, reached up and wrenched the English gun out of Arnie's grasp by its barrel. The pretty horse flinched snorting and backed up a step. Its master looked even more frightened.

"You just let two men take it away from you in one afternoon." The blocky man was breathing heavily, his chest pumping as if from a great effort. "You'll get it back when you learn to hang on to it."

I said, "Do you do that often?"

"Do what?" He was still glaring at the abashed youth.

"Grab a loaded rifle by the muzzle and yank. I knew a deputy sheriff who used to do that with pistols. He's got a pretty widow."

He grunted and turned away, carrying the rifles at his sides like buckets of slop. As he walked he swung his left leg in a half-circle without bending the knee. The limp was more noticeable when he wasn't in a hurry. "Wait here." At the door he turned to nail Arnie again. "You tell Kruger to get someone else to ride line. Man can't drive off rustlers without no gun." The door banged in its casing.

The boy pressed his thick lips tight and wheeled, kicking yard mud over my roan's flanks as he cantered off toward the long low bunkhouse on the other side of the corral. I dismounted and hitched up to the porch railing. The man with the handlebar came out while I was yanking the tie. He was still carrying the Remington, but he had ditched the foreign piece.

"He'll talk."

I stepped onto the porch. "Lead the way, Uncle Ed."

"Name's Strayhorn." He braced his right foot on the threshold and vaulted the other up and over.

We passed through a shallow entrance hall into a large room with a redwood floor and two large windows in the south wall made of rows of eight-inch-square panes that let in plenty of light. Quilted-leather chairs squatted around a fireplace of whitewashed stone big enough for a man to crouch in. Above the mantel, a painting of Napoleon I on horseback scowled from a heavy gold frame, but aside from that, there was nothing French about the room save its owner.

The Marquis was standing in gartered shirtsleeves and a red silk vest to the right of the fireplace with his hands clasped behind his back like a St. Louis shoe clerk and Arnie's rifle on a low mahogany table in front of him. His forelock and pointed whiskers looked even more preposterous in these surroundings than they had in my hotel room.

"Dear me, you have had an accident," he observed.

I'd forgotten about the cheek scratches. "I'll live."

"In my country, marks like those are considered a measure of one's manhood."

"In my country they're considered evidence of rape."

"Oh, but they are not so deep as that. Perhaps just a little rape. Thank you, Edward."

It was a dismissal, but Strayhorn hesitated. "I still think I should take his gun."

"Nonsense. Assassination is not Monsieur Murdock's way." His tone held a sarcastic edge. The other man raked his hard eyes over me as he limped out, still holding the buffalo gun.

"That's a fine rifle," I ventured, nodding at the weapon on the table. "Balanced like a clock."

He picked it up and cradled it lovingly. In his small hands it looked like a cannon. "It is a Martini light four hundred, presented to me by the Empress Eugénie at the time I left Europe. At one hundred yards it has a striking energy of one thousand four hundred and forty-three foot-pounds. It is the only thing of any worth that the English have ever produced, and it comes as no surprise that it was designed by an Italian. The first Napoleon was Italian, you know."

"As I recall, it was an Englishman who defeated him."

"Well, you have not come to discuss history." He replaced the rifle with a startling noise. I had drawn blood.

"I met Pardee last night," I said. "Terwilliger's foreman. He swears neither he nor his boss sent for Chris Shedwell."

"Were I in their position, I would swear as much."

"I believe him."

"My compliments. Your faith in your fellow man is to be admired, if not imitated."

"His reasoning was sound. Why were he and his men in town last night to start something with Mather if he'd arranged for Shedwell to balance the account?"

"Then perhaps you can tell me why he is coming?" When I didn't answer he frowned exaggeratedly, pushing out his lips. "Let us say, just for the sake of argument, that Monsieur Terwilliger has not engaged Monsieur Shedwell's talents and that he is coming only to visit his dear mother, assuming that he has one. How does that change anything? The small ranchers continue to swell their herds at the expense of their larger neighbors."

"How can you be sure they've been rustling Six Bar Six cattle?"

"It is not just Mather's misfortune. The spring roundup has begun, and already the tallies are falling behind estimates. We expect a loss of a thousand calves. Perhaps more."

"Estimates based on book count," I said. "We may be talking about calves that never existed."

"It would be a very large error, would it not? Unpardonable."

"Even if you're right, that's a lot of rustling for one man. He wouldn't have any time left to run his ranch."

"He is not the only small rancher in the territory, monsieur. I do not claim that he alone is responsible for the loss. But he is the leader."

"Let's talk straight," I said. "It wouldn't matter if not one calf came up missing or if you found a thousand more than you estimated. You'd just find some other way to justify clearing out the small fry and claiming the open range for yourself."

I had raised my voice without realizing it. Now I heard footsteps behind me and turned to see Ed Strayhorn standing in front of the door with his ever-present Remington in both hands. I backed away at an angle, resting my right hand on the Deane-Adams.

"Call off your foreman."

"Bookkeeper," Périgueux corrected. "The leg, you see. But it does not hinder his aim. Please leave."

"Not until I've said what I came to say. Last night I made a deal with Pardee to let me handle the situation my way. I was going to cut you in, but since you're not interested, I'll say this: if Terwilliger or Pardee or any of their men is hurt or killed while I'm marshal, even if it's from falling off a horse—hell, even if it's from smallpox—I'll know right where to go. And I'll have help."

"Are you finished?" asked the Frenchman, after a pause.

"Not quite. I need directions to Terwilliger's spread. I want to ask Dale Pardee about some night riders that have been bothering him lately. You wouldn't know anything about that."

"I have heard rumors." He pointed at a framed parchment

map on the west wall. It was shaped roughly like a water jug with a chipped neck. "That is my ranch, and that"—he indicated the missing piece—"is the Circle T, belonging to Monsieur Terwilliger, twelve miles west by northwest."

"That must be like a splinter in your ear."

"It itches from time to time. *Au revoir*, Monsieur Murdock. That means—"

"I know what it means." I shouldered my way past Strayhorn.

# CHAPTER 11

I hadn't time to ride to the Circle T, interview Pardee's brother, and get back to town before nightfall, so I postponed that trip until morning. Night was the time when all hell broke loose in cattle towns. A mile out of Breen I got out the bottle I'd brought in my saddlebag from Helena for the cold nights and drained the eighth of an inch of colored liquid left in the bottom. The temperature had hovered around thirty most nights, and as I said before it was a long ride. I swung out of the saddle and set up the empty on the spine of a low ridge. It was time I found out how much I could expect from the new gun.

I rode out forty yards, dismounted again, passed the Deane-Adams up and down the length of my sleeve just to hear the cylinder clack around and took aim at the neck of the bottle while the roan, ground-trained but pretending not to be, wandered off after new grass. Sunlight glared off the smooth glass, but I didn't change my angle. It glares off a man's belt buckle the same way, and he isn't likely to wait while you find a better location.

I stood sideways to the target because I'm harder to hit that way, sighting down the length of my outstretched arm the way they don't in the dime novels, and was squeezing the trigger when the bottle separated into two pieces with a hollow plop. The neck and the base tilted away from each other like halves of a wishbone, and then the shot crashed, its echo retreating toward the mountains like rumbling thunder. I hit the ground for the third time in two days and rolled behind a clump of bramble.

After half a minute I used the barrel of the revolver to part the brush and peered out. To the west, a man on horseback nosed a carbine into a before-the-knee scabbard, smacked his reins across the animal's withers, and came galloping straight at me.

The sun at his back was blinding. Squinting, I hunkered down with my shooting arm resting straight out in the bramble's crotch and waited for him to move into pistol range.

A hundred yards off he reined in and leaned on his fists on the pommel of his saddle. He wore a linen duster over a town suit and his face was in shadow beneath the brim of a black hat I thought I'd seen before.

"Murdock," he called, his voice rising and falling on the prairie wind, "you are a one for lying down in the middle of the afternoon."

"You son of a bitch," I muttered in relief. But I held onto the revolver. Raising my voice: "Yardlinger, you are a one for asking to get your moustache shot off."

"Not unless that gun Thorson sold you fires Sharps Big Fifty cartridges."

I got up, holding it at hip level. Sometimes it pays to look like you walked out of something by Ned Buntline. "Step down and start leading your horse this way. From the left side, opposite the scabbard. I'll tell you when to stop. And keep your hand away from your belt gun."

He was quiet for a moment. "You don't set much store by friends."

"I had a friend once," I said. "He tried to gut me with a skinning knife when I beat his straight with a full house. Move."

He did as directed, leading his piebald by the bit and holding his left arm straight out to the side like a carpenter carrying a heavy toolbox in the other hand. The rifle on the saddle was the Winchester carbine I'd carried the night before. When he was fifty feet away I motioned him with the revolver to stop.

"Now neither of us has to shout." I relaxed a little, resting the butt of the Deane-Adams on the bone of my hip. "Start with why you shattered that bottle."

"Is that all that's biting you?" He smiled, but it died short of his eyes. "I never could resist a target like that. I'm the champion rifle shot of the county three years running."

I watched him, especially his eyes. At length I sighed and replaced the revolver in its holster. "It was a hell of a good shot." I wanted to say something more, to try and restore the good thing that had been growing between us. Instead I said, "What are you doing out here?"

"Looking for you." His tone was colder than it had been when we'd met. "Pardee rolled into town an hour ago on a buckboard. His brother's in the back. Someone lynched him, and this time they finished the job."

We found the buckboard in front of one of the town's two undertaking parlors. The box was empty but for a coil of rotted twine and about a pound of wet sawdust, wagon stuff. BYRON C. FITCH, MORTICIAN was lettered in gold paint across the parlor's curtained front window.

The interior of the parlor looked more like a cathouse than most cathouses I'd seen. Curtains were drawn across

the front window and lamplight sifted dimly over the
muted carpet and rows of mourners' chairs arranged in
front of a casket on a raised platform draped in black felt.
The sweet smell of hothouse-grown flowers enveloped us
as we entered.

An old man with wispy white hair brushed back over
dry pink scalp and a scowl that had defied the undertaker's best efforts lay in the casket, his head raised on a satin
pillow and spotted hands folded across his vest. We took
off our hats, as if that mattered any more, and went on past
him through a door standing half open into the back room.

Rosy light from the setting sun fell through two small
windows high in the west wall, illuminating a cluttered
pine bench, half a dozen lidless caskets, and a naked corpse
stretched out on a pair of planks nailed together and
propped across a pair of sawhorses. The raw stench of
formaldehyde contrasted sharply with the flowery smell in
the parlor.

A pudgy man in shirtsleeves who had been bent over
the body glanced up and said, "Thank God! Please help
Mr. Pardee out of here, Marshal. He's not doing anyone
any good, especially himself." I recognized him as the man
I had seen riding shotgun on Marshal Arno's hearse the
day before.

Pardee, in rusty range clothes and a Stetson grown colorless from sweat and weather, looked like a man on the
wrong end of a long fever. His face was slack and heavy,
his eyes hot and sunk deep in purple-black sockets. I almost didn't recognize him without a cigar.

"Look at him." His voice was so low he might have been
praying. "Look at what those bastards did to him." He was
gazing at the thing on the planks.

The dead man was whipsaw-lean, tanned from neck to
hairline and from fingers to wrists, and gray-white everywhere else. His eyes bulged, the burst blood vessels in the

whites black and twisted like hairs on the lip of a wash-basin, and his tongue was a dark swollen thing that had grown too big for his mouth to hold. The rope had burned a blue line around his neck and the weight of his body had stretched it twice its normal length. His clothes had been flung to the floor in a heap.

"Pardee said he was last seen this morning, when he rode north after some strays," Yardlinger said. "When he didn't show up by midafternoon, Pardee and some of the hands went looking for him. They found him dangling from a tree a mile inside the Circle T's northwest corner."

"A mile short of the Six Bar Six." The foreman's prayerful moan had fallen to a hoarse whisper. "They didn't even bother to tie much of a knot. They just let him strangle."

"Whose strays was he after?" I asked. "Terwilliger's or Mather's?"

Yardlinger gaped. "Murdock, for God's sake—"

But Pardee was already moving. In one spring he was on me, his big muscular hands squeezing my throat. His eyes bulged like his dead brother's and saliva foamed at the corner of his mouth. I scooped out the Deane-Adams and pronged the barrel deep into the arch of his rib cage. Air whooshed out his lungs, spittle flecking my face. But he held on. My vision turned black around the edges.

I was about to fire when there was a solid *thunk* like an axe sinking into soft wood; Pardee's eyes rolled over white, his hands clutched at my shoulders for support when his grip failed on my throat. I stepped back and he toppled forward, first onto his knees and then onto his hands, where he stayed with his head hanging down.

Yardlinger was standing over him, holding his Navy Colt like a hammer with the butt foremost. When he was sure the foreman's part in the drama was finished he exe-outed a neat spin that ended with the gun securely in its holster.

"Obliged. Not that I needed help." I put up my own gun the conventional way.

"He was in the right. That was a hell of a thing to say."

"Maybe. If those strays had turned out to be Mather's, I'd have known where to look for his brother's killer."

"That won't be a problem."

"Mather strikes me as smarter than that, knowing we'd suspect him. Unless some of his hands decided to do the boss a favor on their own time."

"That's Turk all over."

The undertaker was agitated. "Quick, Marshal, get Mr. Pardee out of here. He makes me nervous."

"I can see why," said the deputy. "Your customers don't usually comment on your work." He'd been watching Pardee, who remained in a daze on his hands and knees. Now Yardlinger looked at the little man. "He had five men with him when I left. Where'd they go?"

The undertaker shrugged distractedly. "They went out right after helping carry in the body."

I said, "Twenty dollars on where they're going," and started walking.

Yardlinger called after me. "It'll be dark in a few minutes. You'll break your neck."

"That'll save Judge Blackthorne the trouble when he hears I let a range war blow up in my jurisdiction. I'll fetch the other deputies. Lock up Pardee and wait for us at the jail." I scattered empty chairs on my way through the parlor.

# CHAPTER 12

We clattered down the freezing, shadow-splashed street at full gallop, five men on wild-eyed horses loaded down with iron, a hellish sight for the curious who had come out to see what the commotion was about. Of the two rifles left in the rack I had chosen a Henry for myself and made Cross give up his shotgun for a Spencer. Yardlinger, who held on to the Winchester, informed me that Earl and the Major knew their way around handguns well enough to do without. The old man, who had no horse of his own, had commandeered one from the livery. Our destination was the Six Bar Six.

Clouds boiled past the moon, merging the solid black of trees lining the road with the smothering wrap of the night itself. The horses were frightened and let us know with whinnies drawn thin as threads of molten silver. Vapor billowed from their nostrils. The air was as cold as the water in a mountain stream.

Yardlinger rode point as guide. At first I had nothing to go by but the feel of his piebald's backdrifting breath on my face, but as my eyes caught up with the darkness I was able to make out his lanky form in the saddle. Now all I had to worry about was the occasional chuckhole in the road, which could splinter a horse's cannon like green wood.

Time stands still at night. It might have been five minutes and it might have been an hour before we heard a crackling in the distance, as of someone crumpling brittle parchment. There was no telling from which direction the sound of the shots had come. I slowed to a canter and finally to a walk, barking at the others to do the same.

"What we doglegging for?" Earl wanted to know. "You got a bet on how it'll come out?"

I ignored the sneer in his tone. "We won't get there any faster on dead horses."

"He's right. Shut up," said Yardlinger.

We alternated between cantering and walking while the animals' sides heaved and their spent breath enveloped us in a shroud of moist warmth. Meanwhile, the distant crackling continued in fits and starts, now pausing, now erupting again in flurries so rapid it was impossible to count the individual reports. It sounded unreal, like fake gunfire onstage.

The horses smelled it first and passed it along to us in exhausted snorts and the dozen other noises they make when approaching a place of rest after a hard ride. It reached us a moment later. I stood in the stirrups and drew in a double lungful of the familiar, faintly pleasant odor redolent of hundreds of nights spent around stoves and campfires. Woodsmoke. I was about to call it to the others' attention when Yardlinger grunted and I looked ahead to see a red glow fanning out across the western sky.

I'd seen something like it once before, riding with Rosecrans' cavalry on the way to hell at Murfreesboro. Coming out of a patch of woods, we had spotted the fires of a Confederate encampment reflected in the low-hanging clouds six miles away. It looked like the sun getting ready to rise, and it only happened when there was a lot of flame . . .

We pushed our mounts the rest of the way. Even so, we were a long time getting there, too long. We heard men shouting and horses screaming and more shots raggedly spaced, and then we heard nothing but the splitting and popping of wood being consumed by fire. *Too late*, said the hoofbeats beneath us. *Too late, too late.* Then we thundered over a rise and were there.

The blaze had passed its peak, but coming straight from darkness I had to shield my eyes against the glare. Flames were slurping at the charred framework of what had been a large barn, clinging to the corner beams, and crouching along the rafters like hordes of magpies stuffing their swollen bellies long after the carcass had been reduced to gristle and bone. An occasional horseman flashed past and was swallowed up in darkness. There was galloping around us, two or three shots fired at nothing in particular, and then there was nothing at all, just the noise of the fire sating itself. I spurred the roan in that direction, fighting it all the way.

"Murdock! Stay back!" Yardlinger's voice was strident. "The barn's coming down!"

The heat on my face was blistering. My mount fought the bit and reared. I threw all my weight onto its neck, and when its forefeet touched ground I swung out of the saddle, landing flat on my heels with a jar that sent sharp pains splintering up my legs. The roan nearly knocked me down with its shoulder as it spun to get clear of the flames and smoke.

Yellow tongues lapped and stuttered at the doomed wood, flicking illumination this way and that. I was alerted to a chilling sound nearby, half snort and half whistling whimper, and saw a horse kicking and thrashing on its side in the barn's blazing doorway, a mass of charred, flaming flesh still fighting for life. Its eyes were gone and its lips had burned away to expose grotesquely leering teeth. I put a bullet in its head from the Deane-Adams. It arched its neck and flopped to the ground like a trout landing, emptying its lungs with a sigh and thrusting its legs in four directions.

The air next to my right ear split with a sharp crack, simultaneous with the deep report. On the edge of the firelight leaned a wagon with a broken wheel; in the right triangle of darkness beneath I spotted a blue phosphorescence on the fade and fired at it, darting for shadow even as I loosed the shot. I waited, but no bullets answered. Instead I heard a voice.

"Don't shoot! I'm wounded."

It was a young voice, breathless and cracking.

I said, "Can you stand?"

I heard grunting and struggling. A pause. "No."

Major Brody was standing just beyond the circle of light, which glinted orange off his Peacemaker's sight. "Cover him," I snapped.

"You bet, Cap'n." He cackled shortly. "Don't make no moves I might regard as hostile, young feller. I'm mostly owl and a little bit bat. That means I can see in the dark."

I circled around and came up on the wagon's blind side, stifling a curse when I tripped over a bulky object on the ground and almost fell. It was a man's body. I bent down, groped for his collar, and pressed my fingers against the big artery on the side of his neck. It was just a useless tube now. I crept around the corpse.

As I drew near the wagon, the flames found an unburned section of rafter and flared up greedily, lighting the space under the broken-down vehicle. The man lay on his left hip, his left arm stretched out along the ground ending in a revolver and his right leg thrust in the opposite direction. His pants leg was slick with blood where he was gripping it with his free right hand. His face was turned toward the Major.

When the light died, I took two long strides and, going by memory, stuck my left foot under the wagon on top of his gun arm and reached sideways and down to clap the muzzle of my revolver to his temple. He stiffened, then struggled to free the trapped arm, but I leaned into it and he gave up.

"Please don't shoot me, mister," he begged again. "I think my leg's busted."

Brody spoke up. "Who's your boss? Turk or Pardee?"

There was no answer. The old man spat. I heard the tobacco splatter the wagon's sideboards. "You called it, son."

"Don't shoot!" I put as much authority into the command as I could muster. The old night rider was in his element and I wasn't sure he could be controlled. "Not unless you want to swing right here."

It made him pause. Skeptically: "You'd do that? A U.S. marshal?"

"Deputy," I corrected. "And you're damn right."

Some more time passed. Finally I heard the slide and click of the Colt's hammer being replaced. Going into his belt the gun made a creaking sound like tightly gloved fingers curling into a fist.

I said, "Fix up some kind of torch and bring it here."

We were left in darkness for several minutes. The wounded man's breath moved in and out sibilantly, fluttering from time to time and catching whenever a spasm of pain shot through him. I heard Yardlinger shouting to Earl and Cross to check out each of the other outbuildings, neither of which had been touched by fire. It was like listening to an argument in the next hotel room, of interest to me but none of my business.

I was beginning to wonder what had happened to the Major when a ball of flame separated from the dying blaze of the barn and bobbed our way, his bowlegged figure hobbling beneath it. At that moment the roof fell in with a noise like a bundle of laundry striking the floor from a great height. Bright orange sparks swarmed upward for a hundred feet and vanished. A corner post tilted, hung motionless for a couple of seconds, and toppled away from the inferno, crunching when it struck ground. Brody didn't even turn to watch. I guessed he'd seen his share of burn-ing buildings.

"I soaked a loose stave in a barrel of coal oil I found back of the barn," he said, squatting to grin at us from the other side of the wagon. His stubbly face was smeared black with soot.

"What do you want," I retorted, "a Johnny Reb medal? Hold it steady."

He cackled again. I never found out if he did that out of habit or for effect. "I still like you."

The wounded man was one of the horseback riders we'd confronted with Mather in Breen the night before. I pried his Navy Colt out of his grasp, stuck it in my belt and lifted my boot from his wrist. He rubbed it with his other hand, bloody from nursing his own wound.

"I'm Murdock." I leathered the Deane-Adams. "You remember me."

He looked at me, blankly at first, and then he nodded. He had brown hair and pimples. "I remember. I thought you was one of them bushwhackers. That's why—" He sucked air through his teeth and gripped his leg.

"Let's have a look at that."

I got down on one knee and gently lifted his hand from the pants leg, stiff with gore and glistening in the torch-light. "Got a knife?"

The Major handed me his, a slasher with a hide-wrapped hilt. I used it to slit the material from knee to thigh and pulled it apart. Bits of white bone showed in a wound as big as a doorknob. I covered it hurriedly.

"It's broken." I didn't tell him how badly. "We'll get help."

"Help's here."

I looked up. A man was standing behind the Major with his back to the flames and a lever-action rifle in both hands, trained on us. Brody dropped the torch and went for the revolver in his belt.

"I'll blow your heart out the wrong side." The deep voice was so calm there was almost no threat to it. Almost. It sounded familiar, but I'd heard too many new voices in the past couple of days to sort them out. The Major let his hand drop from the Peacemaker's butt.

"Who is it?" I demanded.

"Turk."

"It's all right, Abel," broke in the wounded boy. "They ain't with the bushwhackers."

"Then whose bullet is that in your leg?"

There was no answer.

I said, "He fired at me. I fired back. I didn't know if he was with you or Terwilliger."

"Terwilliger." Turk dragged out the name, giving each syllable more than its full value. "I figured it was him."

"I don't know that he was with them. They're friends of Pardee's. Someone lynched his brother today. I don't guess you'd know who."

"You ain't in a position to be asking questions." The rifle barrel was a foot away from my head.

"I'm not in a position to do much of anything, least of all save your cowhand's life. He'll bleed to death if you don't let Brody pick up that torch so I can finish what I started."

The fire crackled behind him. "All right, go ahead. Just don't move too fast."

"Mister, I got to move fast." When the torch was lifted, I took the kerchief from around my neck and twisted it around the boy's thigh just above the leaking wound. The bleeding slowed. "Where can we take him? Someplace with a bed and not too many stairs to climb."

"The main house," said Turk. "I'll fetch help."

He left, to return a few minutes later with four men in

faded denims and bulky cowhide jackets, two of them carrying something that looked like a door. I placed one of them among those I had seen in town last night. The others were strangers.

"The door's from the coal shed," the foreman explained. "We can use it for a litter."

It was slid under the wagon next to the boy and two men took positions on either side. The boy gasped during the transfer but didn't cry out. Meanwhile I supported the leg, and when the litter was slid out into the open and lifted, I went along to hold the tourniquet while the Major bore the torch and Turk led the way.

I kept the boy talking to keep his mind off the pain. He explained that the ambushers had struck while the hands were on their way to the bunkhouse for supper, firing the barn and hurling lead at the men as they scattered for cover.

The main house was a big log structure a couple of hundred yards west of the smoldering shell of a barn. No attempt had been made to disguise the logs, which brought up my opinion of Dick Mather ten percent. The Major ditched the torch and we carefully levered our burden around a shallow, L-shaped entryway and through a spacious room with a sputtering fire and Indian rugs on the walls into a small ground-floor bedroom. A stout woman in a plain blouse and floor-length floral skirt made way for us, babbling away in bastardized French. That, together with her dark round face and flat Indian features, identified her as one of the half-breed Canadians who supplied most of the domestic labor in the region.

We set the improvised litter down on the floor next to the bed while the woman peeled back the heavy counterpane. Then we lifted him onto the mattress, me keeping his leg from flopping. He cursed beneath his breath while the spread was tucked around his chin.

"Fetch Tom Petit," Turk barked. The man thus addressed left.

"Is Petit a doctor?"

The foreman looked at me. Indoors, his hat low over his sloping forehead so that the V of the brim almost touched the broken hump of his nose, he looked more primitive than ever. His eyes were hooded under his low brow. "He was a medic in the war. Now he works for the Six Bar Six. He's the closest thing we got to a doctor this side of town." He jerked his chin toward the bed. "I don't think he can wait for the ride there and back."

I left the tourniquet to another's care and caught up with the cowhand he'd dispatched at the front door.

"Tell Petit to bring whatever he uses to cut with."

He hesitated, then nodded and went out. Yardlinger passed him coming in. His face was streaked with soot and sweat and his clothes smelled of woodsmoke. The Winchester hung loose at his side. I didn't like his expression.

"What's wrong?"

"Earl's hurt." His voice was raspy, either from yelling or from the smoke.

"Bad?"

"It doesn't get any worse."

We hurried out together.


# CHAPTER 13


The barn was a tangle of beams that crossed each other and tilted out from the foundation. Flames continued to flicker in spots, but for the most part everything had burned away that could. Earl lay on his back in the wavering light, pinned to the ground by a charred beam twenty feet long lying across his midsection. His chest bellowed in and out amid breathless cursing. Cross was kneeling beside him, cradling Earl's head in his lap and repeating something I didn't catch over and over beneath his breath. His Spencer lay in the tall grass a few feet away.

"He was walking past the barn when it came down," Yardlinger whispered. "He heard it and tried to get out of the way, but he slipped and fell. He's all busted up."

"Help me."

I looked at Cross. His seamed cheeks were slick. "Give me a hand and let's get this thing off him. We got to get him to a doctor."

Still whispering, Yardlinger said, "That's another thing. One of the wooden pegs they put barns together with is sticking in his belly. We'd gut him like a fish if we tried lifting the beam."

"Poor dumb bastard." Major Brody gazed sadly at the heaving figure. I hadn't realized he'd followed us from the house until he'd spoken. "We best dig a hole right here. He'll mess up something terrible, we try to tote him back to town."

Cross cursed and lunged for his rifle. I backhanded the Major across the face with the Deane-Adams, sending him sprawling, and stepped between them to level the gun at Cross. He froze with his hand on the weapon, then let go, one finger at a time. He settled back on his heels, rocking to and fro with Earl's head in his lap and murmuring gently.

The Major sat on the ground rubbing his bleeding cheek. "What in hell did you hit me for?" he groaned. "He was the one going for iron."

"He wouldn't have gone for it if you rode herd on your big mouth. Next time I'll put a bit in it." I stashed the gun and turned to Yardlinger. "They've got medical help up at the house. Tell him to slap a bandage on the boy's leg for now and come out here."

"He needs a shovel, not a doctor." But he retraced his steps to the house.

"You hear that, Earl?" Cross was saying. "Help's coming. We'll get you fixed up in no time."

The young deputy didn't hear him. His back was arched and his mouth worked, air moving in and out shallowly. Blood bubbled in his nostrils.

I bent over the Major, now supporting himself on one elbow. "I didn't think they were that close."

"Closer'n two toes in a tight boot." He spoke petulantly, holding his handkerchief to the injured cheek. "Earl's old man used to take turns betwixt whaling him and his ma. One time he busted the kid's head with a horse collar. Randy seen it and used a quirt on the old man. Him and Earl been together since."

"Where's that goddamn doctor?" Cross was looking at me, but his eyes were out of focus. Distractedly he lowered them to the boy and stroked his pale yellow hair. Earl began to hiccough, the spasm jerking him. Suddenly his shoulders lifted and his head snapped back, tearing a keening cry from his throat, like the horse had made before I put it out of its misery. For an instant he froze in that position, and then he sank back down and his head lolled to one side. His eyes and mouth remained open.

"That's the ticket," Cross said. "Rest. Save your strength."

"Randy, he's gone." It didn't sound like my voice.

"He ain't." He resumed rocking and petting. "Where's that goddamn doctor?"

In the background, charred wood hissed and popped as it cooled. Beams and rafters glowed in sections, looking like the snakeweed we used to pull apart and put back together as kids. Major Brody got up grunting.

Moments later Yardlinger returned, flanked by a short man wearing a sheepskin coat and a Buffalo Bill beard and carrying a black leather satchel scuffed brown at the edges. Randy looked up at him like a Mexican gazing at a plaster saint.

"He hurts bad, Doc."

"Not any more he don't." Petit—I supposed it was him—glanced from the corpse to me. "You the one sent for medical help?" I nodded. "You look like you should know a dead'un when you see him."

"He wasn't dead when I sent for you."

"Dead or dying, it adds up the same. I got to get back to someone I can save. You been busy tonight." He turned away.

Cross leaped across Earl's still form and spun him around by the shoulder. The Spencer was in his hand.

"What the hell kind of a doctor are you?" He was shouting, waving the muzzle under Petit's nose. "We got a man here needs patching!"

The former medic's eyes sought mine. Sad eyes, calm as a toad's. "He always like this?"

"He's pretty shaken up."

"I noticed that. Can you call him off?"

I held back. Cross had the rifle cocked and his finger rested on the trigger. I didn't want to startle him into spraying Petit's brains all over western Montana. The barn's abused timbers groaned and spat. Then the weapon drooped in Cross's hands and he started to cry. I reached out and gently twisted the Spencer out of his grasp.

"Obliged," said Petit and continued on his way.

I took the rifle off cock and handed it to Yardlinger. "Think you and the Major can undo Earl from that beam?"

"I think so. It isn't all that heavy. A few more pounds on the sunny side and it might only have—"

"And if the barn were made of steel it wouldn't have

fallen at all. Wrap Earl in his saddle blanket and sling him over his horse. Bring the animals up to the main house when you're through."

"What are you going to do?" he asked.

"Pay my respects to the host."

I returned to the bedroom in time to hear Petit ask Turk for laudanum. The foreman turned to the woman half-breed and said something in halting French. She replied, shrugging. Turk turned back.

"There ain't none."

"Whiskey, then."

At "whiskey," the woman's face brightened and a stream of rapid French followed. In the middle of it Turk said, "Three bottles."

"Tell her to get them. All of them."

She hurried out, her skirt scuffing the floor.

The foreman watched Petit open his satchel. "Think that's a good idea? I hear drinking that much in a short time can kill a man."

"There are worse ways to die. Besides, some of it's for me."

By this time the boy in the bed had given up any pretense of bravery and was exhaling curses, his voice rising to a shriek whenever the pain grew acute. His trousers had been cut away and his bare leg lay atop the counterpane with a temporary bandage wound around the gaping hole in his thigh. My kerchief had been replaced by a clean white rag knotted loosely above the wound, the ends left out for quick tightening. Petit did nothing to make the patient more comfortable. I guessed that was so the boy wouldn't notice the instruments the former medic was taking from his satchel and laying side by side on the table next to the bed. The hacksaw's teeth looked sharp enough to shave with.

"Go outside," Turk told the four men who had helped carry in the boy. "Find out how many men we lost."

"Not yet." Petit held the saw over a chipped enamel basin and drenched the blade with liquid from a pint bottle. A hospital stench flooded the room. "They'll be needed."

"For what?"

He left the saw soaking in alcohol and rammed the cork back into the bottle. "Because whiskey is a rotten anesthetic."

"Christ's sake, Tom, you don't mean you're really—"

"I'm a cowhand, not a surgeon." His face darkened. "I don't know the first thing about piecing them slivers back together and neither does Doc Ballard in Breen. That leg'll start mortifying tomorrow. You know how fast gangrene travels? Two inches every hour. It's coming off."

"*No!*"

The boy's hoarse scream buzzed in the rafters. He seized Turk's sleeve. His face was gray, the whites of his eyes luminous by contrast. "Abel, don't let him take my leg. How'll I sit a horse?"

The foreman smiled uncomfortably and blustered, "Nothing to it, Jim. We'll whittle you one of them pegs and you'll be bouncing around like a jackrabbit in no time. Hell, you can tell the girls you lost it fighting injuns. They'll be all over you."

"No peg," Petit said. "Not when it's above the knee."

The lamp hissed on the table.

"Abel." Jim's grip tightened on the older man's arm. "If you let him cut it off I'll shoot myself in the head. If you hide every gun on the Six Bar Six I'll cut my throat. If you throw away my razor I'll set myself on fire with that there lamp. You can have someone watching me all the time, but he's got to take his eyes off me once, and that's when I'll do it."

The woman returned with the three bottles of liquor. Turk took one and yanked the cork with his teeth. "Have a pull, Jim," he said, spitting it out. "It'll make you feel better."

For a moment the boy's gaze remained on the foreman. Then he released Turk's sleeve as if throwing it away and seized the bottle. As he upended it, Petit leaned across the bed and whispered: "Leave me the four men and clear out. I need room to work."

"You going to be able to handle him?" Turk sounded dubious.

"That's what the four men are for."

Turk nodded toward the boy, who was choking from the whiskey. "You reckon he meant what he said? About killing himself?"

Petit glanced uneasily at Jim and slid his hand under Turk's arm, drawing him away from the bed. The bottle made plopping noises as the patient tipped it up again.

"I must of helped the surgeons lop off arms and legs a hundred times in the war," whispered the medic. "Maybe fifteen of them lived. It wasn't on account of blood loss or gangrene or even fever, though they all got that. They just didn't want to. I don't think he'll last long enough to kill himself."

"Well then, why in hell bother, if he's going to die anyway?" He was almost choking with the urge to shout. Petit shushed him.

"I asked the surgeons the same thing. They said it wasn't their job to stand by and watch a man die. If it wasn't theirs, it sure as hell ain't mine."

He straightened, looking like a doctor. "Leave Clarice here with the hands. I'll need a nurse."

"Where's Mather?" I asked Turk, in the living room.

He snatched my collar and gathered it up in both fists.

An inch shorter, he glared up at me. His beard bristled and his eyes were bloodshot.

"I lost three men tonight, not counting that boy. One was in the barn when a bushwhacker's bullet busted a lantern and he burned to death with six horses. Two more to gunshots. There might be more. I been kind of distracted. If you'd let me settle with Pardee last night in town, none of it would of happened. Give me one good reason why I shouldn't bust your neck."

"I'll give you five," I said. "At this range, any one of them would do the job."

He glanced down. In his rage he'd failed to notice the Deane-Adams prodding him in the belly. He let me go with a shove.

I put the gun away and handed him the Colt I'd taken from Jim. "I wouldn't give it to him for a while. What happens now?"

He rotated the cylinder, inspecting the rounds. Only one had been fired. "Now I finish what I set out to do last night."

"I can't stop you," I said. "I wouldn't try, on your own ground with only three deputies. But if one Terwilliger man dies from other than natural causes, I'll pick out a rope for you personally."

"That your kind of law?" Having put the Colt in his pocket, he was jerking spent cartridges from the cylinder of his Smith American and replacing them from his belt. Brass shells plinked to the floor. "It's all right for the small ranchers to do murder but not for the big ones to hit back?"

"If men from the Circle T killed your men and fired that barn, they'll stand trial. That much I can guarantee."

"I heard all about your guarantees. How's that deal you made with Pardee stand now?"

"Pardee's brother was murdered. I'll make an arrest on that too. The rope will decide who's right and who's wrong in this war."

He holstered the big .44. "Funny thing about ropes. The way they stretch and snap back, you can never be sure who they'll hit."

"It's the same with bullets," I said.

"Not when you're standing behind them."

He stalked out, providing me with a fine view of his back all the way out the door. I didn't take advantage of it. I guessed I was mellowing with age.

# CHAPTER 14

Alone in the greater part of the house, I eventually wandered upstairs and saw light leaking out of a door standing open in a narrow hallway. Voices were raised in argument inside. I peered in and saw Dick Mather, in flannel trousers and gray underwear top, seated on the edge of a rumpled bed struggling into calf-high boots. A solid woman in a rust-colored dress took hold of his arms to stop him, but he shook her off. His face matched the dingy, many-times-washed color of his underwear and his eyes looked swollen. He was coughing, the sound hollow and bubbling in his throat.

"Let Abel handle it," the woman pleaded. "That's what you pay him for."

"I pay him to run cattle." His words came in short bursts between wheezes as he tugged at the second boot. "I fought Indians for this land, or don't you remember? I'm damn well not going to give it up to a Michigan cherry picker like Bob Terwilliger."

"I remember," she said coldly. "That boy the Blackfeet killed was my son too."

He paused, then yanked the boot on the rest of the way and stomped his heel. "Anyway, I'm experienced at this kind of thing. Turk isn't."

"Isn't he?"

The woman started and whirled to face me, one fist flying to her mouth. Mather glanced up quickly. His lank red hair flopped into his eyes. He jerked it back with a toss of his head and dived for something under a pillow.

"I wouldn't," I said, without moving.

It made him hesitate. Arm still outstretched he said, "Just how fast are you?"

I snorted. "That again. When I came out here, fast meant women and horses. Thanks to the writers back East it's become a contest to see who can get his gun out first. I've lost that contest six or seven times. They're dead. I'm not."

It was a hell of a speech, but I'll never know if it would have worked, because he resumed coughing suddenly. He doubled over and clawed a handkerchief from his hip pocket. Meanwhile his wife leaned over the bed and plucked his derringer from under the pillow. Holding it firmly by the butt, she tugged open the top drawer of the bedside table, dropped it in and pushed the drawer shut. Her amber eyes glared at me from a strong face.

"Now you can kill us."

I looked from her to Mather, who had passed the peak of his fit and was dry-hacking into the handkerchief, his sunken chest heaving.

"Why is it you skinny guys get all the best women?"

He mopped the corners of his mouth, sat for a moment breathing heavily with his hands dangling between his knees, then returned the handkerchief to his pocket after studying it for fresh spots. "What the hell do you want?" His voice was a raspy whisper.

"Answers to a few questions. Was Turk here all day today?"

"He was out supervising the spring roundup. Why?"

"Someone decorated a tree with Pardee's brother on land belonging to the Circle T. Pardee thinks it was your men did it."

He had gotten up to take his shirt from the back of a chair. In the middle of drawing it on, he paused. "Pardee was here tonight?" Red fever-patches appeared on his cheeks.

"He's in jail, where I put him after his brother was brought into Fitch's undertaking parlor. What about the night Dale was mock-lynched by men wearing pillowcases? Or the other times night riders hit Terwilliger's spread? Was Turk around those times?"

Mather fastened the buttons. "He may be a lot of things, but he wouldn't do his killing from behind a mask. If I thought he was that kind, I'd shoot him where he stood."

"That's the trouble. Men like you using the law when it suits their convenience and throwing it away when it doesn't are what makes men like Turk possible."

He said, "Get the hell out of here before I call him back."

"It's your house." I grasped the knob. "As someone you're throwing out I'm tempted not to give you the warning, but as peace officer for the time being I'm obliged to remind you that snakes don't always come when you call them, and when they do, they don't always bite who you want."

He seemed about to say something in response when the screaming began downstairs.

"What in sweet Jesus—!" He clawed open the drawer containing the derringer. His wife held onto his arm.

"Snakebite," I said and went out. The noise grew louder and more shrill as I descended the stairs, and soon I could make out the shouted obscenities. They were cut off with a gurgle. Someone had gagged Jim to keep him from distracting Tom Petit. But then I could hear the sawing. I barely reached the front porch in time to retch outside.

The ride back to town was quiet. Cross had trouble hanging on to the reins by which he was leading Earl's horse, but our offers of assistance were met with growls. The animal, white-eyed, its hackles standing, kept trying to bite through the ropes lashing the bundled corpse to its back and hurl it off. In front of Fitch's we dismounted to help Cross with the body. He struck away our hands, then gathered it in his arms and carried it through the front door like a father bringing his oversize exhausted son home from a picnic. We stood in the street watching as the little undertaker hastened to close the door and attend to his latest customer.

"Is Randy the kind to hold a grudge?" I asked Yardlinger.

"I don't know what kind he is. He doesn't talk much about himself or anything else for that matter. I don't even know where he came from originally or if Cross is his real name. But then I don't know that about half the fine citizens of Breen."

"Well, keep an eye on him. Let's get these horses rubbed down and square things with the livery over that one the Major borrowed. Then we'll get a drink."

"First right thing you said all night," Brody put in. Yardlinger hung back.

"What about Turk? I thought we were going to secure fresh mounts and head out to the Circle T."

"Why?" I asked. "Terwilliger's men dealt this hand."

He yanked his horse along to catch up. The piebald grunted and dug in its heels, but it was too lathered up from the hard ride to offer much resistance. "You're a peace officer! It's your job to keep the peace."

"That's only true when there's peace to keep."

Pardee was asleep in his cell when we stopped in to lock up the rifles, with one beefy arm flung across his eyes and the other flopping off the cot onto the floor. Nature carries antidotes for its own poison.

The colored livery operator gave us hell about the Major's confiscated mount, but I shut him up by giving him twice what it was worth for the time it was out and wrote out a duplicate receipt for the regular amount so his boss wouldn't know that the help was holding out on him. Yardlinger lagged behind as we approached the Glory.

"I'm not thirsty. Besides, someone's got to watch Pardee to see he doesn't hang himself."

I slid a hand under his arm. "He's too mad for that. If you don't want to drink with me, you don't have to. But I want to talk."

He looked at me with murky eyes. "I don't suppose I'll like what you have to say."

"I don't suppose so. But why start now?"

Alf, the flat-featured bartender from whom I'd taken the Schofield revolver the night before, was measuring whiskey into an ounce glass for a customer when we entered. He blanched when he saw us.

"Not again!"

I smiled and took his chin in one hand, turning his face toward the light. The mark I'd put on his cheek had turned purple and his right eye was a glistening crescent between puffed lids. "That's coming along nice. How's the gun?"

"Stinking." He pulled back out of my reach. "The action's all gummed up with sand and soap. I gave it to Thorson to clean. Meantime all I got's a busted pool cue for protection."

"Get a shotgun. I'll have some from that bottle. Major?"

"Hell, I'll have the bottle."

The saloon was filling with cattle types and girls in balding feathers and tarnished spangles, probably from

Martha's. A sad-faced dandy with a burning cigarette parked behind one ear was dragging "The Ballad of Jesse James" out of the upright piano next to the stairs. Beyond him, an arch led into a smaller room in which Colleen Bower sat dealing blackjack to a gaunt redhead with tired-amused eyes, trail stubble on his chin, and a worn slouch hat on the back of his head.

"That's new." I jerked my thumb back over my shoulder as Alf pushed my drink toward me. He shrugged.

"She said she needed the money and I said all right, so long as she uses the side room. I got the Ladies' Temperance League on my back enough as it is. Anyway, she gives the place some class."

"How much she kicking back to you?"

"House gets half."

"That isn't what I asked, Alf."

He glared at me, all wounded pride. I smiled again and flipped a coin onto the bar for the drink. It rolled, then wobbled over and buzzed to a rest.

"I'm not thinking of asking for a cut," I assured him. "I'm just curious about the going rate here."

"Two thirds," he mumbled and mopped industriously with his rag at the bar. The top was spotless to begin with.

I laughed. "You must have a thing for petticoats. In Helena they'd let her keep a dime out of every dollar. Maybe."

"This ain't Helena."

"Alf," I sighed, "I'm reminded of that every day."

"What did you want to talk about?" Having ordered a drink after all, Yardlinger leaned on one elbow so that he could view the entire room without turning. I was leaning on the opposite elbow facing him. Drinking is uncomfortable for lawmen, but not so much they give it up in droves. Major Brody placed his trust in the advertising mirror in front of him and lapped at his whiskey with both elbows on the bar.

I recounted my conversation with Dick Mather, including my convictions about Abel Turk. While I was speaking, the saddle tramp who had been playing with Colleen unfolded his long frame from the chair with a weary smile and a shake of his head and went out past us, trailing the mingled odors of horse and dust. He wore unmatched six-guns high on his narrow hips.

"You think Turk's a gunman?" Yardlinger signaled to the bartender, who poured him a second shot.

"He feels like one."

We nursed our drinks for a while in silence. Suddenly the Major snickered. "This is getting downright interesting. Chris Shedwell coming, and a hot gun here already. Yes, sir, I'm sticking around for this one."

"If Shedwell's coming," said Yardlinger.

I said, "He's not coming. He's here."

They looked at me. I drained my glass.

"That long drink of water who walked past us a minute ago?" I prompted.

Both deputies shifted their gaze to the front door, empty now.

"Well, well," pronounced the Major, raising his glass to his lips. "Well, well."

# CHAPTER 15

"Why'd you let him go?" Yardlinger's tone was accusing.

"Two reasons," I said. "First, he'll be in town for a while and we'll have plenty of other chances. Breen isn't a place you stop at on your way somewhere else. Second—"

"—You're afraid he'll kill you."

There it was, out in the open. He'd left his slouch and was standing facing me, the cloudiness gone from his eyes. I met his gaze, then caught Alf's attention and made a circular motion with my finger around the inside of my glass. He came forward to refill it.

"Not afraid. I know he'll kill me. He's dropped nine men that we know of, most of them looking at him. He's better than I am. Besides, whether you've noticed it or not, I'm not the most popular figure in this town after last night. I've heard of three men holding off a roomful of angry citizens, but the reason I've heard of it is it doesn't happen often. The next time I see Shedwell I want him alone with his back to me and a shotgun in my hands."

"Heroic."

"What do you want, a shoot-out in the street?" I was facing him again. "I call him out with my gun in its holster and my hands at my sides? Lead flying every which way, stopping who knows where? Who told you we're supposed to be heroes?"

The piano player came to the end of his tune while I was still talking. My voice rang out across the room. Every eye in the place was on us. I tossed a silver dollar to the sad-looking musician, who caught it in one hand. " 'Buffalo Gals.' "

As the music started up again, Yardlinger said: "What you're suggesting would bring you down to Shedwell's level."

"Since when was I ever above him?" I countered. "It's a game without rules and death is the only penalty. Ask the Major. How many men have you killed, Major?"

He swallowed his third drink. "Counting the war?"

"Let's say after, just to keep things manageable."

Thoughtfully he dragged his coat sleeve across his mouth. "Thirteen or fourteen. I can't be sure that redleg I gutshot in Richmond ever come around to dying. I left in kind of a hurry."

"Any of them facing you at the time?"

"Three, but two of them was unarmed and I surprised t'other. He's the one I gutshot."

"How old are you?"

"Hell, I don't know," he replied. "I never knew who my pa was, and my ma died when I was little. I raised myself. Hard on sixty, I reckon."

"You made your point." Yardlinger tossed off what was in his glass and paid for it. "I just don't happen to agree with it."

"No law against that," I said. "Just stay out of my way."

I sent him to look after our prisoner and told the Major to get some sleep. When they'd gone, I settled up with the bartender and went into the side room where Colleen Bower was playing solitaire. She had on something silver-gray with a scooping neckline that showed the line between her breasts, and her auburn hair was arranged in a pompadour with curls like sausages hanging behind her left ear. The bruise on her jaw was fading.

Three stacks of chips stood on the table next to her left elbow. At her right elbow was the handbag, open and leaning to one side from a heavy weight within.

I took the chair Shedwell had vacated and sat looking at her. She played a card, went through the deck without success, then cleared away the layout. She didn't look up.

"You sit, you play," she said. "That's Rule Number One."

I got out the roll of bills. She shook her head.

"Rule Number Two: no cash on the table. Alf will take care of you."

I went into the main room and bought twenty dollars in chips from the bartender. Back in my seat I stacked them according to denomination and watched her shuffle the deck. I anted and she dealt us each two cards, one down, one up. I peeled up a corner of the down card, nodded. She dealt another.

"Eighteen." I turned over the five-spot.

"Twenty." She showed me a ten of hearts to go with the ten of clubs on her side and scooped up my chip along with the cards, depositing it atop one of her stacks. The cards went into deadwood, then I anted again and she dealt two more apiece. I peeped at the hole card.

"Do you know who you were playing with just now? Stand."

She took a third card, the ace of diamonds. "I know. I met him in the Cherokee Strip and again in Fort Smith. Call."

I turned up the ace of clubs. "Twenty."

"Twenty-one." She gave me a look at the four of spades and the six of diamonds and raked in the cards. Her pile grew. I anted again. She dealt.

"He say anything? Hit me."

"He said hello and that my luck had improved since Fort Smith." A card flew to each side of the table.

"I'm over." I pushed the cards away from me. They disappeared, accompanied by another chip. I lost the next two hands and said, "Let's raise the ante to five."

She shrugged and replaced the dollar chip she had in the center of the table with a five-dollar piece to match mine. I accepted two cards.

"Anything else?" I asked.

"You standing?"

I nodded.

"Call," she said.

"Seventeen."

"Nineteen." She turned her hole card. "Anything else such as what?" She claimed the dead cards and her booty, dealt again when I fed the pot.

"Such as, 'Your hair looks nice done like that. By the

way, the Marquis de Périgueux hired me to kill Bob Ter-williger.' Or vice versa."

I lost that hand and had started to play another before she spoke again. "What he does when he's not sitting in that chair is no business of mine. Stand?"

I ignored the question, looking at her. "Withholding information from a peace officer is a misdemeanor. If he kills someone and you know about it, you'd be guilty of accessory before the fact."

Her eyes met mine. The gold flecks glittered hard as metal filings. They changed suddenly, but I was too busy playing the steel-jawed lawman to read the change. A cold snout nuzzled the nape of my neck.

"You first," said a familiar voice behind me. "Then Turk."

Both my hands were on the table. The Deane-Adams was grasped by a third and slid from its holster.

"You better move, lady. His head may not stop this bullet."

"My handbag—" she began.

"Grab it and go!" The shout stopped the piano in the main room.

She reached out as if to snatch up the bag. Her hand disappeared inside.

A bee buzzed just below my right ear and stopped with a hollow thump, simultaneous with the hoarse roar. The answering shot was so loud I didn't hear it or anything that came immediately after; it was a sudden, shocking silence that swallowed up lesser noises in a gulp. Something hot scorched the side of my head. By that time I was already in motion.

I had launched my chair over the instant her hand went into the bag. To this day I don't remember if I caught my gun as Pardee dropped it or if I scooped it up after it landed. But it was in my hand as I rolled, and with my back up against one of the table legs I felt the gun pulse and saw a black hole with a purple rim open where the foreman's left eye had been. It would have been a chest shot except that he was already sinking when it struck, his back sliding down the wall and leaving a bloody slick from the spot where Colleen's bullet had pierced the plaster after passing through his heart. His shot had been pure reflex.

He was slumped in a sitting position at the base of the wall when I scrambled to my feet, his mouth and remaining eye open and Oren Yardlinger's Navy Colt lying loose in his right hand on the floor. The room was thick with smoke. I turned to Colleen.

"Any wounds?"

"Not me." Still seated, she waved a quaking hand in the direction of the shattered plaster behind her. "I can't say the same for my handbag." She showed me the barrel of her Smith & Wesson, still smoking, protruding through a smoldering hole in the material.

Yardlinger pushed his way through the crowd gathered around the arch. He wasn't wearing his hat and his hair was in his eyes. He gaped at the corpse.

"I thought he was still asleep," he stammered. "I turned my back and he jumped me and brained me with the chamber pot. I guess he'd flattened it to get it between the bars. I woke up with my keys and my gun gone."

"Get him out of here."

He commandeered Alf and a customer and the three of them lifted the dead weight from the floor. The crowd made a path for them. Byron C. Fitch was having a big day.

Before the path could close I seized Colleen by the arm, snatched her wrap from the back of her chair, and pulled her toward the door. "Pardee has friends," I whispered, "and gunsmoke is contagious. Let's talk in my room."

She didn't resist. The clerk at the Freestone, a seedy ex-gambler in a cravat and dusty tailcoat, hardly glanced up from the desk as we passed him and continued up the stairs. I closed the door behind us and locked it.

"Every time we meet you sail a bullet past my ear." I could hardly hear myself for the whining in my skull. "Why'd you take the chance?"

She shrugged, exposing the soft valley in the U of her bodice when her wrap slipped from her shoulders. Her composure had returned. I wondered who had really killed those two half-breeds down in Yankton. "I had nothing to lose," she said. "The odds are always with the dealer." She set aside what was left of her handbag. "Is it true what you said before?"

I stared. She looked away, pretending interest in the room's furnishings.

"My hair. Do you really think it looks nice like this, or were you just being clever as usual?"

When I didn't answer she tried to outstare me, then drew the wrap tight and started past. I blocked her with my arm.

"Twenty-one." I drew her to me.

# CHAPTER 16

I attended two funerals the next day, one out of respect and the other as part of my duties. I was on my way to the latter when a small man in a shabby overcoat and bucket hat approached me on the boardwalk carrying a bound stack under one arm. It was the newspaperman.

"You didn't pick these up yesterday. I don't usually deliver." He showed me a sample handbill. The legend $100 REWARD covered a third of the leaf. I gave it back.

"The situation's changed. Wait a minute." I took back

the sample, got out my pencil stub, changed the hundred to a thousand and the phrase "illegal harassment of employees at the Terwilliger ranch" to "the willful murder of Dale Pardee," and returned the handbill. "Think that'll make the front page?"

He read swiftly and tucked it back under his arm. "How many columns you want?"

At the double ceremony for the Pardees the Presbyterian minister, a gaunt man with gray whiskers and salt-and-pepper hair, fixed an eagle eye on me as he said something about the wicked being given to the sword. I responded to his good wishes with a smile and a nod.

The first two pews were occupied by Circle T men in hastily brushed suits, their unruly hair slicked down with pomade and the backs of their necks pink from fresh barbering. They had filed in behind a fierce-looking old stump whose sandy hair going gray swept down past his temples from a natural break in the center when he removed his widebrimmed hat. The pattern was repeated in a magnificent handlebar that covered all but the tip of his chin before swooping back up to underscore his jowls.

I nudged Yardlinger, who was standing beside me at the back of the room. "Terwilliger?" He nodded.

One of the hands I had seen with Pardee the night we'd met had spotted me as they'd come in and said something to the cattleman, whose faded blue eyes swung my way, nailing me to the wall before he'd continued down the aisle and taken a seat in front.

The brothers in the closed caskets before the pulpit were the only Circle T casualties. The Terwilliger men who had taken part in the raid on the Six Bar Six had lain in wait along the road and opened fire on Turk and his followers as they approached on horseback. A horse had fallen and one of Mather's men had taken a bullet in the upper arm, but they had withdrawn without additional mishap.

At least that was the story told by the Mather party when they came to town to have the wound patched up.

According to Yardlinger, who had seen Pardee's companions of the previous night at the Glory, none of them were in attendance at the funeral. Mather's men were absent as well. Just in case, though, I had Major Brody stationed with a shotgun under a shaft of colored light streaming through one of the stained-glass windows. Randy Cross was at home on my orders. He was still broken up over Earl and I was afraid of what he might do in Terwilliger's presence.

The old woman who pumped the organ during the service stayed behind to prepare for Earl Trotter's send-off while we accompanied the procession to the cemetery north of town. We watched the surrounding hills for riders or the glint of sunlight on a rifle sight, and as the minister walked away from the grave dusting his palms I stepped forward to speak to Terwilliger.

I was still coming when he turned and strode toward his buggy, putting on his hat. Two Circle T men moved in to block my path. They were both armed, the horn handles of their revolvers curving over their holster tops. I backed off.

"You don't need to talk to him anyway," advised Yardlinger. "The circuit judge is due tomorrow. You can get a warrant and arrest the raiders."

"For what? Nobody saw any of their faces at the Six Bar Six. We'd just have to let them go. I was hoping to get the old man to call it square until the night riders are in custody."

An hour later we were back at the cemetery, watching Earl's remains being lowered by ropes into an open grave several yards from the fresh black soil that marked the Pardees' twin resting places. While the minister was saying his final prayers, Yardlinger pointed out a man standing where the headstone would go. Heavy-shouldered in new overalls under a shabby suit coat, he had light hair and deep lines from his reddish nose to the corners of his mouth from years of scowling. His eyes were small and shifty and he looked familiar.

"Earl's father?" I ventured.

The deputy nodded. "I'm surprised he came. With Earl's mother gone two years there was no one to drag him along."

"Probably wants to make sure he won't climb out of the box at the last minute."

Randy Cross stood at the other end of the grave with his back to us, hat in hand and head lowered. For the most part he remained still, moving only to stifle something that shuddered across his shoulders from time to time. "Are we going to be able to count on him?" I asked Yardlinger.

"Like a royal flush."

The minister tossed a handful of earth into the hole and got out of the way of the gravediggers, who picked up their spades and went to work. The bereaved father jammed a dilapidated felt hat onto his head and clumped off toward an equally hopeless wagon and team without a backward glance.

"They're burying the three dead Mather men tomorrow." The former marshal tapped a cheroot against the back of his hand, stuck it in a corner of his mouth and set fire to it. "We'll be watching that, I imagine."

I said we would. Fitch, the undertaker, had tossed the extra trade toward his rival across the street, a former partner and a slow worker. "You'd think we were running for office," I added.

"Just as well we're not. We wouldn't get many votes."

"Speaking of politics, have you heard anything from the city council?"

"Only that we seem to be holding a lot of funerals since

you showed up," he said. "They don't think you're doing much for Breen's reputation."

"A lot of people would think having a bunch of night riders going around lynching people isn't good for its reputation."

"They hold you responsible for that too. If you handled things differently, maybe Fitch would be taking the day off."

I looked at him. "You agree?"

He watched the diggers, but for whom Cross was alone at the grave. "Who I agree with has nothing to do with anything. I'm just one of the Indians."

"I know you don't approve of me," I said. "All I ask is that you stick around and see this through. Then you can do whatever you want."

"Last night you told me to stay out of your way."

"I was tired and not in a very good mood. I can use you. Cross too. Even the Major."

As if he had heard his name, the old rebel approached us wobbling on his bowed legs. "This here was a good'un," he announced. "Hell of a lot better'n that one they give the Pardees. I like that part about dust and ashes. Bet I heard it a million times and I still can't get enough of it. Bet you're the same way." He winked at me.

"The Major likes funerals," Yardlinger explained.

"So I noticed. Find out yet where Shedwell's staying?"

"I asked," nodded the chief deputy. "The Breen House, Room sixteen."

I chewed my lip. "He must be in the gold."

"Or expecting to be," he finished.

"Get Cross."

In the office twenty minutes later, I handed around the shotguns, keeping one of the 10-gauge Remingtons for myself. "Does the Breen House have a back door?"

Yardlinger laughed shortly.

"A hotel with a back door? They might as well give the rooms away free."

"Good. You and Randy stay out front and keep an eye on the entrance. Major, I want you watching the windows behind the building. If Shedwell comes out, kill him."

"Just like that?" bristled Yardlinger. "No provocation?"

I stared him down. "If he comes out alone, it means I'm dead. Is that provocation enough?"

"Hell, yes," Brody croaked. "You ain't even in season."

The prissy clerk backed away from the desk as I came through the door. "Afternoon," I said, leaning my palms on top of the desk. "Is Chris Shedwell in?"

"There's no one registered by that name," he replied stiffly.

"You get a lot of transients. How do you know that without looking at the book?" I leaned closer. "We could push this back and forth for an hour: You open the book to prove he isn't registered, I describe him, you say, 'Oh, yes, that's Mr. Dollarsworth, the cattle buyer from Chicago,' I ask you again if he's in, you tell me you're not at liberty to say, I grab you by the hair and shove my gun barrel down your throat. But I don't have that much time and you don't have the teeth to spare. So why don't you save us both the trouble and tell me if he's in his room."

His waxed moustache had lost its curl while I was talking. "Room sixteen, top floor."

"I know that. Do you expect him down soon?"

"I couldn't say." Hastily he added, "He hasn't been down for lunch."

"Fine. I'll wait."

I took a seat inside the curl of the staircase on a settee upholstered in green chintz that reminded me of the furniture at Martha's, the shotgun across my knees. Thoughts of Martha brought me around to Colleen, but I quickly put

her out of my head. I'd once asked an old wolfer the secret behind his impressive kill record and he'd said, "I
just think wolf." I was thinking Shedwell.

I'd been sitting there ten minutes by the standing clock
beside the front desk when the stairs above me started
creaking. I got up quietly and shifted the shotgun to ready.

The noise grew louder, and then a pair of boots came
into view at about eye level on the carpeted steps. I forced
my fingers to relax on the Remington's stock. I was on the
blind side of anyone coming downstairs.

In another moment he had reached the floor and crossed
to the desk, a pudgy drummer type in a knee-length overcoat and a derby cocked at a jaunty angle. He was carrying a carpetbag in one hand and a piece of paper in the
other. I sank back against the wall.

He glanced around the lobby without seeing me, stopped
at the desk, and showed the paper to the clerk, who studied it and pointed at me. The drummer turned and came
toward me. He wore a thin moustache and an embarrassed
smile. I leveled the shotgun at his belt buckle. He stopped
ten feet away. He was no longer smiling.

"Who are you?" I demanded.

His mouth worked a little before he got it out. "Carpenter."

"You don't look like one. What's in there, your tools?"

He glanced down at his bag, as if expecting to see
saws and hammers poking out. "No, no," he stammered.
"Carpenter's my name. Felix Carpenter. I sell harnesses.
The gentleman upstairs asked me to give this to the man
in the lobby." He held up the scrap of paper. It rattled in
his hand.

"What gentleman?"

"Tall, thin fellow. Red hair." The noise the paper was
making almost drowned out his words.

"Put it on the floor and get out."

He bent and placed it on the carpet, then backed away.

"Hey!" cried the clerk. "What about the bill?"

Felix Carpenter fingered a wallet out of his coat and flung a handful of bills onto the desk. The clerk was still counting them when the door closed on his late guest.

Crabwalking to keep an eye on the staircase, I went over and picked up the square of paper. It was hotel stationery. The message was printed unevenly in ink under the name of the establishment.

Dear Marshal,

Cold in the lobby aint it how about coming up for a drink your friends are welcome too.

Shedwell

# CHAPTER 17

The door to Room 16 was partially open when I reached the fourth floor, light spilling across the leaf-patterned hall runner. I stopped a few doors away, wondering if I should have taken Shedwell at his word and brought along the deputies. But I didn't want too many guns going off in cramped quarters if it came to that.

I considered the options, his as well as mine. In his place I might have left the door open as bait and crouched inside a vacant room nearby until someone like me walked past. Then I would have stepped out and emptied my cylinder at his back. Shotgun leveled, I rattled every doorknob between the staircase and 16, alternating between opposite sides of the hallway. All were locked.

There were three ways I could go from there. I could hit the floor as I entered, as I had done at the Freestone when the two ranchers were waiting for me in my room, and hope that any lead that flew would be directed at a standing target, or I could wait for him to make the first move, as I had done a long time ago waiting for a killer at that cabin in Missoula. Or I could walk in bold as brass and give him a clear chance at me.

To hell with it. I'd been brained, drawn on, shot at, and ambushed and I was tired of being careful. I filled my lungs and stepped inside.

Right away I knew I'd made a mistake.

It was a room like Marshal Arno's, richly carpeted and furnished. A trail-battered valise with a rolled-leather handle worn fuzzy sat on the floor next to the too-high bed. A slouch hat I recognized occupied the mattress. No Shedwell.

A voice inside me shouted, *Get away from the door.* But before I could move there was a snick of metal across the hall, two quick footsteps on the runner, and death in a steel case punched my right kidney.

"Move and you're wainscoting."

Then again, if I were in Shedwell's position, I might have figured that my stalker was smart enough to try all the doors and would have locked the one to my hiding place and risked the delay.

The voice at my ear was soft, barely more than a whisper, and carried a lilting accent I couldn't identify from those few words. A hand protruding from a blue-flannel sleeve curled around in front of me and relieved me of the shotgun. The hand was freckled, with fine red hairs curling on the back. I started to raise my hands but stopped when the gun prodded me again.

"Fold your arms across your chest. That's the boy."

While my revolver was being taken from its holster I concentrated on the accent. Irish. The hand reappeared to pat my chest, slide under both arms, press the side pockets of my jacket, and feel my legs down to my boots. He took his time and made a thorough job of it. Clothing rustled as he straightened.

"Don't turn around yet. Go over to the bed and sit down."

I did as directed, perching on the edge of the mattress. This put him within my field of vision. He closed the door without turning and stood to one side of it, a tall man as lean as Yardlinger but not as tense, with an open face dusted with freckles, blue eyes, and rust-colored hair beginning to recede at the temples. Sunburned skin formed scales on his nose and at the tops of his cheeks. He had shaved since last night and he was smiling broadly.

"You'd be Page Murdock. I can tell by the gun." He had holstered his own revolver and was examining the Deane-Adams. The shotgun was leaning in the corner next to the door.

I didn't bother to acknowledge my identity. "You must have seen us coming through the window. I thought of that, but I couldn't see any way around it."

He shrugged. He wore a sheepskin vest over his blue shirt, mottled jeans stuffed into the tops of dusty brown boots cracking at the arches. His gun belt was strapped high, the butts positioned for easy grasping as he brought his hands up from his thighs. The revolver in his right holster was a Remington Frontier .44 with a smooth white grip. Its mate was lighter, constructed along the lines of the Deane-Adams, and its grip was hickory or walnut. I read an article once that said he carried twenty-three notches, but if he did, it wasn't evident during his stay in Breen. I broke the silence.

"Is that a Starr forty-four in your left holster?"

He nodded. "But I don't use it as a double-action. I cock it every time, else I might get confused betwixt it and the Remington."

"The caps jam the action anyway when you don't cock

it," I added. "What about the Remington? I'm told it's barrel-heavy."

"I like them that way. Keeps my hand steady."

A china clock ticked away on the fireplace mantel. Two businessmen whiling away the afternoon talking shop. "Shoot with either hand?" I asked.

"Border shift. I collected some lead in my left elbow down in Lincoln County. These days it's not much good above the waist."

I grunted. "I'm supposed to believe that?"

He smiled again and said nothing. He looked more like an Irish rebel than a western gunman. The writers who were busy shaping his legend couldn't decide whether he was born in New York City or Boston, but his speech and appearance placed him closer to County Cork.

He played with the English revolver, turning the cylinder and taking it on and off cock. "We almost met when I was marshal in Wichita. Did you know that?"

"Enough to make sure we didn't," I replied.

"They told me you was in town shipping cattle with the Harper outfit. You had kind of a reputation then. There was some wanted me to give you a try. I said I reckon not."

"They were saying the same thing on my side. I keep reading about famous triggers shooting it out, but I've never heard of it really happening."

"That's because you don't make a reputation dying young."

He was having fun and we both knew it. Face to face with Chris Shedwell I didn't stand a chance. I said, "Well, that was a long time ago, and now the boot's in the other stirrup."

"I heard you was looking for me. What you doing here anyway? Talk is you're wearing tin for R. B. Hayes."

"I am. The job here is just a hobby to keep me busy during my vacation."

His face looked grim for the first time since we'd been talking. "It's that mail train thing, ain't it?"

"They say you killed the clerk in the express car near Wichita just to get back at the city council for dismissing you as marshal," I said.

"That's stupid. If I wanted to do something like that, it'd be one of the ones fired me I'd kill. Besides, I wasn't dismissed. I had a contract with the council and it run out. Am I the reason you're in town?"

"One of them."

"The main one, I'll warrant. Well, I hope you didn't waste too much public money getting here. Was I a taxpayer I'd write my congressman and complain, if I had a congressman." He set aside my gun and dug a travel-worn fold of paper out of his breast pocket.

I got up carefully and reached to pluck the scrap from his outstretched hand. If civilization was measured by the amount of paper that changed possession in the space of a few days, civilization had come to Breen.

It was a document signed by the sheriff of Sedgwick County, Kansas, and bearing the seal of a notary public, to the effect that Christopher Sarsfield Shedwell had been cleared of all charges connected with the robbery of the mail car on the Union Pacific Railroad and the shooting death of postal clerk Aloysius Garvey on September 4, 1877. It was dated last May 22. I read it twice, refolded it, and put it in a pocket.

"I'll have to confirm it with the Sedgwick County sheriff."

"Figured you would. I'd like that back after. I've had to show it to every lawman betwixt here and Fargo."

"Why didn't you say something before?"

He studied me with eyes the color of lake water when you break through the ice on a clear winter morning.

"Couple of years back I killed a Pinkerton in a fair fight

in a town I don't recollect the name of in Idaho and took to the mountains. That was dead December, and the wind was like razors. I lived in a shallow cave for eleven days, eating sardines cold with my fingers and potting at Pinkertons' heads whenever they showed themselves until they gave up and went back to town. I was found innocent at the inquest, but I still have to cross the street every time I spot a Pinkerton or shoot it out."

"Is there a point to that story?" I asked, when he didn't go on.

"Only that after a man's got through something like that, he don't place a lot of trust in a piece of paper to pry him out of a tight spot."

"If this is confirmed, I'll wire Judge Blackthorne. In a month every jailhouse west of the Alleghenies will have a copy."

"That's if I let you leave here," he said.

I paused. "What's the percentage in killing me?"

"Them writers back East could do a lot with me outshooting Page Murdock."

"Not much. I'm not well known, thank God. I've got better things to do with my time than spend half of it practicing my fast draw and the other half taking on all comers. And I try to avoid mountains in the wintertime."

"I got all the reputation I need anyway." He extended the Deane-Adams, butt first. I was reaching for it when he spun it and I found myself looking down the bore.

"Wes Hardin pulled that one on Hickok in Abilene a few years back," I said. "You're stealing material."

"Who do you think taught it to me?" He handed me the revolver and then the shotgun. "We'll meet again, most likely, but that time the rules will be different."

I put the gun away. "Don't give me rules. You're not talking to one of those eastern writers. Who paid your way to Breen?"

Creases in his face made him not much younger than I, but when he smiled they vanished, the years falling from him like dead bark from a log. "Sure, rules," he said. "I'm supposed to keep why I'm here a secret and you're supposed to find out." He opened the door and held it for me.

He followed me down to the second-floor landing, where he hung back. I felt his eyes on me all the way across the lobby and out the front door.

# CHAPTER 18

"**W**hat is this, the honor system?" Yardlinger sneered. He and Randy Cross were standing on the boardwalk on either side of the hotel entrance, holding their shotguns. "You go on to the jail and wait for Shedwell to turn himself in?"

"I'll explain later. Get the Major." I turned and stepped back inside, leaving them there.

The clerk raised his eyebrows at my return. "Step around in front," I commanded. "Come on, come on. I promise not to shoot you."

Reluctantly he obeyed, cringing slightly as if he'd left his pants behind. Keeping one eye on the staircase landing, now deserted, I stood next to him and measured. I had maybe half an inch on him. Close enough.

"Take off your coat."

He stared, opened his mouth to speak, then drew it shut. Awkwardly he peeled off his black swallowtail. His shoulders came off with it. I shrugged out of my own canvas jacket and told him to put it on. He hesitated, then complied, draping his coat over the desk. He looked like a scarecrow in his new attire, but from a distance he could pass. I took off my hat and put it on his head. It went right past his ears and settled on the bridge of his long nose. I lifted it from him, glanced around, then, ignoring his protests, tore two blank pages from the open register and stuffed them into the sweatband. That made it a perfect fit.

"You'll find three men waiting out front," I said. "You know them, they're my deputies. Go with them to the marshal's office and wait there for me. Tell them I told you to do that."

"The desk," he explained. "Someone has to watch it."

I had him by the shoulders and was pushing him toward the door. "It'll still be here when you get back. Didn't you ever play lawman when you were a boy? Here's your chance to relive your childhood."

"My mother wouldn't let me play. I had to stay inside and practice the vio—" The door slammed on the rest of it.

Striding back across the lobby, I shoved the clerk's coat down behind the desk out of sight and took up my original station inside the staircase curve. I considered the logistics, then lay the shotgun across the chintz-covered settee. In close quarters a long gun can be worse than no weapon at all. Then I waited.

I had time enough to hope that the deputies would take the clerk at his word and accompany him to the office rather than enter the lobby to confirm what he told them, and then there were footsteps on the stairs and Chris Shedwell's dusty brown boots appeared coming down. I stepped back farther into the curve.

The Deane-Adams was slippery in my grasp. I changed hands and wiped my palm on my shirt. Then I switched back, willing myself to relax once again until the revolver snuggled easily into my grip. I had done all this hundreds of times before and didn't have to think about it any more than a woodchopper has to concentrate before spitting on his hands and taking hold of the axe.

He hit the carpeted floor at an easy lope, swiveling his head left and right out of old habit to take in the entire lobby. My nook protected me from observation. He was wearing his hat and a Confederate officer's gray coat with captain's epaulets and powder burns around a patch on the left elbow. He'd ridden guerrilla during the war and I wondered if he'd been wounded in the fighting or if he had told the truth about getting shot in Lincoln County. Or if the coat had come from a dead man.

A third of the way across the room he stopped. The unoccupied desk had alerted him. He grasped his Remington and started to turn. The sound of the Deane-Adams' hammer was like dried acorns crunching in the empty lobby. He froze.

"What you said before about wainscoting?" I reminded him.

He held that position for a beat, and then he slowly raised both hands and started to fold them across his chest. I told him to keep raising them. I didn't know but that he was wearing a third weapon in a shoulder sling.

"Turn around."

He did so, looking amused as far up as his freckled and peeling cheeks. You wouldn't have known it from his eyes.

"The clerk," he said. "I should have figured that wasn't you crossing the street. I used that trick ducking vigilantes in Denver."

"Who do you think taught it to me?"

"Dime novels." He grinned. "Them writers'll kill us all yet."

"And write about it afterwards. Who hired you, Périgueux, Mather, or Terwilliger? Or was it someone else?"

"Don't know the gentlemen. I'm here on a social visit."

"Colleen Bower?"

His eyes widened slightly, then returned to normal. "They said you was fast. I thought they meant guns."

"Breen's the north side of hell. You didn't ride all this way just to see a woman."

"She's got a fine Irish name." He leaned on the brogue. "Maybe I'm homesick."

"Annie isn't an Irish name, and we don't know that that's hers either."

"You don't know mine's Shedwell."

"I think it is. No one would call himself Sarsfield if he had a choice. You're running out of answers."

"But you won't shoot," he said. "On account of I ain't here to sell my gun and that paper in your pocket says I ain't wanted. So what say we get us some supper? I been sleeping almost since I got in. I ain't ate at table going on three weeks."

"No one knows I have that paper but you and me. As far as anyone out here is concerned, you're fair game."

He mulled that over. Then he shook his head. "If you was thinking that way, you'd of put one through me before this."

"I never could bluff," I sighed, letting down the hammer. "Eat your supper and clear out. Just remember that the next time a cowboy dies within a day's ride of town you won't survive him by long."

"I don't intend to."

He wasn't smiling as he said it, and I was still thinking about it after he had gone through the door that led into the hotel restaurant.

I went back to the office to put away the shotgun and trade coats with the clerk, who on his way out muttered something about the wisdom of staying in Chicago. Cross and the Major had gone home. Yardlinger watched me from behind the desk. He was still wearing his hat, something he rarely did indoors.

"I guess I'll have to wait for your autobiography to find out what all that was about," he said.

I dropped into one of the other chairs, suddenly weary. "It won't take up much space. See what you think of that." I flipped the folded document Shedwell had given me onto the desk. He read it swiftly, then looked up.

"Think it's genuine?"

"What am I, a forgery expert? Wire Sedgwick County. If he's like any other lawman the sheriff will be eating supper about now. Tell them to send the reply here and get something to eat meanwhile."

He got up and stretched, bones cracking. "Want something sent over?"

"I lost my appetite at the hotel." I tilted my hat forward.

I must have dozed, because when I opened my eyes again it was dark out. I turned up the lamp just as Colleen Bower walked in. She was wearing something that caught the light and threw it back, and clutching her wrap at the neck. Her cheeks were rosy from the cold, or maybe it was rouge.

"Someone steal your handbag?" I asked. "It can't be worth much with that hole you blew in it."

She stopped halfway between the door and the desk. "You're drunk."

"I'd like to be, but I'm just tired." Then I read her expression. "What is it?"

"Dick Mather's hands are going to hit Terwilliger's Circle T tomorrow morning."

I started to rise, then sat back down. Playing it close to the vest. "How do you know?"

"Some men from the Six Bar Six are at Martha's. I overheard them discussing it in the parlor. They're drunk and loud."

"Sure?"

She tilted her chin. "That they're drunk or that I overheard them?"

"That they're making plans. Never mind." I remembered that I was still wearing my hat and took it off, placing it on the desk. Mother would have approved. "Why come to me?"

"I thought you might be interested." Her tone dripped ice.

"I mean, why should you care? You'll excuse me if I look this particular gift horse in the mouth, but what good is even a free mount with bad teeth?"

"Don't you trust me by now?"

"If you're talking about last night, that doesn't have much to do with anything."

"Miss Jessup was right. She told us that men lose their respect for women who say yes." She started to turn away, then stopped. "Maybe I wanted to make your job a little easier. Maybe I think there's been enough murder done in this vicinity."

I waited, but she didn't say anything more. "What time tomorrow morning?"

"First light."

"Thanks. Anything else?"

Her lips parted, then pressed together, etching unbecoming lines from mouth to nostrils. She drew the wrap tighter about her shoulders, spun, and flounced out, her heels knocking the boardwalk until the noise was lost in the waning traffic outside.

Minutes later a boy entered with my answer from Wichita. I paused in the midst of checking the loads in the long guns to tip him and open the envelope. A cowhand convicted of the strangling death of his common-law wife north of Hays had confessed to the lone robbery of the mail train the night before his hanging, lifting suspicion from Chris Shedwell.

"I'll be damned."

"Is that your answer, Marshal?"

I'd forgotten the messenger was still there. I shook my head and sent him off. Yardlinger returned as I was locking up the guns. I showed him the wire and briefed him on what Colleen had told me. Sitting in the customer's chair, he played with a pen and listened in silence until I finished.

"You believe her?" he asked then.

"I was going to ask you the same question. You've known her longer than I have."

"But not as well."

I grinned. "For some reason, given my obvious appeal, I've never been able to convince myself that I'm the Lord's gift to womankind. When one of them starts confiding secrets I always feel for my poke."

He tested the pen's nib on the ball of his thumb. "There's another explanation. Remember what I said about the second rule of successful gambling."

"If she wants to stay on the right side of the law, she wouldn't dangle false bait," I agreed.

"And she did save your hide last night."

"Hers too, don't forget. You never know where a bullet's going to land in a small room. Besides, leading us into an ambush would improve her standing with the cattlemen on both sides. They'd be calling the shots once we're dead."

"Sounds like you've talked youself into disbelieving her story." He stopped playing with the pen.

I shook my head. "I've talked myself around in a full circle. One thing's sure, though. We can't ignore it."

He pushed himself out of his chair, flipping the pen so that it stuck in the stained blotter for a moment before flopping over. "I'll get Randy and the Major."

"No hurry. Just say what's on the fire and tell them to meet us here at three o'clock. We'll need all the sleep we can buy between now and then." I stood and put on my hat. "I've got some doors to try before I turn in."

"Think you should?"

"If I don't, Mather's men will suspect something. Besides, ducking lead is one of my many talents."

With darkness, the action in town had moved indoors, leaving the streets deserted but for the occasional transient making his unsteady way between saloons. A shoe-heel moon shed milkwater light over the east side of the street. I confined the early patrol to the facing side, where the shadows lay. That's one thing you gave up when you accepted a star, the right to walk in the light. City marshals were targets at the best of times, but in a wide-open town they were always in season. I'd kept to the shadows so long that I was beginning to grow leather wings and sleep upside down.

Piano music spilled out of the saloons as I walked past, snatches of tunes mingling with the general racket of loud talk and drunken laughter, now riding a wave of warm air tainted with stale smoke and old beer, now fading to a whimper as I left the barrooms behind to rattle the doorknobs of darkened shops and peer through shuttered windows. I took my time crossing alleys, where a tongue of blue flame licking from the darkness could send me rolling for my life in the dust or kneeling in my own blood, depending on whether I detected anything before the trigger was squeezed. But they were quiet.

I was on my way back across the street when Yardlinger emerged from the Pick Handle with Major Brody in tow. We met just off the boardwalk.

"Randy's inside," reported the chief deputy. "Dead drunk."

I cursed. "He picked a fine time for it."

"He's still busted up over Earl. We can't talk to him."

"Think we should start pouring coffee and salt into him, Cap'n?" Brody asked.

"That depends on whether he's a mean drunk."

He grinned toothlessly. "There's other kinds?"

"Then let him go till he fags out. We'll have enough people trying to kill us in the morning without starting early." I gave Yardlinger what was left of the roll I'd brought from Helena. "Hand that to the bartender and tell him if Randy isn't in a bed—any bed—by midnight I'll close him down permanently."

"Honey and vinegar in one dish. You don't take chances." He went back into the saloon.

Alone with me, the Major sawed an inch off his tobacco plug and popped it into his mouth. "Shooting tomorrow, I hear."

I confirmed it with a nod. Coal-oil light from the saloon clung to us dirty and yellow.

"I do believe for the first time in my life I've had enough already."

I studied him. "That mean you want out?"

"Didn't say that." There was a twinkle in his eye that, had I still money, I'd have bet was the last thing a lot of men had seen this side of Gabriel's horn.

I was still watching him when the shooting started.

# CHAPTER 19

I didn't hear the hoofbeats until they were right on top of us. Later I found out they'd stopped before the city limits and bound the horses' feet with gunny sacks to muffle the noise. At the time, all I heard was a strange thumping behind me and turned just as a demon bore down on me, riding a black horse with red fire at its eyes and nostrils and swinging a cavalry saber that snatched the light as it came around and swept my hat off my head. If I hadn't ducked at the flash, my head would have come off with it. Then the horse was pounding past, sideswiping me and knocking me staggering. But I caught a glimpse of the rider's face, or lack of it, dead white with black holes for eyes.

The street was alive with them, hollow-eyed and faceless astride coal-black horses, their muffled hoofbeats sounding like rapid shots miles away. Only these sounds were right here and I was in the midst of them. Sabers whistled. Once I heard a noise like a cook's cleaver striking half-boiled meat, a nauseating sound. Then there were real shots, hard and sharp, like derisive coughs, and metal-gray smoke that mingled with the white vapor exhaled by the horses.

The rider who had swiped at me spun his horse and came back for a second try. I tore out the Deane-Adams and snapped off a quick shot, not hoping to hit him, just teach him some respect. Lead was singing all around me. I didn't wait to see if my bullet had any effect, but dived between the horizontal logs that supported the boardwalk and scrambled around until I was facing out, my cheek resting on the hand holding the gun.

There might have been twelve riders. There might have been a hundred. With their frantic galloping this way and that and the layer of black-powder smoke that hung in the still air, there was no way of counting them. The boards above me creaked and I heard a hammering above those and knew that Yardlinger had left the saloon to make use of his Navy Colt. A deeper roar announced the arrival of Cross's shotgun. Another revolver joined in, probably the Major's. I fired at a white head, but then it was lost in the confusion and smoke and I didn't know if I'd hit anything.

Presently a horse went down whinnying, rolled completely over, and struggled to its feet, favoring its shattered left rear leg and leaving its rider spread-eagled in the dust, his pale oversize head bobbing like an India rubber balloon on a string. Hoarse screams wound their way through the popping pistols and thudding hoofs. Then they stopped altogether. The galloping and shooting continued, around and around, this way and that, as if a gang of children had been turned loose in a fenced-in playground.

Something landed on the boards overhead like a sack of grain and an arm flopped in front of my face. It wore a black coat sleeve. The hand uncurled and Oren Yardlinger's Navy Colt swung loose from the trigger guard hooked on his index finger.

Bitter rage swept through me. Working mostly by feel, I thumbed out my spent cartridges, replaced them, and squeezed the trigger again and again, moving my arm in a wide arc along the ground from left to right and back, the gun throbbing in my grasp. I felt its kick, saw the smoke whooshing out the barrel and through the space between the cylinder and the frame, but I was too intent on my fleeting targets to hear my own reports. I heard glass shattering on the other side of the street and knew that I was responsible for some of it. Whether or not I was hitting anything in between made little difference in the general uproar. Horses turned and galloped and shook their manes and reared to paw the air with their sack-clad hoofs, blue and orange spurts lashing across their necks and over their heads behind a motionless veil of smoke, like something going on outside a clouded window. And then they were gone.

As quickly as that. One moment the street was alive with men and horses and the next only the smoke remained, drifting cautiously now as if unsure that it was safe to depart. Silence crackled.

I kept cover for what felt like an hour. Then impatience overcame caution and I wriggled out of my hiding place inches at a time, ready to scramble back under at the first shot. None came. I was alone on the street, or so I thought.

I stood, brushing unconsciously at the dust and dried manure on my front. The opposite side of the street was even darker now, with blank spots where before there had been window panes to throw back the light from this side. The air was raw gunsmoke. Somewhere in the shadows a sheet of glass the size of a dinner plate dropped loose and struck a sill, parting with a clank. I whirled and squeezed off in that direction from reflex. The hammer snapped on an empty shell.

On both sides it seemed there was scarcely a building whose woodwork wasn't bullet-chewed and whose windows didn't sport missing panes and dollar-size holes. A sign that had swung from chains under the porch roof of the harness shop swayed dangling at the end of a single set of links, its legend shot away and the broken chain trailing like a kite tail. Even the hitching rail on this side looked worm-eaten, though minutes before its new wood had stood out nakedly against the weathered planking behind it. The next day's edition of the Breen *Democrat* would report that more than one hundred and fifty shots had been fired within six minutes, and I would wonder if the editor had crouched behind one of his typecases tallying them on a pad.

Most of the lamps in the business section were out, either destroyed by bullets or turned out when the shooting started. Yellow light flared and faltered in one of the saloons, where an aproned bartender and one or two volunteers labored with wet towels and slop buckets to put out a fire probably started when a lamp broke.

The rider I had seen go down under his horse lay still in the street with arms and legs spread like spokes in a wheel, crushed into the two-inch-deep dust and resembling a pasteboard doll discarded and forgotten. He wore a pillowcase over his head with circles cut out for his eyes, which accounted for the swollen white heads I had been shooting at. It was tucked into his collar and tied down with a cord. I stepped over and tore it off.

He was young, hardly more than twenty if he was that. His moustache and side-whiskers barely covered the flesh beneath. A soft moist glaze coated his eyes and his mouth was frozen open. I had never seen him before.

A whistling snort brought my attention to a lone black horse standing near the livery, where it had undoubtedly been drawn by the familiar smells of manure and feed. It was strapped into a scaled-down saddle like cowboys used and held its left rear leg aloft at an unnatural angle. I had seen it fall when that leg shattered and I was standing over the man who had fallen with it.

Sighing, I reloaded the Deane-Adams and took aim at the animal's head. Page Murdock, the Fearless Horse-Slayer of the Plains. Before I could fire there was a hard, flat bang and the black folded down onto its right side with a grunting sigh.

I pulled down on the bullet's source and held back at the last instant. Major Brody came rocking toward me, trailing smoke from his big Peacemaker. He was as dirty as I was in front, having just crawled from under a buckboard next to the dry goods emporium. His left shoulder was smeared with something darker than the dust on the street.

"That's twice someone's claimed a target of mine since I got here," I complained. My voice sounded strange in the silence following the final shot. I put away the gun, nodding toward his stained shoulder. "Bad?"

He shook his head. His face was black with powder. I supposed mine was too. "Bastard glanced a saber off'n it. I shot him in the guts, though. He won't get far."

I remembered the noise of a cleaver striking meat. "Let's have a look at it."

"We'll tend to Oren first."

I realized with a pang of guilt that I hadn't thought about the chief deputy since his arm had dropped in front of me. Yardlinger was lying on his face with one boot hooked inside the threshold of the Pick Handle, his hat bunched forward and the hand holding the gun still hanging over the edge of the boardwalk. We turned him over as gently as possible, considering his one hundred and seventy pounds of muscle, and laid him on his back. The right side of his face was covered with blood and I thought at first that half his head was gone. Then he groaned.

"Water!" I barked. The Major ducked into the saloon, to reappear moments later carrying a full bucket. When he set it down I soaked my kerchief in it, wrung it out, and, supporting the wounded man's head with my free hand, used the makeshift washrag to clean off the blood.

A bullet had carried away part of his eyebrow, leaving a two-inch long furrow along his temple. As I dabbed at the congealing leakage, his eyes fluttered open and he tried to speak.

I said, "Don't bother explaining. Anyone who stands up in the middle of all that flying lead deserves to lose a lot more than his good looks. Is he hit anywhere else?" This to Brody.

He searched Yardlinger for blood spots, loosened a button here and there and then did it up. He shook his head.

"Fetch the doctor," I said.

"No need."

The speaker was built small, with thin wrists protruding like brittle sticks from too-short coat sleeves, no cuffs, and carrying a black leather bag that looked new. He wore a sandy moustache and looked about fifteen but for that. "Orville Ballard," he introduced himself.

I stared at him. "Discovered girls yet?"

"What did you expect?" he snarled. "An old, established

practitioner? They don't come out here. Only drunks, charlatans, and untried medical school graduates."

"Which are you?"

He smiled thinly behind the moustache. He was down on one knee already and rummaging through his bag. "You got lucky. I hate alcohol and when I lie my ears get red."

I watched suspiciously as he examined the wound. Then he lit a match and pulled open each of the wounded man's eyes to study them in the flickering light. That done, he unstoppered a small bottle of peroxide, inserted a cotton swab, and applied the strong-smelling stuff to the gash along Yardlinger's temple. The patient flinched and said something about the doctor's ancestry.

At that point I relaxed, rocking back on my heels. Out there you were grateful when what passed for the local physician didn't strap feathers around his head and cut a chicken into pieces to read the entrails.

"Where's Randy?" I asked the Major.

He was holding his injured shoulder, fresh blood seeping between his fingers. His head tilted toward the saloon. "Warming a chair with his shotgun on his knees. Fagged out."

I got up and took a step toward the door. There was a deep bellow and six inches of door casing disintegrated next to my head. I ducked.

"Reckon he woke up," Brody suggested.

I raised my voice. "Randy, it's me, Murdock. If you do that again I'll ram that shotgun down your throat. Sideways."

There was a silence, then: "C'mon in, Page. Damn. I thought you was one of them bushwhackers come for another go." He slurred his consonants.

I started forward again, then twisted around and picked up the bucket of water the Major had brought from the saloon. To the doctor I said, "When you're through with Yardlinger, take a look at the old man's arm."

The moonlit barroom was a shambles of overturned tables and broken glass. I crunched through it to where Cross was slouched in a chair, hat pushed far back on his head, and the short scattergun in his lap. The back door stood open, marking the path of the other occupants' retreat at the height of the melee.

"You all in one piece?" I asked Cross.

His teeth gleamed in a slow, lopsided grin. "Hell, yes," he drawled, and belched. "Why shouldn't I be?"

"Good." I swung the full bucket back in both hands and dashed its contents into his face. It struck with a noise like wet rags slapping a fence, drenching him from crown to sole. He coughed and sputtered and pawed his face with his big hands.

His mouth was working like a fish's, but before he could say anything I hurled the bucket away and said, "Climb into something dry and ride out to the Circle T. Tell Terwilliger if he wants the men who lynched his foreman's brother to arm his hands and send them to town. There's a tracking moon and I need special deputies. Get going!"

I shouted the last two words. Galvanized, Cross sprang from his seat and lurched dripping toward the door, considerably more sober than he had been moments before. I followed him out.

Yardlinger was sitting up with his back against a porch post, a white bandage holding a patch of gauze to his injury. In shirtsleeves now, the doctor was kneeling over Major Brody, lying coatless on his back with his head resting on the physician's folded garment. Someone had provided a lantern that shed cheery light from a nail on the post. A lot of blood stained the planks around the old man, too much.

"Why didn't you have me look at him first?" spat the

doctor as I emerged from the Pick Handle. "His arm al
most came off with his coat!"

I squatted next to the Major, whose blackened face glistened in the lantern light. "You told me the saber glanced
off."

He grinned without teeth. It might have been a wince.

"It must of." His voice was a harsh whisper. "Else the
arm would of dropped off right then."

I smiled in spite of myself. One-armed he'd have taken
on all hell's host if he smelled a ruckus in it.

"Now's as good a time to tell you as any," he said then.
"Day you taken over you said something about a deputy
selling information to the Frenchie."

"I knew it was you the minute we met," I put in.

He looked puzzled. Then his face twisted into a mask
of agony. Ballard was using a short pair of scissors to cut
his shirtsleeve away from the wound.

"It stood to reason," I went on. "Périgueux could afford
to pay a stiff price for intelligence. Randy was too loyal
and Earl was too stupid. You were the only one left."

I had to bend closer to hear what he said next. "It was
just that one time. I only done it 'cause I was bored. I ain't
been bored since you come."

"Forget it. You did a damn fine job tonight. Without that
Peacemaker we'd still be dodging lead."

The bewildered look returned. "Hell, I was reloading
when they decided to chuck it. I thought it was you."

I let my hands dangle between my knees. "That doesn't
make any sense. I was banging away like an idiot under
the boardwalk. Yardlinger was down and Cross only fired
one barrel. I . . ."

My silence alerted the doctor, busy trying to staunch the
flow of blood from Brody's mangled shoulder. He glanced
up at me, then followed my gaze. Chris Shedwell was
crossing the street in our direction.

# CHAPTER 20

**H**is face meant nothing to the doctor, who resumed his labors at the Major's side. I stepped off the boardwalk to meet the mankiller. He was wearing his Confederate coat.

"Why?" I asked. "Or don't you shed enough blood in your work?"

His eyebrows went up a quarter inch. He had an expressive face, not at all the kind you'd expect a professional gunman to possess. "I figured gratitude was too much to hope for," he said. "I didn't expect to be called out, though. Next time I'll maybe mind my own business."

"I wish I knew what your business was."

He favored me with the famous Shedwell smile. "Don't jump to conclusions. The fact is I decided to make an early night and I got sort of smoked with all that noise under my window. Thought I'd pick off an ear or two just to spread some education."

I watched him. I've said he didn't have a poker face, but his expressions didn't necessarily match his meaning. "Well, thanks for the help. You wouldn't care to carry the lesson out of town?"

"That'd be vindictive," he said. "I mean, just over a few minutes' sleep lost."

"Suit yourself." I left him, approaching the fallen horse. Its eyes were frozen with the whites showing and its tongue was dusty between its teeth. The saddle blanket covered the flank. I flipped it up to get a look at the brand. A vertical bar with a numeral 6 burned on either side—Mather's Six Bar Six. What else? I spotted the Negro who ran the livery standing among the spectators nearby and called him over.

"Yess'r?" His face was like dull, crumpled foil under a floppy hat and he was wearing three shirts over dingy flannels, the tails hanging outside his gray, shapeless trousers.

I nudged the dead horse with the toe of my boot. "Drag this carcass into the stable and hold it till someone comes for it. It's evidence in an assault case and possibly a lynching."

"I gots to talk to the boss," he said, rubbing his chin with a big horny hand. "We ain' never kep' no dead aminuls in the stable before. I wouldn't know what to charge."

"It ought to be half. You won't have to curry or feed him. I'll pay double the regular rate. See Yardlinger for your money when he's on his feet."

The doctor hailed me. "I'll need help getting these men over to the Freestone. I can't treat them out here."

"Devil take the Freestone." Yardlinger gathered his legs under him, attempted to rise, lost his footing and slammed down on his tailbone with an impact that shook the saloon's porch. He blinked dazedly. A nervous titter rippled through the growing crowd.

"Concussion," said Ballard, adjusting the deputy's bandage. "Couple of days' rest will fix that up."

I designated a number of townsmen to help with the injured pair and started walking. I was striding as I turned onto Arapaho Street, my boots clomping on the boardwalk and echoing like shots in the porch rafters. People who had come out to see what was going on made way for me when they saw my face. Sensing excitement, some of them followed me, and then some more, so that by the time I reached Martha's place I was heading a motley parade. On the strip of grass that separated the house from the street

I turned around, glaring. They stopped and I mounted the steps to the door alone.

The door crashed against the wall as I went through it without knocking. A vase of flowers fell from a window sill and broke, water darkening the floral print carpet. An overripe blonde in a thin cotton shift threw me a startled glance from the settee. Her eyes traveled over me, and then she smiled, fingering back a stray tendril of yellow hair gray at the roots. She had freckles on her teeth like an old horse. Seated next to her, a thickset man in a prickly suit and a paper collar too small for his bull neck started to rise, then sat back down. He had a tea cup and saucer balanced on one knee and his lips were pursed under a bristling moustache. I recognized him as the town barber and a member of the city council.

"Evening, Marshal." He transferred the crockery from his knee to the arm of the settee. It rattled slightly. "What was all the shooting about? This young lady was kind enough to invite me in out of the line of fire."

I wasn't paying attention to him. Martha was standing before the beaded doorway leading into the next room, all six feet of her, the good eye cocked in my direction. "Where's Colleen?" I demanded.

She said, "This carpet was woven in Asia two hundred years before I was born. If you've stained it—"

I repeated the question, advancing on her. She placed a hand over the brooch at her neck. Another woman might have swooned or begun screaming. "Upstairs. First door on the left." She moved away from the opening.

I dashed aside the beads, found the staircase, and vaulted up two steps at a time. The door was locked. It flew open on the second kick, overturning a pedestal table and an earthenware pot containing a fern whose fronds hung to the floor. My heels ground the spilled black dirt into the rug. I'd graduated from horses to plants.

"Who the hell do you think you are?"

She stood next to a vanity, wearing a thin flannel nightgown and holding a tortoiseshell brush. Her red-brown hair flowed loose over her shoulders, glowing in the lamplight from the fresh stroking.

My anger had been building from the moment I'd exposed the Six Bar Six brand on the dead horse's flank. Face to face with its source, my rage leveled off. I closed the door almost gently and stood with my back to it.

"Nice touch, brushing your hair," I said. "Salome danced."

Something fluttered over her face, I couldn't tell what. When she spoke again her voice was no longer shrill. "What are you talking about? What was happening downtown? I heard the shooting. I thought some cowhands were blowing off steam." Fear gripped her then, draining the color from her features. "Why is your face black?" It was almost a whisper.

"Who'd you take up with?" I said calmly. "Mather or Turk? Whose idea was it to tell me that Mather was hitting Terwilliger in the morning so that I wouldn't expect him to attack me tonight? Pick one or all three. Just give me an answer."

Her fingers went to her mouth in admirably feigned fright. If it was feigned. I was in no condition to judge. "I didn't know." This time I barely heard it.

I didn't say anything. I hadn't the faintest notion of what to say or do. What had I been thinking all the way there? It angered me that she wasn't a man, and it angered me that that angered me. A few years earlier I'd have shot her where she stood without regard to her sex, but that was before the dime novels came and ruined me along with every other Westerner who read one just because there was nothing else to do in the middle of all that emptiness. Life was hard enough on the frontier without having to conform to a creed. I started to leave.

"You're not hurt." She was barefoot and made no noise hurrying across the rug. The top of her head barely reached my chin. Her hands grasped my shoulders. Tiny hands. It was hard to imagine them palming an ace. Her hair smelled of the scented soap they used downstairs, and something else.

I might have been gnarled wood in her hands for all the response she got. "One of my deputies is down with what might be a cracked skull," I said quietly. "The other one may lose his arm and probably his life. Me? I'm indestructible."

Her nails dug into my skin. "It wasn't a lie, Page. I did hear them planning to raid the Circle T. They didn't say anything about attacking you. They didn't. I'd have told you if they did." The gold flecks swirled in her eyes.

I shook off her hands and grasped her wrists. I could have broken them both with little effort.

"Maybe you weren't lying. Maybe Mather's men knew I depended on Martha for information and spread that story knowing it would reach me sooner or later and put me off guard when they hit town. But I can't chance it, understand? I can't chance it."

She grimaced. I was hurting her wrists. I slackened my hold. The smell of her made my head swim.

"I'd never be able to relax with you," I continued. "I couldn't hold you without wondering if you were signaling someone over my shoulder. We couldn't go riding but that I'd think you had a sniper laying for me along the road. It wouldn't last a week, and when it was over we'd carry away the bitter taste."

She lowered her eyes. I released her wrists and she turned away. Then she faced me again, across a distance of four feet.

"When I was three years old my father took me from Ohio down to the Nations and married a Cherokee woman for her land," she said huskily. "He called himself a farmer, but he spent most of his time gambling at the trading post. At night he'd teach me to play poker, and when the other players complained about his dealing he'd have me sit in for him. At thirteen I could shave an ace in full view of a roomful of people and no one would notice. A year later my father sold me to a whiskey peddler named Bower for his route and a four-horse team.

"The reason Bower got rid of his route was he was his own best customer. He went crazy when he was drunk, and since I was always close by, he'd beat me until his arms got tired. One night after he'd done an especially good job of bloodying me I waited until he was snoring face down in the back of our wagon, and then I dug his Dragoon Colt from under a feed sack and emptied it into his back. I went clear around the cylinder and squeezed the trigger three times on empty chambers."

Lamplight haloed her head and painted shadows in the folds of her nightgown. With her hair loose and her feet bare, she looked like the thirteen-year-old girl she was talking about.

"He had three hundred dollars in gold in a strongbox," she went on. "I grabbed it, put on his riding clothes, unhitched a horse from the team and lit out. No one ever came after me. I don't think anyone much cared who had killed him as long as he was dead. When I got to Arkansas I invested in a new wardrobe and a finishing course in Little Rock. I was young, but I knew that without an education I'd never do better than Bower for a husband.

"I soon learned that rich husbands were out unless your family was old and established, and mine stopped at an unmarked grave outside Muskogee where they buried my father after he was murdered by a drunken Osage. So I came back to Miss Jessup's School for Genteel Young Ladies and took a job teaching. For a year I helped mold a dozen little Colleen Bowers until I couldn't stand it any more and left. By the time anyone missed me, I was twenty miles inside the Nations. *I was seventeen years old."*

Someone was calling my name on Pawnee Street. It sounded like Cross, back from the Circle T. I heard horses outside, a lot of them. "Why tell me?" I asked her.

"Can't you see I'm sick to death of crime and treachery? Are your instincts so deep you can't put them behind you long enough to believe that? What else do I have to do to buy your trust?" Her hands were curled into tight little fists in front of her.

"I don't know." I fished for words. "I don't know that it can be bought. If I were a bootmaker or a farmer or even a whiskey peddler in the Nations, it might be for sale. But I'm not and it's not. The price is too high. I wish it weren't."

"It doesn't have to be." Her eyes were shining in the darkness on her face. "You don't have to stay a lawman."

I opened my mouth. I almost agreed. Then I remembered the two dead half-breeds in Yankton and wondered if they'd heard this speech. I closed it. "I'm sorry it didn't work out." I pulled open the door.

She might have said, "So am I." I couldn't be sure. The door closed on whatever she did say.

# CHAPTER 21

**R**andy Cross met me coming around the corner from Arapaho Street. Beyond him, the main four corners were a jam of men and horses. Light from the windows slid along the oily barrels of rifles and shotguns and sparkled off modest raiments. Metal rattled, leather creaked, animals snuffed and blew. Steam curled around the mounts' fidgety legs like locomotive exhaust. Some of the men were carrying torches, and black smoke columned up from the flames and merged with the darkness above. The scene smelled of tobacco and burning pitch and sardines. A number of the volunteers had filled their pockets with stores in anticipation of a long ride.

"I been looking all over for you," complained the deputy. The ride to the ranch and back had sobered him. "I got your posse."

"So I see. How many?"

"Fourteen's all I can spare." The stout man I had seen at the Pardees' funeral called down from his perch astride a big sorrel. The brim of his slouch hat touched the hook of his nose and he was huddled in a coarse woolen overcoat cut for a much larger man, the sleeves turned back and the tails spread to cover his saddle. His stirrups were adjusted as high as they would go to accommodate his short legs.

"Who's running the ranch, Mr. Terwilliger?" I asked.

His fierce eyes smoldered in the shadows. "It was your business, maybe I'd say." He had a thin voice for his build, and his tone was Midwestern flat. "You're Murdock? You know none of this'd be necessary, you let Pardee treat with Mather when he wanted to."

"I'm not so sure Mather was behind the raid. Or the lynching."

"You got a dead horse with the Six Bar Six brand. What more you need?" His nervous excitement passed to his horse, which scooped its neck and danced from side to side. The rancher seemed to be holding the animal in check by no other means than sheer force of presence.

"May I speak to your men?" I asked him.

He took a beat to consider, then nodded abruptly. In my absence Cross had saddled and bridled my roan and brought it from the livery to hitch to the riddled rail in front of the Pick Handle. I slipped its tether and mounted, then trotted out in front of the others. They had been conversing among themselves in growls, but lapsed into silence when I appeared. I pinned on the star.

"This isn't a vigilante raid," I announced, after introducing myself to a chorus of muttered obscenities. "You're to be sworn in as special deputies. That means you'll take my orders and no one else's. It doesn't give you leave to commit murder. We'll fire if fired upon, but if not, we'll give the men we're after a chance to surrender before we start busting caps. Who objects to that?"

"Me." This from a lean horseman near the center, with cracks for eyes and a trailing moustache that completed the oriental effect. "Why should they get any more chance than they gave Dale Pardee?"

Agreement rumbled through the group.

"Ain't you the one killed our foreman?" challenged a voice from the rear. The rumbling grew loud. I urged the roan forward into the flickering torchlight. The noise died.

I addressed myself to the oriental-looking cowhand, whom I had picked out as the spokesman for the group.

"Pardee gave me the same treatment his brother got. I'm not his brother."

He said nothing. I raised my voice to take in the group. "I was told when I came here you wanted law. You don't get it by trampling over it when it doesn't suit you. Any man not in agreement with that is free to leave. If you decide to stick, I'll make holes in the first man who goes against me."

"Whose law is that?"

A new voice, deep in the assembly. I couldn't locate the owner.

"Mine." The roan started fiddle-footing. I squeezed my thighs together and it settled down. "One thing more.

There's reason to believe Abel Turk is leading these night riders, not Mather. For sure Turk's with them. I know an experienced gunman when I see one, and it's only safe to assume he's surrounded himself with others as good. If that bothers you, go now. No one will think poor of you."

I stopped talking. The riders stirred, spoke to each other in murmurs that rose and died like sounds coming from a crowded room as a door swung open and shut.

"You sure Turk's part of it?"

The question had come from the porch of the Breen House, where a lanky figure was outlined dimly between the lighted windows. I couldn't make him out but I knew Shedwell's brogue.

"Fairly," I said. "Why?"

He stepped forward. His coattails were flung back to expose his guns. "I'll be one of your deputies. Unless you got objections."

Some of Terwilliger's crew recognized the mankiller. His name buzzed through the gathering.

"Get your horse," I told him.

He struck off toward the livery, moving with an easy lope. "What about it?" I asked the others. "Any dropouts?"

Terwilliger kneed his horse into the space in front of the cowhands, facing me. "My men don't shy from a fight, Marshal. Swear away."

When Shedwell returned straddling a bay stallion, I had everyone raise his right hand and recite the oath I'd heard often in Judge Blackthorne's chambers when new officers joined the fraternity. The words didn't vary a lot between the federal and local levels and didn't mean much of anything anyway. After the "I do's" I said, "Kill the torches. No sense advertising," and led the way in the direction of the night riders' retreat. The dead raider had been removed from the street, which explained the light in Fitch's undertaking parlor.

We made good time until we reached the point where our quarry had left the road to ride across country, after which we had to stop from time to time and dismount until someone picked up on matted grass or a similar sign of recent passage. Moonlight is deceptive. We wasted precious minutes following false trails that dead-ended where the fugitives had doubled back on themselves to throw us off. Finally we came to a spot where the tracks stopped heading north and turned east.

"That ain't the way to Mather's spread," Terwilliger reported.

"Could be another sour lead," suggested Cross.

"I doubt it." I pointed to a spattering of dark spots on the beaten grass. "Whoever's bleeding has been doing it for miles. They're running out of time for clever tricks."

"How many of them are there, you reckon?" asked the rancher.

"Shedwell got the best look at them," I said.

"Eight." The gunman looked thoughtful. "Nine. I was sort of preoccupied."

I frowned. "Looked like more."

"Could be. Like I said, I didn't keep no tally."

"Think Périgueux knows they're on his land?" Terwilliger asked.

"It wouldn't surprise me." I clucked the roan into motion.

Half a mile farther on we came upon a bundle of clothing dumped alongside the trail. The horses were downwind of it and shied as we approached. It wasn't a bundle of clothing. I stepped down and turned it over with my foot.

The front of his shirt was black and glistening in the pale light. An empty scabbard like the kind cavalry officers wore was hooked to his belt. I remembered Major Brody saying he'd gutshot the man who had tried to lop off his arm. He wasn't wearing a pillowcase now. I recognized him as one of the men I had seen at the corral near Périgueux's headquarters. I felt his neck.

"Still warm," I said, mounting. "We're gaining."

An hour later we topped a rise overlooking several sections of undulating grassland. Nestled in a furrow between swells was a wooden line shack with a slant roof and a covered window with a gunport where the shutters met, left over from the Sioux wars. A brush tail flicked into view from beneath the roof of the lean-to stable in back and was gone. We withdrew below the ridge.

"Might be a decoy," Cross whispered. "They got a horse to spare now."

"If they've got wounded, they'll need shelter," I said.

"If they got wounded."

I considered. "I'm betting on the shack, but let's make sure. Circle around on foot. Stay low. If there's only one horse in the stable, fire a shot in the air and wait for us. Otherwise come back and report. Just a second."

The deputy had started off in a crouch. I clutched his sleeve. "If you start anything without orders, I'll kill you."

His eyes glittered in their slits but he said nothing. I let him go.

The rest of us stood around listening to each other's breathing. The prairie wind came up at ragged intervals, humming through the grass and plucking at our hat brims so that we had to hold on to them with both hands, but for the most part nothing moved. Even the moon seemed nailed in the sky. At last we heard Cross's heavy footsteps in the frost-brittle grass.

"There's nine horses." His breath came in shallow, excited bursts.

"Fan out," I said. "Surround it. No one fires till I give the word."

Cow horses all, the animals held their positions from the moment the reins touched earth. I kept Shedwell with me and divided the men between Cross and Terwilliger, thus balancing the command. When we were alone, the gunman and I crawled to the crest on our bellies. I had the Winchester from the office, he a Spencer repeater with a folding sight. I noted the moon's position.

"Sun will be up in about an hour. We'll call them out as soon as it gets light."

He made no reply. In the hollow, the lonely shack cast a shadow solid enough to trip over. Miles away a coyote hurled its sad challenge at the moon.

I blew on my fingers and worked the stiffness out of the joints. "Where do you know Abel Turk from?"

"Centralia, eighteen sixty-four." He was watching the shack.

"You were riding with Quantrill then."

"Anderson."

"Was Turk a guerrilla?"

"He was second in command." His voice was low. "We'd been picking Centralia all morning and was feeling pretty good. Along about noon we stopped the train from St. Charles and ordered everybody out. There was twenty-five armed Yanks aboard, going home on furlough. We lined them up and made them strip to their flannels. Anderson found out one was an officer and ordered him out of line. Then he told Turk to muster out the rest."

The broad brim of his hat drenched his face in darkness. His breath curled in the brittle air.

"I was pretty fresh then," he said. "I thought that meant Anderson was going to turn them loose. I laughed to think of all them bluebellies hobbling down the tracks in their long handles and stocking feet. Then he started shooting at them.

"He blasted away with a pistol in each hand, and Yanks fell like dominoes. Some of them tried running and went down with holes in back. One blubbered and stuck out his hands like he thought he could stop the lead. There was this yellow-haired sergeant that let out a roar and charged Turk when he was reloading. Turk didn't hurry. He finished and shot the sergeant twice in the chest and once in the neck, and even then he had to step back or the Yank would of fell into his arms.

"By this time we was all shooting, me included. It wasn't hard at all. You'd be surprised how easy it was when everyone else was doing it too. Thing is, I don't think any of us could of touched it off except Turk. When it was over, the only Yank left standing was the brass-buttons Anderson took out of line."

He chuckled dryly. "Old Bloody Bill, he did hold a soft spot for brother officers."

We listened to the coyote again, farther away this time, the mournful note warped by distance. When it had ended I said, "Is Turk the reason you came to Breen?"

He didn't answer. We waited in silence for the sun.

# CHAPTER 22

It's quiet at that time of year, with no crickets singing or bugs thumping through the grass. We lay there watching the shack while the cold sniffed at us and crept down our collars and up our pants legs and lay like metal against our skin. Even the faraway coyote had ceased crying. I warmed my hands in my armpits and creaked my toes in my boots when they grew numb. The grass crackled when I changed positions. Shedwell didn't move a hair.

For a long time I watched a leaden sliver on the eastern horizon before it lost its hard edge and melted into the black that surrounded it, spreading with the painful slowness of a bad dream drawing to a close. The sky bled gray, then pale blue, and then a wedge of red sun appeared like a raw wound in the Little Belts. The shadow cast by the line shack shifted and shortened, becoming more dramatic as coppery light washed the foothills.

I waited while the sun cleared the mountains and its glare grew less direct. Then I gathered my legs beneath me and, squatting on one knee, drew a bead on the shuttered window. Beside me, Shedwell remained prone, supported on his elbows, with the Spencer trained on the door.

My own voice surprised me, booming out over the hills after so much silence and bounding off the tall rocks to east and west. "Surrender" continued to ricochet long after I finished speaking, altering its shape each time it struck until it was just a grumble in the distance, then a whisper, then nothing. More minutes passed before my answer came screaming straight at me and buried itself with a *whump* in the earth at my feet. Blue smoke slid sideways from the port in the shutters.

"Open fire!" On "fire" I squeezed one off, levering another into the chamber and shooting again even as the silvery tinkle of collapsing glass reached me. The door jumped in its frame as Shedwell's bullet smashed through the weathered wood.

Reports crackled across the surrounding hills. Balls of smoke were blown elliptical and shredded by the mounting wind. Pieces of shingle flew from the shack's roof. Lead whined off solid objects inside and clanked against ironware. The horses in the exposed stable screamed and kicked at the posts supporting the roof, the impacts sounding like small explosions even at this distance.

The men trapped inside returned fire sporadically. A black snout would poke itself through the port, sneeze fire and smoke, then withdraw as more bullets chewed at the shutters. Reports from the opposite side testified to the existence of at least one other window. Meanwhile, hurtling bits of metal hammered the weatherboard. I remember thinking of a magician I had once seen in St. Louis who shut a pretty girl up in a box and proceeded to thrust swords through the sides at all angles, and I wondered now, as I had wondered then, how anyone could survive such an assault. But the answering fire continued.

I was reloading when the shutters and door burst outward simultaneously as if a powder charge had gone off inside. Four men spilled out, arms and legs uncoiling like loosely baled rags as they struck the ground and straightened running, revolvers and rifles blazing. Bullets tore up grass all around me.

The one who had come through the door, working the lever of a Henry now and backing with the others toward the stable, wore a dark beard. Turk. Shedwell recognized him too, but before he could take aim the earth heaved in front of his face, spraying dirt into his eyes. He cursed and rubbed at them with his fingers.

I chambered a cartridge and got a bead on Turk just as he darted around the corner of the shack. My bullet splintered wood. One of the men who had leaped out the window was down, spread-eagled on his stomach with his six-gun still in his hand. Seconds later two horses bolted from the stable, their riders hugging their necks bareback. I fired and one horse went down with a scream. Its master leaped clear. It was Turk again.

I had him in my sights when his partner swung his horse around and crossed in front to give him a hand up. Someone on the other side squeezed off at the same time I did. The rider arched his back and slumped forward. Turk pushed him off and mounted in the same movement. He was a hundred yards away before his rescuer stopped bouncing. Dark geysers erupted around horse and rider. They disappeared over a hill, and when they came into view again atop the next they were well out of range. A number of desultory shots were hurled after them none-theless.

Then it got quiet.

I waited for the appearance of the fourth escapee. When he didn't show I assumed one of the others had gotten him. I learned later that the others were thinking the same thing on our side. The missing man would be found draped over the hitching rail, where he had succumbed to a wound suffered while still in the building.

I asked Shedwell about his eyes, red-rimmed now and blinking. He waved the question aside.

"Turk get clear?"

I said he had. "He'll head toward Périgueux's for supplies and a fresh mount. It's closer than Mather's house."

"Don't shoot!"

The shout came from the shack, where moments later a rifle and two revolvers flew out the open door in order and landed on the ground twenty feet away.

"We're unarmed!" The voice was hoarse and desperate. "We're coming out!"

"Hands on your heads!" I shouted.

I gave the order to cease fire. Two men staggered out the door one after the other, hands clasped on top of their heads. The second man was limping. Blood slicked his right pants leg to the knee. I called for them to halt and stood up. Brass casings tinkled from my lap to the ground.

"What about the others?" I kept them covered.

The uninjured man answered. His hair and short beard were snarled as if he'd just risen from bed.

"One's dead. The other, almost. He got it in the lungs and he's coughing up bloody pieces. That's it."

I called for Cross. There was a pause while his name banged around the mountains, and then a solid figure rose from the ridge on the other side of the shack. He waved the Spencer he'd taken from the rack at the jail and started down the slope. Terwilliger and his men followed suit. I was waiting for them when they got to the building, having taken possession of the prisoners and their discarded weapons. As he was closing in, Cross pivoted suddenly and smashed his rifle stock across the wounded man's face.

I dropped the confiscated guns and lashed out even as the man fell, catching the deputy full on the chin with my left fist. This was the same hand I had used to silence Colleen and Earl. I felt tiny bones snapping when it connected. My bones.

He staggered back a dozen steps, roared, and brought up the office Spencer. I sailed a bullet past his ear from the Winchester before he could pull the trigger.

"I don't miss twice," I barked, when it looked as if he was going to try again. He dropped his arm. Blood trickled out a corner of his mouth. I turned to Shedwell. "Can you handle things here?"

"You handle them," he said. "My business is with Turk."

Terwilliger was roughly helping Cross's victim to his feet. The night rider's nose was broken and bleeding copiously. "You're in charge," I told the rancher. "Try and see that no one gets lynched while we're gone."

The sun was clear of the peaks and losing its bloody color when Shedwell and I rode within view of the massive skeleton of the Marquis' new chateau. The numbness had worn out of my left hand, and each time the road lurched, tiny bursts of pain shot straight up my arm. In spite of this we drove our mounts hard for the next half hour and thundered into Périgueux's yard just as Turk was emerging from the ranch house.

In his arms he cradled a bedroll bulky with foodstuffs. A sleek dun was ground-tethered by the corral, saddled and ready to run. We drew our revolvers and fired over its head. It whinnied, reared and took off at a mad gallop toward the hills, reins flapping.

Turk dropped his bundle and answered with his Smith & Wesson, backing away fast. I'd never seen anyone get a gun out that quickly. A furrow appeared across the horn of my saddle, exposing dull lead under the leather. Shedwell circled to the end of the porch and whipped his horse up onto the boards, ducking to clear the roof and block that line of retreat. We had him between us now.

The foreman sank into a half-crouch, swinging his gun to cover us both as he backed toward the corner of the house. I danced the roan in that direction, herding him in the other direction like a contrary bull.

My hat was snatched off my head by a bellowing explosion from above. Startled, I glanced up and met Ed Strayhorn's gaze at an upstairs window, behind the sight of his big Remington rifle. I'd completely forgotten about Périgueux's bookkeeper. I snapped off a hasty shot before he could take aim again. He ducked behind the wall and the window frame splintered.

A battering ram struck my chest. My horse reared and I cartwheeled from the saddle, turned over with agonizing slowness as in a terrifying dream, and stopped suddenly with an impact that dwarfed the first. What breath I still had left me with an animal grunt.

When my senses returned I raised my head to look for my horse and pain tore through me. I laid it back down, but not before noting that my shirt front was clotted with gore. I knew I was dying. I had seen what a bullet from a .44 could do to bone and muscle too many times to believe otherwise. Vaguely, not too far away, I heard a series of reports, a pause, and then one more. The last one carried the finality of an exclamation point. I remember thinking that that was important, then reminding myself that it wasn't, not any more, not to me. I could hear the squishy sound of blood pumping through the hole in my chest.

I may have blacked out. In any case, I don't recall any other thoughts until I heard a crunching and Chris Shedwell moved into my field of vision. His expression was grim and he was plodding like a man in the final stages of exhaustion. His right arm hung limp at his side with the Remington revolver dangling at the end. His other hand was clasped to his rib cage, where a red stain was spreading around his fingers. He stopped, looking down at me, and opened his mouth to speak.

A shot rang out, very close. His mouth opened a little wider along with his eyes. For a long moment he remained like that, back arched, elbows drawn in, and then the gun dropped from his hand, his knees buckled, and he fell out of my line of sight. Behind where he had been standing I now saw young Arnie Strayhorn holding the rifle his father had taken from him until he could show he deserved to carry it. The last thing I was aware of was his thin, bespectacled face wreathed in blue smoke.

# CHAPTER 23

I dreamed of naked women and oceans of blood, of diabolic, laughing faces erupting from the muzzles of guns and scaly hands slippery to the touch that grasped my limbs in grips like steel cables and strained to pull me apart. One of the laughing faces belonged to Doc Ballard. The hands belonged to Alf, the bartender at the Glory. The blood was mine and so were the naked women, dredged up from my imagination and forgotten since I was fourteen years old. From time to time I'd see a man strapped to a bed and raving. I felt sorry for him, and sympathetic tears would roll down my cheeks and leave burning furrows. I found myself dreaming of him more and more often. He wasn't raving any more and the straps were gone.

"Murdock?"

It was the first time I'd heard human speech in my dreams. I strained to understand what was being said.

"Murdock? Wake up."

My eyelids were weighted at the bottoms, like curtains on a saloon stage. When I got them pried open, I was looking through a red haze. I closed them again and opened them. Again. The haze dissipated slowly, like frost on the inside of a window as a room warms up. The doctor's face hovered over me. He wasn't laughing.

"I've been having some crazy dreams." It came out gibberish. I started again, but he'd understood.

"That was the laudanum. You've been out for six days. You were feverish when Terwilliger's men brought you in. I didn't dare drug you until it broke. I had to get someone to hold you down when I extracted the bullet. You screamed bloody murder."

"Alf?"

He looked surprised. "Yes, it was Alf. I didn't think you'd remember. The Glory had the nearest bed. That's where you are now, in the back room. You were delirious for days; I didn't think we'd pull you through."

I glanced down at my chest. I was shirtless. A white bandage swaddled my right shoulder above a coarse gray blanket.

"You took a bullet in the chest," he explained. "It just missed your right lung." He held up a conical lump of dull metal. "You were lucky twice. Ordinarily the lead would have pierced the lung, glanced off the shoulder blade, and torn a path through your vital organs before coming to rest.

In this case it entered at an upward angle, scraped along the bone and became entangled in the muscles and ligaments of your shoulder. There was substantial tissue damage. You may lose some of the use of that arm. It's too early to tell. But it beats dying."

I lifted my left arm. My fingers protruded from a plaster cast that reached to my wrist. Cross's jaw had been harder than expected. The doctor smiled.

"When you decide to hurt yourself, you don't stop halfway. It'll take six weeks for those bones to finish knitting, but you can write and feed yourself."

"When can I get out of here?"

"Whenever you want to. But you won't want to for a while. You lost a lot of blood and you don't take too well to being fed, as this eye can attest." He indicated his left eye. It did look a little discolored and puffy.

"Shedwell," I said.

He looked grave. "There was nothing anyone could do for him. He died instantly." He paused. "Major Brody is gone too. He lived for a day after his arm was amputated, but the shock was just too much for his heart. He had an attack a couple of years ago. I guess you didn't know that."

I said I didn't. His manner lightened.

"You have a visitor. Shall I show him in?"

I don't remember how I answered. I must have said yes, because he went out and a moment later Yardlinger appeared at the foot of the bed. He was carrying his hat and had a patch over his eyebrow. I levered myself into a sitting position, stifling an exclamation as pain streaked down my weakened right arm.

"How's the head?" I asked.

"Stuck together with crepe and spit." He fingered the patch. "I won't be as pretty as I used to be, but few people are. How's the shoulder?"

"Ask me again when the laudanum wears off. I'm sorry

about the Major. For a bloodthirsty guerrilla he had the makings of a first-class lawman."

He smiled wearily. "Just as well he didn't live to hear that. You know you left me in the lurch. Randy and I have had the devil's own time keeping our prisoners from being lynched. We had to club a couple of heads last night, but it looks as if they'll live long enough to face the circuit judge this afternoon."

"Who've we got?"

"Well, Périgueux's the star. It was his idea to form the band of night riders. The two survivors have confirmed that and we've got Mather's testimony that he sold a string of black horses to the Marquis a month before the raids started. He suspected the Frenchman was involved but was afraid those horses would implicate him so he kept quiet. I'm convinced he wasn't in on the raids and that he didn't know his own foreman was leading them. If he's guilty of anything, it's being afraid to ask questions."

"Where's Périgueux now?"

"Terwilliger's men are guarding him at his place. They're still sworn and they know what's in store for them if anything happens to their prisoner. The jail's at capacity."

"Who's there, besides the two night riders?"

"Actually, there's only one. Doc Ballard's treating his partner at the Freestone for a hip wound. Both the men who were still in the line shack were dead when Randy and the others found them. Three Circle T hands involved in the raid on Mather's ranch. The other two rode out that night. I don't have any evidence other than my testimony that they were with Pardee when his brother was brought into Fitch's, but I'm going with that. Then there's Ed Stray-horn and his nephew Arnie."

"They were with Turk?"

He shook his head. "The old man thought he was just

protecting his boss's interests when the shooting started. I mean to put in a word for him at the trial. As for Arnie, well, I don't see him pulling much more than a suspended sentence considering Shedwell's reputation. The Judge takes a dim view of professional killers."

I was having a hard time keeping up. The laudanum had dulled my comprehension. "What about Turk?"

"Terwilliger got there just in time to see it from a distance." He spoke slowly. "After he shot you, Turk took cover in what there was of Périgueux's new chateau. Shedwell went in after him standing up. The night rider wounded him first shot. From then on Shedwell might have been invisible the way Turk's bullets just kept stitching up the ground all around him. Shedwell fired once. Just once."

I considered. "Arnie must have seen it too. When he realized who it was, he must have gone to get the English rifle, thinking that killing Chris Shedwell would make him man enough for his uncle."

"Men have died for lots less," he said. "Anyway, Terwilliger's the one to thank for saving your hide. He threw you in one of the Marquis' wagons and trundled you into town more dead than alive."

"Damn nice of him, considering I saved him a few dead men himself. Any messages?"

"I almost forgot." He reached inside his coat and drew out a sheaf of telegraph forms. "Guess who."

"Answer them. Tell the Judge I'll report in person." I searched his face. "Anything else?"

"No word from her. She hasn't budged from Martha's since you were brought here." Angrily he thrust the forms back into his breast pocket. "She's no good, Page."

I laughed nastily. Even that hurt. "Who am I, the Pope?"

"You know what I mean."

The doctor returned. "That's enough visiting for now. He needs rest."

As he said it I realized how tired I really was. I held out my left hand. "I can't say you didn't keep me entertained."

Yardlinger grasped my fingers in the cast. "Don't worry about Doc's bill or the rent on this room. The city's taking care of it, though the council doesn't know that yet. Your horse is at the livery and I've got your gun. Anytime you're ready for them."

I grinned. "Marshal, are you ordering me out of town?"

"Maybe." His tight smile flickered behind the lank moustache. "The sooner you're gone the quicker I can get the citizens of Breen accustomed to orthodox law enforcement." He left. I was asleep before the door closed.

That afternoon I was walking around the room, and by the next day I could dress myself and venture out to the barroom for a beer and some conversation with Alf. There was no news from the new opera house, where the trial was in its second day. The bartender caught my attention wandering toward the deserted side room.

"She ain't been around," he said, polishing a glass. "Talk is she's leaving."

I paid for the beer without a word and returned to the back room. My shoulder was beginning to act up in spite of the sling.

The trial lasted three days. Michel d'Oléron, Marquis de Périgueux, was found guilty of conspiracy to commit murder and sentenced to life imprisonment. He never spent a day behind bars. The sentence was later commuted to ten to twenty years at hard labor, then suspended. He sold out his holdings in Montana and returned to France, where rumor had it that he married into another fortune after his first wife, a woman of frail constitution, perished during the ocean crossing. The two night riders were hanged in Breen for murder. The jury found Ed Strayhorn innocent of complicity in the raids and he was released. His nephew Arnie received six months on a work detail clearing land for the Great Northern Railroad, scheduled for completion in 1883. After that he joined a theatrical troupe and toured some eastern cities as "The Man Who Shot Chris Shedwell." I lost track of him in succeeding years.

In a separate action, the circuit judge dismissed out of hand the case against the three Terwilliger men for lack of evidence. No one ever came to trial for the raid on the Six Bar Six and the murder of three employees of the ranch.

Dick Mather died of consumptive bronchitis in 1882.

By a six-to-four vote of the city council, Oren Yardlinger was appointed to a two-year term as Breen city marshal. The appointment wasn't renewed and he drifted down to Wyoming, where he took a job as deputy sheriff in Cheyenne and was shot in the back by an unknown party while making his rounds. He died with his Navy Colt still in its holster. I didn't hear of Randy Cross again until 1899, when he refereed the Jeffries-Fitzsimmons fight in Coney Island, N.Y. After that, nothing.

The last I heard, Bob Terwilliger was still alive and living in comfortable retirement on his ranch, now under the management of his son.

Against doctor's orders I testified on the last day of the night-rider trial and retired to the Glory during the recess for a drink. Colleen Bower was in the side room, dealing blackjack to a man in a suit with an eastern cut.

I peeled enough off the roll Yardlinger had returned to me for my bills at the hotel and livery, bought some chips out of the rest, and slapped what was left down on the table in front of the easterner. "Try your luck at the wheel."

He glanced up, annoyed. Then he saw the sling I was wearing and went a little pale. He scooped up the bills and his chips, mumbled polite excuses to the lady, and went out. My reputation was spreading.

"Any news?" She dealt two cards apiece without looking

at me. Her hair was done up the way I liked it and she was wearing blue.

"Judge turned it over to the jury. Nothing to do now but wait. Twenty-one." I turned up the ace of hearts.

"Twenty."

I took in her ante. She dealt again. "Been sick?" I asked.

"I needed a little vacation. Nineteen."

"Seventeen." I watched my chip go onto her stack and fed the pot again. "You knew Chris Shedwell pretty well, didn't you?"

She didn't answer. Cards slithered over the table's polished top. "I'm over."

I claimed her chip. "Well enough to scout for him, I'd say."

She hesitated, then resumed dealing. Her eyes never left the cards. I grabbed her hand. She glared.

"It was convenient for Shedwell," I said. "Not every killer has someone he can blame for his profession. He could fancy himself a soldier until that day in Centralia when Abel Turk made a murderer out of him and the others in Anderson's crew.

"Being confined to a bed gives you a chance to think. I kept wondering what it was that made Shedwell hate him enough to want to kill him. When he told me about Centralia I thought it was because of what Turk had done to those unarmed Union soldiers, but that wasn't it. It was because of what he thought Turk had done to him. It's been eating at him all this time. Maybe he thought destroying Turk would wipe out the last sixteen years and let him start over clean."

Still she didn't say anything. I held on. I knew from experience that she had to be a captive audience to listen.

"Then I started wondering how he found out Turk was here. That wasn't too hard to answer. You were the only person he knew in Breen. How did you send the wire, in code? Something you fixed up together before he sent you in this direction to nose around and find out what you could? It doesn't really matter how you did it. But it was smart. Who'd suspect a lady gambler of spying for a killer?"

She had a new handbag. I caught her eyes wandering toward it and released her hand to slide it toward me. It was heavier than most reticules. She sighed resignedly and sat back.

"It wasn't like that at all." One of her fine white hands went up before I could interrupt. "Oh, I sent him a wire, and I used a simple code designed to stand up to a first glance. But he didn't send me here. I recognized Turk by accident from Chris's description when Turk visited Martha's. Chris didn't depend on women to lay his groundwork. And he didn't come here to kill Turk. I thought you understood that."

I summoned a sneer. Then I spotted my reflection in the glass chimney of the lamp on the table and stopped. "He didn't go out to Périgueux's ranch to swap old war stories."

She shook her head, exasperated at my density. "I'm not saying Chris wouldn't have tried to kill him if he thought he could. He didn't think he was good enough. As it turned out he was, but he couldn't know that. He had nothing but memory to compare with."

I stared at her, trying to put what she said in order. This time I couldn't blame it on laudanum. "You're saying he came here to die."

"Is it so hard to accept?" She pushed aside the deck of cards. "Some people slash their wrists. Others take a gun and blow their brains out. Chris chose the way he thought was best for him. I like to think that Doc Ballard was wrong and that he had a chance to realize what had happened when that unexpected bullet hit him. That way he would've died content."

"He hated living that much?"

"Not living, waiting to die. Have you ever heard of the law of diminishing returns? They talk about it a lot back East. The more durable you make a product, the lower your chances of selling a replacement because the first one never wears out. When you're best, you sow the seeds of your own destruction. With Chris, it stood to reason that if he kept killing off the gunmen who weren't as good as he was, the odds of his meeting one as good or better increased. No, it wasn't living he hated. It was waiting."

I didn't say anything. After a few moments she retrieved the deck and dealt. We played a few hands, winning each other's money, then: "Alf tells me you're heading out."

"Soon as I can hire a wagon." She dealt herself twenty-one. "I don't need one, but a lady of my breeding can't be seen riding horseback across the prairie."

I won the next turn. "Ladies don't travel alone."

"Is that an invitation?"

"If you're headed west."

She shook her head. "If you can survive the Nations without an escort, you can survive anywhere." She won the last hand, drew in the discards and shuffled the deck. "Care for another go? Maybe we can break this deadlock."

"I wish we could." I got up, taking my chips. I started to say something else. She put more energy into her shuffling, the cards hissing. Her eyes remained on the deck. I moved toward the door.

"Planning to hang around Helena for a while?"

I stopped, my back to her. "For a while."

There was a pause, then: "Thanks for the warning."

I left. Outside, it was a bright spring day.

# CITY OF
# WIDOWS

For Debi, *mi arma y mi salvación.*

"These widows, sir, are the most perverse creatures in the world."

—JOSEPH ADDISON (1712)

"Be wery careful o' vidders all your life."

—CHARLES DICKENS (1837)

# CHAPTER 1

**G**eneral Lew Wallace had a grip that could crack corn and no chin at all under a beard that was like a fistful of nails fused together by rust. He had small sharp gooseberry eyes under straight brows, an aggressive nose, and fine hair plastered to his forehead in the classical style. He had on a fresh collar and there was something of the uniform in the way he wore his clawhammer coat and vest with no chain or decoration of any kind.

"Have a seat, Deputy. How is my old friend Harlan Blackthorne?"

"He's well, General. Your honor. He sends his regards." The horsehair chair felt strange after the hard seats in the day coach. No Pullmans for a deputy United States marshal from Montana Territory.

The office was done up in that Spanish frontier style I'd gotten my first taste of the moment I crossed into New Mexico Territory and had my fill of long before I reached Santa Fe: brick-reinforced adobe, squaw rugs on a pine floor, and an oak desk as big as a porch with leather stretched drum tight across the top and secured with brass tacks the size of ten-dollar gold pieces. A walnut bookcase with glass doors contained mustard-bound law books, Bowdler's Gibbon, and at least ten copies of *Ben Hur*.

At the window overlooking the plaza stood a beanpole in a ready-made suit, all elbows and Adam's apple, a big-eared, knob-knuckled Missouri farmer got up for Sunday with pomade in his hair and moustache. He was as red as a skinned rabbit and looked hard on fifty, which in that country meant he was closer to thirty. He regarded me with pale unfriendly eyes and made no move my way when Wallace introduced us.

"Page Murdock, this is Pat Garrett. Garrett's sheriff in Lincoln County."

"Hard place." I didn't recognize his name, although it was clear from the governor's tone I was supposed to.

Garrett said nothing. Wallace lowered himself into his leather swivel. "Mr. Garrett's here for my advice. Not as a politician or as a military man, but as an author. He's considering a book about his experiences and he has it in his mind I know something about the subject because of my little tale of the Christ." He was being modest. *Ben Hur* had been on sale barely a year and already shared a shelf with the Bible in most of the homes I'd visited.

I raised my brows politely. "Experiences?"

"Mr. Garrett shot and killed Billy the Kid last month down in Fort Sumner."

I shook my head, feeling ignorant. Wallace stared, then sat back slightly and twitched his shoulders. "You wouldn't have heard of him up in your country, I suppose. The little bucktoothed killer put us through six kinds of perdition after that circus in Lincoln County." He looked at Garrett. "Mr. Murdock rides for Judge Blackthorne up north. His employer and I served together in Mexico. He was a fierce campaigner then and if what I hear from Helena is true, he hasn't changed a great deal."

Garrett was back looking out the window. I said, "He speaks well of your military record too, your honor. General." What the Judge, who had also known the New Mexico governor when he was prosecuting the conspirators in the assassination of President Lincoln, had actually said was that as a lawyer Wallace proved a consummate soldier. He'd added that he couldn't write, either.

Wallace blushed exactly like a girl and fingered his whiskers. "I asked my publishers to send him a copy of the book. Did he read it?"

"Yes, sir. He said it was a splendid example of the current condition of American letters."

"Yes. Well." He cleared his throat. "Was there anything else, Mr. Garrett?"

The sheriff from Lincoln County said he guessed there wasn't and excused himself. His petal-soft Alabama drawl didn't go with the rest of him. He left without having spoken to me once and I never heard anything more from him until his book came out a year or so later. I read it and made up my mind there and then never to write one. One more promise I haven't managed to keep.

Wallace tugged a yellow telegraph flimsy out of a sheaf pinned to his desk by a bronze bust of Alexander and straddled his nose with a pair of egg-shaped spectacles to read it. "Harlan's wire says to expect you and to show you the same courtesy I would him. It says nothing else. I assume you're in Santa Fe on business."

"Yes and no, General. Your honor."

"'Your honor' is sufficient. I sent down the uniform after Appomattox. Which is it, yes or no?" He hooked the spectacles into an oystershell case and snapped it shut.

"Well, it's business but not law business. I'm no longer in government service."

"How old are you?"

"Forty next month." I had to fish for it. I wasn't expecting the question.

"Only fancy men and laggards retire before age sixty. You don't dress well enough for the former and for a man who just spent forty-six hours on the rails you still move too quickly to pass for indolent. Were you dismissed?"

"Forty-eight," I corrected. "We hit a cow. I handed in my badge and papers."

"Differences, after all this time? Judge Blackthorne's wire says you've been with him six years. I'll warrant he's a difficult man, but surely by now—"

"Your honor, I'm too tired for tact. It isn't my strong suit when I'm fresh. I stand a whole lot less chance of tangling myself in my tongue if I speak directly."

"Please do."

I sat forward, resting my forearms on the desktop. I saw then what he meant about not dressing gay enough to be kept by a woman with cash. The one good suit of clothes I wore for court and genteel travel needed brushing and my shirtcuffs were as raveled as old crepe. "Bear Anderson was a difficult man. You wouldn't have caught wind of him down here any more than I heard of your Billy the Kid. The Flathead Indians, what he left of them, were ready to stop hunting him and make him into a god when I pulled him down out of the Bitterroot Mountains four years ago and stood him on a scaffold. A one-eyed buffalo bull with a belly full of crazy weed and an arrowhead stuck under its tail is difficult. Judge Blackthorne is the cruellest, pigheadedest, most vindictive and contrary mother's son that ever trod cobble. That wasn't bad enough but some damn fool in Washington City saw fit to put a gavel in his hand and place him in sole charge of a territory bigger than most countries. It didn't improve his temperament."

He might have smiled behind the beard. I couldn't tell for sure but there was humor in the sharp eyes, or what passed for it in that old-soldier circle. "And so you feel you've had your life's portion of Harlan A. Blackthorne and all his works."

"It isn't just that. What with the war and trail herding and upholding the duly constituted law between Canada and old Mexico I've spent the best part of the last twenty years either too hot or too cold or too shot at, and most of it horseback. I'd like to try a town job for a while. I'm a fair hand with cards and I've been offered the chance to buy a half interest in a saloon down in Socorro County."

"Congratulations, Deputy. That's good cattle country and they're prospecting for silver in the vicinity. You should do a fair trade. Unfortunately, I don't gamble and I've never trafficked in spirits. Just what is it you're expecting of me?"

"I'm not expecting anything, Governor. The Judge and I parted on friendly terms and he offered to put in a good word with you in honor of our long association. I'm told there's been trouble in Socorro County and the sheriff there has blocked the establishment of any new saloons until it sorts itself out. My partner, Junior Harper, doesn't feel that order will affect our transaction as the Apache Princess has been operating for six months, but the Judge thought I might benefit from a letter of reference signed by the governor of New Mexico Territory, just in case."

"Attesting that you are a man of family and good character."

"The character part, anyway," I said. "I never did find tracks in that family country."

He sat back again, not far, gripping the arms of his swivel. All those drills had pounded into him the posture of a Springfield rifle. "Word travels faster down here than you suppose, Deputy. Allow me to show you a popular item available at the mercantile down the street. I would that my book sold as well." He took something out of the top drawer of the desk and placed it on top, square in the middle.

It was a pamphlet, bound in dirty yellow paper the size of a newspaper folded in quarters but not as thick. The cover bore a steelpoint engraving of a fierce fork-bearded jasper straddling a lathered horse. He had the reins clamped between his teeth and a hogleg belching fire in each hand. Ran the legend:

SATAN'S SIXGUN:
Being a True and Authentic Account
of the Adventures of Page Murdock,
the Lawless Lawman of Helena.
By Jack Rimfire

I grinned at the illustration. "I can't wear whiskers," I said. "I tried but they come in all colors."

"Are you acquainted with this fellow Rimfire?"

"Aaron Hookstratton's his right name. I ran him out of Helena last year after I shot Jordan Mercy. He was running a medicine show and seemed determined to foment a rebellion over Mercy. It sounds just like that counterfeit colonel to take his revenge in this way."

Wallace sat silent for a long time. Then he jerked his head in a manner I took to be positive. "A good answer. Had you denied knowing him I might have assigned weight to his tale. There was either truth or bad blood behind it."

"Does that mean you'll provide the letter of reference?"

"Nothing would give me greater pleasure than to grant Judge Blackthorne's request. It's a rare enough thing for him to make one." He fished a gunmetal watch out of his vest. "Where are you stopping in town? I'll have the letter delivered tomorrow."

"Don't trouble yourself, your honor." I slid the cowhide wallet out of my coat, removed the letter the Judge had dictated, and spread it out on top of the nickel novel on the desk. It was damp from the long ride plastered to my ribs.

He put on his spectacles. "Indeed. Most glowing. I see he employs a type-writer. I had no idea the nineteenth century was so firmly entrenched that far north."

"His niece took a course in Chicago."

"Comely, no doubt. I knew his wife when he was courting her."

"She's his sister's child."

"Oh." He unstuck his pen from the blotter, dipped it, and signed his name to the bottom of the letter. "I won't guarantee its efficacy in Socorro County," he said, sprinkling sand on the ink from a little glass container bearing the United States seal. "Frank Baronet is the sheriff. He and his twin brother Ross rode for the Dolan-Murphy syndicate during the late unpleasantness in Lincoln County. Ross was wounded in a raid on a ranch house that left a small cattleman and his wife slain and is believed to be either recovering and in hiding or dead somewhere below the border. No witnesses came forward to connect Frank to the raid but he rode off anyway and got himself elected down there; Jimmy Dolan has friends all over the territory and they throw a wide loop. My predecessor was a Dolan man. You can draw from that the extent of my influence in that country."

I thanked him for the letter and put it away. "I shouldn't have too many dealings with him after this one. He's in Socorro City and the Apache Princess is in San Sábado."

Rising from his seat, he hesitated. "That is a harsh place to spend your retirement from law enforcement. The town has a rough history. It's sheltered bandits and revolutionaries since the time of Cortez. Three times in the past, vendettas have wiped out its male population. The Mexicans call it *La Ciudad de Las Viudas*."

I stood. "I didn't get much opportunity to practice my Spanish up in Montana."

"It means The City of Widows." He extended a grave hand. "Go with God, Deputy."

# CHAPTER 2

Sheriff's Office
Socorro County
City of Socorro, N.M.T.
Aug. 15, 1881
Mr._____:
Your Presence is requested at the Execution of
       HERNANDO PADILLA
For the Murder of Ernestine "Mexican Red"
Grosvenor. To take place in the Yard of the
Socorro County Jail on
       Monday, August 22, 1881.
          (signed)
    FRANCIS S. K. BARONET, Sheriff

**A**bout a dozen of the invitations, printed on coarse gray stock with a black border, stood in a pile on the yellow oak counter separating the customer's side of the office from the side where the serious business was conducted. It was a big swept room smelling of oiled wood and sun, uncluttered, with lath and plaster over the adobe and two big brick-framed windows in front. The door to a hallway leading to the cells in back stood open. There were two desks with chairs and a big worktable supporting a parchment-colored map of the county, its corners held down by odd office items and an empty tequila bottle. Wanted readers and telegraph flimsies layered a corkboard like shingles and a buffalo gun with an octagonal barrel shared a wall rack with matched Winchesters, a Henry, and a Stevens ten-gauge cut back to within an inch of its usefulness. It looked like every other place on the frontier where the local law was upheld. I think I must have missed the issue of *Harper's Weekly* that set the standard.

"Go ahead."

It occurred to me as I turned that I was getting out of marshaling just in time. I hadn't heard the owner of the voice coming in behind me. He was at least half Indian, or all Mexican, which that close to Chihuahua amounted to the same thing. Short, thick, and brown, he had eyes as black and shiny as beetles in slits without lashes and a wide mouth with triangles of moustache at the corners. He wore a Stetson the way it had come from the factory, with neither dent nor dimple in the crown and as flat in the brim as a tortilla, a clean white shirt buttoned to the throat, and striped trousers reinforced with leather and stuffed into the tops of stovepipe boots. His age was indeterminate. A Smith & Wesson .44, the Russian, with the slim black rubber grip and a bow spur on the trigger guard, rode high on his hip in a left-handed holster and he was carrying a Remington Creedmoor rifle with a folding sight. The brass star on his shirt bore no engraving.

"Go ahead," he repeated, "take one. Be sure and fill in your name before you present it."

I said, "I don't expect to be in town on the twenty-second. Do you always give out invitations to whoever blows in?"

"Not as a matter of general practice. The sheriff likes a good crowd for a hanging—he says that's what separates a lynching from a legal execution—but Nando was the town barber and a good one and nobody much wants to see him dangle. Jury might not have convicted him except the town needs whores more than it needs barbers. Mexican Red had a following." He leaned his rifle in the corner by the front door. "You'd be the fellow from the train. Oz

Alanson at the freight office seen three people get off. You don't look like a pipe drummer from Detroit and you sure ain't Ernst Schwimmer's wife Gretchen."

"Page Murdock." I grasped a hard sandy palm with more strength in it than he was bothering to employ. "If you're Frank Baronet, I have a letter for you."

He showed me two gold teeth. "Hell, you ain't that much bigger than me. What kind of wages is that Satan paying these days?"

"I hoped that hadn't got down this far." At that moment I wanted that half-dime novelist standing in front of me more than a woman.

"Oh, we get all the latest since the A.T. and S.F. came through. The name's Jubilo, I'm the full-time deputy. This time of day you'll find Mr. Baronet at the Orient. He owns the game there."

"Just Jubilo?"

His face now looked as if any smile that tried to light there would curl up and blow away. "I don't use the other. It was just my mother's."

I thanked him for the information and went out to find the Orient.

Walking felt good after another eighteen hours in the cars. I'd dropped off my necessaries at a hotel named for the town and county, visited a bathhouse that brushed suits while you washed, and with a shave and a change of shirts I felt closer to civilized man than I had at any time since Montana. My interview with Governor Wallace in Santa Fe had been just brief enough to allow me to catch the next train south, which was how my luck had been running lately.

Socorro City showed all the signs of a town on the grow. Buckboards and buggies outnumbered saddle horses on the street. Frame buildings were clattering up among the adobe and lumber was stacked everywhere, some of it un-

der armed guard because by the time it was cut and milled
in the mountains to the west and transported by wagon to
the building sites it was worth nearly as much as a shipment of silver. Four men in shirtsleeves and paint-drizzled
overalls were at work in front of a sign shop, where a dozen
fresh placards were already curing against the side of
the building. Most of them seemed to advertise real estate
brokers. There were a stove works, a billiard hall, and
four saloons on a main street as wide as a pasture. Prospectors came there for supplies and trail herders stopped
there to cut the dust on their way across the border to
borrow cattle from the old Spanish grandees.

The pride of the Orient, and likely the inspiration for
its name, seemed to be a paneled bar as long as an express
car, lacquered black with cherry blossoms painted on the
front. Antelope heads decorated the back wall and a six-
foot painting of a belly dancer in a frame crusted over with
gilt cupids dominated one end of a room built along the
lines of a shotgun to accommodate a narrow lot. At that
afternoon hour all the tables were occupied. When I asked
for Frank Baronet a bartender with a strawberry mark on
his forehead and a bulldog pistol standing in a water tum-
bler at his right elbow pointed out the faro table.

"You playing?" he asked.

"Not today."

"You'd best wait then till he finishes off that fellow.
When it comes to kibitzers Frank is no Christian. There's
an empty chair at that corner table if you're drinking.
Billy the Kid sat there when he shot Feeny MacAdo last
December. Straight through the heart at fifty-four feet."

"This Kid must have been hell on a stick. It can't be
twenty feet from there to the door."

"Nineteen and a half. Feeny was eating his breakfast in
the Chicago House across the street when Fate struck him
down."

I left the corner table to the Kid's ghost and went over to watch the game.

A sallow-faced man in a bowler and fresh collar that made his skin look even more unhealthy was bucking the tiger. He had a large stack of chips and eyes that never left the board except to follow the dealer's movements when he slid a counter in the cue box. The dealer was as lean as a lodgepole and sat as stiffly, with an embroidered pillow doubled behind his back for support. He was sheathed in a black vest and green-striped shirtsleeves with garters to match the stripes and parted his black hair in the center. He had modest handlebars, a predatory nose, and an odd habit of batting his eyelids rapidly, like a sporting lady. It seemed a clumsy signaling device, but as there was no one standing behind the player I assumed it was some kind of tic. They say Jesse James suffered from a similar affliction.

A counter moved. The player studied the board, sucked on his cigar. He put it down and slid a stack of reds onto the five of spades. The dealer drew two cards out of the box and laid them face up on the table. The first was the deuce of hearts. The second was the five of spades.

The dealer exhaled softly. "Sid, you are part Irish to-day. I never saw such a run."

"How many turns left?" Sid asked.

"Nine."

"Wrong again, Frank. It's ten."

"Well, why the hell did you ask if you knew the answer?"

"I got a side bet with Lyle Ring on just how big a liar you are." He moved his chips to another card. "Draw again."

"Sheriff Baronet?" I said.

The dealer winced and reached back to adjust his pillow. Three points of a nickel-plated star poked out of a pocket in his vest. "Later, mister. I have just ten more chances to bust this gentleman out. After that you just might be bringing your business to Sheriff Sidney L. Boone."

I recognized the name. "The real estate broker. I think your sign's done."

The player picked up his cigar and drew on it. His attention remained on the board.

"I'm Page Murdock," I told Baronet. "I guess you know me better around here as Satan's Sixgun."

"Give me a minute, Sid." The player shrugged and sat back smoking and glowering at the board. Baronet blinked, regarding me. "You're a lot south of your pasture, Marshal. We've had our sorrows with that cow crowd, getting drunk and shooting up innocent greasers they take for Don Segundo's vaqueros, but we are on top of it. It never was a federal matter."

"That's all behind me," I said. "I'm fixed to go into private enterprise in San Sábado. Junior Harper has sold me half of the Apache Princess. I'm here to see if that's all right with Socorro County."

"You no longer keep the peace?"

"Only my own."

He counted his chips. His other hand dangled off the hook of his chair near the pillow. "I'm concerned about this yellowback business. It might draw fire. Some pissant *pistolero* reads his nickel's worth and decides to find out for himself if you sizzle on the griddle. He shoots you or you shoot him. Either way somebody has to dig a hole. The newspapers forget all about Tombstone and here I am sitting on six hundred thousand square miles of sand and scorpion shit and no prospects. It's happened in milder places than this."

"Maybe they'll decide to publish this instead." I handed him Governor Wallace's letter.

He read it quickly and handed it back. "That carpetbagger. Things were just becoming settled in Lincoln County when he brought in the federals and stirred them back up. It killed my brother, Ross."

"I heard he was wounded in some kind of raid."

"He ran wild, I don't deny it. Ross hadn't my temperament or he would not have lashed out. He died last month of the blood fever in a cave in Chihuahua."

"I saw him three weeks ago in Juarez," Sid Boone said. "He looked fit to me."

"You're mistaken." Baronet batted his eyes at me. "I went through there on my way to bury Ross. We were twins. People confused us often."

"Ross is two inches shorter and twenty pounds heavier. I guess I can tell you apart."

"Someone else, then."

I put away the letter. "What about the partnership?"

"The Princess has a quiet reputation," Baronet said. "Anyway the ordinance against any new saloons expired last week. I look forward to trying my luck at your table."

I thanked him, hesitated. "How large is the caliber in that pillow?"

He had good teeth behind the moustaches, blue-white against the New Mexico tan. From behind the embroidered pillow he drew a Remington Rolling Block pistol with a fifty-caliber bore. I could have reached inside with my fingers and plucked out the ball.

"I didn't know buffalo came this far down," I said.

"Single-shot." He turned it sideways, admiring its lazy-J lines. "I've found that in indoor shooting, one slug this size is sufficient. What's that you carry?"

I pulled aside my coattail to show the chicken-bone butt

of the five-shot in the dropover holster. "Deane Adams. English gun. It fires Colt's forty-five, but only if I load the cartridges myself."

"Frank." Sid Boone put out his cigar.

The sheriff laid down the Remington and dealt two cards. I thanked him again and left.

The Socorro Hotel was one of the older adobe structures on a side street. My room was cool in the daytime desert heat but included a scooped-out fireplace for the chilly evenings. A Navajo saddle blanket did for a rug on the planks. There was a crucifix on the wall above the iron bedstead and a cornshuck mattress that felt like spun clouds when I stretched out on it in my clothes, and to hell with the rustling and scratching when I turned over. A Mexican as old as cornmeal and frijoles, shriveled down no bigger than my thumb in peasant cotton and rope sandals that slapped his feet like shutters, came in at sundown with an armload of sticks and started a fire. When he left I got one boot off and dropped into the warmest blackest hole I had been in since childhood.

I woke up just after dawn, feeling sore all over and more rested than I had at any time since quitting Helena. I thought about treating myself to a barber shave, then remembered that Hernando Padilla was in jail thinking about his own neck, and shaved myself. I put on corduroys, a fresh shirt, and a mackinaw against the morning cold and reported for breakfast to the Chicago House, where Feeny MacAdo had had the black fortune to sit in the line of Billy the Kid's magic fire.

I had a short wait. The room, plastered and wainscoted, with framed lithographs of Greek ruins leaning out from the walls, was just big enough for six tables and was clearly the most popular place to eat in town. At length I was seated by the owner, a bald, loose-jowled German in his fifties whose waistline was his best advertising. He brought out my steak and eggs in good order and filled my cup from an old campaigner of a two-gallon pot.

"Big doings at the Orient last night, you bet," he said. "You heard shooting?"

"Last night I'd have slept through Shiloh." The coffee was thick and black and strong enough to float a fifty-cent piece. It scorched a furrow all the way down to my stomach. "Who got shot?"

"Sid Boone, the real property man. They are saying he had a bad run at the sheriff's table and went on the prod. He took out his pistol. Mr. Baronet put a round in him while he was still cocking. He is dead as Judas."

He spotted an empty cup and boated off before I could ask questions.

My steak had had all the fight pounded out of it. Cutting it up, I reflected on how rapidly a man's luck could change in a game of chance.

# CHAPTER 3

The sun was barely above the Oscuros when I stepped out of the Chicago House and already the heat was crawling off the dirt street. It lay across my shoulders like an oak beam when I took off the mackinaw.

The larger of the town's two liveries was an unpainted barn with a roof that extended four feet past the front, throwing a triangle of shade on a man sitting on a bench in overalls with one strap gone, brogans with black steel toes poking through the leather, and a slouch hat with no more shape than a bar rag. He was shirtless and the hair on his chest was pale against the boiled skin.

"I need a saddle horse for a couple of hours," I said. "What's the best you've got?"

He had to tip his head all the way back to see up from under his flop brim. He was a towheaded twenty, a surprise. He had slat shoulders and the general dilapidated posture of a man in his seventies.

"Depends on what you want it for. I got a buckskin wouldn't throw a child or a fly but you'd have to carry it back from the lip of town on your hip."

"It has to carry me out to the Whiteside ranch and back. No flies or children."

His head dropped. "Patch get you."

"I heard the Apaches were raiding Arizona this year."

"Patch don't know when he's across the line." He spat. The spittle evaporated in the air.

"I'm obliged for your time," I said, turning. "There's another stable."

"Don't get your bowels in an uproar, mister. She's too hot to argue." He stood, stretched, and went inside. The sun moved, and then he came back out leading a gaunt bay by its bridle. Its hip sockets showed and its right eye was milky.

"That's as good as it gets?"

"Good as *you* get anyway. You don't have to stand in front of my uncle and tell him Patch et his sorrel for noon dinner." He tipped his head. "What's that for?"

I had drawn the Deane-Adams. I plugged a cartridge into the empty chamber and spun the cylinder with a diamondback buzz. "I want to be sure I have enough shells to hit a swift-moving target like you once I finish putting this sack of umbrellas out of its misery."

"Hold on, mister. There's law in this county."

"Curious thing about the law. It almost always gets off the second shot." I holstered the revolver. "Ten minutes from now I'm going to step out the front door of the

Socorro Hotel and throw a leg over an animal with some kind of pulse. If I should fall off the porch for lack of anything to break my drop, the law in this county is going to hold an inquest over your remains. That's if it can find a difference."

"Two dollars for the day," he said after a minute. "Saddle's fifty cents extra."

"I'll use my own." I handed him two cartwheels and left.

A sorrel with some years left on it was hitched at the rail when I came out carrying my gear. The boy was there and so was Frank Baronet. The sheriff had on a Prince Albert and a pinch hat squared over his brows. His thumbs were hooked inside the armholes of his vest and the gutta-percha handle of the large-bore Remington poked out of the notch above his belt buckle. He looked like an election poster.

He blinked up at the sky. "There's worse days for a ride."

"Not in Montana." I set down the saddle and Winchester and smoothed my faded blanket over the horse's back. "Is it always like this?"

"Nine months out of the year. Then it heats up."

I slung the saddle into place, jerked the cinch before the animal could puff itself up. It whickered and tried to crawl out of its skin. "I heard you had a row."

"Yes sir, I did. I'm going to miss old Sid. It's sad what the love of money will do to a Christian."

"The cards must have gone sour for him all at once. He was a piece ahead when I left."

"They will do that. I won back the table stakes plus an interest in his real business when he got frisky with that belly gun he carried. His widow can keep the store. I only let him wager it because he was determined to quit even. If I knew how determined I'd have shut down the game."

"I guess you had a crowd by then. When a man loses that much that fast it generally draws an audience."

"No, it was late. It was just Sid and me and Mike Henry behind the bar. Mike was asleep on his hand at the time. He fell off it and chipped a tooth when I fired."

"You're proficient with that buffalo pistol."

"I was elected to keep the peace. I don't play at it." He blinked. "I'll have that hip gun."

When a man says that, right out of the blue with both hands occupied, you look around. Jubilo, the deputy sheriff with no last name, was standing at the end of the hotel porch with his Creedmoor rifle resting on top of the railing. The bottom half of his face was a desert beneath the shadow of his flat brim. At that range he didn't need the folding sight.

I looked back at Baronet. "I'm headed into Apache country."

"You should have thought of that before you threatened the life of young Ole here. I'll have the whole rig. Just hang it over the hitch."

I unbuckled the cartridge belt and draped it next to the sorrel's tie. The sheriff stepped forward and lifted it off. "Hang on to that." He thrust it at the boy, who seized it eagerly, his head tilted back to watch me. His face was all anticipation.

"You don't wear the tin, you don't abuse a free man." Baronet jerked the Remington out of his belt and back-handed it in the same motion. A drop of red paint on the front sight caught my eye just before the sun exploded. I missed the fall. I was lying on the porch boards looking at the remains of my steak and eggs.

"Aw." Ole was disgusted. "He got something on my pants."

I rolled over quickly. The sole of a boot fastened on my throat.

"Come around here waving a letter from the governor," Baronet said. "I kill a man, I don't eat for three days. You can thank Sid Boone for your life, him and the fact I don't take to starvation. Otherwise you'd be bucking the devil's tiger right along with him."

"Aw, kill him."

"Shut up, Ole."

I was having trouble squeezing wind down my pipe. The sheriff leaned in, shutting off the rest of the supply. I clutched at his boot, but the blow to my head had done something to my connections. I had no feeling in my fingers.

"There's one law in Socorro." His upper body blocked the light. "It isn't a yellowback former federal named Murdock and it sure isn't that carpetbagging Wallace in Santa Fe. Let me hear you say its name."

I couldn't talk. He leaned harder. My vision broke up into black-and-white checks.

"Say its name."

The white checks shrank to pinholes. I could feel the blood swelling the veins in my eyeballs.

He leaned back then, relieving some of the pressure. I sucked in air and coughed.

"Frank Baronet."

He removed his foot, straightened. His face was an oval blur inside the circle of his hatbrim with sharp blue sky behind it.

" 'Satan's Sixgun,' " he said. "My ass."

I lay there for a space of time. I knew Baronet had left and probably Ole and the deputy, but I was aware that I was still an object of curiosity for a portion of the local tax base. My hands were starting to tingle when I pushed myself into a sitting position. My cartridge belt slid off my chest and the Deane-Adams clunked against the boards. I hadn't even felt its weight when it was dumped on me.

I picked it up along with myself, found my hat, Win-

chester and canteen, and went back inside to use the basin
in my room. The barrel of the sheriff's pistol hadn't broken the skin but the entire right side of my head felt like
rotten wood. I inspected the loads in the five-shot, gripped
the handle hard until I could feel it as far as my elbow. I
brushed the sawdust off my corduroys and went out.

The countryside was ablaze with that dry heat that opens
your pores and sucks out the moisture like lemon carbon-
ate through a straw. For all that it was a green land, dotted
over with juniper and scrub oak connecting in the distance
to create the illusion of a grass ocean. The mountains too
were flecked with green, cloud-capped, the air so clear
around them I might have been looking at them through a
glass. The sky came down to the ground.

The ranch road led past a long low adobe house with a
red tile roof and a corral next to it containing half a dozen
horses. Behind the house I found a Mexican cook and his
Negro helper scalding a hog in a cauldron the size of a
bathtub. The cook said I'd find *Señor* Whiteside stringing
fence in the northwest corner. I didn't waste time leaving
the pair to their work. I don't mind the smell of singed bris-
tles, but a dead hog looks too much like a naked man to
my taste. On my way back to the road I paused to look over
the horses in the corral.

John Whiteside is in most of the history books now as
the man who opened up New Mexico to the cattle trade.
Severely wounded at the head of his own regiment at Cold
Harbor and mustered out, he got a head start on the other
barons who went west after the war, rounding up the red-
eyed, ladder-ribbed descendants of Cortez's longhorns
wandering wild in Mexico and booting them up into the
territories, inventing a new business in the process. Co-
manches raped and killed his Mexican wife of six months
and ran off his first herd, and when he got through fighting them the Apaches came and burned his headquarters

and strung his partner head down over a mesquite fire until his brains boiled. Whiteside was still fighting them at the time I caught up with him in the summer of 1881, but his fame had not yet spread north of Taos and I didn't know him from General Grant. He was just a short twist of rawhide seated on a wagon loaded with spools of barbed wire in a faded blue flannel shirt, canvas breeches, and a wide Mexican sombrero, holding the team while a trio of men in overalls and leather gauntlets spun the jacked-up left rear wheel to seat the wire around a fence-post. He had brown whiskers going gray around his mouth and restless blue eyes in a thicket of wrinkles. His left arm was gone above the elbow, the empty sleeve pinned back.

"I require all the horses I have." He'd glanced at me when I rode up, then returned to his seemingly aimless study of the horizon. If an irregularity appeared there he'd spot it.

"I'm no hand at bargaining," I said. "The truth is I stink at it. I'll pay two hundred for that claybank in the corral."

"Murdock, is it? Mr. Murdock, I'm in the fence business. I used to trade in cattle but right now I spend most of my time restringing wire. I've strung this section six times. Billy the Kid showed the world how easy it is last October when he cut it the first time and spirited out five hundred head. Between the goddamn thieves and those Apache bastards and that greaser son of a bitch Don Segundo del Guerrero down in Chihuahua and every lost tramp who cannot be bothered to ride half a mile to the nearest gate I have strung more wire in this one corner than Western Union. You will pardon me if I don't feel the necessity to add a livery operation to this here booming fence trade I have going."

"The sheriff gave me your name."

"Sheriff." He snarled the word. "Dolan men counted the

ballots. They were only just through counting when the first silver shipment to the bank in Socorro City went missing. It was Frank's brother Ross done it and he has been behind all the others since. I supply beef to all the bigger mining companies in the territory and what injures them injures me. When I suggested taking this to Lew Wallace, Frank started arresting my best hands for shooting up Mexicans."

"He said something about it. He didn't say your men were involved."

"My hands were swapping lead with Don Segundo's vaqueros over the ownership of cows when the Baronet brothers were still abusing themselves to cigarette cards. Anyway I took his message. It isn't my silver, and I need men to run a ranch."

"You must have choked on it."

"It wasn't my first choice. However, times are different. Sooner or later some ass would decide to call in the army just like they done in Lincoln County. That is bad for business."

"The fence business." I grinned.

He turned his blues on me. They were as austere as the sky. "I see someone has used you."

I let the grin slide. "Baronet. I was foolish enough to give him a reason, but his real purpose was to warn me. I was there last night when a man named Boone caught him in a lie about his brother being dead in Mexico. He killed Boone later. He said it was an argument over cards, but he was the only witness."

"I don't mourn Sidney L. Boone. Those land men are slicing up the country like a steer. Are you fixing to call Frank out?"

"Fights are easy enough come by without provoking them. Anyway I haven't time. I'm just passing through on my way to San Sábado."

"What's in the Widow City?"

"A place called the Apache Princess, and my signature on the operating agreement. Cattlemen welcome. Fence men too," I added. "What about that claybank?"

His attention hesitated on something, then moved on. An antelope or a low cloud.

"Three hundred," he said. "This wire costs money when you order it by the carload."

We shook on it.

# CHAPTER 4

"Well, Murdock, I guess you have had your fill of the county seat."

I exhaled slowly, letting some of the tension out with the bad air. After checking out of the hotel and packing my worldly possessions aboard my new mount I had hoped to clear the place without running into the sheriff. I'd begun to think I might succeed when I pulled over to let a buggy pass coming in from the east road and Frank Baronet drew rein to blink up at me from under the roof. He had on a linen duster over his town clothes and a Henry rifle that might have been the one I'd seen in the county office leaning against his thigh. The embroidered pillow was wedged between his lower back and the leather seat. I had dismissed that as a ploy to conceal his pistol, but since the handle of the Remington was visible in the notch of his vest I decided the pillow served another purpose.

"I've been in town less than a day and already there's been a killing and a pistol-whipping," I said. "I left marshaling to get away from that."

"If that was your intention you should have gone back

East, where I hear a man can wet his beak of a Saturday evening without a weapon on his person." His eyes went to the claybank's brand. "I see you took my advice and went to Whiteside. What that man knows about horses and cattle comes close to making up for what he don't know about people."

It was a conversation I didn't feel like getting into. "When I saw that rig I thought you were a doctor." It was a handsome construction of pebbled black oilskin and good leather on yellow wheels, hitched to a patient-looking gray. Brass fittings caught the light.

"A walleyed mustang threw me into a ravine in '78. I haven't been able to ride more than eight or ten miles at a stretch since the brace came off. Misery of the back is a hellish thing, worse than being shot. It has taken all the fun out of collecting taxes." He adjusted the pillow and leaned back. Pain brushed across his features like a cloud. "Don't forget to register with the marshal's office when you get to San Sábado. It is required of new saloon owners."

"Your order?"

He spread his moustaches. "When it's one of mine I enforce it with enthusiasm, as I think you know." He gathered the reins. "*Buena suerte,* Murdock. I will be in one day soon and try my luck at your table." He rattled off.

My destination was a day's ride from Socorro City in gentle weather, slightly longer in the dead-blow hammer heat of August. The way led south along the foothills of the Oscuros and San Andres, broken peaks bleached white above the timberline like the molars of fighting dogs, through a region covered with cactus nettles and white alkali, charmingly named *La Jornada del Muerto.* I kept a weather eye, but of course I didn't see Apaches. There never were enough of them in any one place to make a show of strength on a ridge like in the five-cent dreadfuls. Their strategy was to run among the rocks like those little hot-blooded lizards you saw in the tail of your eye and take you from behind. At dusk I made camp in the lee of an old rockfall with the claybank tethered to my wrist and my Winchester across my lap. In the morning I found the charred foundation of a house nearby and the rocky oblongs of four graves, their markers long since gone if there had been any to begin with. It was raw country, stolen many times from determined hands at great cost. The white man was only the latest in a long line of misguided thieves.

You don't haggle too hard over the price of a good horse in country where your life depends on what you're riding, and the claybank was proving to be a wise investment. It was a gelding, fifteen hands high with a big rump and an arrogant manner, which meant a keen sense of self-preservation. This last was a credit, as a suicidal horse is less than useful when scalp fever is abroad. Of course the beast hated me. All my mounts do out of instinct. They know I'll shoot them for a breastwork the minute we fall short of room to run.

Not missing San Sábado entirely required knowledge of the ways of open country. Coming over a rise I saw what looked at first like Indian mounds or a prairie dog town, but was in fact a collection of adobe buildings swept up around the base of a sixteenth-century mission, with a few frame structures straggled east like a thread unraveling, and everything baked the same dun color on a flat that hadn't known shade since the last glacier. Something inside me sank at the sight. I felt like the consumptive who had come at last to the place where he would die, and it wasn't Atlantic City, New Jersey.

Closer up, things were more encouraging. The bell in the mission tower began to swing, the thud of its clapper humming along the ground and shaking loose activity behind windows and inside the covered walkways. That would be the end of the noon siesta. There was, in addition to another saloon besides the Apache Princess, a livery, an emporium, and a combination bathhouse and barbershop, the last in a building that had started out adobe, then split in the middle like some kind of hybrid grass and wound up clapboard with a shake roof. Best of all, a harness shop advertised itself in two windows on the second floor of the livery. That meant cowboys. The bare fact that I would welcome that obstreperous lot was evidence enough I had stopped thinking like a lawman and started thinking like an entrepreneur.

Other windows, particularly those in the old mud huts, were less cheering. Muslin curtains stirred but did not open. Behind two of them I glimpsed the black weeds of the widows who gave the town its popular name.

I stepped down in front of the livery, removed my necessaries from behind the cantle, and told the Yaquí who came out from inside to rub down the claybank and give it water and feed. The Indian, short and thick in peasant dress with his hair cut short and no shine in his black eyes, took the reins and said nothing. That breed got most of its talking and all of its laughing done by age ten.

THE APACHE PRINCESS was painted in circus letters two feet high across the windowless false front of the last wooden building in the row. They would have flared out in bright barn red when they were new, but in just six months the New Mexico sun had dulled them the color of dried blood. I pushed aside a half-door on a leather hinge and stood inside the dim interior, blinking like Frank Baronet. The sudden shade chilled the back of my neck.

"Page! Goddamn!" A chair scraped back and my hand was seized by a narrow wiry one crackling with nervous energy. "The red bastards didn't scalp you after all. There's a bet won."

"It's good to see you, Junior."

I did see him now, all five and a half skinny feet of him, splendid in lilac-colored shirtsleeves with red plush garters, paisley vest, and a green silk cravat stuck with a ruby pin. His collar was too big by half and his fingers stuck out of the cuffs like a child's. He looked as out of place in the rig as he had in range clothes when we both worked his father's spread in Montana. Junior Harper had fair hair darkened with pomade and slicked flat to his skull, large luminous eyes, and a long rectangular jaw like a sewing machine treadle that slid to the side rakishly when he showed his big horse teeth. At first glance, and maybe at all the others, he looked like a hereditary failure beside Ford Harper's bull shoulders and red beard shot through with iron gray, and in fact two physicians, including a specialist whom Ford had brought in from St. Louis for a second opinion, had predicted Junior wouldn't live to see twenty; but he had made them both liars by fifteen years and counting and there wasn't a hand who had worked with him who didn't have some story attesting to his strength and endurance. He was a pale reed with a taproot that went clear through to China.

"You're some older," he said, stepping back to take me in from hat to heels, "but you are still one mean-looking son of a bitch. I'm guessing Geronimo took one look at you and hared right back to Arizona."

"You look like Christmas Day. Is that what they're wearing on the border this year?"

He grinned his sloppy sideways grin and stuck a hand inside his vest like an oil painting. "Men of property don't dress like spring roundup. I hope you aren't fixing to deal cards in that kit."

"I had a suit fitted before I left Helena. It's probably following me right now. Is your mother still living?" I remembered a frail brown sparrow, small-boned like her son and withered beyond her years in Ford's shadow.

"She's well and in Chicago. She moved in with my aunt after the old man died. You heard he was dead."

"Apoplexy, I heard." My bet had been on either the Shoshones or a fall from a mad horse. He'd continued to insist on breaking his share of the string well past his sixtieth birthday.

"I sold the ranch to pay his debts. Ma got most of the rest and I put down what was left on the Princess. That's why I needed a partner, to buy the fixtures and inventory. What do you think of her?"

My eyes were adjusting to the dusty light coming in through the windows. The room was larger and simpler than the Orient in Socorro City, with wood chips on the plank floor and the standard lithographs razored out of eastern publications and framed on the walls, racehorses and boxers. The bar itself was plain pine and lacked a rail. The mirror behind it was a giveaway, carrying an advertisement for the Hermitage Distillery of Franklin County, Kentucky, dressed up a little with red-white-and-blue bunting. There were eight tables, including a faro layout in the corner, and three hurricane lamps swinging from the ceiling.

"Who supplies the stock?" I asked.

"Distributor in El Paso. We're on the route. That bar's temporary. I put in a bid on a honey in El Paso del Norte across the border. Mexico City closed the place down for treating with enemies of the republic. This here's Irish Andy. He won't tell me his other name. I hired him right out from under the Mare's Nest down the street."

I shook hands with the man behind the bar, blue eyes and a sheared head on a buffalo neck with shoulders to match, aproned from his neck to his knees. He had one of those fixed smiles you wanted to trust but knew better. I asked him what part of Ireland he was from.

"Frankfurt." His accent was as thick as a Prussian lance. "What can I pour you?"

"Bet you could eat the asshole out of a skunk," Junior put in. "We got a stove in back."

"I'll have a steak and a bottle."

Andy stood a bottle and a glass on the bar and went through the curtain in back. Junior and I sat down at a table out of the sunlight. He folded his blue-veined hands on the table and watched me drink. "Ever throw a lip over any whiskey smoother than that?" Liquid eyes pleaded.

"I've had loads worse. I guess you still can't drink hard liquor."

"Ties my guts in square knots." He kneaded his hands. "Page, I'm sore glad you came in with me. To tell you the truth I never thought you would when I wrote you. I figured after all this time you had that star tattooed on."

"Six years is as long as I do anything. I was grateful you kept the offer open. It took me three months to make up my mind."

"You pulled me out of more than one bog. I calculated I owed you that much time and then some." He chewed the ends of the moustaches he'd been nurturing for as long as I'd known him. They disappeared in strong light. "Shit, whose hind leg am I pulling? The Lord's truth is I didn't have no other takers."

The thing that had sunk in me when I got my first look at the town sank again. "You swore to me it was a sound investment."

"Oh, the Princess is a hell of a lot more than just that. We got the Butterfield coming through four times a month and there's talk the Atchison might run a spur out here, and until then we have those trail herders stealing Mexican beef, which is thirsty work. I just don't inspire confidence. Folks that don't know me look at me and think I am bound to crumple under the first hard rain."

"They don't know you for certain."

"Well, there you have it. I was thinking of selling out to Eille MacNutt at the Mare's Nest when the wire came with your end. That money came in handy, I can tell you."

A whiff of hot grease reached my nostrils from in back. My stomach started to gnaw. I poured whiskey into it. "When's the next herd come through? It's been a long time since I played with house money. I need to practice."

"That's the other thing. You won't be the only one playing with house money."

"You hired a dealer?"

"No. No, not exactly." He looked down at his hands.

I stuck the cork back in the bottle. "Who'd you cut in and for how much?"

"Now, Page, I had expenses. The carpenter I hired never done a roof before. It leaked and I had to bring in somebody else to do it right. Lumber's dear. The wholesale price of whiskey went up. Then the note came due on the town lot. There was other things. It's all in the ledger." He pried his hands apart and laid them palms down. "It was a third interest."

"You sold half of my half without telling me?"

"You'll get your end."

"It isn't that I'm concerned about. I came all this way thinking I owned fifty percent of something and now I find out I'm part of a syndicate. We had a deal, Junior."

"You want out?"

"What if I said yes? That ruby stickpin wouldn't bring today's interest on what you owe me."

"I'll go back to ranch work if I need to. My old man would pay you your time in the middle of a stampede if you asked, and I am his son. If it takes twenty years I'll settle the debt."

"Hell." I took the cork back out and refilled my glass. "For all we know they won't even honor cash money come the new century. Sheep will be the coin of the union. That or silk hats."

"Does that mean you're still in?"

"Ask me again after I meet our new partner."

"That will be Friday when the stage comes in. I won't tell you any names until then. You're ripe for a surprise, partner. Eille MacNutt too, though not one so pleasant. He has the notion that string of whores of his makes him king of the alkali flat."

"I won't run whores," I warned him. "Keeping the peace for Judge Blackthorne is as low as I've crawled or ever plan to."

"Whores are trouble I don't require. You feed them and put clothes on their backs and pay the doctor when they catch a cold in their pantaloons and then they run off and marry the first drunk cowboy who asks. I say let them get drunk here and take their proposals down the street."

My steak came, trailing black smoke off a blue china plate. It crunched like hardtack when I chewed, but I finished it and washed it down with whiskey. Not counting a pemmican cake at my cold camp the night before, my last meal had been a tortilla and chili peppers in Socorro City; a mistake, as I'd found out after two hours on the trail.

I pushed away the empty plate. "I feel I should explain this Satan's Sixgun business."

"I always heard he carried a pitchfork."

There was no irony in his expression. The phrase meant nothing to him. I felt my face grinning. "I may just take to this place after all."

"It grows on you. It does for a fact."

"I didn't see a hotel or a boardinghouse on my way in. Where do I sleep?"

"Your room's over the faro game, thought you'd appreciate that. Mine's over the bar. The stairs are outside. I guess you want to put up your boots."

"After I visit the bathhouse. Also the marshal's office. The sheriff says I have to register there."

"The son of a bitch. I don't know which is worse for business, him, his brother, or the Apaches. At least the savages don't smile at you when they're cutting your balls off."

"He claims Ross is dead."

"That's horseshit. He stays below the border where the American authorities can't arrest him and plans robberies of pack trains from the mines. Does a little rustling too, but that's practically legal around here. After each silver robbery Frank sends out posses in every direction but the right one. Them James boys up in Missouri could learn something from watching the Baronets."

I changed the subject. "What kind of man is the town marshal?"

His face lightened. "Oh, you have a treat coming in Rosario Ortiz. He is the biggest thing to hit this place since Billy the Kid shot the blacksmith."

We talked for a little while longer and then I went up to drop off my things in my new quarters. I was thinking that just a few days ago I had never heard of Billy the Kid, and now I was sick of the name.

# CHAPTER 5

The combination barbershop and bathhouse that couldn't make up its mind whether to stay adobe or go wooden was just as undecided inside. There was a clear joint where the new tongue-and-groove floorboards met the old worn planks with cracks between them into which a careless barber could sweep ears and things, and someone had tacked up tent material to keep out the weather where the original mud wall didn't quite bunt up against the fresh studs. The proprietor was a small dour Mexican who scraped my face with half a dozen expert strokes. Mexicans are generally good with razors and don't bore you with conversation.

The room I returned to from the shave and a bath was clean and smelled of sawdust. It had a clothes-press, a basin, a bed with a feather mattress, and a lantern on a nail. The inevitable Indian rug lay on the floor waiting to deaden the noise from downstairs, of which there was none at that hour of the afternoon. The soft enveloping mattress was a poor choice for the climate, but I stripped to the skin and slept two hours without interruption. Instant oblivion, in my late line of work, was a prize you either won or failed to acquire and learned to function at half your natural capacity three quarters of the time.

I put on my town clothes and stepped out under a rusty sky to present myself to the local law. I didn't look west. The color spectacle would go on for the best part of an hour, and I had seen enough of them lately to last my life. I would have to stop missing the sudden sunsets in the Bitterroots before I called this place home.

The building I had been directed to by Junior Harper stood at the north end of town on the other side of a plank bridge over a dry riverbed, inconvenient to everything but the ancient mission in whose shadow it spent twelve hours of every day. It was small, adobe of course, built in the old Spanish style without brick reinforcing, and patched many times with mud and clay that dried to varying shades, its roof poles extending two feet into the desert air for the purpose of stringing up hides and reluctant Roman Catholics. The stick door hung as crooked as an Indian agent.

A fat Mexican in overalls and a cavalry coat, so stained and weather-faded I couldn't tell which army it had belonged to, knelt in a strip of loam protected by rocks next to the door, probing for feathergrass roots with a bayonet that had seen all its glory days and cursing softly in that bastard border dialect you heard all over that territory. A snaggle of yellow roses that were more thorn than blossom appeared to be the beneficiaries of all this industry. They hardly seemed worth it, but then I had seen a man lose his life defending his wife's imported china from a group of drunken buffalo hunters in a restaurant in Cheyenne. In a land of spines and diamondbacks some men will go to any length on behalf of beauty.

"Marshal's office," I said.

The Mexican started, shielded his eyes up at me, and stood, snatching off his sombrero. His gray hair was cut in a bowl and his handlebars, untrimmed and tobacco-stained at the ends, underscored a twenty-weight of pock-marked jowls. His nose was the size of an avocado.

"*Allá, mi jefe.*" He gestured toward the door with the sombrero. "In there."

"*Gracias.*" I pulled the latchstring. The door flopped open.

As soon as I was inside I knew the Mexican had misunderstood my question. It was a house like a thousand others in and around old Mexico, decorated with bunches of dried chili peppers hung from the ceiling and straw pallets on the dirt floor. There was a dugout fireplace with a trivet for cooking, a square plank table stained all over and scored many times by knives used to slice meat and tortillas, and on the other side of it a piano stool that had been rescued from a wagon trail or some white family's trash, discharging horsehair out of its burst seat. A naked child no older than two sat there trying to spin itself sick. The little house, in fact, was filled with children of every age and both sexes, all of them engaged in something destructive that required noise. One, a boy of about six, had discovered that the back wall had a timber frame and was busy chipping away adobe with a carving knife to expose it further. The din was enough to make you yearn for the serenity of a slaughterhouse in St. Louis.

I was turning to leave when the fat Mexican stepped past me and barked a single syllable that knocked dust out of a rafter. It was like the last shot at Appomattox. The children stopped what they were doing and turned as one to stare at the entrant with large dark shiny eyes like wet olive pits. He strode through the silence, accumulating authority as he went, and paused by the table.

"Josefina."

This time he spoke gently. The naked child slid off the stool and scampered around behind him, peering out at me as if from the cover of a post. He shooed it away with a pat on its split behind, straddled the stool with a grunt and a sigh, and fished inside first one, then the other side pocket of the cavalry coat until he came up with a bent star and hung it on the tobacco pocket in front.

*"Buenas tardes, señor,"* he said. "What can I do for you this day?"

"You're the marshal?"

*"Sí,* part of the time. By trade I am a master carpenter. I am called Rosario Ortiz." He didn't offer to shake hands. His were filthy from the flower bed.

"Page Murdock." There was no reaction. "I'm new part owner of the Apache Princess."

He smiled with all his teeth. It was like a sunburst. "The Princess, *sí.* I do the roof right. The other fellow, he makes privies." Suddenly he stopped smiling. "The roof has a leak? I fix it for free. Ortiz stands behind his work."

"I'm sure it's fine. I've come to register."

"Register?" He blinked. "Oh, *sí, sí.* Yes. By order of the sheriff." He looked around, including under the table, lifted his sombrero off the top and put it down. Finally he shot a stream of Spanish at one of the children, a grave faced boy of fourteen or fifteen, who said, "*Sí*, Papa," and went out the open door at the back.

"I apologize for my worthless children."

"I've seen worse," I said, "though not so many in one place."

The boy returned carrying a green ledger stuffed with loose pages. Ortiz spread it open carefully and leafed through it until he came to the page he wanted. He went through the ritual search once more and said something to another child, a girl this time who had begun to develop breasts under her white cotton shift. She went to a painted cabinet with a bucket on top, opened a door, and came over to the table with a horsehair pen and a bottle of purple ink. He unstopped the bottle, dipped the pen, and turned the ledger to face me, holding the pen out.

"Your signature please, *Señor* Murdock. Your mark will be sufficient if you cannot write."

I accepted the pen and scratched my name between ruled lines. There were only two others on the page: Ford Harper, Jr. and Eille MacNutt. Someone had neatly printed MacNutt's name next to a ragged *X*. I handed back the pen.

"The registration fee is five dollars."

I whistled. The marshal looked apologetic. "I keep not a penny, *señor*. It all goes to the county seat."

"The county seat being Frank Baronet's faro bank." I flipped a gold piece onto the table. It bounced and he caught it against his chest. He bit down on it, studied the result, and entered the transaction next to my signature.

"A carpenter can work anywhere, and I do not care to keep the peace," he said. "I would leave, but my wife is buried behind the mission."

"I'm sorry."

"It is not your sorrow. I am the one who shot her."

He placed the coin inside the ledger, closed it, and

returned the star to his side pocket. Rising and giving me a slight bow, he set the sombrero on his head and went out to tend his roses. As soon as he crossed the threshold the children resumed their loud destructive activities.

The faro equipment at the Apache Princess was strictly basic. The layout was an oilcloth with the card denominations crudely painted on it and there was no cue box. Instead the dealer was obliged to keep a running tally of the cards dealt with a pencil and paper or by transferring chips from one stack to another with each deal. The cards were worn and the painted tiger on the card box had had so many thumbs run across it the stripes were all rubbed off. I played three miners, slab-faced failed farmers in flannel shirts beaten clean on rocks, traces of black clay crusted behind their ears, but they all left before I could get a rhythm going either way. Even the one that quit ahead looked as glum as if he'd lost his grubstake. Junior, who had been tending bar while Irish Andy ate his supper in back, flipped him the towel and came over and sat down. "Odds against the house tonight?"

"Who could blame them? I saw fresher decks in Leadville, where they threw the slops in the street."

"I have a trimmer here somewhere."

"I arrested a man once for shooting a man for owning a card trimmer. Some places that's all the evidence they need to lynch you."

"I never heard evidence was required. Anyway, not everyone uses them to shave cards, just to tidy up the fuzzy edges. New decks are expensive out here, especially when you order them by the case. Who cares if the jack of diamonds has a clean collar?"

"Let me ask you this." I dealt us each a hand of poker. "What makes a cowboy come to a place like this and gamble?"

"That's an easy one, to win money, Two," He discarded two pasteboards from his hand. I replaced them and stood pat.

"Wrong. He can do that back at the bunkhouse without having to put on a clean shirt. What makes that same cowboy come to a saloon and pay for his whiskey by the glass when he can buy a bottle for less and drink it at home?"

"You're the one making the point. What are we playing for?"

"Education."

"In that case I call."

I turned over four sixes. He threw his hand into the deadwood. "Deal another."

I shuffled and dealt. "He comes here for the noise and colors and things going on. Music, if there's any, but there doesn't have to be. Other men and loud talk and the naked lady on the couch in the picture over the bar. Something he doesn't have at home. Dealer takes one." He did the same. "Gambling's no different," I went on. "He likes to hear the counters click and slide his fingers over the wax on the cards and he wants that tiger on the box to look so real it might take his arm off if he bets wrong. Call."

He laid his cards face up. He had a ten-high straight. I showed him a heart flush.

"One thing he don't want." Junior sat back. "He don't want them cards coming off the wrong end of the deck. If you're fixing to keep on doing that in here, you best get a whole lot better at it fast. John Whiteside's hands will sew you up in a green hide and leave you out in the sun to cogitate on your sins."

"I only cheat when it doesn't count. How about a new layout?"

"I have the catalogue. Pick out what you want and we'll order it. No billiard tables, mind. You will find all you need strung out along the Jornada del Muerto, complete with the bones of the wagoneers that tried to slide them past the Apaches. Those killers have got a Philadelphia Ladies League mad on against that game. Old Cochise must have had him a snookering." He watched me laying out a hand of patience. "Did you make the acquaintance of our local James Butler Hickok?"

"Oh, Marshal Ortiz and I are old friends. He showed me his children and his roses."

"Ten years from now those kids are going to make Quantrill's raiders look like *East Lynne*. We had the frame up on a schoolhouse when two of them burned it down. Almost wiped out San Sábado. Rosario only has the job because he will work for found. Did he tell you he killed his wife?"

"It came up during the conversation."

"It generally does. It's the only thing ever happened to him worth talking about. Story I heard when I came was he caught her on the floor between pews in the mission with a Yaquí mine worker, missed him, and shot her clean to hell. Personally I think he done it by accident while seating a charge in that old ball-and-percussion pistol he uses to shoot stray dogs and coyotes. If them kids can't get him mad enough to beat the devil out of them I don't see how his wife could do it just by misplacing her vows."

"You never married, I guess."

"Did you?"

"I thought about it. I can see how it could make you mad enough."

"Hell, yes, *you*. Not Ortiz."

I placed a red deuce on a black trey. "Did he soak you five dollars when you registered?"

He nodded. "Eille MacNutt too, and a dollar for every whore besides. Our sheriff must have enough to retire on registration fees alone, when you figure in all the saloons and sporting houses in the county. Then there's the percentage he gets for collecting taxes."

"That's a job of work. Cattlemen are a rough cob when it comes to paying their fair share."

"Not when you have an assassin like that deputy of his siding you," he said.

"Jubilo? He didn't strike me as the kind."

"Nobody knows a Mexican but another Mexican. The talk is a firing squad's waiting for him across the border. Then there was that business up in Lincoln with both Baronets. Ross or Frank killed this poor dumb rancher, but they say Jubilo done for the wife. Spooner, their name was. Dave and Vespa. Shot dead in front of their own house."

"I heard Frank might not have been in on that."

"Ross never done a thing that Frank didn't know about it. If he wasn't there you can be damn sure he told Ross where to put the slugs. All them Spooners done wrong was to side with Chisum against Dolan and Murphy. I guess they were what you would call an example."

"The sheriff seems to favor those." I touched the swelling along my temple where he'd laid the barrel of his Remington.

"Frank done that? I noticed but I didn't want to ask. What did you do that stirred him up?"

"Not much. I threatened to kill a stable hand."

He grinned and shook his head. "I swear, Page, you always did draw fire. I remember that time in Missoula—"

"So do I." I went bust and gathered up the cards. "I sure do shine at picking a spot to settle down."

# CHAPTER 6

I wasn't in town Friday when the stage came in from El Paso. A saloon is a low place to be mornings, with sunlight lying on the cheap stain that passes for elegant mahogany at night and the human debris hunched in the corners over the first glass of the day with their buttons all undone because their hands are shaking too hard to fasten them. No one is gambling, at least not with anything as meaningless and as much fun as money. I put on my trail clothes and rode out for some target practice in the bright blue open. The trigger pull of the Deane-Adams needed sweetening from time to time and so did my aim. Marshaling wasn't the only profession that required those things up to the mark. There were a lot of bad gamblers out there who weren't aware that money was meaningless and as much fun to lose as it was to win.

The claybank liked the snappy cold of a desert morning, arching its long neck and cocking its legs high as if running involved less effort than standing still. I tethered it to a low piñon tree and walked away fifty yards to pot at stones and elbows on branches, watching out the corner of my eye for its reaction to gunfire. It snapped up its head after the first shot, then reached back to bite an itch. John Whiteside, who had fought Indians and Mexicans and Johnny Rebs both on foot and from horseback, had trained it well.

The coach driver, around thirty with a full beard and that facial twitch you saw often in men who spent much of their time trying to keep arrowheads and bandits' bullets out of their backs, was checking the team for fistulas in front of the freight office when I returned. I saw that rather than waste one of his pretty Concords on a flyspeck like San Sábado, Mr. Butterfield had sent a common mud wagon, open on both sides with only canvas flaps between passengers and the weather. The seats were empty now and the luggage gone.

I found Junior conferring with the cedar chief in front of the Apache Princess, smoking a tailor-made with lady-like puffs to avoid drawing smoke too far into his finely balanced system. The day was warming up but he still wore a sheepskin over his frock coat and vest and a wide-awake hat that made him look like something stunted in the shade of the great brim. "Our partner got in an hour ago and is waiting for us at *Señora* Castillo's boarding-house," he said. "The *señora* is one of our celebrated widows. Ugly as a washboard and cooks like one, but it's the only place to stay in town until we get a hotel built. I didn't know we'd need another room when I put up this place."

"Who is he, Jay Gould? Why can't he meet us here?"

"You saw the stage. Would you feel like walking this distance once you finished scrubbing off New Mexico?"

"This rig okay to meet him in, or do I need a morning coat?"

"Let's go. You are the complainingest partner."

The house was on an alley off the main street and was probably the oldest wooden building in town, built of barked logs with the chinking as thick in places as a man's wrist. *Señora* Castillo, older yet, greeted us at the door holding a straw broom in the fashion of a weapon. She was as dark and wrinkled as a chili pepper and bent nearly double in a coarse black dress with a dusty hem and hundreds of black bead buttons up the front. A plain gray scarf completely covered her hair. No eyes showed in the black crescent hollows between the puckered lids. I had seen more life in Aztec masks. When Junior told her what we were about she turned and led the way inside, dragging both feet with a sound like a locomotive champing at the platform.

The parlor was a combination of Mexican and Chicago Victorian. Oval portraits of bitter-faced men in whiskers hung on the log walls, a serape covered most of the worn spots on an overstuffed sofa, a tea table with yellow pottery on it stood on an earthen floor swept as bare as tile. The place smelled of extinct meals and dry rot.

"Good morning, Marshal. I suppose it is Mr. Murdock now."

I stopped, letting Junior walk past me to the middle of the room. The voice coming from the direction of the sofa was husky for a woman, slightly roughened from years of calling for wagers in smoky barrooms full of loud men in a fever to lose their gold dust and coppers. She had aged some—her cheekbones were more pronounced and there was a vertical crease where before there had been only white forehead as smooth as glaze—but her hair, done up loosely, was still Indian black and the eyes, set just a shade too wide, were clear blue with tiny gold points floating in them like snowflakes in a crystal paperweight. The mouth was excessive too for fashion but well formed, the chin cut delicately but firm. Her dress was cambric, plain white and cut simply to her clean figure and closed at the throat with an amber brooch set in rose gold. The contrast with her black patent leather high-tops, and with the dark colors that surrounded her, was marked. But then I knew from old experience that it was her business to stand out.

"Just Murdock will serve," I said. "Is it still Mrs. Bower, or have you gone back to Poker Annie?"

"I never went by it. That was a mistake on a circular that went out in Dakota and it stuck. The circular was a mistake as well. I see you are as sweet-natured as ever."

"Mrs. Colleen Bower, Page Murdock," Junior said. "The

old man always insisted I was born a day late and managed to fall behind an hour a year. I had a notion you two were old acquaintances. It had to be more than just your reputation that almost backed Mrs. Bower out of the deal when your name came up."

She had been dabbing at her throat with a lace handkerchief when we entered, blotting the moisture that surfaced in the dry heat through pores freshly open from the bath. Now she returned the pretty to the reticule in her lap, white satin with a black drawstring. "Breen, Montana, is a ghost city now. Lumber rats got the boards after the cattle interests pulled out, leaving just the foundations and broken glass where the saloons were. Two years ago it was wide open and filled with desperate men. Mr. Murdock held his own."

"Mrs. Bower is a fair judge of that breed. She's known so many."

"That's small even for a killer."

I pointed my chin at the purse. "Do you still carry that pocket pistol in your bag, or have you stitched the holster to your petticoat by now?"

Junior interrupted. "A gentleman never discusses underwear with a lady. Anyway we are here to talk business. Sundays are for reminiscing."

"Sit, Mr. Murdock. I assume you still bend far enough for that."

I thought about answering. Instead I stepped past a walnut rocker and pulled up a ladder-back that someone had promoted from the trash pile and put back into use with splints and buckhide thongs. A thousand acres of dust had settled since the last time I had wanted to be comfortable in Colleen Bower's company.

"Now we are all friends." Junior perched on the opposite end of the sofa, placing his hat in his lap. "Let's not show off our Spanish, by the by. The old hag has ears like

a bat." *Señora* Castillo had removed herself through a
doorway behind a hanging shawl.

"I will come to the point. As I recall, you favor that approach over all the others." Flecked blue eyes fixed me. "As
Junior said, when we met in El Paso and he told me you
were involved I considered withholding my end. However,
my situation there was hardly an improvement."

I nodded. "Poke Allyard was marshal there last I heard.
He isn't the kind to be gotten around with paint and scent
like the late peace officer of Breen."

"The circuit is a cruel enough place for a man. Try being a woman and see if you don't employ what God gave
you to keep you in biscuits and sardines. To continue. This
is a business relationship as Junior pointed out. Men are
finding silver all over this country and the butchers in Chicago are standing by the U.P. tracks with their knives out
just waiting for that cheap Mexican beef. El Paso—"

"Cheap meaning stole," Junior said.

" 'Every great fortune begins with a crime.' Balzac." She
kept looking at me. "El Paso is too far for these cowboys
and miners to go to spend their money on cards and liquor.
There are too many Apaches on the way to Socorro City
and a bandit behind every piñon tree between here and old
Mexico. San Sábado promises to become the next Tombstone. I'm certain you know what that signifies."

"For starters I'm happy it's not my job to keep the peace.
All the news I hear from Tombstone has hair and fangs."

"A fine peace you kept in Breen."

"It got kept. I didn't seek the post. Your benefactor strangled on a piece of gristle and Judge Blackthorne appointed me."

"Beside the point. I should not have brought it up. What
I am driving at is people are making their fortunes in
Tombstone. We could make ours here if we will only for-
get the back trail and pull together between the traces."

"I have nothing against making a fortune."

"Then perhaps we should start by shaking hands." She offered me one of hers.

I let out air and took it. It was as cool and smooth as I remembered, all except the small callosities on the finger-tips from handling pasteboards and chips. She had been clutching her reticule with it, and when she changed hands I admired the plain band on the third finger of the left. I knew her as a self-made widow who didn't wear one. "I guess good wishes are in order."

"Thank you." She withdrew her right and placed it on top of the other, covering the ring. "Now that we have smoked the peace pipe, you can settle a point. For weeks now Junior and I have been burning up the wires arguing over whether the Apache Princess should be renovated. I hold that it should."

"Why renovated? It's only just built."

"That's what I said." Junior pushed the dents out of the wideawake's crown and put them back in.

"You and I and Junior Harper are not the only people on the frontier with vision," she said. "Once we begin sep-arating these miners and cowboys from their pokes, just how long do you think it will be before this town has more saloons than widows? If we are going to draw more than just a grubstake to start over somewhere else when the oth-ers crowd us out, we must plan to meet the competition now. Junior informs me that you are adamant about not keeping whores."

"I am."

"He holds the opinion that my presence alone will draw customers away from the women at the Mare's Nest."

I looked at him. "You said that?"

"Not first thing," he said. "They will all want their turn, women of easy virtue being an improvement over a knot-hole in the side of a buckboard, if you'll disregard my coarse language, ma'am." He'd have tipped his hat if he were wearing it. "My guess is you haven't seen the Mare's Nest women yet."

"That bad?"

"Coyote girls, the lot. You know, when you wake up to find one laying on your arm and you chew it off to get away. Once they have all had their turn they will come here to look at something that reminds them of a female. Don't forget these are men who will ride forty miles to see a picture of Lillie Langtry. All the renovation we require is to paint 'Poker Annie' in big yellow letters under the Cold Beer sign and they will bet on there being fifty-three cards in a standard deck just for the opportunity to sit across the table from Mrs. Bower and tell their friends about it back in camp."

I grinned. "Junior, how is it no one sold you the governor's palace in Santa Fe on your way down here?"

He looked blank. "I came by way of El Paso."

Colleen reached across the sofa to pat his knee. "You're a ring-tailed dreamer and that's why I took you up on your proposition and came here. Boomtowns attract good-looking women. In six months I will look like *Señora* Castillo next to some of them. Ask Murdock."

"That's true enough. They follow the market."

"Lumber is cheap now," she said. "We need to expand, build a gaming room in back. That will allow more than just faro and poker and free up space here for more drinking and a stage. I know a theatrical agent in Saint Louis who can supply talent, singers and tumblers and Shakespearean companies. It would surprise you to learn how starved these illiterate tinpans are for *Troilus and Cressida*. Next month they are auctioning off the fixtures at the Crystal Palace in El Paso. The owner shot himself over a marital misunderstanding and his widow needs cash. We

can pick up a hickory bar and brass pulls and a chandelier
with gimcrackery and doodads. Items like those are bound
to impress the rubes clean out of their overalls and everything in the pockets. People will read about the Apache
Princess in Boston."

"I have a line on a bar." Junior was petulant.

"What will we use to acquire all this elegance, besides
a six-shooter?" I asked.

"We can borrow the money and offer the saloon as collateral."

Junior bared his teeth. "Borrow from who, Geronimo?
The nearest bank with that kind of capital is in Santa Fe
and it won't gamble on anything this close to the border.
It's the first place I went when I decided to become a saloonkeeper."

"There has to be someone in the vicinity with means
and the itch to increase them. A rancher."

He shook his head. "That'd be John Whiteside, but
everything he has is tied up in cattle. I doubt he would invest in an enterprise in town anyway."

"Frank Baronet."

Four eyes met mine. Junior's treadle-shaped jaw fell
open. "That diamondback son of a bitch? Your pardon,"
he said to Colleen.

But she wasn't listening. "Who is he? Does he have
money?"

I told her who he was. "Sheriffing is a porkbarrel job
out here. He gets to claim a percentage of the taxes he col-
lects, and the registration fees and whatnot he imposes by
his own order probably go into his personal war chest. On
top of that he has the gaming concession at the Orient in
Socorro City and who knows how large a piece of how
many others. It's his county, he answers to no one but the
governor, and he doesn't answer to this governor. Then his

brother is a desperado, a dead one officially but alive probably, and successful. Brothers share. Yes, I would say he has money."

"You don't make him sound like a friend. Would he be interested in investing?"

"I've only known him a short time. With some people that's all you need. My impression is if this place has as much potential as you say, he'll find a way to cut himself in even if we don't invite him. Especially if we don't. This way at least we'd have some of his money to play with."

"And his hand in our pocket till Gabriel blows." Junior stood and tugged on his hat. "You know my position. The notion of cutting Frank Baronet in as a fourth partner don't sweeten the tea."

"That's one vote. Murdock?"

"I've sided worse. At least we can trust Baronet to deal us dirt if he sees the chance. It's the not being sure that makes most arrangements go south."

"Call that a vote yes. Carried. We'll discuss the details tonight. I'm dealing."

I was looking down at her now. "Friday is the first good night of the week. I might have known you'd claim it."

"The Princess has more than one table, and I have my own board and cue box. Deal or don't." She lifted a book off the arm of the sofa and opened it. The title on the pebbled cover read *The Gentleman's Guide to Percentages in Games of Chance*.

Outside, Junior asked, "Are you really fixing to climb into bed with Baronet after what he done to you in Socorro City?"

"That was personal. This is business. The protection of his office is worth something. Anyway he'll nickel and dime us to death if we don't."

"I'm opposed to it." Suddenly he grinned; his disposition had more varieties than the weather in Montana. "I thought for a minute there you and Colleen was going for your irons."

"I wish you'd told me she was the partner."

"Swear to God, you spend a winter with a man in a line shack you think you know him. I never suspected."

"Suspected what?"

"That you could fall in love so hard."

# CHAPTER 7

As it happened, Colleen Bower and I didn't have the chance to discuss renovations that night. Early on the gamblers were stacked six deep at her table to play and watch, and later I had to kill a man, which makes concentration difficult.

I dealt a few hands of faro and finished ahead, no slight accomplishment when you consider it's the serious ones who keep track of the cards who will sit at a man's table when someone like Poker Annie is dealing in the corner. Tonight she had a silver comb in her hair and a red silk choker around her neck that just naturally drew the eyes down the front of her dress, which was some kind of layered thing of lace and percale that made you think it was cut lower than it was, anchored at the shoulders by two simple bows. It was a rare bettor who could pay attention to the pasteboards when it looked like one of those bows would work loose any second, spilling her femaleness out over the table. Men have no understanding of costume architecture.

About ten o'clock I ran out of dedicated players and went to spell Irish Andy behind the bar. You couldn't have pounded a shim between customers there and for half an hour Junior and I were too busy washing and filling glasses to talk. When at last there was a lull he mopped his face and slung the towel over his shoulder. "I always wanted a job with a collar," he said. "I never thought I'd be sweating into it so much. I might as well be roping and throwing."

"This pays better and doesn't smell as bad. How are we doing?"

"Not as well as she is. What do you suppose it is makes a man bet so foolish with a woman he can't even have?"

"Judge Blackstone told me once there's no desert harder to cross than the two feet that separate a man's brain from his penis. He was hanging a man for rape at the time."

"It ain't my business asking what soured you on her."

I drew a beer for a miner at the end of the bar, sliding it down the side of the glass to cut down on foam, and skidded it into his hand. "She is too much cards for me. There were three sides to take in Breen and she laid side bets with all of them. If I lived she won. If I got killed she won too. A situation like that is hard on a man's good opinion of himself."

"Might could be you were expecting too much."

"No might-coulds about it," I said. "But I won't compound the mistake by repeating it."

"I don't know. Some of my best mistakes was made on the second run. How's the keg?"

I pulled the bung-starter out of its socket next to the sawed-off and gave the beer keg a couple of raps. "Better have one ready."

"First one generally lasts past eleven on Friday. You have to stop being so generous, running the beer down the glass that way. We charge the same for air."

I was putting away the starter when three fresh customers came through the flap door. Trouble clung to them like wolf scent.

Men had been coming in and going out, but when they arrived in a bunch they either stayed together or split between the bar and Colleen's table. This crew peeled off in three directions. One, puny and consumptive-looking in a duster snagged with nettles and a miner's cap made of greasy ticking, went straight to the table without pausing. Another, larger and bulkier in a slouch hat and a hide coat too heavy for the weather, stepped to the side wall and placed his back against it, the one spot in the room that yielded an unobstructed view of the tables, the bar, and the door to the street.

The third didn't look like he belonged with the first two. The shortest of the three and stocky, he wore a corduroy shooting coat with leather patches, a black plug hat with a feather in the band, and a cartridge belt slantwise across his chest loaded with rifle shells belonging to the .45-70 Springfield drooping lazily in his left hand. There was something about the set of the bones in his face, with its neat beard and swooping moustaches, that reminded me of someone, but that wasn't the thing about him so much as the way he took in the room, rotating his head without moving his eyes, and the easy unhurried way he stationed himself at the door, looking as if he had just stopped there to search for a familiar face.

I figured he was the one with the orders, but it was the man in the hide coat with his back to the wall I chose to favor. Any heavy wrap worn out of season is likely to conceal something you'd rather not have exposed. While I groped for the shotgun the man by the table tugged an 1860 Army Colt with a Theur conversion out from under his duster and pointed it at Colleen Bower's head, crackling back the hammer in the same motion.

"Lay back or she gets it."

This from the man in the hide coat, who took advantage of my instant's hesitation to bring up a full-length

Greener with both barrels already cocked. At that range the Apache Princess stood to lose two part owners, a number of paying customers, and several feet of bar. I laid back.

The room was quiet, painfully so after the rumble of male voices and thump and rustle of human activity that had been constant since just after sundown. Colleen was motionless behind her cue box.

"You." Hide Coat gestured at Junior with the Greener. "Put the cash box on the bar and slide it down towards the door."

Junior hung on a second, then lifted the tin Beacham's bread box into which he'd been stuffing notes and cart-wheels all night off the shelf under the bar and placed it on top. It turned a little after he pushed it, upsetting a shot glass and splashing the lanky young cowboy whose drink it was. He did nothing. The box now was within reach of the man with the Springfield but he made no move to pick it up.

Duster spoke for the first time. His speech was a shrill twang, the opposite end of the scale from Hide Coat's half-humorous baritone. "Now you, honey. Toss over that purse."

It was the white leather reticule, resting in her lap. Something might have fluttered over her face as she reached for it, the shadow of the reflection of the ghost of a smile, but then I was a gambler too and I noticed those things.

Irish Andy chose just that moment to come in from the back.

His close-cropped head was tilted down and he was tying his apron as he walked, unaware as yet of the silence in the room and what it signified. Hide Coat, startled by the sudden development, jerked his shotgun in that direction. I swung up the sawed-off, backing up a step to clear the top of the bar, and squeezed the rear trigger. Colleen fired at the same time but I didn't look for the result. Hide Coat was off his feet and headed for the wall backward, propelled by a pattern of buckshot as solid as a croquet ball, when I swung the second barrel on the man with the rifle, my finger wrapping the front trigger.

He was braced for a hipshot, both hands on the Springfield steadied alongside his pelvis with the hammer back. I saw him calculate the odds in an instant, a single rifle ball against shotgun spray, and I watched his muscles relax. Then he raised a palm in a brown jersey glove with the fingers cut out and backed away through the door.

*"Du lieber Gött."* Irish Andy goggled, his hands still behind him on his apron strings.

Junior was the first to move. As he strode to the end of the bar to rescue the cash box the tension broke apart in two halves. Voices and creaking floorboards came through the space between.

"Jesus. Christ Jesus."

Duster was still standing by the faro table, bent over now with his hands pinned between his knees. A pattern of fresh dark circles kept changing and growing on the floor between his feet and I couldn't tell which hand was hit. His Army Colt lay under the table. Colleen's bag rested on the table with her hand inside, smoldering from the powder flare of her pocket pistol.

Hide Coat was still alive and squirming in a muck of blood and sawdust on the floor, making wet sounds. I couldn't tell how much of his midsection remained beneath the mess I'd made of the hide. I came around the bar and stooped to pick up the Greener. I knew of two lawmen who'd been killed by men already dead for neglect of that chore.

The flap door opened. I swung that way, a shotgun in each hand. Rosario Ortiz stumbled in pulled by the weight of a Walker Colt as long as his forearm, a cap-and-ball model designed to ride in saddle scabbards and anchor rowboats. He had traded his overalls and cavalry tunic for a gray suit buttoned at the top of the coat and vest and no-where else. His white-shirted belly hung out almost be-yond the brim of his sombrero. The bent star sagged from the buttonhole in his lapel like one of his yellow roses.

"Hell's fire, Marshal, don't shoot one of us!" Junior stood cradling the bread tin in both arms.

All the customers were eager to report what had hap-pened. I left them to it and went over to retrieve the Army pistol from under Colleen's table. The man in the duster had found a chair and sat in it now rocking to and fro, sup-porting his dripping right hand with his left and finding Jesus with every other breath.

"I understand Bill Cody is hiring precision shooters for his exhibition," I told Colleen. "You will need to practice some before you can pluck a half-dollar from between a man's fingers."

"I hadn't the luxury of taking aim. I wanted to hit the thickest part of him, but he hadn't any." She was frown-ing at the ruined reticule. "This one came from Monkey Ward's. I waited three months for delivery."

"It didn't go with that rig anyway."

Having established that there was no need for it, Marshal Ortiz threaded the long barrel of the Walker Colt inside the waistband of his trousers, obliging himself to walk stiff-legged as he made his rounds among the wit-nesses. You had to smile at the sight. That swift-draw thing was mostly an invention of novelists of the Jack Rimfire stamp, but a man could have eaten the free lunch in the time it would take the fat Mexican to bring that big pistol back out into the open. He listened to the accounts with his head bent, nodding energetically when he comprehended something and lifting his sombrero to scratch at his fore-lock with a black fingernail whenever some point differed from the others. Several times he crossed in front of the man dying on the floor, being careful each time to avoid treading in the blood with his boots, which were old-time Mexican cavalry issue worn round at the heels but blacked to a high shine on the toes. At length he stopped before the wounded robber in the chair and said something in a polite tone that was too low to make out from a distance of six feet.

"You go to hell, greaser."

Ortiz straightened with a sad look and came over to me. "I need your help, *señor.*"

"If you're deputizing me to ride with the posse I'm not interested," I said. "I left all that behind when I came south."

"Posse? No posse. I need assistance removing this man to the mission."

I wasn't sure which man he meant. "Why there? Can't the padre come here? I never heard where the Last Rites in a saloon didn't take."

"You misunderstand, *Señor* Murdock. San Sábado has no jail. When it is necessary to hold a man for the sheriff we use the mission cellar. It has a trapdoor. The old fathers and brothers hid women and children there from Indians in times past. The doctor can bind his hand here but I will require someone to help me get him down the ladder afterward. The shock, it makes a man weak."

"Can't someone take care of that while you go out after the third man?"

He scratched his forelock. "*¿Por qué?* Why? You have your money."

"That doesn't make what he did any less illegal."

"The only reason to chase a man at night is to get back what he has taken, no?"

"What's to stop him from trying again? We don't even know who he is."

"Oh, we know his name."

"We do?"

The toothy smile behind his handlebars was eager to please in a way that made me want to push it in. "I apologize, *señor*. I forget you are new. The man with the hole in his hand is Abel Freestone. The man you have killed is called Dutch Tim. Everyone in this country knows who they favor with their company."

I glanced toward the door the man with the Springfield had gone through. I remembered the vaguely familiar set of his features. "For a twin, Ross Baronet doesn't look that much like his brother, does he?"

"They are not, how do you say, identical."

"Like hell they're not," I said.

The man on the floor had stopped squirming.

# CHAPTER 8

The bell in the mission tower began to bang out Mass a few minutes before seven Sunday morning. The sun wedging its way over the San Andres was pretty but the color reminded me of the corruption we'd had to scrape off the floor of the Princess Friday night. The planks would still need sanding and a fresh application of sawdust to remove Dutch Tim's final traces. As for the rest of him, I'd given five dollars to the little Mexican who sheared hair at the barbershop to scratch a hole in the cramped patch of unconsecrated ground east of town and erect a board. He doubled as town undertaker.

He weighed the gold piece on his palm. "A board for a bandit?"

"I want his friends to see what his line of work got him."

"You wish an inscription?"

I thought. " 'God's finger touched him and he slept.' "

"More like a full load of double-ought buck," said Junior when he heard about it.

That was Saturday morning. Now, after four hours' sleep on top of the Saturday night crush, I was in front of the Princess lashing my bedroll across the claybank's big rump. Junior came out yawning bitterly in his morning sheepskin and wideawake hat.

"You got a good day for it," he said, leaning against a porch post.

"Yes. I can cook my noon dinner on a rock without having to make a fire."

"Damn shame sending you back out into it. You just got here."

"No help for it. Your feelings about the sheriff are too strong to negotiate with him and I doubt Colleen's purse pistol shoots far enough to keep her out of some three-legged buck's wigwam."

"Baronet's bound to think Ross scared you into offering him a cut."

"I disagree. Ross is out two men because of us."

"Think he knew what Ross was up to?"

"Maybe. If he did he'll offer me special protection before I even bring up our proposition." I checked the magazine of the Winchester and scabbarded it.

"Here come *las viudas*."

I turned in time to see the last of perhaps a dozen old women step off the boardwalk on the other side of the street and turn in the direction of the mission. They were dressed all in black from bonnets to shoes, their dark hems dragging like crows' wings in the dust of the street. One or two fingered rosaries; the rest clutched their shawls at the throat and stared straight ahead as they walked, moving with a kind of bicycling gait that raised a yellow plume in their wake. The group swept along like some low-hanging cloud and seemed to drain the life from everything it passed.

Junior said, "California has its swallows and we have our magpies. They gather at one or another's house at first light and go to Mass in a flock. That's how it's been every Sunday for as long as anyone can remember."

"I thought it was just some leftover legend. I didn't think the widows were real."

"In a few years they won't be. Eille MacNutt says when he came to town there was twice this many, and three times that many twenty years before that. This is what's left from the last vendetta. Any town that is running out of widows can't be all bad."

"I'd feel better if I didn't think someone probably said the same thing just before the last vendetta."

No sooner had he mentioned Eille MacNutt than two women came out the door of the Mare's Nest, tying on head scarves as they followed the widows. Their dresses were more subdued than what they would wear for work and cut for the parlor, but they seemed as bright as plumage against the group that had passed ahead of them.

"It's a sad day when a whore gets religion," said Junior. "Next comes married and babies and then the Wednesday League to stamp out the things that bring them here to begin with."

"That's civilization."

"Now you sound like the old man. And every time he said it he jacked the ranch house up on rails and moved it farther back toward the mountains." He tipped his hat back with a knuckle. "If that's civilization, what do you call this here?"

I followed the slant of his chin. Another woman had come to the corner from the side street that led to *Señora*

Castillo's boardinghouse, paused to check for traffic, and turned in behind the women from the Mare's Nest. She was dressed in blue gingham and had a lace scarf tied under her chin, concealing her hair completely. If it hadn't been for that brief turn of the head I might not have recognized Colleen Bower. Just in case she was bound somewhere else I went on watching as she crossed the bridge over the dry creek and entered the mission behind the others.

"I'll be damned," I said.

"What kind of odds you giving?" Junior asked.

Three Apaches mounted on slat-sided ponies trailed me most of my first day at a distance of five hundred yards, not even bothering to conceal themselves when I turned in the saddle to look back. That meant either they were just curious or had enough reinforcements nearby to make any action I might take a topic of conversation that night while they were waiting for my brains to come to a boil. Since they knew where I was anyway I built a fire after dark and cooked my supper, but when I turned in I led the claybank a hundred feet away from the embers and spread my blanket there. In the morning they were gone. Frightening the water out of lone white travelers is an Indian sport as old as Montezuma.

The streets of Socorro were crowded even for a town that size of a Monday. I threaded my way between the buckboards and buggies and stepped down in front of the livery, where Ole, the white-haired youth with the tired bones, was sitting on his bench in the shade of his flop brim.

"Give him oats and rub him down." I held out the reins.

He tipped his head back carefully, as if it might fall off its hinge, and screwed up his face against the sun. "I thought the sheriff run you out last week."

"I ran back. Oats. Rubdown." I jiggled the reins under his nose.

"Well, I ain't certain we got the room. Lots of folks in for the hanging. I'll tether him out here for a dollar, though. Feed's extra."

I chewed on it a second, then reached inside my pocket. His tongue bulged his cheek as he watched.

"Maybe two dollars," he said.

Without taking my hand out of my pocket I hooked the heel of my right boot under the edge of the bench and shoved. He showed me two soles in need of repair and went right on over in a creditable somersault. Lying on his stomach on a patch of ground past due for shoveling, he spat out gravel. "I'm going to the sheriff!"

"Save the leather, Ole. I'm on my way there now." I came up with a cartwheel and flipped it. It landed in front of his nose. "Rub him down good. I'll know if you give him anything but oats. Hay makes him windy. And I want him in a stall."

"We're full up!"

"Give him your room. He's not choosy."

The door to the county office was locked with a sign on it reading EXECUTION TODAY. I took the alley to the fenced-in courtyard behind the building. Jubilo No-Last-Name, the full-time deputy, was standing inside the gate. He had his Creedmoor rifle and any joy his half-caste face might have held had died in the shade of his flat-brimmed Stetson.

"Where's your invitation?"

"I didn't take one, remember? I didn't think I'd be in town for it. I need to talk to the sheriff."

"He's a mite busy just now."

"I'll wait."

Nothing went on in his features. "Might as well wait inside as out."

"Without an invitation?"

"We're hanging a man today, mister. I don't see nothing to joke about."

"They're hanging someone somewhere every day," I said. "I don't see anything but."

He turned sideways to let me pass. It was a big yard, and popular as the condemned man might have been, Baronet could have spared himself worry about filling it. Even in a town as large and lively as Socorro, events worth attending and talking about after were separated by long quiet times during which many a frontiersman found leisure to wonder why he came west in the first place. Next to Shakespeare and a lewd woman an execution was the best excuse to avoid so much unwelcome self-knowledge. There was the usual ratio of three men to each woman, but plenty enough of the latter to warrant shaking the shelf creases out of the store suit and putting it on. In those days we duded up for hangings the same way we did for funerals and church, and in my trail clothes I was seriously underdressed for the occasion. Not that anyone paid me more than passing attention. That was reserved for the four men on the scaffold.

This was an impressive structure as such things went, it being low-bid business on the county budget and generally a good excuse for the builder to get rid of his warped and knotty lumber. The cornerposts were six-by-sixes, planed smooth as white siding, and appeared to have been set as many feet below ground as they stood above. There was a proper staircase of eight steps instead of a ladder, which as far as getting a man up it who doesn't want to go is no better than a rope, and the gallows itself was six-braced to the platform and mortised at the yardarm. The whole thing looked as solid as a new barn.

Frank Baronet, in his black frock coat and gray pinch hat, shared the scaffold with a priest in full raiment including the swan's-neck headgear, a much less picturesque pudgy party with his shirt ballooning out under his vest whom I took for the hangman, and the guest of honor. Hernando Padilla would have made two of his Mexican barber counterpart in San Sábado, standing three inches taller than the sheriff and nearly twice as broad across the torso. He was in white shirtsleeves, striped pants, and stockings, with a leather harness strapped around his waist pinning his arms to his sides, and just before the hangman dropped the black hood over his head—standing on tiptoe to reach—I saw that his face was large and badly pockmarked, with the elaborately curled moustaches that are the signature of any tonsorial artist who takes pride in his profession. I wondered which he had used to dispatch Ernestine "Mexican Red" Grosvenor, a razor or just his big hands with their long, oddly graceful fingers. I found out later he had split her skull with a cuspidor.

There being no final statements from the condemned, and the priest having finished reading from Ecclesiastes, the hangman snugged the big knot up under Padilla's left ear, paused with his hand on the lever, and tripped it. The bottom dropped out from under the man in the hood. His neck broke with a sharp report like a log snapping in a fireplace. He bounced twice, pumped his right leg several times as if trying to climb back up onto the platform, and swayed around in a half-circle. The audience let out its breath in a collective sigh and began shuffling toward the gate.

The priest was one of the last to go. Just as he passed me he broke wind, reached back to pluck his cassock out of the crease in his buttocks, and picked up his pace.

As Jubilo herded out the stragglers, Baronet and the hangman loosened the rope and lowered the dead man through the trap, under which two men with funeral coats on over clean overalls caught him and laid him in an unlined cedar box, grunting a little as they wedged in his shoulders. The sheriff shook the hangman's hand and glanced at me distractedly as he came down the steps. I fell in beside him and we entered the building through the back door. The cells were empty on both sides. He unlocked the door to the office, tossed his keys at the desk, hung up his hat, and began opening and closing drawers in the desk.

"How many of those you been to?" He found a bottle and a glass and stopped looking.

"A few."

"Ever get used to it?"

"I never thought I would until I was hanged myself," I said. "It didn't take and now it's just like watching a branding."

"You won't require this then." He heeled the cork back into the bottle and emptied the glass down his throat. After putting both away he took the embroidered pillow off the swivel behind the desk, pounded it twice, and sat down, poking it behind his back and squirming around until he had contact where he wanted it. He looked up at me, blinking hard. "One of Whiteside's hands was at your place Friday night. He sat at my table yesterday. He said you had trouble."

"Marshal Ortiz is holding a prisoner for you at the mission. He'll never play any violins with his gun hand."

"I heard there was a man killed."

"You heard it all then. The third man got away." I watched his face, but that blink was distracting. It would serve him well at poker. "That's not the reason I'm here."

Jubilo came in the back way and I stopped talking. The sheriff told him to go eat. He looked at me without expression, then went out the front carrying his Creedmoor.

"Does he sleep with that rifle?" I asked.

"I wouldn't know. We haven't shared a bed." He waited.

I leaned back against the high counter and crossed my ankles. The big-bore Remington pistol was sticking out of the notch in his vest but I didn't think he could use either end of it in his present position without alerting me. "Before we talk you ought to know I just left Ole in front of the livery with his face in a pile of manure."

"How could you tell them apart?" He rocked back and forth on the swivel, stopped. "Give me the rest of it."

I gave him the rest of it, including the details Colleen and I had worked out the day after the shooting. He listened, blinking and lifting a hand on occasion to smooth one or the other of his handlebars.

"How much are we discussing?" he asked when I stopped.

"Two thousand. Less if we can get a good price on those fixtures Mrs. Bower mentioned."

"She is your best collateral. If she is as comely as they claim on the circuit, and maybe even if she is not, there isn't a cowboy or a miner in the territory who wouldn't lather up a good horse in order to say he played cards with Poker Annie. Or any female, comes to that. There is the little problem of a county ordinance against women gambling in public."

"Yours?"

"It was on the books when I came. Some fracas over a tinhorn from Kansas and his redheaded companion; I disremember the circumstances. I'm told that in Dodge City they get around a similar law by declaring the gaming room private and banning Chinamen from entering."

"We have no Chinamen in San Sábado."

"Then they should be easy to keep out. What are the terms?"

"Three percent per month and the note comes due at the end of a year."

"Ten percent is customary for me."

"No percent is customary for me. Three and a half percent."

"Half percentages require too much arithmetic. Eight."

"Five."

"Eight is as low as I go."

"Who supervises the collection at that rate?" I asked. "Your brother Ross?"

He had stopped blinking. "Ross is dead. He died in Mexico of wounds received in the fighting in Lincoln County."

"He handles a Springfield rifle well for a corpse."

He shifted in his seat suddenly and I placed my hand on the butt of the Deane-Adams. Crossing his legs, he smiled. "Five percent. I will send someone to collect the first of every month. Not my brother. You are mistaken about him."

"The papers will be ready for you to sign when you come to claim Abel Freestone. He is the man Marshal Ortiz is holding at the mission."

"Ortiz couldn't hold his dick in a high wind. Are you heading back today?"

"No, I am stopping at the Socorro and going back in the morning. I saw Apaches yesterday. If I have the choice I'll be rested and fresh when I see them next."

"They intended no mischief if you saw them. If you wait a few days Jubilo will go with you. I'm sending him for Freestone and he can bring back the loan papers. I cannot leave the county seat at tax time. He is an artist with that Creedmoor."

"I'll think about it. If you don't hear from me before he leaves I went back already."

I went from there to the railroad station to wire the details to Junior and Colleen. The operator, bald and green-faced under his eyeshade, squinted at my name. "You're

Murdock? I was just about to relay this on to San Sábado."
He tore a flimsy off his spike and held it out.

YOU LEFT YOUR WALKING STICK IN HELENA STOP
YOU WILL FIND IT WAITING LARAMIE W T UNTIL
THIRTY AUGUST TRACK THREE

It was unsigned. "When's the next train north?" I asked.
The operator called across to the clerk at the ticket
window, who checked his board and called back. "Five
fifteen."
"I need to add something to that telegram I gave you."
He handed it back. I thought, then added:

HAVE LINE ON PURCHASE PIANO LARAMIE BACK
IN TEN DAYS

The operator looked up from counting. "I was in Laramie last month. I don't remember seeing a piano works."
I stared at him until he returned to his totaling.
The ride north was uneventful, meaning it was hot and
sooty and about as smooth as sitting on a rockslide. Educational, too; when you sleep on your tailbone you discover
parts of your body you never knew you had. At the station
in Laramie I shaved in the gentleman's water closet beside
two other bleary-eyed travelers along life's highway. We
couldn't have shed much more blood if we'd started a razor
fight.
A porter directed me to Track 3, a siding with grass
growing between the rails, occupied solely by a redwood
Pullman with curtains in the windows. I mounted the platform, rapped on the door, received an invitation, checked
my boots for mud, and entered. The inside was all panel-
ing and red plush and crockery lamps with milky glass
shades, in the midst of which its only inhabitant, seated in

a big yellow leather wingback chair with studs, looked like a plain stone in a baroque setting.

"Well, Deputy, you are almost late," announced Judge Blackthorne. "I hope this saloonkeeping episode hasn't made you forget whom you're working for."

# CHAPTER 9

**H**arlan A. Blackthorne had once been described by a member of the party to which he ostensibly belonged as a "vest-pocket Lincoln." The statement was not intended as a compliment. Built along Honest Abe's narrow lines, with chin whiskers, a high arid brow capped with a swirl of blue-black hair, and prominent bones, he would have required something more lofty than his bankers' heels to deal with the Great Emancipator on any level other than face-to-cravat. A forty-year-old error in his military record reckoned his height at five feet six and he was vain enough to cite it still, but I knew for a certainty that the army had been uncharacteristically generous by at least three inches. The toes of his custom boots barely touched the floor while he was planted in the big chair.

His smile, which was a fixed thing with no amusement in it and a source of consternation for his political enemies and the defendants who appeared before him, was more reminiscent of President Washington's in the portrait that hung in his courtroom. It concealed his total want of teeth. I'd never known him to wear his temporaries at any time except when he was trying a case. I had long since left off asking myself why a man who spent so much time and personal assets on his tailoring—today it was a gray Norfolk and matching trousers with his lucky gold horseshoe

tacked to a purple ascot—never took the trouble to visit a
dentist who knew his trade. But then I will go to Glory not
knowing the man, though I spent the better part of my
middle years earning his good opinion.

"I wouldn't make light of this saloonkeeping business,
sir," I said, looking for a place to lay my hat. "The hours
are better than federal work and I don't have to pay to bury
the men I shoot."

"You've shot someone so soon? If I thought your intention was to improve upon your previous time I never would
have agreed to let you go."

I gave up looking and sat down in a padded rocker,
crossing my legs and hanging the hat on my knee. "They
don't call me Satan's Sixgun for sport."

"Yes, it seems all of Helena is reading the man Hookstratton's gentle prose. I expect to see it entered into the
Congressional Record any day. Those carpetbaggers in
Washington will stop at nothing to cause me grief." He
rapped a finger on the arm of his chair for lack of a gavel.
"I am sorry I had to bring you all this way, Deputy. Rail
travel is a trial in this climate."

"More so for some of us than for others."

"I have temporary use of the salon car, no more. I am
fortunate in my acquaintances. The apology stands."

"It's unnecessary. You can't know what a relief it is to
be someplace where Billy the Kid didn't shoot anyone."

"Who?"

"Nobody important, sir. We have to discuss this walking stick device. I doubt there is anyone in Montana who
hasn't seen through it by now."

"I did not employ it to deceive anyone in Montana. So
far as the territory of New Mexico is concerned, Blackthorne is a name from your past. In any case it brought
you here."

"The question is, what brought you? Your honor."

"We shall come to that presently. What have you to report?"

"I'm in partnership with Junior Harper as planned. He thinks I took him up on his offer because I'm weary of keeping the peace. It might surprise you to learn how little convincing that required."

"You are impertinent. Proceed."

"Something we didn't plan on is named Colleen Bower. Junior cut her in for a full third before I arrived."

"The name is not unfamiliar."

"She's known more widely on the circuit as Poker Annie. I had dealings with her two years ago in Breen."

"Ah." His *Ah* had more sides than a roundhouse. How much he knew or speculated beyond what I had told him of the happenings in Breen was anyone's guess.

"She has San Francisco ideas for the Apache Princess. All of them involve money. I suggested we borrow it from Frank Baronet."

"Elephantine."

"You haven't met him, sir. Anything less is lost on him. Mrs. Bower agreed to the proposition, although Junior did not. It was a majority decision and I took it to Baronet. He went for it like a steer for water. He is all cash-and-carry."

"Anything else?"

I told him about the pistol-whipping I had received in Socorro City and the man the sheriff killed who claimed to have seen Ross Baronet alive in Mexico. The Judge smoothed his whiskers, always a sign he was troubled.

"A dead man who happened to say something in your presence and a battery on your person which you confess to have invited through your own intemperance; is that the extent of your grounds?"

"Yes. Well, except for Ross Baronet attempting to rob the Princess Friday night."

*"Thunderation!"*

I had seldom heard him bellow, and then only at certain attorneys from back East who thought the law they had learned from their professors assayed out higher than the grade he had panned behind his rude bench. It made the glass in the car ring. He gripped the arms of the chair hard until the spasm passed.

"Again I apologize," he said in his customary judicial tone. "You are in San Sábado as a favor to me and I have no right to dictate the manner in which you impart information. I do request that you refrain from the dramatic."

"I'm sorry, sir." I gave him the full account, ending with Dutch Tim's burial. As he listened he crossed his legs, something he did when particularly pleased, an event more rare for him than shouting.

"A distinct touch, that headboard. Tweaking Ross Baronet over the loss of his man should help to draw suspicion from your eagerness to enter into a transaction with his brother." He put the leg down. "My purpose in arranging this meeting is to inform you that we must move up our schedule."

"I wasn't aware we had one."

He went on as if I hadn't spoken. "It has come to my attention that certain Democrats in the Congress are conspiring to propose amnesty for all those currently wanted for crimes committed during the war in Lincoln County. The measure will be introduced in the Senate next month in time to pass through both houses before the November elections. Given his preference the American voter will see a scoundrel set free. It is that old revolutionary curse."

"Do you think the president will sign such a bill?"

"Who is to say who will be president when it reaches the White House? Garfield does not appear to be recovering from that assassin's bullet he took last month. Chester Arthur is a Hudson River hack who blows with Tammany, and that Irish crowd will side with Dolan. If we do not move swiftly we may be forced not only to release our covey, but to present them with the net as well in fee simple for the inconvenience."

He paused a beat in case I cared to jump in. I didn't, and he sat back as far as he ever did, perhaps an inch.

"Grapeshot tore open my belly at the siege of Monterrey," he said. "My intestines were lying on the ground beside me. A medical officer commanded an orderly to let me die and go help some other wretch who could still be saved. Sergeant Uriah Spooner leveled his musket at the officer and informed the orderly that if I were not removed to the field station immediately the American expeditionary force in Mexico would be shy one brass-buttons. For this offense he was arrested, court-martialed, and sentenced to death. I was too ill to testify at the first hearing, but when another was convened to review the evidence I appeared on a stretcher. I dislike quoting myself. Suffice it to say I found my calling that day and I have cleaved to the law ever since. Spooner's sentence was commuted to five years' penal servitude and a dishonorable discharge.

"I was present at his wedding ceremony and again at the christening of his only son. I missed his funeral two years ago as I was hearing a capital case at the time. When I learned that Ross Baronet and whoever was with him had killed young Dave Spooner and his wife in Lincoln County, the scars of that old injury began to sting for the first time in thirty-five years. They are stinging yet. I can only conclude that they will continue to vex me until justice is served."

He tapped the arm of his chair. Tension fled from the car like heat through a shattered window. "One man's sore stomach is scarcely grounds for federal action. My jurisdiction does not cover crimes committed in New Mexico. I therefore accepted your badge and papers and wished you Godspeed on your sojourn into private enterprise. The fact

that the enterprise should be located in the county where
Frank Baronet presides was mere coincidence."

"Helped along by a good memory," I said. "Dave and
Vespa Spooner were still nursing cattle and enjoying good
health at the time Junior approached me. I always did take
a while deciding my future."

We were coming perilously close to an expression of
gratitude, but he side-railed it as only a civil servant can
who has managed to survive three presidential adminis-
trations and an impeachment attempt. "I want the men responsible for these murders arrested, tried, and convicted
before the politicians can act. Since the territory was under martial law at the time of the atrocity I want the case
heard in federal court where the Dolan influence is less
profound. I do not insist that it be my court, but neither will
I shirk my responsibilities should the venue shift to Montana to avoid local prejudice. I fear that the delay of even
a month may be fatal."

I uncrossed my legs and circled my hatbrim through
my fingers. "Well, we can arrest Ross for the attempted
robbery of the saloon. We can try to peg Dutch Tim's
death on him. It's a stretch, but if we play him smart he
might be persuaded to talk about the raid on the Spooner
ranch in return for the promise of a sentence lighter than
death."

"If he pulled the trigger he will hang."

"He won't talk then. You can bend a rifle barrel over the
skulls of these southwestern road agents for twice your
month and they will just laugh at you. They all fear the
rope, but if it's swing for Dutch Tim or swing for the
Spooners I don't see the choice in it. Nor will he."

He touched his beard. "Life then. But only if he gives
up his companions and the name of the man who planned
the raid."

"That would be Frank or I miss my guess. There is the

little problem of tracking Ross down. The trail is cold. I had hopes of getting to him by way of Frank's wallet but that will require more time than we have. Also if I take out after him alone it will look wrong. I'm not a lawman down there, remember. As a saloonkeeper I'm only out the price of a burial. The holdup didn't go through."

"Who keeps the peace in San Sábado?"

"No one. A fat Mexican named Ortiz pins himself to the town star when he is not weeding his roses or shouting at his many children."

"Ortiz? Intriguing. We captured a young lieutenant by that name at Cerro Gordo. On the second night he strangled one of the sentries guarding him and shot another with the man's musket. He bayoneted a third on his way over the stockade. The following day he was observed fighting alongside his countrymen. I haven't thought of him in years."

"It isn't the same Ortiz."

"Likely not. The surname is a common one. You must try to bring this man around. Fewer questions will be asked if you assist him in Ross Baronet's arrest."

"It will be like assisting a boulder up Granite Peak. One question, sir."

He read the face of a mantel clock mollusked over with gilt cupids. "Make it brief. You have just time to board the Santa Fe southbound. It leaves at one forty-five."

"Pinholster is the deputy with all the experience under cover. He was a Wells Fargo agent for four years. Arnsen knows that Socorro country like the clay under his nails and O'Donnell has been with you longer than anyone and has more of your trust than all the rest of us put together. Why did you ask me to help in this?"

"I do not submit my decisions to committee, Deputy. You will miss your train."

"That's too thin, sir. It works when we are judge and

officer of the court, but you said it yourself, this is a personal favor. The question deserves an answer."

"You may be right. I may even concur. That does not mean I will provide it."

I rose. "It doesn't signify anyway because I've guessed it. Pinholster and O'Donnell are as straight as a short drop. They bring their men in alive. So does Arnsen, but for a different reason. He's close with his purse and would avoid paying a federal burying fee at the cost of his own skin. I make the effort, but it doesn't always answer and I will kill a man without thought if he brings me grief. That's why you chose me, not because I'm loyal or dependable. The odds are better than even I will spare the United States the bother of a trial, which might delay things long enough for Dolan to get back from Washington City with his box of pardons. This way he will be forced to nail them up in matching coffins."

"You are misled."

"I've never thought so."

"Good hunting, Deputy. Wire me in Helena when you have something worth sharing."

I left him then surrounded by his borrowed bric-a-brac. You can read about Judge Harlan Amsdill Blackthorne in the florid memoirs of the tenderheel attorneys who pleaded in his courtroom, about his Old Testament views and the forty-six men and one woman he sentenced to hang in their observance, and it's all true. But something he said on the subject of justice while handing down one of those sentences is carved over a doorway at the Harvard School of Law, and the memoirs are all mustering dust and dead flies on some forgotten shelf. The fact that I don't understand those chiseled words any more than I did the man who spoke them is neither here nor there. He had more enemies than Custer on his hill but few peers.

# CHAPTER 10

The same three Apaches, or three from the same litter if not them, locked on to my trail half a day out of Socorro City on the way home, and inside two hours had closed to within a thousand feet. That was close enough to show their long shirts sashed about the waist and their hide leggings, proof against mescal spines and diamondbacks, and too close for me. Two had lances. The third carried a carbine behind his shoulder and what looked like extra cartridge belts slung from the horn of a proper saddle. Sensing them, the claybank told me in a hundred little ways what it thought of the situation, but I held it to a brisk walk, conserving vinegar for when a dash might be required. It seemed to understand and made only a token try at throwing the bit.

Another good reason not to run was I was in no hurry to quit that rolling foothill country west of the Oscuros until nightfall, when I might have a chance to cross the Jornada del Muerto under cover of darkness, which was the only cover that flat desert land offered. That was the plan, and the only thing wrong with it was it depended largely on Indian patience, a commodity rarer there than spring water.

It ran out in another hour. Something struck the parched earth in front of us and to the left with a *tuck* sound and a ball of dust. The report reached me a beat behind, bent in the middle and dulled by distance, *palop,* a pebble dropping into a shallow pool. I didn't look around, but quirted the reins across the gelding's withers and leaned over the pommel, offering less opposition to the wind while reducing the target. The bottom dropped out of the horse's gait.

Its long legs chewed up ground and the wind pasted the front of my hatbrim to the crown. I thanked John White-side and myself for our taste in mounts. A big rump has all the mechanics necessary to push an animal along.

There may have been other shots. Probably there were. I didn't listen. I was too busy looking for a place to come to ground. You can't outrun Indians, there is no use trying. Apaches especially will overtake you on a bag of buffalo grass and bones no matter if you are riding von Bismarck's finest. They run them on pure mean, of which they have an unlimited supply.

The outlook held small promise. The foothills them-selves lay too far to the east and there was nothing handy in the way of a breastwork. I risked a look back and saw all three riders closing, the one with the carbine foremost. He would be coming hardest to give himself time to draw rein and make a stationary shot before I fell out of range. Savages were poor marksmen as a rule and disliked wast-ing lead on a moving target from a moving platform.

Well, hell. Three hundred dollars doesn't go as far as it used to.

I reached back and unsheathed the curve-bladed skin-ning knife I'd carried since my winter wolfing days up on the Cut Bank. Shooting horses is preferable to cutting their throats for a variety of reasons, but not when you are in for a long siege and can't spare the ammunition. Next to a clay hill a supine carcass is the best thing in nature for stopping enemy fire.

I was just about to dig in, leap off, and cut when I spot-ted something sweet to the southwest. This was a long gentle swell of land much like all the others in that region but with the attraction of a line of junipers behind which a man could crouch and give battle without making a bull's-eye of himself into the bargain. I veered that way and raked the claybank's flanks, drawing blood and a squeal of pain and rage and a burst of speed that almost snatched my hat off my head. A spark flew off a flat rock just to my right, a snap shot intended to steer me away from the junipers. I hoped the nearness was a fluke. Trust me to draw the only sharpshooter in moccasins this side of Buffalo Bill's Wild West.

Going around the end of the juniper bank was the long route. I headed straight for it. I hoped the gelding was game and not one of those treasures that set their brakes at the prospect of leaving the earth for any reason. In the end it wouldn't matter, though, because either way I was going over, and if I made the trip alone and landed on my head and broke my neck I'd make a poor subject for the Apache notion of entertainment. I clawed for meat once again. I could tell by the answering shudder that I had made a friend for life. It's just as well they don't have trigger fingers.

And then we were airborne, the drumming gone from below and only the wind whistling past my ears to take my thoughts off what was behind and what might be ahead. The claybank grunted when it pushed off. Only the whites of its eyes showed on the way aloft. A branch brushed my leg and then we were clear. Open ground swept away in front of un. My teeth snapped together when we struck down, a pair of disks scraped against each other in my lower back. I gave the horse a few yards to find its footing and then I leaned back on the reins, turning its head and slipping my left foot out of the stirrup. When it went down I leaped clear, landed on both feet, and snapped the Winchester out of its scabbard. By the time the claybank got up and shook itself I was down on my stomach and drawing a bead between junipers.

The three braves had slowed their approach, reading my mind. At that distance I couldn't tell if they were painted, but then I'd gotten drunk in Helena one night with a former aide of General George Crook's who told me Apaches wore theirs on the inside where it never rubbed off. Resting my forearms on the slight rise, I laid the front sight on the arch of the rib cage of the one with the carbine, took a breath, let out half of it, and squeezed the trigger. A rooster tail of dust bristled in front of his mount's left forefoot.

Damn the duplicity of that sand country. The heat made a long lens of the air near the ground and made everything look closer than it was. All three Indians hauled back on their hair bridles and retreated farther out of range.

While they parleyed I crawled back toward the claybank for my canteen and the extra cartridge boxes in my saddle wallets. The damn beast was still indignant over having been made to soil its coat and shied, but I lunged for a dragging rein and hauled it close hand over hand. When I had what I needed I crawled back to my rise. One of the Apaches was missing along with his horse.

How they manage to move around in open prairie and stay invisible is one for those eggheads in Chicago who take them apart like frogs and study the pieces and publish papers on the subject. It didn't much matter, because I knew where he was going. I measured the height of the sun with my hands and decided there would still be enough light for him to see what he was doing by the time he got behind me. At least I still had a view of the one with the firepower.

Not that dying from a lance thrust instead of a bullet makes much difference beyond what they carve on the headstone.

Desert heat doesn't follow any of the standard rules. You'd expect it to be worst when the sun is straight up, but a hat will protect you from it then. When the only shade for miles is on the wrong side of the shrubbery you're using for cover, there is no hiding from that afternoon slant. I turned up my collar and unfastened my cuffs and pulled them down over the backs of my hands, but I could feel my skin turning red and shrinking under the fabric. Pinheads of sweat marched along the edge of my leather hatband and tracked down into my eyes, stinging like fire ants. The water in the canteen tasted like hot metal. I wanted the Montana snow, blue as the veins in Colleen Bower's throat with the mountain runoff coursing black through it carrying shards of white ice. All this time the two Indians sat their ponies, as motionless as buttes and just as easy to reason with. I was just something to break up the day, that and a horse and a long and a short gun to bring the two braves with lances into the nineteenth century.

I thumbed a fresh cartridge into the magazine to replace the one I'd fired and took another shot at the man with the carbine. There was no reason for it other than to spook his horse and spoil his mood. For all the reaction the pinto showed I might as well have waved my hat and sung Dixie. I guessed I was becoming addled by the heat and worry.

A rifle cracked. I swore it was behind me, but that country was full of distortions and I wasn't thinking right to begin with. I did know that the Indian with the carbine hadn't moved and there was no smoke in his direction. I rolled over, reversed ends, and squinted through the ground haze to the west at a rider coming hard my way. I swept a sleeve across my eyes to clear away the sweat, polished them with the heels of my hands, but he was still there, and closer. His horse's hoofbeats reached me then, hollowed out by distance and warped by heatwaves. I worked the Winchester's lever and settled the iron sight in the middle of the shimmering bulk. Either the man they'd sent to shut the back door had a long gun I didn't know about or a fourth had joined the fracas. I fired. I will still testify that

I saw the bullet leave the barrel and find its mark. Fear and sunstroke are like peyote. You will see things.

What counted was my target heeled over and struck the ground with a grunt that was real enough. After a couple of seconds it separated into two pieces, one smaller than the other, and when the smaller piece rose from a crawl to a crouch I knew I'd deprived the rider of his horse. I racked in another shell and took aim on the man.

"Mother of God, don't shoot *me*!"

I knew there were Christian Indians and had met one or two, but rarely enough to make me hesitate with my finger on the trigger this time. That was sufficient time to see that this was no Apache. He ran like a white man for one thing, long strides with his toes pointed out, and his high boots and striped trousers and white shirt were store-bought. In another second I recognized the flat-brimmed Stetson and the rifle he carried, ready to raise against me if I failed to lower the Winchester.

"Jubilo, is that you?"

"Murdock?"

I said it was. The deputy sheriff of Socorro sprinted the rest of the distance and dived headfirst into the shallow depression, holding up the Creedmoor to keep sand out of the action. He crawled forward to face me. "I just shot a damn Apache off a horse for you. If I knew you was fixing to shoot *my* horse I'd of caught his."

"Next time raise a yell. I didn't know you from Geronimo."

"See if I come help a white man out of a hole next time." The expression on his half-caste face was unreadable. "Did you even know you had a red bastard climbing your back fence?"

"Knew it. Couldn't fix it. Care to see what's up front?" Without waiting for an answer I rolled over and slithered back up to the shrub line. He joined me a second later.

"Shit, I'd of thought Satan's Sixgun was more than a fight for two little *mimbreños*."

"Three. And I didn't write that book."

"They'll be getting restless in a minute. They're thinking their pard should be on you by now."

"Maybe they'll come in range to investigate."

"Why wait?" He rolled back the Creedmoor's Remington block, removed the long cartridge, blew inside, and replaced the cartridge. He rolled the block forward.

"You any good with that competition rifle?" I asked.

"I was Lincoln County champion two years in a row. One thing they like to do in Lincoln is shoot." He unfolded the sight, locked it into place, looked through it at the waiting Apaches, adjusted the slide, looked through it again, and stretched out full length, finding a comfortable spot to rest his cheek. The Indians were straining their necks to see past the junipers. They didn't appear agitated. They knew they were well outside the Winchester's reach.

Jubilo pressed the trigger. The gun roared, backing up against his shoulder. Far away across the plain the Apache with the carbine, still craning for a good look, threw back his arms and slid over sideways. While he was still falling Jubilo opened the block, plucked out the hot shell, poked in a fresh cartridge, slammed home the action, and took aim again. But the other Apache was already moving, wheeling his horse and slapping its rump. Jubilo fired again.

"Miss."

"Maybe." He extracted the casing and reloaded. "The sons of bitches are like antelope and will run forty miles with the top of their heart blowed to hell."

But he didn't fire the third cartridge. The Indian now was out of range of even the big rolling-block and moving fast. Jubilo glanced at the sun. "We'll wait here till dark.

No telling how close his other friends are and this is the only cover for miles. Such as it is."

The Apache he'd shot wasn't moving. His horse had bolted when he fell. I calculated the distance at right around four hundred yards.

"The sheriff said you were an artist," I said.

"I am when it comes to drawing a bead." He sat up and brushed sand off his cheek. "What you doing way out here? I thought you went back to San Sábado a week ago."

"I had business up north. What are you?"

"Sheriff sent me your way to pick up a prisoner. I'm just on my way back."

"Where's the prisoner?" I had almost forgotten about Abel Freestone.

"Dead as Andy Jackson. When that hand swoll up and turned black he wouldn't let the sawbones take it off and he was gone the next day."

"Hard luck."

"Not so bad. I had to bring back some papers anyway."

I watched him wiping dust off the Creedmoor with his bandanna. He had slender hands for a Mexican and appeared to be fussy about the nails. That was an old story among gun men. It started with taking care of your weapon, spread to your hands, and before you knew it you were wearing red velvet coats and perfume in your hair like Hickok. "How long have you been working with Frank Baronet?"

"Just since last fall as deputy. I come back up from Mexico after he got elected."

"I mean since before that."

"Two years. I knew his brother Ross and we all hired on to regulate for the Dolan-Murphy combine. We had us some times, Frank and Ross and me, till that carpetbagger Wallace took over and brung in the army. There was a stir over this cow thief that got killed, him and his whore wife, and Ross and me went down to Chihuahua. He had a ball in his hip and died of mortification there."

"Were you with him then?"

"No, we split up and I only heard about it when I come back here. I scouted some before Lincoln County. Before that I worked for Juárez."

"You fought in the revolution?"

"The last part. I was just a yonker. This old one-eyed colonel stuck a Jaeger needle gun in my hands and showed me which end to point and which end to pull on and before I knew it I was knocking down *federales* like apples. Turned out I had a gift for it. Then the war went and ended."

"What does a sharpshooter do in peacetime?"

"You'd never guess. Growing up on the border I had as much English as I had Spanish, so they gave me a job collecting taxes in El Paso del Norte." He shook his head. "Gawd Almighty, don't them butchers and barbers hate to pay their share. I shot one by accident and that's when I decided to come north the first time. The revolution had went to hell anyway by then. Juárez didn't turn out to be no better than what we had before."

"That why you threw in with the Baronets?"

"You're just down on Frank on account of he buffaloed you that time. That weren't nothing. If he didn't like you they'd of scooped up your brains with the horseshit."

"That's no answer."

"I guess not. Someone told me they got this fancy notion back East about always mounting a horse from the left. I figure they don't ride much. Out here it don't matter which side you climb up on. They're both of them just as bad." He watched me peering between bushes. "Don't expect him back. Moving at night's just smart in case there are other parties out haring around. They ain't cowards, mind. That ain't the reason he lit out. Those lazy sons of bitches get ants when something starts to look like work. I'm Comanche on my father's side and I guess I know them."

"I'm glad you happened along. Dealing with them alone might have cost me another day."

"Not to mention your hair and both ears. Apaches are partial to ears. They string them around their necks so they can listen to the other side."

I reloaded the Winchester's magazine. "I heard the same thing about the Sioux. Also the Nez Percé and the Cheyenne and the Blackfoot. I've fought them all and a few others whose names I can't pronounce and I never saw an ear necklace on one of them."

"Well, if it ain't true it ought to be. You can make a case for them tribes you mentioned defending their land and all. Patch got nothing to defend. Nobody wants this here desert country but him. There's nothing meaner than an Apache brave, unless it's an Apache squaw. Neither one will eat snake. They say it's because of their religion. I say it's professional courtesy."

"I'm starting to understand. You don't like them."

"The other tribes don't like them any better than me. That's why they drove them out of every place worth living in."

"Going just by that," I said, "you're just as wicked as they are."

He smiled for only the second time since we'd met. "Well, hell's bells. I never said I wasn't."

That was the end of conversation. We settled in to wait for darkness. I didn't want any more talk in any case. I was on the edge of liking him, and it would just get in the way when the time came to kill him.

# CHAPTER 11

**W**hichever god looks after snipers and saloonkeepers was on duty that night, and we stole away under a rustlers' moon bright enough to show prairie dog holes but not us. Jubilo's horse, a blaze-face roan fifteen years old, was cold when we stopped to strip it of as much gear as we could carry. The claybank didn't encourage being loaded down with two full-grown men and their necessaries, but it seemed to sense how close it had come to sharing the roan's fate and didn't become obnoxious. We entered San Sábado at first light, iron shoes chiming against the empty hardpack street. In front of the livery we stepped down and I kicked the door until the Yaquí came out to take the reins. He wasn't long coming and was fully dressed. I don't know when he slept.

He led the claybank to a stall and brought out a bay mare for Jubilo's inspection. The deputy checked its teeth and fetlocks and looked in its ears.

"Hundred," he said.

"*Doscientos,*" said the Indian.

"It's too early to dicker. Hundred and twenty-five."

"*Doscientos,*" said the Indian.

"She's twelve if she's a day. If she was a woman I wouldn't pay more than fifty cents for all night."

"*Doscientos,*" said the Indian.

Jubilo looked at me. "That the only Spanish he knows?"

"You're the Indian expert."

"Hundred and fifty. Now, that's the limit."

"*Doscientos,*" said the Indian.

"Shit. I'll give you a county marker."

The Indian shook his head. "Cash money."

He said shit again, unbuttoned his shirt, and unwrapped a money belt from around his waist. Thick white scars curled around his brown hairless torso from behind in a pattern familiar to me. I wondered whose lash it had been, Maximilian's or Juárez's.

He gave the Yaquí another dollar to feed and rub down the bay and we walked out carrying our gear. "You can bunk in my room," I said. "I guess I owe you a roof."

"I'll spread my roll uptrail."

"I'm told I don't snore."

"It ain't that, it's the being shut in. I got me a little room off the cells in Socorro but I don't use it much."

We divided without a word in front of the Apache Princess. I didn't know if we'd see each other again except through our sights.

I caught two hours' sleep and was shaving over the basin in the room when the door opened from the outside stairs. Ford Harper's only son grinned at me sloppily past the barrel of the Deane-Adams. He had on his sheepskin over the paisley vest and was carrying a bundle under one arm. "Put it up, son," he said. "I didn't steal that much while you were gone."

I returned the revolver to the belt hanging from the bed-post. "You've been around these townies too long, Junior. In the old days it was knock or get shot."

"Knock on what? I've went through more doors to see you in the past month than I did all the time we punched cows. How was Laramie?"

"Same as Virginia City, only smaller and farther north." I scraped my throat.

"Where's the piano?"

I hesitated. I'd almost forgotten the wire I'd sent from Socorro City. "They wanted too much."

"That's a long way to go to come back empty-handed."

"Well, once you're on the road." I changed the subject.

"I see you're not in the same condition. What's in the bundle?"

He threw it on the bed. "You tell me. It came for you Friday on the Butterfield. Not knowing what's in it I didn't think it was safe to leave it in your room unattended." He slumped into the room's only chair, a Morris with faded tapestry cushions. "I hear you rode in double this morning with Baronet's deputy. Run into trouble?"

"He killed two Apaches. I killed his horse and we quit even."

"Is he as good with that rifle as they claim?"

"He is if they claim he hits what he aims at." I wiped off the remaining lather and reached for my shirt. "I hear Abel Freestone didn't make it."

"The padre wasn't happy. The ventilation is poor at the mission and there is not enough quicklime in the territory to kill the smell of putrification coming up from below during High Mass. He has asked Ortiz to find another place to store his prisoners."

"Has anyone heard anything of Ross Baronet?"

"Someone stuck up a pack train outside Las Cruces Sunday and got off with six thousand in silver. They left eight Mexicans dead and the mules aren't talking. My better judgment says it was not Jesse James."

"Eight dead. That's raw even for a Baronet."

"Did I mention they were Mexicans?"

"Still it's taking a chance. Frank cannot have approved of it."

"Possibly not. Two of those killed were vaqueros hiring out before the fall drive. Talk is President Díaz will wire an official protest to Washington City by way of Governor Wallace. The vaqueros belonged to Don Segundo and guess who bankrolled the Díaz revolution?"

"No wonder Frank insists Ross is dead," I said. "It's a fond wish."

"The business will come to nothing. Garfield is busy bleeding into a pan and Wallace can't move without federal help. Meanwhile Ross is no concern for us. By now he's in a cave in Chihuahua counting his booty."

I sat down on the bed with my back to him and pulled on my boots. He was a good poker reader and might see the disappointment on my face.

"What's Colleen about?" I asked. "Shot anyone lately?"

"She's out riding with Eille MacNutt."

I turned to look at him. His treadle jaw was set.

"It started the day you left for Socorro City. She has the notion we can come to some sort of business arrangement with the Mare's Nest. You will have to get it from her. Every time she explains it to me I get a headache." He forked out a nickel-plated watch I recognized as his father's. "They should be getting back about now. No buggy horse will tolerate hauling around a man of MacNutt's size much past an hour."

"I thought the whole idea of this investment was you wanted to run a saloon. It seems to me all you've been doing is watching someone else run it."

"I admit I'm not the man you are, Page. I can't manage a business and Poker Annie too."

I stood and put on my hat.

"Ain't you going to open your package?" he asked.

"Later. I know what's in it." I went out.

The Mare's Nest conducted business in an adobe pile that probably dated back to San Sábado's founding and showed every repair job that had ever been done on it in a hundred mottled patches like a topographical map. Its name was painted directly on its surface in large inexpert capitals without an apostrophe. At the moment an obese yellow cat was the only thing inhabiting the front porch, curled up in a splayed rocker wired together at the weak points. Thus far in my tenure I had never seen anyone else in the chair except Eille MacNutt. He was there when I came out in the morning and he was there when I climbed the Princess's outside stairs to bed, and he never seemed to feel the urge to rock, really an inhuman feat when you thought about it. He couldn't have weighed less than three hundred and might have gone four; I had yet to see him standing and so didn't have a height to figure in. I was certain he'd taken on most of those pounds since coming to town, because I couldn't picture him in his present state sitting on a wagon seat, much less a saddle. The very thought of him riding in a buggy, with or without female companionship, brought forth visions of a glacier on a velocipede.

"Don't be shy, long-tall. There's lots more to see inside."

The woman slouching in the doorway of the building wasn't the prettiest in a string not known for its beauty. Clad in an undyed muslin shift with enough sunlight coming in the back windows to show she wore nothing underneath, she was gaunt with bad skin and worse teeth that she covered with one hand when she talked. The paint she wore might have been applied by whoever had done the sign on the building, emphasizing all her worst features, and her brown hair was cropped suspiciously short, as if to discourage lice. She went by Clara California. I doubted she came from there. San Sábado was the kind of place you left behind on your way to California. She looked forty and was probably twenty-five. It was cruel work for the pay.

"That's a lie," I said. "I've seen inside. And I'm not tall."

"You're all of you the same height laying down." There was Texas in her speech, or more likely the Nations. She had Cherokee bones. "Everyone else is asleep. You can have the morning rate."

"Thanks. I'm waiting for someone."

"Not that Adabelle. She's all shine and no heat. It'll freeze and fall off."

"Someone else."

"Too bad, long-tall. Too bad." She withdrew inside.

In a little while a green phaeton with ivory trim rattled up the street behind a gray and a black with blinders and stopped in front of the building. Actually it didn't do much rattling. The ballast provided by the man in the driver's seat pasted the wheels to the hardpack as solidly as a load of iron stoves. Eille MacNutt was a tailoring challenge in several yards of crinkly seersucker and a straw skimmer with a red silk band, tilted rakishly over one eye. His features were crowded around a toothbrush moustache in the exact center of his big face like too little furniture in a huge room and when he winched himself up, using both hands and leaning the carriage far over on its springs, a thick cloud of lavender flooded my nostrils. I didn't fault him for it. Fat men suffered in that desert heat and he had done what he could about the inevitable acrid odor with the help of the toiletry section in the Montgomery Ward catalogue.

He got down to the street without help and reached up a hand to his passenger. Colleen Bower laid her gloved one in it, lifted her hem, and stepped down. She wore an embroidered wrap to protect her blue dress from dust and a wedge-shaped hat planted with flowers and secured by a plain white scarf tied under her chin.

"Thank you so much, Mr. MacNutt. You're a wizard with horses."

"I claim no credit. Your charming presence is more effective than any quirt." His voice was callow. The weight made him look older, but he was probably still in his twenties. He saw me and nodded. "Murdock."

"MacNutt." It was as much conversation as had passed between us since we'd met.

"Good morning, Page. I hope your trip was pleasant."

Colleen raised a hand to let me help her up onto the board-walk.

I kept both of mine in my pockets. "I still have my hair. That's pleasant for New Mexico."

MacNutt mounted the walk and performed the gentle-manly duty. "There's no need to end this just because the animals are tired," he told her. "I have a bottle of Napoleon in my office."

"Another time, perhaps. Thank you for an enchanting drive." She took my arm and inserted pressure on the bicep. We started walking in the direction of the Apache Princess.

"It's at least a hundred yards to the door," I said. "Shall I hitch up the buckboard?"

A muscle worked in her jaw. "The first time I heard your name I thought it sounded chivalric. I had much to learn."

"Is that what it took to get you to go riding with the Great Divide?"

"A trim waist is hardly a substitute for good manners."

"If you're that smitten I'm surprised you didn't take him up on the brandy."

"Do you want to hear the proposition I put to him or not?"

"Does it matter what your partners want?"

"It helps when they are here to consult."

"I am here."

"So you are. It occurred to me while you were gone that we are not in competition with the Mare's Nest at all. Our customers come to drink and play cards. They can do that at MacNutt's as well, but it is not their primary concern."

"Yes, Clara California gave me that impression."

"Oh?"

"I interrupted you."

"So you did. I proposed to MacNutt that since we are not in the same business we could help each other by issuing vouchers. If they visit the Nest first and spend money they will receive a certificate to be redeemed for chips or a drink at the Princess. If they visit the Princess first and spend money we will issue them a token to be applied against the price of companionship at the Nest. As things stand, fully half our respective clientele winds up spending the entire evening at one establishment or the other. This way they will patronize both."

"At a discount."

"Just for one turn of the cards or one drink. If they stopped there we would have been out of business before this."

"It's not the same with companionship," I said.

"That's the beauty of the arrangement. MacNutt's head runs toward figures, not the nature of man. Most of the advantage is ours."

"Sooner or later he is bound to see that."

"By then there will be customers enough to go around. Meanwhile we will have more capital to invest in the improvements we discussed."

"And until then you intend to buy time by going riding with Eille MacNutt."

We were in front of the saloon. She stopped walking and intercepted my gaze. "Yes."

"What happens when he finds out what you've been doing?"

"I grew up on the circuit," she said. "I would not have done so had I not learned how to take care of myself."

"That purse pistol won't get you out of everything."

"It has so far."

"Is this what you were up to when they ran you out of El Paso?"

"That was a misunderstanding."

"Did it have to do with that band you're wearing?"

She touched it involuntarily; smiled, but not with her eyes. "For someone who no longer keeps the peace you are asking a lot of questions."

"You're forgetting our silent partner. Frank Baronet is already worried about his brother's banditry and what it may mean for his position as sheriff. A falling-out involving an enterprise he's connected with could bring this whole thing down around us."

"Is that what you're concerned about?"

"Isn't it enough?"

"I thought perhaps you just didn't want me going riding with any man who's not named Page Murdock."

"That door closed in Breen."

"Doors have been known to open."

She went through one then, leaving me alone on the boardwalk with the cedar chief.

# CHAPTER 12

"**N**o, no, *Señor* Murdock. *Es imposible*. It cannot be done."

"Why not?" I said. "He's wanted for the stickup at the Apache Princess. You identified him yourself."

Rosario Ortiz shook his head. I wasn't sure if it was at the prospect of getting up a posse to track down Ross Baronet or the determination of the stalk of feathergrass he was grasping in both hands to hang on to its place among his yellow roses. He had on his gardening outfit of overalls, army coat, and sombrero, and the effort had him red and sweating. In truth I couldn't picture the fat part-time lawman at the head of a mounted party of armed men.

"To begin with, he is by now among the caves in Chihuahua. They are a honeycomb and have been known to swallow a platoon of cavalry for a week."

"You don't know he's there. You're only guessing."

"In the second place, he has nothing that belongs to you. You have the lives of two of his *compañeros,* in fact. If anyone should be hunting anyone, it is he who should be hunting you. But you see he is not. This is because he is a man of reason."

"Tell me, does that star the city gave you mean anything?"

"*Sí, señor.*" He gave one last tug. The stalk tore loose suddenly, leaving the root below the ground. He bared his teeth at the fragment in his hand, threw it aside, and sat back on his heels to take off the sombrero and drag a sleeve across his eyes. "It means five dollars a week and ten cents for every rat and stray dog I shoot in the city. Upon this and what I am paid for my work as a carpenter I put clothes on the backs and tortillas in the stomachs of eleven children. *Por favor,* look around you, *señor.* Do you see much carpentry work to be done? Do you see any?"

"Your front door has a broken panel."

"I must be sure and pay myself to replace it. No, *señor,* San Sábado is not Socorro City. A man can live on the rats he shoots there. Here he must clean cisterns and hang doors and make repairs at the mission. He would sweep the floor there as well, except that is Yaquí work and if they catch him at it they will wait for him outside and cut his throat when he leaves. Having told you all this, I hope that you will excuse me if I do not spring into the saddle to run after a bandit who has not stolen anything."

"The families of eight Mexican muleskinners may not agree with that last part."

He crossed himself. "*Lo siento,* it was an infamous thing. But it is not my concern officially. That incident took place outside this jurisdiction. If I were to go after these swine, who would pay for the provisions?"

"The Apache Princess will, along with a fee for your time."

"Your pardon, *Señor* Murdock." He unfurled a lash of Spanish at a miniature version of himself urinating against the wall of the house at the end of the flower bed. The boy buttoned his fly hastily and ran inside, tears on his face. Ortiz sighed. "You have children, yes?"

"None I know about."

"They are a treasure and a trial. If you spare the rod they will grow up to disappoint you. So will they if you employ it overmuch. These things I suppose are obvious. What is not so obvious is how little is too little, and how much is too much. This business of keeping the peace is simpler by far. I am told you were once a lawman, *es verdad?* You nod. Then you know that to track a man requires the existence of tracks. The Las Cruces pack train robbery is almost a week old."

"If you're so sure about Chihuahua we can go down there and sniff around."

"You do not know that country. It is not just the caves. The place has sheltered brigands and revolutionaries since the time of the Aztecs. Everyone who lives there is either a bandit or the great-great-grandson of one, and strangers are their enemies. Have you ever seen a man cut to pieces by a machete?"

"Sabers, in the war."

"I would not die such a death if it meant the lives of my children and their grandchildren. Chihuahua? No."

"Then what do you suggest?"

"I? Nothing."

"Nothing?"

He shrugged. I've seen all manner of men do that and I'm bound to say no man does it like a Mexican. "You have kept the peace. We may act only when the peace has been broken."

"That's no good. Ross Baronet just made off with six thousand in silver. A man can stay underground a long time on far less."

"I see. You are in a *hurry* to apprehend this man whose actions have cost you nothing."

This time I shrugged, not as well. "If you like you can call it a defensive maneuver. He isn't accustomed to failing, and we did cost him two men. I doubt he's Christian enough to turn the other cheek."

"Your reasons are your own, *señor*. I am not refusing your offer. I cannot make adobe without mud."

I said nothing for a long time. I despised him thoroughly, not so much for his sloth as for the bare fact that he was right. I suppose I hated Judge Blackthorne too, for his deadline, but I was so accustomed to hating him I gave it no thought.

"How can I get word to Don Segundo del Guerrero that I want to see him?" I asked.

He nodded, as if he'd expected the question. "His foreman, Miguel Axtaca, is sometimes at the Mare's Nest Friday night. He has a favorite there, Clara California."

"I know Clara. Axtaca doesn't sound Spanish."

"It is not. It is Indian, very old Indian. He claims kinship with Montezuma the Great."

"I guess it's too much to expect him to have forgiven us Cortez."

"It is difficult to picture Miguel Axtaca forgiving anyone anything, including himself."

"Friday night?"

"When he is not attending to ranch business." His eyes followed me as I got to my feet. "A word of caution, *Señor* Murdock. He is never without friends."

"Do these friends carry machetes?"

*"Por supuesto,"* he said. "Of course. It is a dangerous land."

Colleen was playing a hand of patience when I returned to the Princess. Her morning tea steamed at her elbow in a blue china cup on a saucer. I asked Irish Andy for coffee and he went into the back room for the pot.

"No kibitzing," she said when I brought my cup over and sat down opposite her. "It's a game for one but everybody seems to have an opinion about how it should be played."

"You needn't worry. I've never played it."

She paused in the middle of placing a black four on a red five. "Never?"

"The use of it escapes me. What have you won when you've beaten yourself?"

"Fifteen or twenty fewer minutes between you and the grave. That's where we're all headed anyway."

"Speak for yourself."

"You speak like a man with a system."

"You don't win with a system," I said. "You have to beat the system to win. You're born, you grow up, you settle down, you have children, you die. Being born is something you have no control over, but if you avoid any or all of those in the middle you stand a better than even chance of avoiding the last."

"Don't tell me. You chose not growing up." She turned over the king of hearts.

"I considered it. In the end I decided that playing games to live was for other people."

"Instead you played with guns."

"That wasn't play."

"Wasn't it?"

I met her blue stare. "No."

"Perhaps not." She went bust and gathered in the cards. "I heard you had trouble with Indians."

"They had all the trouble. Jubilo told me he picked up the papers for Frank Baronet. Did you write them up the way we discussed them?"

"Yes. Don't you trust your partners?"

"I trust Junior."

"You would. He's a man."

"He hasn't gone riding with Eille MacNutt."

She shuffled the deck the way she never did with rubes present, watching me over the blur. "Why don't you say what you mean? You're not concerned over any trouble with the Mare's Nest in connection with our business arrangement. You wouldn't be if Junior had proposed it."

I sat back, grinning over my coffee. Irish Andy had faded away at the beginning of the conversation. A discreet Prussian is a rare beast. He was undoubtedly listening from the back room.

"You know, I think I like you better when you're not smiling," Colleen said. "It makes you look hydrophobic."

"There's no help for it. I never met a woman who looked to her clothes and face and hair the way a gun man looks to his weapons and didn't complain about how every man she spoke to wanted to bed her. I think about that and before you know it my teeth are showing."

She fanned the deck. "I think you mix up comment with complaint."

"Who gave you the ring?"

"Who did you go to see in Laramie?"

I sipped from my cup. The conversation was becoming dangerous.

"Quiet morning," I said.

"They are all quiet. It's my favorite time of day in a saloon, when the air is still clear and the glasses are all polished and twinkling and the man behind the bar is crisp with starch and means it when he says welcome. Before the punchers and the miners and the tumbleweed tinhorns blow in all stinking of horse and lime water and the air fills with smoke and noise and stale beer. From heaven to hell in the space of a few minutes."

"You seem to handle it well enough when they line up at your table."

"It's the old conflict." She turned over the cards with a rippling movement of one finger and they were all black. "What you do to live versus what you live to do." She rippled them the other way, and now they were all red.

"You won't live long if you do that in front of the customers."

"Since the only customer in the room just passed out in the middle of the free lunch I would say the point is moot. In any case when they come in this early, it isn't cards they're desperate for."

"How shall we kill time until the rush?" I asked.

"There is always blackjack."

"Not with your deck."

"I haven't marked a card in four years," she said. "I am too good to have the need."

"The last three card-markers I shot all said the same thing. I have a deck upstairs."

She did the trick with the reds and blacks one last time, then stacked them and smoothed the edges. "I'll help you find it."

Upstairs, in the half-light edging in around the crooked window shade, I managed all her hooks and buttons but had trouble with the stays, which she undid herself with a deft movement. She had put on weight since the last time, but not much, and she wore it well. We started out awkward and unsure, and the feather mattress was no improvement on the one in Breen, but we found the middle ground together and she cried out softly, once. Later she watched me open the bundle that had come on the stage and put on the new shirt and the suit of clothes I'd had

made to my measurements before leaving Helena. The
coat was a simple charcoal-gray frock with stepped lapels
from which I'd had the black satin facing removed on the
same principle that prevented me from wearing a star, to
avoid drawing fire. The only other adjustment involved a
double-reinforced inside breast pocket designed to carry
the Deane-Adams. In the wavy mirror over the basin the
sober material lay flat across my shoulders like a good saddle blanket. The trouser cuffs broke at the insteps of my
boots and the low-cut vest hugged my ribs without con-
stricting them when I moved. This attention to movement
was remarkable on the part of this particular tailor, who
had an exclusive contract with Judge Blackthorne's court
to provide burial clothes for officers slain in the line of
duty. It was probably the first suit he'd made in years that
didn't fasten loosely up the back.

"What's your opinion?" I tugged at the hem of the coat
and adjusted the string tie. I could load a revolver in the
dark with my teeth but I couldn't tie a cravat straight to
preserve the Union.

"It's wrinkled in back. You should have hung it up as
soon as it arrived."

"The sleeves are too short. I told him not to show more
than an inch and a half of cuff."

"No, two inches is what they were showing the last time
I visited Saint Louis."

"I look like a crooked banker."

"The suit isn't *that* good."

"Aside from all that."

"Do you need a compliment that badly?"

"I need truth. If I were going out after someone for the
first time I'd ask someone who knew about it if I had
everything I needed. I never ran a saloon before."

She was sitting up in bed with the counterpane tucked
under her arms, resting a hand with a cheroot smoldering

between two fingers on one raised knee. With her black hair undone she looked younger, girlish. "Not bad for an aging mankiller," she said.

"I mean the suit."

A pillow whipped past my head and flattened against the door, coughing feathers out a burst seam. "Clear out while I get dressed."

"I'll wait for you outside."

"Why?"

"You won't let me wait inside."

She took in smoke and didn't let any out. "This didn't signify anything. Breen's an empty spot along the U.P. right-of-way. So is everything that happened there. It's not even history."

"I didn't hear myself proposing."

"That's just as well. Whatever you think of me, I only marry one man at a time." She threw the cheroot at the basin and slid out of bed, stark naked. "Make sure the latch catches."

Junior was behind the bar in his shirtsleeves when we entered the Princess a few minutes later. He looked at us and said, "Well, I'm glad there's one man in town doesn't depend on the Mare's Nest for his entertainment."

# CHAPTER 13

I don't know why even now, but somehow I knew Miguel Axtaca wouldn't be at Eille MacNutt's place that Friday night. Probably it was my lack of faith in my good fortune. I went there anyway, and stretched half a bottle of gin over three hours listening to MacNutt's mulatto pianist making a hash of Gilbert and Sullivan on an upright someone had salvaged from a wagon trail and buying the occasional drink for Clara California and Adabelle. The latter was easily the least resistible of the string, five feet and eighty-two pounds, most of it bust, in a tight shift with nothing but perfume between it and her, and short coppery hair that hugged her head like a bright helmet. If she was as frigid as Clara claimed, there was a thaw on that night; she accidentally brushed my arm with her breast at least a dozen times and insisted on cleaning up the debris by hand after she upended a dish of hard candies into my lap. She was either dedicated to her work or the clumsiest woman I'd seen in a long time.

The place was finished off with flocked wallpaper over plaster and complicated further with framed steelpoint engravings of nymphs and satyrs going about their traditional business in pastoral settings and embroidered pillows scattered among the skirted sofas and lamps with fringed shades. MacNutt made no appearance. The responsibility of greeting customers fell to a small, straight-backed woman in a plain gray dress buttoned to the throat and her hair in a bun who shielded her weak eyes behind rectangular spectacles with tinted lenses. I hadn't seen her before, but this was my first time inside the establishment during business hours, and when she introduced herself as Phyllis MacNutt I assumed she was the proprietor's sister, although it developed in conversation later that she was his wife. What she thought about her husband going riding with someone like Colleen Bower was well concealed behind those opaque shards of glass.

I got out of there around eleven with what was left of my virtue intact. I spent the next week letting my new suit grow acquainted with my angles and hollows while I dealt faro and spelled Irish Andy behind the bar and took Colleen upstairs twice. Neither the gold ring she wore nor the reason for my trip to Laramie came up again. Both times she was affectionate and eager, but with the exception of a good poker reader like Junior Harper anyone who saw us together downstairs would have thought we were no more than partners.

And he'd have been right. Whatever intangible thing that had existed between us in Breen was as gone as that town itself, torn up along with the timbers and siding when the economic balance shifted and transported farther down the line in the hands of strangers. Taking her to bed was like playing a friendly game of cards with someone you once had much in common with and don't anymore; then the cards were just an excuse, and now it was just the cards.

And September crept along in its sluggish way, growing golden everywhere but in that desert climate, where the days melded together without a seam and everything was the color of adobe and dried blood.

On the second Friday I reported to the Mare's Nest just as the last rusty streamer was spiraling down behind the Cristobals; and I knew as soon as I opened the door, before my eyes adjusted to the dim interior, that he was there. A pungent mix of old sweat—layers of it dried in separate sheets—and open-air wood-smoke abraded my nostrils. It was a stink I knew well and had worn often enough myself, the kind that accompanies men who haven't spent a day under a roof in weeks.

I spotted them over Phyllis MacNutt's shoulder, three men seated in kitchen chairs along the back wall facing the door and passing a bottle of mescal back and forth. Clara California was sitting on the floor near the one in the middle with her feet gathered under her, stroking her cheek with his left hand.

Three identical pairs of obsidian eyes observed my approach. "Miguel Axtaca?"

The question floated like a feather descending a mine shaft. Then the man on the left spoke. "Who is asking?"

I gave him my attention briefly. He was thick through the torso in a white peasant shirt and canvas trousers with an ammunition belt slung slantwise across his left shoulder. The man on the right was dressed the same, and the two looked enough alike to be brothers. Both had large brown faces scored all over, shaggy moustaches, and masses of black oily hair that they combed straight back with their fingers, the tracks of which showed as clearly as furrows in fresh loam. Their machetes leaned against the wall beside their chairs, thonged grips close to hand.

"Page Murdock." I was addressing the man in the center. "I'm part owner of the Apache Princess down the street."

He said nothing. There wasn't anything Spanish about him. He was lean for a Mexican in his middle years and his features resembled primitive architecture. A block of brow rested like a lintel on the thick post of his nose, his mouth slicing straight across underneath. He wore his black hair in bangs chopped off square above the eyes. The rest stopped just short of his shoulders, as coarse as broomstraw. His costume matched those of his companions except for the lack of a cartridge belt or any other indication that he carried a weapon of any kind. That was worrisome. I knew he had one, I just didn't know what it was or where he kept it. A man who arms himself in secret is a man who will come at you from behind.

And there was something else. I'd dismissed that claim of descendancy from Montezuma as an empty boast; now I wasn't so sure. I had always heard Aztecs were extinct, but once when Judge Blackthorne had kept me waiting in his chambers I saw a woodcut in one of his thumb-blurred books showing ancient Indians greeting the Conquistadores, and Miguel Axtaca was the closest thing to them I'd encountered. Indians in general are easy to read, but whatever thoughts were going on behind that crudely hewn face were as hidden as his weapon.

"We do our drinking here." Evidently the Mexican on the left was the spokesman for the group.

"I'm not here to drum up business. I have something to discuss with *Señor* Axtaca."

"No *señor*." This from the man himself, in a voice that grated from disuse. "Just Axtaca. Miguel to my friends. What do you wish to discuss?"

"It's private."

"Everything is private with you white men. Then you whisper it in the ears of your whores and it is known all over."

"It's about Ross Baronet."

"I have heard this name and so have these men. Speak if you will speak."

"It's really for your boss. I want to meet with him to discuss bringing Ross Baronet to justice."

"Mexico is a republic where all men are free. You may go there and see him. My permission is not necessary."

"That's not how it works," I said. "Not in your country, and not in mine. It's supposed to but it's not. Where and when can I meet with him?"

The man on the right spoke for the first time. His Spanish was too rapid for me to follow. Axtaca replied more slowly in a dialect I had never run across before. The conversation took place with neither of them taking their eyes off me. I felt like something on the auction block.

The foreman switched back to English. "We go from here tomorrow at first light. You may come or not. We will not wait."

"How far is it to the ranch?"

"You are on it now."

I wanted to pursue that one, but he exerted pressure on Clara California's hand and she rose from the floor and climbed onto his lap, and I decided the interview was over. I took my leave.

"Old Don Segundo's got a bug up his ass about San Sábado," Junior said when I joined him at the Princess, where he was drinking his nightly glass of hot water before retiring. "His great-great-granddaddy or somebody got five million acres from King Ferdinand for burning heretics or somesuch and no Mexican War is going to change his conviction that we're all of us squatting."

"Give a man a grant for all eternity and he will take it seriously every time," I said. "Does he do anything about it besides write angry letters to Santa Fe?"

"Fifteen years ago he got up his own army and led it into the field for Juárez. He had three horses shot out from under him at Santillo. They say he is still known down there as the White Lion. Then when the new president had the *cojones* to tax him he backed the Díaz revolution. That came close to busting him when it fell apart, but when Juárez died and Díaz came to power the old bastard found himself right welcome in Mexico City. They say he personally hung better than a hundred men for rustling his stock before he lost the use of his legs. Then he got surly."

"What happened to his legs?"

"Horse fell on him or something. I guess he learned you don't go around busting remudas past seventy, but I wouldn't count on it. He's a stubborn old cob. What makes him so interesting all of a sudden?"

"I ran into his foreman tonight at the Mare's Nest."

His forehead creased. "You talked to Miguel Axtaca?"

"If you can call it that. He is no conversationalist."

"He's a savage is what he is. He sacrifices goats and the reason he only sacrifices goats is Don Segundo was running out of vaqueros. Clara California's the only whore in MacNutt's string will go with him. She's as crazy as a duck that flies backwards. What would you have to talk about with Miguel Axtaca?"

"He's taking me to see the old man tomorrow at day-break."

He had started to raise his glass. Now he set it down. "You looking for cattle work? I can tell you now, I've had a bet with Colleen since the day you left to go talk to the sheriff that you wouldn't last six months in the saloon business, but I thought it was marshaling you'd go back to. I was sure you had your fill of leather on the hoof a long time ago."

"Colleen bet I'd stay with saloon work?"

"She couldn't pass up the odds. If you miss ranching so much, what's wrong with working for John Whiteside? He's American and the climate beats old Mexico."

"I wouldn't go back to the cattle trade for a Yankee dollar. I thought you knew me better than that."

"I know you good enough to know when you don't answer a question it means you don't like the question any better than I'm fixing to like the answer."

Irish Andy had stopped polishing glasses. I sat forward and lowered my voice. "I'm going after Ross Baronet. I figure the only man in the area who wants him more than I do is the old don. I'm hoping he'll help me outfit a posse."

He grasped my forearm suddenly. The tensile strength in Junior's fingers always came as a surprise to those who shook hands with him. "Page, he didn't get anything from the Princess. Two of his men dead is what he got. What are you out to prove?"

"You wouldn't understand it. It doesn't make any sense. I never stood still for a stickup all the time I rode for Blackthorne. The only difference is this time I'm riding for myself."

"Maybe you forgot he's Frank Baronet's brother. Apart from the fact he's our new partner, this is his county. You calculate he's going to just sit there on his fancy pillow while you ride Ross down?"

"I'm curious to see just what he does. He's on record as

having Ross dead and buried in Mexico. His constituents might fall to wondering what he stands to gain by protecting a corpse."

"You know what I think? I think he don't care what his constituents think. I think if it's you or his brother he'll pick his brother a hundred times out of a hundred, dead or alive. You're my friend and I'll miss you, but this don't figure to stop with you. This here is the first chance I've had since my old man died to show I pump Harper blood. I'm not about to lose it on account of you can't remember you handed in your papers. Don't do this thing, Page."

"It might not pan out. If it does, Marshal Ortiz has agreed to head up the posse. It's every citizen's duty to help out when the peace is broken."

"Ortiz couldn't head up an expedition to locate his fat ass. Baronet's going to know who's in charge."

"I'm not asking your permission, Junior. I'm just letting you know what's in the wind so you'll be prepared. If the sheriff comes around looking for answers, tell him you don't know where I've gone."

"I kind of hoped my last words would have a better ring."

"He's not going to hurt you or the Princess. He's not going to do anything that will jeopardize his investment."

"That's what you had in mind when you brought him up, isn't it?" he said. "You had this worked out even before Ross hit the place. What's your game, Page? It sure isn't poker."

"I'll tell you what it is."

Colleen Bower had closed her faro game and seen off her last customer. Now she swung a chair out from the table next to ours and sat down. She had a black choker around her throat with a green stone that drew the eye down the front of her dress and away from the cards. The pupils of her eyes glittered as large and bright as dimes—

the application of belladonna without causing instant death is an art—and her hair was arranged in sausage curls the way it was the first time we met, two summers and a thousand years ago. Irish Andy was there immediately with the cup of tea she favored when her work was done. The big squarehead had a crush on her the size of Düsseldorf.

When he had withdrawn she said, "Being the law, that's Mr. Murdock's game."

"I admit I have a turn for it," I said. "I thought I could quit cold, but maybe I can taper off. There's always a call for men to ride posse."

"I don't mean it's in your blood. I mean it's your game. The same game you've been playing since before we met. You're still playing it."

"Get it out of your craw, Colleen," Junior said. "I'd have been married before this if I could just find a woman who says what she means the first time."

"I mean the reason Murdock can't stop being a marshal is he never stopped." She opened her reticule, removed a travel-worn fold of familiar-looking yellow paper, and spread it out on the table. YOU LEFT YOUR WALKING STICK IN HELENA, it read. "Next time you leave a woman alone in your room with all your things, think about emptying your pockets first."

# CHAPTER 14

"Walking stick?" Junior looked lost.

"Blackthorne," said Colleen. "You men are always playing games with codes and symbols, as if no one could see through them with half an eye. That telegram was sent the same day you wired us you were on your way to Laramie to look at a piano. That piano wears black robes and swings a gavel. It makes sense. It never did that you left Judge Blackthorne. The only way it does is you never left him to begin with. If this were wartime, you'd be hanged for a spy. I'm not so sure you still won't be. I'm just wondering who is going to be standing in line behind you on the scaffold."

I said, "That's a good deal to draw from an old piece of paper."

Quick as thought she drew the pocket Remington from the holster inside her reticule, cocking it in the same motion. I could see grains of dust inside the barrel. Not many; she took as good care of her weapon as she did her clothes and her cards and herself. "Junior, if I shoot him and testify he was pressing his attentions upon me, will you side me at the inquest?"

I said, "You're forgetting Irish Andy."

"Andy would side me if I shot Bismarck."

That was true enough. With the shotgun I had used on Dutch Tim well inside his reach the big German was standing with both hands on the bar and that cow-eyed look you saw on young girls gazing at a rotogravure of Edwin Booth. Not much help there. The Deane-Adams was just as inaccessible with a two-inch-thick tabletop between it and my hands. Jack Rimfire could retire on such a fix. Move over, *Satan's Sixgun*. Make room for *The She-Devil of San Sábado*. The cover would feature Sylvia Starr in form-fitting buckskins with a Colt in each comely hand.

"Junior?" I said.

"Is it true, Page?"

That startled me. His narrow face looked young, the lower lip pushed out slightly and his eyes as big as poker chips. I didn't open my mouth. I didn't have any words for it.

"We go back some," he said. "I shot a Nez Percé off his

pony with a long gun when he was coming at you with a
war club, and you up to your hips in river mud with a calf
in your arms and your back turned to boot. You done as
good for me a couple of times. I didn't ask you down here
to partner me because I needed your gun. I done it because
we're friends. Anyway that's what I thought."

"We're still friends."

He shook his head. "I don't know what we are, but
friends sure ain't it. I don't know who you're after or
why and I don't care. I hope you get him and it's worth
it." He pushed back his chair and stood. "Shoot out a
lamp if you don't want to put that pistol up cold. If you
was going to shoot him you'd of done it before this." He
went out.

"He's got a point." I held out a hand.

This time Colleen shook her head. "Firearms cost
money. You lawmen are always taking them off people and
never giving them back. It's no wonder there are coming
to be so many of you out here. You can eat for the rest of
your life on what you make off the resale." She seated the
hammer and returned the revolver to her purse. "I shot a
police officer in the lip in El Paso. I might as well have
finished him for all the yell they put up about it. I've got
a policy against running foul of the law twice in one season or you'd be colder than my tea."

"Why the lip?"

"I was aiming between his eyes but the floor was slanted.
What kind of errand are you running for Blackthorne?"

"We haven't established I'm running any kind of errand."

"I know it's not me. I haven't shot any federals lately.
A stray card or two isn't worth your train fare. Anyway
you didn't know I was going to hook up with the Princess.
*I* didn't know until I messed up that policeman's lip." She
pushed her tea away untasted. "It's Baronet you're after,

isn't it? Frank, not Ross. Bad lawmen always did upset your appetite."

We were speaking too low to be heard from the bar, but I leaned back in my chair and told Irish Andy to go home. I said I'd clean up. He took off his apron, got his mackinaw from the back room, said goodnight—more for Colleen's benefit than mine—and went out.

"That wasn't necessary," Colleen said. "You can trust Andy not to carry stories. Not because he's loyal. He just doesn't care."

"That's why I don't trust him." I got up and went behind the bar. Under the top, covered by a mouse-chewed feedbag, was the bottle of sour mash whiskey that Andy ordered special from the distributor every month and kept hidden. I filled two glasses and brought them to the table. When I sat down we touched rims and drank. "When Judge Blackthorne took over in Helena he found a man sitting in the city jail waiting to hang for killing a Wells Fargo express agent during a robbery. The man claimed it was his partner who shot the expressman, but he was the only one caught. After interviewing witnesses, Blackthorne wrote to the president, got him to authorize a new trial, and acquitted the man for lack of evidence. The man's name was Cocker Flynn. You never saw it in a newspaper or a dime novel, but he was the first deputy marshal appointed by Judge Blackthorne and he was the best peace officer I ever knew. Everything I know about the work I either learned from him or didn't and went and found out later he was right."

"I assume this story has a point." Her face was unreadable, her success at cards being in no way dependent upon the natural distractions of her person.

"Just that the Judge didn't much care if an outlaw turned lawman, or for that matter a lawman turned outlaw, unless he had something to gain or lose from it. My standards are no different. In any case the situation in Socorro County, New Mexico Territory is of no concern to the federal court in Montana."

"If your aim is to convince me that saloonkeeping is your only interest in San Sábado, you went the long way around the barn for nothing."

"I didn't say that."

She turned her palms to the ceiling. "Call."

I told her then, starting with Harlan Blackthorne's intestines lying on the ground at Monterey and finishing with his vow to avenge the murders of Sergeant Uriah Spooner's son and daughter-in-law by the Baronets. I didn't tell it as well as the Judge, but then he was the kind of man you didn't interrupt, and I had to talk fast to get it in between questions from the other side of the table. When I'd finished, and didn't need it anymore, she gave me silence.

"It doesn't signify," she said finally. "For it to do that, I would have to credit the Iron Jurist with humanity. Everything I've ever heard about him says he pounds that gavel to circulate his blood in place of a heart."

"I'd never play cards with the Judge. But I believe him in this case. No other explanation covers it."

"I hope my taxes are not financing this personal vendetta."

"You never paid a tax in your life."

She took another drink and rolled it around, appreciating it. Most of the stock we sold was best rustled past the tongue like doubtful cattle across a border. "What are you going to do about the Apache Princess?"

"I've been thinking about it. If I apprehend Ross Baronet I'll no longer require it as a cover. Junior offered to buy me out the day I came. I'll sign over my end and you can reimburse me later, possibly out of Frank's end."

"I cannot believe you think that transaction will go through."

"Why not? There's profit all around. Frank knows a good deal when he sees it and you and Junior might as well have the use of his money for as long as he's at large. Gold itself isn't wicked, only its source."

"When were you going to tell Junior and me about this plan?"

"When Frank and Ross Baronet were standing side by side on the scaffold in Helena."

"The conundrum to me is whether marshaling made you the bastard you are or you took to marshaling because you were born a bastard." There was less heat in this than the words implied; yet there was heat. She finished her whiskey, picked up her purse, and rose. Looking down at me: "You didn't say what happened to the man Flynn."

"A fugitive shot him last year. He died while I was talking to him."

She considered it. "Was that better than the rope? I'm curious about your answer."

"It was later, anyway."

"Serves me right for asking." She started toward the door.

"Where are you headed?"

"*Señora* Castillo's. It's late."

I reached for my hat. "I'll see you get there."

"I have the Remington for that. Your day tomorrow starts early, or have you forgotten?"

I let her go. There's no worse company than an angry woman, unless it's one who is right.

A bluish glow, the kind that edges sharpened steel, limned the broken peaks beyond the Jornada del Muerto when I led the claybank from the livery to the Mare's Nest, where Miguel Axtaca's vaquero companions were slouched against the hitching rail, passing a cheroot back and forth.

In the saffron light of the lamp that had been burning

in the front window for as long as I had been associated with the city, they looked even larger than they had the night before, their shadows stretching nearly as far as the boardwalk on the opposite side of the street. I couldn't believe they were just cowboys. They had on last night's clothes—I wouldn't have given odds that they had ever had them off—with the addition of burlap serapes and dull brown sombreros that from the looks of them had held many a horse's fill of water. Their stovepipe boots were caked with dust and from crown to heel the two men were the same dun color with nary an inch of exposed metal to catch the light. Even an Apache would have been hard put to spot them at any distance in the desert. A trio of well-fed sorrels were hitched nearby, loaded down with gear, including water bags and Mexican Winchesters on two of them and the ubiquitous machetes, slung from the saddle rings in special scabbards. The animals all bore the same brand, an inverted *V* inside a square tipped up on one corner.

"*Cuerno Diamante,*" said the more garrulous of the pair when I asked about it. "Diamond Horn. It is the sign of Don Segundo as it was of his father and his father's father, the crest of the Guerrero family, a gift from King Philip at the time of the great Armada."

"The Armada sank, I heard."

For answer he drew deeply on the cheroot and handed it to his partner. They were a sharing party. I swear that after one inhaled the other blew smoke.

Presently Axtaca emerged from the building, carrying what looked like a bundle of sticks eighteen inches long bound in a rawhide wrap with symbols painted on it. He too had thrown a serape on over his peasant dress, but it was more elaborate than those of his fellows, embroidered with a fine design in dusky red that would nonetheless be invisible beyond a hundred yards. He wore no hat, only a plain bandanna around his head. Seeing him upright for the first time I realized he was no taller than I, long of waist but short in the legs and bowed unheroically at the knees, and I might have been reminded of an orangutan I'd seen in a medicine show in Helena but for the overall dignity of his bearing. Without a word or a glance in my direction he tied the bundle across the throat of the saddle belonging to the nearest of the three sorrels, the one that carried neither machete nor rifle, untied the reins, and stepped into leather. The less talkative of the two vaqueros threw away the cheroot and the pair followed his lead.

Straddling the claybank, I thought I recognized the bundle as a distant relative of the medicine bags carried by some of the northern tribes. It was a talisman against mishap and, so far as I could determine, the closest thing to a weapon that Don Segundo's foreman carried on his person. In that rough country he was either the bravest man I'd yet encountered, or the most arrogant.

## CHAPTER 15

It was September everywhere in America except along the Journey of Death. From the time the molten-copper sun cleared the San Andres, the air grew warmer by the minute. The tiny fiery blossoms that opened to drink the condensed moisture by dark and blazed in the early bright curled in on themselves under the mounting heat and vanished like the stain of breath on glass. My coat and my companions' serapes came off early and went behind our saddles. Within minutes I felt the first pricking drops of sweat where my hat met my forehead. You don't wipe away the first sweat of the day in the desert; you let it cover you in a transparent sheet like thin varnish. Another day, another layer, curing your hide in the salt of your own system until it was as scaly as a lizard's back. You can build a house from the human bones you will find bleaching in the desert, but you won't see a gila monster's skeleton.

I was traveling with a silent crew. The most open of the three would have been considered laconic in any company I had ridden with, and some of those would have made a monastery sound like Independence Day. He at least answered questions, although the pauses before his responses were long enough for me to forget what I had asked. The others were as stony as the buttes that appeared and began to multiply as we moved farther south, and he was too polite to reply to a comment not addressed to him directly. His name was Francisco. He took pains to point out that it was not to be shortened to Pancho, Saint Francis having some specific importance to his family whose nature I wasn't able to draw out of him. As I'd suspected, the other vaquero was his brother, younger by ten months, called Carlos. The surname was a mix of Spanish and Indian I could neither pronounce nor remember. They had come to work for Don Segundo when the counterrevolution against Juárez failed, having fought for it with machetes, loyalty, and little else in some backwater of Mexico's remotest province so wild it appeared as only a blank on the best maps. Miguel Axtaca had accompanied them, or rather they him, and it was clear from the outset that their pledge was to him and that he held a position in their regard somewhere between *El Cristo* and the old gods. They would no sooner depart from his course than two drops of water would leave the Bravo to start their own river.

By midday I had begun to think fondly of the winter I had spent in a dugout in the Rockies trapped under twenty feet of snow, wondering if I would have enough toes left to walk out when the thaw came. The sun was a white coin nailed to a naked sky, and when the hot wind gusted I felt the glue that held my joints together drying out and cracking. Even the claybank hung its vain head. I stopped twice to give it water from my cupped hand and to take some for myself, but the others kept riding without touching their water bags. I'd heard tales of Apaches and their mounts subsisting on sun and dust and nothing else and had charged them to the same kind of frontier storytelling that had grangers in windy Wyoming feeding their chickens buckshot to keep them from blowing away, but here were three men who could outparch any of those mythical Indians. I hadn't felt this far out of my class since the day I tracked a white scalphunter into a railroad owners' banquet in Denver.

When night came we camped south of Las Cruces, where the others watered at last, built a small fire for warmth, and handed around twists of jerked beef. They didn't offer me any and I didn't ask. From the outset it was clear I was just someone who happened to be going in the same direction they were, and if I expired for lack of provisions or water, the occurrence had no more to do with them than the czar's assassination. I opened a tin, ate sardines, drank the juice, and wished for coffee.

The next day was more of the same, with the addition of a few new flat spots on my body thanks to a night spent on the hard earth. If I was adjusting to the heat, that heat was yesterday's; we were nearing the border now and the oven of Chihuahua. Already the scenery looked alien, dotted with plants and bushes I had no name for and corrugated like a brown ocean frozen in mid-roll. And I felt something undefined, an inner caution born of being foreign and alone.

I noticed a change in my companions as well, but in the opposite direction. As we continued south, some of the tension seemed to go out of their posture and they began to look around, not so much in the way of a small party expecting trouble as of travelers noting the changes and samenesses in country they called home. Now they talked among themselves in that boundary mix of Spanish, English, and Indian, and once one of them laughed, a deep open male guffaw that said as clearly as if I understood the language that some mention had been made of a woman. I knew then, from my position not only outside their circle but outside the great vast space that their circle now encompassed, something of how these three men and all their kind felt when they crossed the border heading north.

Somewhere during that trip—I think it was the third day, shortly after we broke camp at the base of a dead volcano still steeped in the stench of sulfur—I turned over another year. I wondered how many other forty-year-old men were still traversing unknown territory on horses that hated them in the company of men who would never be their friends. It seemed that by the halfway point a fellow should have more to his name than he can carry away in two hands.

That afternoon we struck Indian.

There had been signs, although no more than one would expect of a people who drifted along the ground like chaff, leaving little behind to prove they existed: a thread of smoke scratching a faded exclamation point against naked sky, a wrinkle of movement atop a distant butte. It was a big country but not as empty as it looked, and they had been there long enough to know when something as unnatural as Man interrupted the pattern of its days. Tiny fleeting impressions of activity, and then they were there, fifteen of them strung out in a ragged line across an open space without sufficient cover nearby to conceal a moccasin. It was a trick I'd have given much to learn, but I suspected it wasn't something that can be taught, only known.

Of course they were Apaches, as ugly and toadlike as the terrain they ruled. Naked but for breechclouts, they sat hollow-hipped pintos and carried Springfield rifles with the barrels upright, some of them trailing feathers from the ends. It was a lot of firepower in one place for a tribe with nothing worth trading. This was no ordinary raiding party, I decided, but an escort of some kind. As unobtrusively as possible I reached behind my saddle and loosened the Winchester in its scabbard.

There was no movement on their side except for their mounts' nervous heads and the wind stirring their hair, unfettered and without decoration. A mile above them an eagle—I hoped superstitiously it wasn't a vulture—hung suspended from its broad wings, painted there. The three Mexicans conferred. Then Miguel Axtaca kneed his sorrel forward. In one hand he held his reins high while he lifted the other with the palm out to show he had no weapon. He'd advanced ten feet when one of the Springfields spoke.

The barrel came down, the butt went up to the Indian's shoulder, white smoke puffed from the muzzle and slid sideways with the wind. Something tugged at the dry earth several yards in front of Axtaca's horse. He drew rein, Francisco and Carlos hoisted their carbines and worked the levers. Six or seven days later the sound of the shot reached us, a hollow *plop* like a frog jumping into a pond. Axtaca dropped his hand and pushed the palm back, stopping the others from returning fire. It had been a warning shot.

At the end of another week the Apache mounted at the center of the line raised one hand and made a sign. After a moment Axtaca responded. Then—it had to be for my benefit—he spoke his first words of English since the night we had met in the Mare's Nest.

"He wants all of us to come."

A pause. The vaqueros lowered their Winchesters.

Once, in Dakota Territory, I'd ridden ninety miles with a Cheyenne arrowhead between my shoulder blades to Yankton and the nearest doctor. The arrowhead was poisoned with toad spume and human manure and I lay for three weeks in delirium. From start to finish the experience wasn't as long as the half-mile we crossed that afternoon. The Apaches made no move to shorten the distance, remaining as impassive as foothills.

When we were about fifty feet apart the Indian in the center barked. A linguist might have made something of the guttural syllable, but it was the closest approximation to the sound a big dog makes when its hackles are standing as I had ever heard from a fellow human. Its meaning was clear enough and we stopped.

During the conversation that ensued, carried on entirely between Miguel Axtaca and the Apache who seemed to be in charge in a language completely unrelated to the one the Aztec had been using for days, I had plenty of opportunity to study the other side. They were all males and mostly young, one or two barely old enough to have passed whatever test for manhood that tribe observed, and in general they were lean almost to the point of emaciation, their rib cages standing out like umbrella staves beneath burnished flesh. Here was a predatory people, half-starved like wolves and therefore dangerous. Many were scarred—one in fact had come close to having his head split open from the way the new hair stood out like quills from a crescent of fresh pink skin on the right side of his head, as wide as the spread fingers of a man's hand. Despite their alien features, the broad flat faces, slit eyes, sharp noses, and mouths like razor cuts, there was about them that grim weary faithless air of the veteran killer that I had breathed in more places than I could count, from Shiloh to Adobe Walls to the massacre at Sand Creek. It observes neither race nor creed and jumps all the barriers between.

All of this and a good deal more was present in their leader. He was easily the oldest of the band, nearly three times the age of its youngest member, with iron gray in his relatively short hair and deep creases crosshatching every square inch of his face. His eyes, small and close-set, smoldered steadily in the deep shadows of his brow like embers in a cave. There was no decency in them, nothing that passed for mercy, no capacity for any emotion but hate. Somewhere I have a photograph that was taken of him much later at Fort Sill, and after forty years the raw hostility in those eyes has not lessened; it spans the decades like a scar on the land. At the time I had barely heard his name, but its four syllables have come to sum up my experiences in the Great Southwest of 1881 in a way that no whole book or paragraph could.

At one point during the conversation, the Apache gestured toward the medicine bag tied across the pommel of Axtaca's saddle. Don Segundo's foreman touched it with the ends of his thick fingers and said something in a tone softer than any I had heard him use previously. On the other side, the harsh flame in the eyes belonging to the granite head altered, then became pitiless once again. The head nodded slightly. More talk followed, punctuated by hand signs on both sides. At length the line of Indians turned, collapsing upon itself like a cotton clothesline, and moved off toward the east. Not one of the riders looked back.

"What did he say to them?" I asked Francisco. I was sure some trick was involved. The Apaches knew no prayer but Death to the Enemy, and they had no enemy they despised worse than Mexicans. Since 1840 the State of Chihuahua had issued a bounty of one hundred dollars for each male Apache scalp and fifty for each female.

Francisco rearranged his thick shoulders. "I do not speak Apache."

Axtaca turned in his saddle and fixed his obsidian gaze on me. He had neither looked at me nor acknowledged my existence since San Sábado. In that desert glare his face looked like something shaped by erosion.

"I lived with the Chiricahua Apaches from the time I was six until I turned fourteen," he said. "I am the only man not a Chiricahua who is allowed to display their symbol upon my traps. I know the secret name of God. Geronimo is a Chiricahua. All these things I told him and he wished me good medicine on my journey."

"That was Geronimo?"

"It is the name by which the Mexicans and the Americans know him. I addressed him by his warrior name, which your *norteamericano* tongue could never manage." He pitied me that.

"I thought he'd be taller," I said.

# CHAPTER 16

With two hours of light remaining we passed a longhorn skull polished white and set on a flat piece of shale. The Diamond Horn brand had been burned into its forehead above letters in faded red paint reading PROHIBIDA LA ENTRADA. It was the only indication that we had entered the region acknowledged by two governments to belong to Don Segundo del Guerrero, the White Lion of Chihuahua. Here and there across that rocky plain, knots of surly beeves stood around munching the short tough grass that did nothing to fill out their hollow hips and exposed ribs.

Another hour went by before we came within sight of ranch headquarters, an adobe oblong with a thatched roof and the long veranda unique to the Spanish gentry, as if shade itself were the special property of the wealthy. But for that it might have been any one of a thousand such structures you saw down there and scarcely noted. Whatever pretensions the old man might have inherited from his noble ancestors had apparently been leeched from him by the dirty stuff of revolution.

We dismounted before the porch and tied up at the rail. My legs felt as stiff as uncured leather. One of those yellow dogs of indeterminate breed that proliferate in that country lifted its chin from its paws on an ancient glider, growled, and went back to sleep. Its coat was tattered with mange and glittered with flies.

The front door was opened by a bell-shaped woman in a print blouse and a dark skirt whose hem swept the floor. Her gray hair was caught with combs behind her head, tight enough to pull the creases out of her face, which held no expression. I assumed she was the housekeeper, but at sight of her the two vaqueros removed their hats and Miguel Axtaca addressed her as *Señora* Guerrero. On further study I realized too that she was a good deal younger than she at first appeared. That raw land was full of women whose youth had been burned away by the struggle to survive both the climate and the force of their men's character.

After a brief exchange in Spanish, and with barely a glance at me, she stood aside and we entered. Francisco and Carlos paused to cross themselves before an impressive carved wooden crucifix mounted on the wall opposite the door, but Axtaca went on through the shallow room and out the open door on the other side.

It was a pleasant room, running nearly the length of the house and elegantly furnished in contrast to the building's exterior. There were bright rugs on the oiled floor, tasteful religious paintings in ornate frames, camelback sofas upholstered in wine-colored velvet, and silver everywhere, twinkling in the late-afternoon light sliding through the small curtained windows. The place was well ventilated and noticeably cooler than the veranda. That was its chief luxury and the thing that spoke loudest of the old don's position in the community.

Outside, a shot rang out.

The vaqueros and I caught up with the foreman on a back porch as long as the one in front just as another report sounded. There, a very old man in a wicker wheelchair with a Hopi rug spread across his lap sat at a long bench facing the open plain. In spite of the heat he had on a heavy brick-colored sweater with a shawl collar and all its buttons fastened and a straw hat that had seen all its best years, sunlight dappling his face through gaping holes in the broad floppy brim. His hair was white, startlingly so against the deep brown of his skin, curling over his collar, and he wore the spade-shaped Castilian beard and a pair of those elaborate moustaches that required suspension in a special hammock when their owners slept; trimmed, waxed, and coiled at the ends. His long hands were spotted and clawlike, but the fingers were dextrous as he laid a rifle with a long brass barrel on the bench and accepted another from the man standing at his side. There were eight rifles lined up on the bench, including three Hawkens, a Sharps, a pair of large-bore Remingtons, a Springfield, and a foreign make I couldn't identify. They were all single-shot and long-range. Sharpshooter's guns.

The ungainly hands, shriveled and plainly rheumatic, came alive when they gripped a rifle—in this case the Springfield—drew back the breech to inspect the load, and slammed it home. Resting his elbows on the bench, he socketed the buttstock in the hollow of his right shoulder and sighted down the barrel with both eyes open. The rifle pulsed when he squeezed the trigger, but his grip remained as steady as a sunken post. He said, "Bah!" and laid the Springfield next to the gun with the brass barrel.

The man standing next to him lifted and proffered one of the Hawkens. This was a plain-faced Mexican nearly his age, but in full possession of his legs, dressed in sandals and the white cotton uniform of the peasantry. He had a fringe of white hair around a bald head and a pair of moustaches that had never known a hammock, drooping like tired wings to cover his mouth and chin. Houseboys come in all ages.

Don Segundo—the old man in the wheelchair could be no other—was raising the Hawken to firing position when Axtaca cleared his throat.

"*Sí*, Miguel." The don fired. I searched for his target but could detect nothing worth spending ammunition on as far as the Sierra Madres. I had been to Mexico before and had never seen anything to equal the price of an ounce of powder in the entire country; but that was just me. People as different as Cortéz, Louis Napoleon, and Montezuma the Great had chosen to gamble their fortunes on the place without taking me into their confidence.

An exchange of Spanish followed between rancher and foreman, too rapid for me to catch anything beyond an occasional reference to cattle, while the old man inspected the Hawken's hammer, working it back and forth. Apparently he was taken with the rifle. At length he laid it aside and sat back, fixing me from under the ruined straw brim with eyes as blue and clear as matched terrestrial globes. "*¿Y usted?*" It was less a question than a command.

"*No español, jefe.*" It was the only phrase I'd acquired that had any use for me.

"A grave error. In my eighty-one years I have spent a total of only six months in your country, and yet I took the trouble to learn the rudiments of the language."

His accent was heavy, but I suspected this was due not so much to ignorance as to lack of practice.

"My range is Montana Territory," I said. "I'm a good deal closer to Canada than I am to Mexico." I told him my name.

It meant nothing to him. "Are you a hunting man, *Señor* Murdock?"

"Elk, a little. And men."

"Man, bah! As quarry he is truly overrated. He lacks instinct. His senses are inferior to the armadillo's, who flees his own shadow. There is no sport in hunting men."

"I never did it for sport."

He didn't pursue it. "Lions are the thing. You begin by hunting them, and if you are not watchful you find that they are hunting you. I have been entreated by tenants of my ranch to bring to an end the marauding ways of a certain cat that lives above the Río Santa Maria. He is a *viejo*, an old one that eats people because it can no longer outrun antelope. You see by this my meaning when I say that man offers no challenge. I am to prevent it from making away with any more small children."

"That's rough country for a wheelchair."

"The chair is a poor enough substitute for a horse but more easily maneuvered inside a house. I shall of course be mounted. What my legs have forgotten my arms remember. *Quita las otras*, Jesús. I shall use the Hawken."

The old servant gathered the other rifles into his arms and carried them inside. Don Segundo picked up the Hawken, drew a bead on something in the distance, and snapped the hammer on the empty chamber. "Miguel informs me you are on a mission."

"One that may interest you. I want to arrest Ross Baronet and bring him to trial."

"And you have come to ask my permission?"

"For your help. In order to make it official I need the cooperation of the marshal of San Sábado, but he's reluctant. With the support of one such as you I think I can bring him around."

"Refresh an old man's memory, *Señor* Murdock. I have not been across the border in more than forty years. Who is the marshal of San Sábado at present?"

"A man named Rosario Ortiz."

He had been tracking something through the Hawken's sights, sliding the barrel along the horizon. Now he lowered it. "I know this name. What has he to do with the man Baronet? What, for that matter, has *La Ciudad de las Viudas* to do with him? The ambush in which my vaqueros were slain took place near Las Cruces."

"The crime I intend to charge him with is the attempted robbery of the Apache Princess, a saloon in San Sábado."

"How many were slain in this attempt?"

"Two. Both belonged to Baronet."

"I think I understand. *Dinero* takes precedence over eight Mexican lives."

"I didn't say that, sir. Once he's in custody he'll likely be charged with the assault on the pack train, if there's evidence to place him at the scene. My interest is the saloon robbery. I own a one-third interest in the Apache Princess."

The magnificent moustaches twitched. "This I *do* understand. A man protects what is his. Tell me this. What have I to gain from this transaction? I have access to a thousand men at arms. I hardly require the assistance of one gringo and a soft city lawman."

I threw the dice.

"If you thought he was hiding out anywhere in this country, you'd have run him down and strung him up by now, in which case you would have sent me on my way before this. That means he's up north, and you have too many ties with Mexico City to risk sending an armed force across the border and giving the United States Army an excuse to come down here and try out its new Napoleons in a war with Mexico. But with a duly appointed city marshal and a former United States deputy marshal—that's me—riding up front, the entire affair can be represented as a joint action involving two friendly nations equally concerned about the lawlessness along their frontiers. Instead of an invasion, it would be an act of diplomacy."

Miguel Axtaca and the two vaqueros were watching us both through all this. Francisco and Carlos were plainly confused, not so much by my blinding example of logic as by all this English. How much the Aztec was following I couldn't say. He was a stone idol.

"You are a lawyer, *Señor* Murdock?" Don Segundo asked after a long silence. His gnarled old hands were folded atop the long rifle resting across the arms of his wheelchair.

"I rode for the federal court up in Montana Territory for six years. I guess some of that speechifying was bound to rub off."

"You have stated your case well."

Again I waited. Jesús, the manservant, came out carrying a heavy brocaded rug and draped it across the old man's shoulders. The landscape beyond the porch was swimming in heat.

"I invite you to stay here tonight. Dolores is an ordinary cook, but I think you will enjoy her tortillas more than the camp food you have been eating. In the morning I shall tell you what I have decided."

Without waiting for a response, he returned the Hawken to the bench and nodded at Jesús, who turned and pushed him into the house. Axtaca and the vaqueros glanced at me—high praise, but then I had become one of the anointed—and followed.

As a cook, Dolores del Guerrero was Mexico's best-kept secret. Her tortillas were thin enough to read a newspaper through, yet strong enough to hoist a plateful of chili peppers without crumbling, and they melted on contact with the human tongue. The wine was blood-red and strong, poured by Jesús from a green bottle whose label bore the Diamond Horn crest. All the food was served by the woman. Axtaca, who on the trail would have outstarved a Spartan, filled his plate three times and drained the bottle into his glass when the rest of us had had enough. Francisco and Carlos were absent, probably sharing a table with the other vaqueros in the bunkhouse.

The foreman appeared to be a favorite with the woman of the hacienda, who seemed to know no English but was extremely vocal in her native tongue, addressing Axtaca softly but aiming sharp barbs at her husband, whose one small portion of food washed down with plain water was evidently a nightly habit and interpreted by *La Doña* as a comment upon her abilities in the kitchen. By contrast, his responses, if they were responses, sounded conciliatory, even meek. It was clear enough that while the White Lion of Chihuahua held full reign over an area of land larger than the Commonwealth of Massachusetts, the den belonged to his mate. I earned a shy approving smile from her direction by accepting a second helping gratefully.

Jesús gave up his quarters for a cot in the bunkhouse and I passed the night on a straw pallet under a heavy quilt—welcome in the cold of the desert at night—in a tiny room at the end of the house. It was just big enough to contain the pallet and a portable altar with a candle guttering before a miniature painting of the Virgin and Child, inestimably ancient, in a frame three times its size. Outside, coyotes yipped, mourning the loss of the moon. I went to sleep fast and didn't stir until I smelled breakfast cooking.

Someone knocked at the door while I was pulling on my boots. Jesús, looking none the worse for his night outside the house, entered at my invitation, inclined his head, and informed me in halting English that Don Segundo requested my presence in his bedroom.

"Thank you, Jesús. I am sorry to have come between you and Mary."

His eyes went to the icon and he crossed himself. "None can do that, *señor*." He bowed again and withdrew.

The room, two doors down from the one where I had slept, was not much larger and filled almost to the walls by a four-poster of ornate old carved mahogany with a brightly colored counterpane of native workmanship folded at the foot. The old man, attired in a plain linen nightshirt, sat propped against a number of embroidered pillows with a footed tray across his lap supporting a thick slice of corn bread and a pot of steaming coffee. He was pouring some of its contents into a yellow china cup when I entered. Without the hat, he displayed a fine head of creamy white hair brushed straight back behind his ears from a dark widow's peak. The ends of his moustaches continued to defy gravity, and I was more sure than ever that he wore some kind of device to support them while he slept.

"Breakfast is corn bread and hotcakes with honey," he said without greeting. "Jesús has a cousin in Sonora who keeps bees. I cannot abide it myself. Once you have eaten, Miguel will escort you as far as El Paso del Norte, where you may cross the bridge to the American side and ride the stagecoach from there to San Sábado. Miguel has a way with the Apaches. They will not harass you."

"You're turning me down?"

"Hear me out before you speak. I am sending you home to make your arrangements with Marshal Ortiz. On the twenty-second of this month you will go to Las Cruces and meet with my vaqueros under Miguel's command.

Together you will ride to the place where this dog Baronet is hidden."

"You talk as if you know where that is."

His disconcerting blue eyes nailed me over the rim of the cup.

"But of course. He is with his brother, the sheriff of Socorro County. I supposed everyone knew this."

# CHAPTER 17

I've done a fair amount of traveling in my time, very little of it under ideal conditions. I've frozen in the leaking holds of sailing clippers, sweltered by the fireboxes of tramp steamers, counted the joints in the rails between Dodge City and Abilene on the floor of a cattle car, lashed oxen through blizzards with a wagonload of stoves behind waiting to burst their moorings on the downgrade and crush me like a tick, and rubbed sores in my person on the backs of all manner of horses from racing thoroughbreds to a gunnysack full of bones and bad temper. In 1914 I even took a spin in a kitelike contraption built of sticks and canvas and held together with piano wire that lifted me above the Colorado Rockies and deposited me in a tangle of torn fabric and broken ribs in a place called Fair Play. You could say I've seen the elephant from all five sides. But even in my present extremity I'd choose any one of those methods of transportation over twelve hours in a Butterfield coach.

They called them Bozeman bone-breakers, and for once they weren't exaggerating. The leather straps upon which the body of the vehicle was suspended were designed for the comfort of the horses, not the passengers, and the four of us—a Creole lawyer from New Orleans named Dupont who smelled of trade whiskey and lavender, a grizzle-bearded Texas ferryman wearing a stiff new Stetson and linen duster over his only suit, an old woman named Newkirk in a sturdy dress and one of those cinderproof tie-down hats who claimed a daughter and son-in-law in Fort Sumner, and me—jounced and swayed and caromed off the mud wagon's ironwood frame all the way from El Paso to the City of Widows, sickening of the pervasive dust, one another, and above all our own company before we'd gone ten miles. When the ferryman learned Mrs. Newkirk was bound for the place where Billy the Kid was slain, he honored us with his firsthand account of the time the Kid stuck up a bank that was holding the mortgage of a destitute widow, gave the money to the widow so she could settle the mortgage, then stuck up the same banker again as he was leaving the widow's house with the money. The Bonney legend seemed to be taking a new turn, from efficient killer to crafty saint. If I hung around long enough I'd hear of him changing the Alamosa River to wine.

Approaching San Sábado, the coach slowed for a boot-jack and I spotted a familiar lumpy figure on hands and knees atop the unfinished roof of a frame building that hadn't existed when I left. I shouted to the driver to stop, hopped out without a word of farewell to my fellow passengers, and hobbled on pins and needles to the back to untie the claybank. The shotgun messenger threw down my saddle, bedroll, and Winchester, the driver snapped the reins, and the whole improbable waste of good firewood rattled off towing a plume of New Mexico topsoil. I hadn't been so glad to see the back of anything since the mustering-out camp in Maryland.

Rosario Ortiz, trapped out in his customary work kit of overalls, cavalry coat, and stained sombrero, sat back on his heels on the rooftree and spat a mouthful of nails into the palm of his hand.

"*Buenas tardes, Señor* Murdock! Shake the hand of my worthless eldest son Arturo, whom I despair of ever teaching a trade."

I accepted the strong grip of a black-haired youth of around sixteen who had been engaged in passing planks up to his father. Gaunt where the other was fleshy and more guarded in the face, Arturo nonetheless possessed the Ortiz eyes—large, dark, and all-absorbent—and the tonsorial bowl of a big family with plenty of hair to cut and not much time to observe the current modes from the East. I saw too a potent strain of rebellion, barely masked by the perfunctory politeness. I wondered if he was one of the pair who had burned down the schoolhouse.

"Not another saloon, I hope," I said to the marshal.

"Better than that, *señor.* Colonel Ripperton's harness shop has outgrown the second floor of the livery and he has secured a loan from the bank in Socorro City to build and stock a new store on this spot, where the cattle companies will see it first thing as they enter town. There will be rooms to let upstairs and space in back where the ladies may purchase hats and gingham. This is progress, yes?"

"I hope he plans on stocking plenty of black."

"A merchant can starve serving the widows. He is preparing for the ladies to come. Everyone is talking about the sheriff's investment in the Apache Princess. It is said that he can smell gold. There is talk of a hotel and a theater, and perhaps even the railroad will come to San Sábado someday. If all this comes to pass I shall have to hire an assistant. Arturo is less than no help at all, and his brothers and sisters are worse." He removed his sombrero and mopped his coatsleeve across his forehead. It must have been hot enough to fry bacon up on that roof.

"Anything new in town?"

"I do not know. I have not been there in five days." He pointed at a bedroll spread out on the floor of the half-finished building. "I think no one has been shot, or someone would have come out and told me."

"Ortiz, how did you ever come to be marshal?"

He clamped the nails between his teeth and spoke around them as he lined one up between thumb and forefinger at the end of a joist. "The old padre, he says, 'Rosario, you have served in the Army of Mexico, you can shoot a gun, yes?' I say yes, but it has been a long time. 'Rosario, at night the coyotes come down from the hills. They dig in the church garden looking for moles, drop their waste in the cemetery, and get in fights outside the door during Mass. I appoint you marshal so that you may shoot them. The city will pay you five silver dollars at the end of each week for keeping the peace and ten cents for each coyote you shoot inside San Sábado.' The carpentry business, it is not so good at this time I am speaking of. I say yes. This was five years ago. Now the old padre is in the cemetery and the coyotes no longer come down from the hills, but I still go to the back door of the church at the end of each week and there the new padre hands me a sack containing five dollars and counts the dead rats I have brought and gives me a dime for each one. The coyotes ate the rats, you see." He pounded the nail home with his hammer.

"Can you come down from that roof? My neck is stiff enough from the ride without having to look up at you while I talk."

"*Lo siento,* I cannot. I have but two hours of daylight in which to work. The colonel wants to move in Sunday."

"He'll have to wait. I've got marshaling business that has nothing to do with rats or coyotes."

He sighed a Mexican sigh, full of revolutions and piety,

and climbed down the ladder. On the ground he picked up an Arbuckle's sack and expectorated the nails into it, then handed it and the hammer to Arturo. He stood in front of me, waiting, with his feet splayed and his hands open at his sides. I tried to picture him as a soldier but couldn't. Well, the Army of the Potomac had succeeded in spite of the excess baggage in its ranks.

"I'm just back from old Mexico and the Diamond Horn Ranch," I said. "Don Segundo has agreed to provide men for the posse and will meet us in Las Cruces on the twenty-second."

"Why do you pursue this, *señor?*" He sounded like the despairing father. "This thing that happened at the saloon, out here it is like a flood or a high wind, a thing that no one can predict or control. You cannot chase the wind."

"I spent six years chasing it up in Montana. Your problem is you think because you can put on and take off that star the job's the same way. You don't stop just because the coyotes have returned to the hills. You have to follow them there and finish them off. Otherwise they'll just come back, and then they won't stop at digging up the garden and disrupting services."

"I think you forget you are in business with Ross Baronet's brother. What will happen to our new prosperity when he learns what you are about?"

"Which do you represent, the law or the chamber of commerce? You agreed to head up a posse once I had Guerrero's support."

He folded his arms across his chest. It was a large expanse and they barely reached.

"I have given my word. I require truth in return. It is a small enough request when a man of my family responsibilities offers his life. What is your difference with the Baronets? I reject the robbery attempt."

I nodded. I'd been expecting something of the sort.

"That's fair. Two years ago in Lincoln County, Ross gunned down a rancher named Spooner and his wife. Spooner's father saved the life of the man I work for at the time of the war with Mexico. The man I work for believes Frank was involved in the shooting, either as a participant or as the man who planned it. He wants to try them both in Helena and see them hang."

For a long time the Mexican said nothing. Then he unfolded his arms.

"This I understand. I know of Judge Blackthorne, and of his character, since long before he was Judge Blackthorne. You should have told me this at the beginning." He rummaged inside his pocket and hung the battered star on the front of his coat.

"What have you to offer besides that hunk of tin and your old cap-and-ball?" I asked.

"I shall go to see John Whiteside, with whom I am friendly. He too has reasons to see the soles of the feet of both Baronets. He and Don Segundo have been stealing each other's cattle for fifteen years, but I think this is a business in which they can set aside their quarrel. He will match the don in men and horses and guns."

"You'd better get started. We have less than a week."

He barked at Arturo, who picked up his father's toolbox in both hands. It was three feet long, made of solid maple, and filled to the handle with iron implements. Ortiz stepped up onto the floor of the building and bent to roll up his bedding. I joined him, curious about something he'd said.

"Where do you know Blackthorne from since before he became a judge?"

"I too fought in the war you mentioned, *señor*. I was a prisoner for a time. He was among the *norteamericanos* who held me."

A light dawned. "Cerro Gordo?"

"*Sí,* that is the place where I was captured." He tied the bedroll.

"He told me about a young Mexican lieutenant who killed three of his guards and escaped to resume fighting the next day. He said the man's name was Ortiz. I didn't think it could be you."

"We grow old and fat, *Señor* Murdock. We change. But on the outside only. The eagle does not die a swallow."

*Of course,* I thought. *And I am President Garfield.*

I rode the claybank into town, turned it over to the Yaquí at the livery for a rubdown and feeding, and carried my gear over to the Apache Princess and my room upstairs. I looked at the bed, wanting it down to my toes, but when you reach forty it's a sound idea to lubricate the aching joints if you expect them to work properly the next day. I went downstairs for a shot, but I never got it. Colleen Bower got up from her table when I entered and intercepted me on the way to the bar. The cowboy she'd been playing with scowled at me and counted his chips.

"Where have you been?" she asked. "I thought you'd gone back to Helena."

"I went south for *Señora* Guerrero's tortillas and a talk with Geronimo. You look like you're rigged for church." It was a sober dress for her, dark blue and buttoned at the throat. Her black hair was tied back and there were tiny fissures at the corners of her eyes where she'd missed with the powder.

"I expected you back before this. Junior's gone. I think he went to Socorro City to kill the sheriff."

I didn't credit it. "Why would he want to do a thing like that?"

"Right after you left he started drinking. It made him sick, but he'd go out back and throw it up and come back in and order another. I told Irish Andy to cut him off. Look what he did to him."

The bald German was polishing the bar, holding his head at an awkward angle to watch his progress. One eye was swollen almost shut and gone rainbow-colored.

"He's lucky. Junior's been known to break jaws when he's on a tear. That little frame of his fools you."

"He got it in his head somehow the sheriff had come between you. If he weren't around you'd forget about up-holding the law and take care of business here. It didn't make sense so I didn't pay much attention."

"That's when you have to pay attention to him most. But you couldn't know that. When did he leave?"

"Yesterday early. I wasn't up yet but the stable hand at the livery said he hired a buckskin. He had on a duster and he was carrying a Spencer rifle."

"I know the one." I'd traded it to him in '72 for a bay mare that splintered its right foreleg in a prairie dog hole the following spring.

"Where are you going?"

"To find Ortiz." This from the door.

"What good is a carpenter going to do you in this situation? Page?"

He was at the mercantile, shoveling food tins from the counter into a canvas sack while the clerk, a schoolmaster by trade and a dish-chested consumptive forced into commerce in the absence of a house of learning, totaled up the order in his ledger.

"I'm glad I caught you," I said to the marshal.

"There was no need for haste, *señor*. I cannot leave before morning. The days grow short."

"There's been a change in plans. I won't be meeting you and Don Segundo's men in Las Cruces. I'll be waiting for you in Socorro City." I told him about Junior.

He frowned, the ends of his tobacco-stained moustaches nearly meeting. "Frank Baronet is not a man to call out. It is more than just his badge that makes him sheriff. I hope that you and your friend did not exchange cross words before you parted. Surely he is dead. All that remains is for him to fall down."

"You haven't seen him use that Spencer. He's a good man with a rifle."

"Jubilo is better, and he is always within rifle range of his friend Baronet." He paid for his purchases—in silver dollars—and gathered up the sack. "You have not told me where I should look for you in Socorro City."

"I'll find you. It shouldn't be so hard with all that firepower you'll have along, with or without John Whiteside. When you see him, tell him he did a fine job with the claybank."

"I will do this."

I went back to the Princess, truly too tired now to sit up and drink. Instead I climbed the stairs to my room with no thought beyond sleep; concern for Junior, with dusk rolling in and my bones turning to lead, would serve neither of us. I felt as if I'd walked all the way from El Paso.

Someone knocked while I was climbing into bed. I pulled on my trousers, hooked the Deane-Adams out of its holster hanging on the bedpost, and took aim at the door from the far corner. "Who is it?"

"Colleen."

I took the revolver off cock and went over and opened the door. She was dressed as she had been earlier, but either she had done something about her makeup or the failing light canting in through the window had decided to be kind to her. She looked little more than school age.

"There's gray in your hair but not on your chest," was the first thing she said. "I've wondered about that."

"I use my brain a lot more than my heart. Is anything wrong?"

"No. Yes."

I closed the door behind her, returned the gun to its holster, and set fire to the lantern. Orange light spread.

"I didn't tell you everything today," she said. "Junior proposed to me."

"I'll be damned."

"It happened in the saloon the day you left. He caught me off guard. I didn't realize he felt anything toward me more than one partner to another."

"I'll be damned."

"He was drunk at the time. I didn't think he was serious. I laughed. I told him I was already married."

"Did you tell him who?"

"Yes." She licked her lips; something I had never seen her do. "That's when he started talking about killing Frank Baronet."

*I'll be damned.*


# CHAPTER 18


"**F**rank Baronet." It was as if I had never heard or said the name before. Like Billy the Kid he was something I had not known existed until recently and already he was filling my life.

She said nothing. There was murk in the blue depths of her eyes, as if something had stirred near the bottom, churning up silt. Just what it was, I had no hopes of ever understanding.

I felt my head nodding. I had the impression it had been doing so for some time. "I don't know why I didn't guess.

When I met you, you were the mistress of a dead city marshal. Then you started keeping company with me. You always did feather your nest by latching on to the local law."

"You were different," she said. "I'll never make you believe it but it's true. I don't apologize for the others. You don't know what it's like for a woman on the circuit. When you fall into a fix you can fight your way out of it and if the odds don't favor fighting you can jump into the saddle and ride hard. I cannot fight, and I cannot jump in these petticoats. I've been beaten and jailed and raped. That can happen to you only so many times before you realize you need the same edge in life you look for in cards."

"What became of your edge in El Paso?"

"There is too much law there and it is all split up." She changed the subject. "In Socorro City, where I set up last year, you either dealt faro at the Orient or you cut Frank Baronet in for fifty percent. I chose the Orient. It turned into something."

"It generally does, although not always marriage. How did that come about?"

"You wouldn't notice, but Frank is an attractive man, and wealthy. Jim Dolan has his eye on him for governor when statehood comes."

"Do you believe that?"

"I did then. I do now. That old fool Fremont did less for Garfield than Frank did for Dolan before Lew Wallace came, and now Fremont is territorial governor in Arizona. I was in a tight, Page. The Civic Betterment League ran me out of Leadville with nothing but the clothes on my back and a pearl necklace that got me as far as Santa Fe. I picked a pocket there and took another train. The pocket belonged to a Dolan man who wired my description to Frank. He was waiting for me when I got off in Socorro."

"Is that when he proposed?"

She was silent for a moment.

"I cannot talk to you," she said then. "I could in Breen. You've changed."

When she started to turn away I grasped her arm and pulled her into the room. She tried to pull free. I took her other arm and held on. The material of her dress touched my naked chest.

"So it was jail or a table at the Orient," I said. "Baronet is not a man to overlook a good draw. And he favors a corner, so he dangled a wedding ring. You liked his chances, and marriage to the biggest gun in the county comes in handy when those cowboys and miners forget what side of the table they're supposed to sit on. Then Wallace settled the war up north and Baronet's chances didn't look so good, so you left. You never were one to hang around when the glitter wore off a thing."

She tried to knee me in the crotch. I let go of her to make distance. She backed up a step, but she didn't leave. Instead she raised her hands to her head and spread her hair to the left of the part. There was another part there, jagged and white and freshly healed. It would be a long time before hair grew along it, if it ever did. She said:

"I don't even remember what the argument was about. He slapped me around, not for the first time, and then he drew that big rolling-block pistol and backhanded it. If I hadn't turned my head it would have split my face open from forehead to chin. He tried again, but I got hold of my bag and the pocket Remington. At first he was surprised. Then he laughed, called me a whore, and turned his back on me. His *back*. I shot him. He fell on his face. I guess I should have made sure he was dead, but I had blood in my eyes. I was afraid he'd cracked my skull.

"It happened in my room over the Orient," she went on. "It was Saturday night, the place was noisy. No one heard the shot. I went down the back stairs and bled all the way to the doctor's office, where I got my scalp sewn back together. I said I fell. Doc Sullivan was no idiot—he'd patched me up before after Frank and I had words—but he didn't say anything. He gave me something to make me sleep, but I poured it out when he wasn't looking. His wife gave me some old clothes to wear back to my room and they left me alone to change. I let myself out the window. I never stole a horse before, but I was sure I'd be hunted for a murderess. I caught up with the train in San Marcial and rode it to El Paso."

"He told me he hurt his back when a horse threw him."

"Would you expect him to say a woman shot him?"

"Why did you come back to New Mexico?"

"By the time Junior Harper came to town to buy fixtures for the Princess, I'd heard Frank had recovered, which meant I wasn't wanted since he'd never admit what happened. 'Unknown assailant,' the wire reports said. My run was going sour and I had just enough capital left to take Junior up on his offer to buy in. You could argue that I was just swimming back into the same net, but it was a net I knew. You don't always have choices. You almost never have choices."

"You didn't put up an argument when I suggested cutting the sheriff in on the Princess."

"His money spends just like anyone else's. And I was curious to know if getting shot by me had changed his outlook."

"Risky."

She moved a shoulder. "That's why they call it gambling."

"Not when you throw someone like Junior into the pot. Then it's called something else."

"We both did that, Page."

I said nothing, agreeing.

She turned her head slightly, reading me like a deck. "You love him, don't you?"

"We go back."

"Maybe he'll turn around when he sobers up."

"He never has."

"What are you going to do when you get to Socorro City?"

"What I should have done the first day I saw the place." I had turned and was thumbing cartridges out of a Union Metallic box into the empty loops on my gun belt. "Vote the sheriff out of office."

# CHAPTER 19

For a mile under the creeping crimson in the east, my route and Marshal Ortiz's were the same, and we rode together. He sat a well-fed gray with a brand I didn't recognize and his sack of provisions knotted unceremoniously to the horn of a Mexican cavalry saddle. The saddle's fenders had been trimmed and pared many times for leather to make repairs. A brass-framed Henry rifle hung from the ring.

If we hadn't been the only things stirring in town when we encountered each other in front of the livery, I wouldn't have known him. He'd traded his overalls for faded cavalry breeches with a stripe up the side and a knitted blue pullover of a type I hadn't seen since my last skirmish with the guerrillas in Missouri. The greasy somberero was gone, replaced by a slouch hat with all the nap worn off the brim in front where he gripped it to tug it down over his eyes, and on top of the cavalry coat he wore crossed bandoliers crammed with .44 cartridges with only their blunt lead noses showing so as not to catch the sun on the brass. The curved butt of a Schofield .44 fitted with black walnut grips showed above a plain holster worn in front like an Elizabethan codpiece. With his high-topped riding boots sporting long jingly Mexican spurs, he looked taller and fitter in the outfit than he had at any time previously, and more a part of the land; one with the snakes and scorpions and lean rangy beasts of prey that slunk among the shadows carved by the rocks in the desert.

"That rig hasn't been sitting in any trunk since Cerro Gordo," I said by way of greeting.

"I scouted for Colonel MacKenzie in 1874." He handed the sleepy stable boy a coin and took charge of the gray.

"You fought Quanah Parker?"

"He was just Quanah then. Parker came with the reservation."

I had been riding the line at the Harper Ranch with Junior when the news came of Ranald MacKenzie's defeat of the Comanche Nation in Palo Duro Canyon in 1874. It had brought a sudden end to more than thirty years of fighting in Texas. Nearly everyone involved in the engagement had been decorated for valor. On the road he made a coarse noise when I asked him about the battle.

"It was a slaughter of horses. I do not talk about it."

Where the road forked we drew rein. I told him again I'd see him near Socorro City and offered my hand. He hesitated, then took it.

"I hope *Señor* Harper is all right."

"Me too."

Once we parted I began paying special attention to the irregularities in the landscape, rock piles and buttes and thickets that held so much appeal for hostiles who didn't wish to be observed. By midday, however, the absence of Apaches had begun to become obvious, and when eight hours later I made camp I felt certain I was alone. Well, Geronimo and his band had been headed somewhere when Axtaca and the vaqueros and I encountered them below the border, and there were rumors that the Apaches were concentrating on Arizona. That placed them in General Crook's wheelhouse, which was good enough for me. There was a strong case to be made in favor of all the tribes but that one. If they were alone on the planet they'd have picked a fight with the moon.

On the ridge overlooking the county seat I paused to gaze down at the teeming sprawl at my feet. Hammering and sawing, the heartbeat and respiration of civilization birthing in the wilderness. While it was going on, life glowed. When it stopped, decay set in. Only sometimes the rot was present in the fresh lumber, growing unheeded during the construction, spreading to the healthy timbers and eating away at the joints and pegs, so that six months or even six weeks later the entire structure collapsed, taking lives with it. Often that rot was human. Sometimes it wore a badge.

I conferred with my dented pocket watch, the posthumous gift of a Confederate captain. Unless Frank Baronet had altered his routine, he would be dealing faro at the Orient about now, leaving Jubilo No-Last-Name in charge of the jail. It seemed a likely place to start.

The gate leading inside the board fence that enclosed the gallows and surrounding courtyard was latched as simply as possible, with a piece of lath secured by a nail. I'd been counting on that, breaking into jail not being as popular a practice as breaking out. On the other side, the scaffold threw a shadow that clasped the back of my neck like a clammy hand. The back door to the building was solid oak, set flush to the frame, and probably bolted and padlocked inside, but that wasn't how I was planning to get in so I ignored it. The single barred window on that side of the building, designed to allow light into the cells rather than to let the residents see outside, was nearly seven feet from the ground. I grasped the brick sill in both hands and chinned myself up.

No lamps burned inside and the sun was coming in at a flat angle. In the murky light I couldn't tell if any of the cots in the cells were occupied. I tried tapping on the thick glass.

"You won't find him in there."

I didn't turn my head at the sound of the voice behind me. I let go of the sill and spun when I landed, gripping the butt of the Deane-Adams.

I didn't take it out. The tunnel I was looking down belonged to Jubilo's Creedmoor. Its owner was standing at the other end with the butt against his shoulder and his finger on the trigger. The gallows rose gaunt and empty at his back.

"Well, toss it over."

I slid the five-shot out of its holster between thumb and forefinger and gave it a low flip so that it landed gently at his feet. He lowered the rifle but kept it balanced along his forearm as he crouched to pick up the revolver. He found the catch and thumbed the cylinder around, tipping the cartridges out onto the ground. His eyes remained on me. They were almond-shaped after his Indian ancestors. The face under the flat brim of the Stetson, with darts of black whisker at the corners of the wide mouth, was unreadable. He handled the long-barreled rifle in one hand as easily as a sidearm. So far I had never seen him make use of the Russian on his hip, and I decided it was an ornament of office.

"Always keep a live round under the hammer?" he asked.

"Empty chambers attract drafts. I catch cold easy."

"Shoot your dick off someday."

"That's what everyone says. But it's still there and I'm still here."

He tossed it back. I caught it. "I guess you know where the gate is."

The rifle was resting on his shoulder now. I blew dust out of the pistol's action, returned it to its holster, and preceded him into the alley. Behind me he paused to set the latch on the gate.

On the street we walked side by side to the end of the block. He carried the rifle with the muzzle angled down. He stopped in front of a new brick building, opened the door, and held it. The lettering on the plate glass show window read:

P. JOHNS & SON
UNDERTAKERS

It was a dark, heavy room, thickly carpeted and swaddled in wine-colored velvet and black oak. A mahogany casket with brass handles lay open on a padded dais with a bald-headed geezer propped up inside wearing a morning coat and a stiff collar. Another one, nearly as old and dressed similarly but more lively looking, with a rubber face and small bright eyes like shirt studs, bustled out of a back room at the sound of the entry bell, buttoning his vest. Jubilo pointed at the curtains the man had just come through and kept walking. I accompanied him.

The back room was nearly as large as the parlor but made no pretense at ornamentation. Large windows set near the ceiling allowed sunlight to pour in onto a bare plank floor strewn with packing material, a long oilcloth-covered workbench at the back, and sawhorses. Two of the sawhorses supported a plain pine box without a lid. The air was thick with ammonia and formaldehyde.

Jubilo hung behind while I stepped forward and looked down inside the box. The undertaker had done little more than wash his face. There was dust in the creases of his Prince Albert and fancy vest—he hadn't bothered to change clothes for the long ride—and a couple of stitches had been taken in the hole in the silk where the bullet had either gone in or come out, but nothing had been done about the bigger hole in his left sock where two of his long sharp-nailed toes stuck through. His dark hair was plastered back with water, accentuating the narrowness of his skull, the caverns in his cheeks, the long treadle jaw and the bulbous eyes, barely closed, resting like billiard balls in their sockets. Those eyes had never warmed the air with their moist glow. That face had never slid off-kilter to illuminate a room with its crooked grin. His skin had the gray translucence of paraffin.

"Two questions." My own voice sounded hollow, like someone else speaking in a room at the end of the house.

"Me," Jubilo said. "He was standing in the street in front of the Orient, waving a Spencer and calling the sheriff every kind of a son of a bitch. That made him a public menace. I shot him from a window on the second floor of the Chicago House. I couldn't wait for him to turn around. I guess that's the second question."

"Did Baronet even get up from his table?"

"Hell, he wasn't even in town. He's off collecting taxes. I hated to do it, if it means anything. I liked the little guy right off when we met in San Sábado. He didn't make no secret what he thought of Frank even when he was asking him for a loan."

I turned to face him. "How far out is Baronet's ranch?"

After a pause he showed his eyeteeth.

"Well, all he told me was to say he's out collecting taxes. He didn't say nothing about anyone guessing. Head straight east for a day. Keep Chupader Mesa square in front and you can't miss it. It's a thousand acres. I won't ask who told you about it."

"The White Lion of Chihuahua."

His face didn't change. "You do get around," he said.

"Might could be there is something to this Satan's Sixgun business after all."

"What happens now? Am I under arrest?"

"What for, trespassing on public property? Go back to the Widow City, Murdock. Socorro County will bury your friend."

"Tell the undertaker to put him in the icehouse. I'll be back for him."

"Don't go after him, amigo."

His tone made me turn back. "How many guns does Ross have?"

"Ross is dead."

"That train pulled out a long time ago, Jubilo."

"Habit." He moved his shoulders. "A dozen. More, maybe. They drift in and out. Not all as good as those two you killed in San Sábado, but good enough to side the Baronets is good enough for anyone, and they know the ground. But they are not Ross's guns. They answer to Frank. Always did. Ross never pulled up his britches but that Frank gave him leave."

"Don't read over me just yet. I should have been dead twenty years ago and a hundred times since. Others keep taking my place."

"I just hope it isn't me kills you," he said. "It wouldn't be the first time I done it to someone I liked. I can do without what comes after."

"Did you like the Spooners?"

Light dawned. Absently, he nodded. "That's what this is about. I wondered. What was Dave Spooner to you?"

"To me, nothing." I told him about Judge Blackthorne, Sergeant Uriah Spooner, and the siege of Monterrey. He nodded again.

"I was there when Dave and Vespa got it," he said. "I didn't pull the trigger. Ross done that. It was Frank sent us out there. A lot of Chisum's men looked up to Dave.

Frank thought if we killed both of them the rest would see Dolan meant business."

"Did they?"

"It never works that way. Dolan got mad as hell. He didn't order it or know about it until it was over and done with. He said if there was ever a chance of Wallace not bringing in the army and spoiling everything, that chance went into the ground with Dave and Vespa Spooner."

"You're telling me when you and Frank and Ross left Lincoln, it wasn't the army you were running from."

"You can always avoid an army. I don't think Jimmy Dolan shot a gun in his life, but if he ever come close to using one on anybody, it would of been Frank. I think the whole reason he got Frank elected sheriff here was to keep him out of Lincoln. I think he thought if he didn't and Frank came back, Dolan would of killed him sure as hell."

"Frank's living on borrowed time," I said.

"Not borrowed. Stole."

"What keeps you with him?"

"What keeps you with the Judge?"

"It's different."

"For you, maybe. Not me. When you're half greaser and half Comanche and you know one end of a rifle from the other, backing someone like Frank Baronet is as high as you can reach. It's one hell of a lot higher than if you didn't have the rifle."

"Where were you when Colleen shot him?"

"I don't follow him into bedrooms," he said. "She told you, I guess. In that case you can take her a message from Frank. Tell her he don't hold what she done against her. He wants her back."

"So he can finish beating her up?"

He blinked. "Did she tell you he done that? Frank never done that."

"Just in bedrooms, I guess."

"I've known Frank right around five years. Rode with him, camped with him, stood up with him when he hitched up with Colleen. He'd maybe kill a woman, but he never beat one up. Should of, some of the ones he run with. He never did. It's a failing."

"She showed me the scar."

"Her head, right?"

I said nothing.

"A Mexican whore done that. They called her Juanita Pistola on account of this old pepperbox she carried around to scare folks with. It wouldn't shoot. She tried splitting open Colleen's head with the barrel when she found out about the wedding. Frank shot her."

"Then why did Colleen shoot Frank?"

"Like I said, I don't follow him into bedrooms."

I exhaled. All my energy went out with the bad air. I felt bone weary.

"Ride south, Jubilo," I said. "Don't stop before old Mexico. There's an army coming you can't avoid."

"I figured out that much when you mentioned Don Segundo. I reckon I'll stick. I got more enemies down there than I do here, and there's nothing waiting for me up north but a rope. What the hell, I never was no good at making a choice anyway. Just where are you riding with this here army?"

I dug the nickel-plated star engraved DEPUTY U.S. MAR-SHAL out of my trouser pocket and pinned it to my shirt. Once again he nodded.

"Out front. I guessed that too," he said. "By the by, a wire come in this morning from Santa Fe. Garfield died last week."

"Sorry to hear it. I voted for him." I waited.

"Point is, if the office of president don't turn away bullets, how much protection do you think you'll get from that tin plate?"

# CHAPTER 20

The rifle report rang thin and insignificant in the vast night air. I caught the fading phosphorescence of the muzzle flash in a clump of cottonwoods to the north and stood in my stirrups, waving my Winchester over my head. A three-quarter moon washed the open plain in watery silver.

"I'll need a name," called a voice.

"Page Murdock. Ortiz knows me."

"Step down and come ahead. Keep your hands in sight."

He was small and young and well turned out for his work in a pinch hat, leather vest and chaps, and those torturous boots with pointed toes that bowed their legs and made them hobble around when not in the saddle. His rifle was an old Volcanic with scrollwork on the receiver and someone's initials carved into the stock in big childish capitals.

"Your father's?" I pointed at the rifle.

His lips were tight behind his puppy moustache. "Walk ahead."

The campfire smelled inviting after a week of cold prairie nights without a fire lest I attract the attention of Jubilo or one of Baronet's bandits. I had seen the dust of a large band of horses shortly before sundown and cut a course for the glow of the fire after dark.

"I figure you're with Whiteside," I said, walking. "You don't look like one of Don Segundo's vaqueros."

He grunted.

"Bad enough I got to ride with them without getting took for one."

I spotted Ortiz first, squatting by the campfire with a stick in his hand, drawing designs in the dirt between him and John Whiteside, also squatting on his heels. The marshal had on his slouch hat and cavalry clothes but had removed the bandoliers. The old rancher, built even slighter than his lookout but lean as a salt rind, wore his big sombrero and a sheepskin coat with the left sleeve hanging empty. His whiskers looked grayer in the firelight. Both men were intent on what the Mexican was doing with the stick.

"Chupader," Whiteside muttered. "I seen easier places to defend but not lately. I and forty men fit eleven Apaches there for a week back in '68. All it takes is one good man with a rifle."

"They've got that."

Both men turned their heads my way. Whiteside's blue eyes scarcely lingered on the badge I wore. "Took on weight, I see."

The young cowboy said, "He come riding up bold as Maggie's nipples, Colonel. Asked for the greaser marshal."

"I know him. Get back to your watch, Abbott," he said when the man started to turn.

"Yes, Colonel?"

"You might want to hold off on that greaser talk till we get back home. Half the men you're riding with are greasers and they might not all be as accommodating as Marshal Ortiz."

"I don't know why we're riding with them a-tall. I guess the men of the Slash W can handle one slippery sheriff without dragging along a bunch of pepper-guts."

"You were still on the tit the first time I crossed lead with pepperguts from the Diamond Horn. They put better men than you in the ground. If it was a case of one slippery sheriff I'd of done the job alone. Once you've put your first ball through something that can defend itself better than a colicky prairie hen, you can bellyache all you want. Till then, get back to your watch."

"Yes, Colonel." He left.

"Pup."

"He is young." Ortiz rose, dropping the stick, and pulled his sleeve down over his hand to scoop a two-gallon coffeepot off a flat rock by the fire. "When was the last time you thought you could fight bad *hombres* all the day and make love to bad *mujeres* until the dawn?"

"Cold Harbor. And if I'd had this new batch with me then there would still be slaves in Carolina. Pull up a piece of ground, Murdock. How you getting on with that claybank I sold you?"

"I haven't eaten him yet. He's tied up back there. I fed and watered him before I broke camp."

"I gelded that one myself. Hated to do it, but there was no help for it. Stallions have a way of catching some Apache filly's scent and blowing just when you're looking for quiet. I was pleased to see he kept his spirit."

The marshal handed me the tin cup he'd filled from the pot. He searched my face. "Have you seen *Señor* Harper?"

"I saw him. He didn't see me." I took the cup in both hands, warming them, and poured the hot bitter stuff down my throat. It brought a glow to my stomach like good whiskey.

"*Lo siento.* He was a good man."

"He was a jackass. I don't know how he lived as long as he did."

Brushing past me on the way back to his spot by the fire, he laid a hand on my shoulder briefly.

"You said they have a good man with a rifle," Whiteside said. "That would be Jubilo."

"I saw him snatch an Apache brave off his pony's back at four hundred yards. If the mesa's as good a perch as you say, he could take his time and pick us all off one by one like ticks."

"Not at night."

Miguel Axtaca had slid from the shadows outside the firelight, making no noise at all in a pair of soft Apache boots designed to pull up over the knees in cactus country; the flaps were secured around his calves with thongs. His square features, less flexible, were unchanged from when I had seen them last in El Paso del Norte on the way back from the Guerrero ranch. As always he appeared to wear no weapon.

"We have a hundred men," Whiteside told him. "You cannot move a party that size in the dark. They would trip over each other."

"One man alone has no one to trip over."

"Only himself. What will you do when you get there? It's a big mesa and you don't know where he will be."

"I will once he starts shooting."

"What then? Do you intend to place a hex upon him with that medicine bag you carry?"

"The bag is for the protection of my soul. For the protection of my body I use this." He reached behind his neck and produced a knife with a nine-inch blade, its handle bound with rawhide.

I said, "That's close work. Are you any good at it?"

"Ask Francisco and Carlos."

"How are you with that rifle?" Whiteside asked Ortiz.

The marshal had picked up his stick and resumed making marks in the earth. "A Henry is not a Creedmoor. Within its range I am adequate."

"Just so you're good enough to shoot this Indian son of a bitch if he cannot do all he claims."

Axtaca returned the knife to its sheath without another word. The animosity between the Aztec and the old campaigner was as thick as the woodsmoke in the air.

"Baronet took over the old Sherman spread," said the rancher. "The headquarters was just a dugout shack last time I was there."

"He has built a fine house with many rooms with good lumber from the Oscuros," Ortiz said.

"How do you know this?"

"I built it."

"Well, now, that's right handy." Whiteside was disgusted.

"I am a carpenter, *señor*. I am the son of a carpenter and if just one of my sons proves to be less worthless than I fear, he, too, will be a carpenter. You are a cattleman. *Señor* Murdock is a saloonkeeper. Miguel is a ranch foreman. We are none of us warriors, yet we have all made war and we are all still living. In the light of this I do not see cause to defend what each of us does when he is not fighting."

"Save it for Sunday. What's the layout?"

While we had been talking the marshal had drawn a floor plan in the dirt. Now he used the stick as a pointer. "It is a house a man might conceive whose conscience is troubled. This is a tower room of three stories, open on all sides, from which a man with good eyes may observe a rider approaching from a great distance. The windows on the ground floor have oak shutters two inches thick, with gun ports. All of the roofs are pitched steep, that none who is not part fly can hope to scale them. Of course there is no ground cover within rifle range of the house."

I said, "Is that all?"

"*Lo siento,* no. The basement is eight feet deep, lined with stones and mortar, and has many shelves and cabinets for the storage of provisions. The well is there. With only a small trapdoor to defend, a man in that dark hole might withstand a siege of many months."

Whiteside stared at him. "Didn't any of this make you curious?"

"The sheriff said he wished to secure the house against an Indian attack. I thought it was excessive."

"It shouldn't, but it always surprises me," I said. "The lengths some men will go to in order to stay out of jail."

"Even build one of his own." Axtaca eyed the plan gravely.

"It *is* a jail," Whiteside said. "Ain't it?"

We looked at him. His eyes were as bright as pennies.

Axtaca left camp twenty minutes later. Francisco and Carlos, unchanged from when I had last seen them at the Diamond Horn, wanted to go with him, but he rebuffed them in harsh Spanish, bundled his sorrel's hoofs in rags torn from his only other shirt, and rode off at a walk armed with only his knife and medicine bag. Whiteside had turned in by then, having dispatched a rider to the Slash W on an errand, and the entire encampment was settling in for the night. Men snored, spoke in low rumbling voices of past battles won and lost in and out of town, cleaned and loaded weapons, and scraped mud off their boots in the glow of dying fires. I poured myself a second cup of coffee and drained the pot's remaining contents into Ortiz's.

"Any trouble getting Whiteside to throw in with Guerrero's men?" I sat down beside him.

"Very little. When two men have been fighting as long as they, the thing they share is not so different from love. It was this way with my wife and me." He crossed himself and drank.

"You said you killed her."

"I took no pleasure in it. She pleaded with me to do it. I swore the day we married that I would deny her nothing."

"She asked you to kill her?"

"She said if I did not agree to do this thing she would

find a way to do it herself. I could not let her soul go to hell and so I agreed."

"Was she ill?"

"Her body was healthy. In here . . ." He touched his head and shook it.

I said nothing. The wood in the fire separated slowly into coals, and I thought the conversation was ended.

"It was in the church," he said then. "She knelt before the Virgin, and as she was praying I shot her once in the back of the head. She died in a state of grace."

"I'm sorry."

He moved one of his heavy shoulders. "I lost her long before that day. My sorrow is that we cannot be together in the next life. The bullet that spared her from hell has damned me."

"Did you confess to the padre?"

"No. If one is to be forgiven, he must first be repentant. I would do this thing again."

"The rumor around town is you found her with another man."

"That is the story I told at my trial. A jury of twelve men, husbands all, found me innocent of murder. And Serafina's torment is not spoken of in the saloons of San Sábado."

I drank the rest of my coffee in silence. I had ridden through thickets and mountain passes crammed with ice that were easier to penetrate than his tragedy.

At length I threw the wet grounds into the fire. "Earlier tonight you called Miguel Axtaca by his Christian name. Even Francisco and Carlos don't do that. How far do you go back with him? Spare me the peon humility," I said when he started to reply.

"*Sí.*" He raised and lowered his chin. His jowly profile was a blank cutout against the slightly lighter sky. "In truth we did not meet before Las Cruces, five days ago. However, I read his name many times in dispatches in the old days when we were on opposite sides, and I came to feel that I knew him then."

"Opposite sides of what?"

"The revolution against President Juárez. I was a colonel in his army."

"Ortiz, you're a damn liar."

"I do not lie about these things, *señor*."

"Not about that. I mean before, when you said you weren't a warrior. I'm wondering when you found time to practice carpentry."

"It is not what we do that makes us what we are, but what we feel. I have not known a day since I learned to think for myself when I did not run my palm along the grain of a piece of wood and feel the life that resides there. Death is nothing. What have you done when you have brought nothing to your fellow man?"

"With some men," I said, "there was nothing there to begin with."

"You are wrong, *Señor* Murdock. There is always something. When you destroy a man you take upon yourself the burden of never knowing what it might have been. When you have spent much of your life destroying men, the burden is sufficient to cause your own destruction."

"If you feel that way, why are you here instead of back in town finishing the harness shop?"

He breathed deeply and drank the rest of his coffee, which must have been ice-cold. "You ask that question of the wrong carpenter, *señor*."

Soon after that we rolled ourselves up in our blankets, and within minutes Ortiz was snoring. What dreams he dreamt I could not fathom.

# CHAPTER 21

There is an old Zuni legend, nearly as ancient as Creation itself, that maintains that when Father Sun made the world he dumped all the parts he had left over in New Mexico. The story makes sense when you see Chupader Mesa for the first time pouncing straight up out of the planed country east of Socorro City, fluted at its base and blunted at the top like a spent bullet, with the sun, no longer young and red-faced from the effort, hauling itself over the edge. Faced with such momentous physical evidence in support of a pagan belief, it was no wonder the early Spanish missionaries had made so little headway bringing the natives around to a faith in a tale of floods, apples, and shrubbery ablaze.

Rich as it was, I doubt the local Indian canon encompassed anything as strange as the party now approaching that geological non sequitur: one hundred men and change riding together but separated by their dress, loyalty, and philosophy into two distinct bands with a destination in common. Behind them trailed a pack train and, lurching along a good quarter-mile behind that, a small supply wagon new to the expedition since early that morning, its driver a man whose lost face said he had long ago abandoned his ties to life. His name, if it mattered, was Wendigo, and behind his seat rode death in a box measuring three feet by two.

"The sticks are old," Whiteside had explained when the wagon arrived. "They sweat in this heat and nobody but Wendigo will come near them. He lost his wife and two sons to the cholera last year. He don't care if he blows to pieces."

"Don't you have anything more stable?" I'd asked.

"Governor Wallace has placed an embargo on explosives and ammunition in quantity until the dust settles in Lincoln County. I tried old Mexico, but the lid is even tighter there on account of the revolution, I forget just which one. I have had to give up my mining aspirations for a spell. Not that them two holes in my southwest sixty ever coughed up anything shinier than a salamander."

The vaqueros from Don Segundo's Diamond Horn were a disciplined-looking lot, riding mustangs by and large with both hands on the reins, elbows out, backs as straight as the Springfield carbines and El Tigre Winchesters slung behind their shoulders. Their flat-brimmed hats were secured with strings ending in tassels and worn at an identical angle. It was clear that the White Lion of Chihuahua had not laid aside his military sensibilities when he had turned from fighting men to raising cattle. John Whiteside's cowhands looked almost slovenly by comparison, but they were armed as heavily and rode like men who did everything but defecate in the saddle. The one-armed rancher who led them wrapped the reins of his big black around his wrist and manipulated the horse with his knees.

There had been incidents. Breaking camp, a vaquero and a cowboy had disagreed over the ownership of a canteen, a knife had been produced, and a Mexican arm splintered when two other cowboys intervened; and in an epilogue, Francisco, who had apparently been placed in charge of Guerrero discipline in Miguel Axtaca's absence, slashed his quirt across the face of a Whiteside man on his way to reopen the argument with pistol drawn, laying the flesh open to the bone. The marshal of San Sábado, mounted also, broke up both fights by inserting his gray between the combatants, one hand resting on the butt of his Schofield. I remembered the stern father frightening a roomful of unruly children into paralysis by his presence alone on the day we met. It seemed that with each mile he progressed from his sleepy life in town, he lost another layer of Rosario Ortiz the fat part-time peace officer, paring down closer to the young Mexican Army lieutenant who had impressed Harlan Blackthorne so many years before.

Abbott fell first.

The callow cowhand who had challenged me at the edge of camp the night before was riding a few yards to my left and a little in front when he grunted and slid sideways out of his saddle. He grasped at the horn, but his fingers refused to close. For a second his left boot snagged in its stirrup. Then his momentum tugged it free and he fell hard on his shoulder and rolled over half onto his back, broken in the middle. All this took place before the report reached us, drawn so thin by distance it bent double. Near the north end of the mesa a scrap of tissuey smoke scudded across the crags.

*"Down!"* Whiteside's roar bounded off that rock wall. Most of us were off our mounts before the echo made it back, our long guns rattling out of their scabbards. I hauled the claybank over onto its side and was pleased to see it stayed put. For all his grousing about how much time he spent stringing fence, the old rancher still took pains to train his horses for combat.

The same wasn't true of the pack animals, whose death wails drifted our way as the wranglers cut their throats to make breastworks of their carcasses.

"It is Palo Duro all over again." Ortiz was down on one knee behind his supine gray with the barrel of his Henry resting across its ribs. "All day and all night we slaughter the horses. When Quanah returns and sees what we have done, it is his sickness at the sight that makes him surrender."

Patting the claybank's flank for courage—the animal's

or mine, it didn't matter which—I crawled on my belly over to where Abbott had fallen. After a minute I crawled back. Ortiz read the news on my face.

"His spine, *sí?*" He shrugged at my reaction. "From the way he fell."

"I said Jubilo slept with that Creedmoor."

A spout of dust erupted in front of my horse. It snorted and stirred, but I reached across to grasp its bit and it subsided. The sound of the shot followed. Somewhere among us a Winchester spoke back.

"Hold your fire, you damn idjit!" Whiteside. "You're just throwing away cartridges."

"I hope that sorrel of Axtaca's didn't put its foot wrong last night," I said.

"I think it did not, *señor*. Even if it did he would continue. He was the only soldier not of rank whose name appeared in the dispatches."

"Oh, Mama, I'm hit!" This from a point somewhere ahead. We heard the shot.

I said, "Right about now I'd settle for something a lot less showy, like a buffalo gun."

Something moved at the top of the mesa then. A human silhouette separated itself from the rock, craning high. More smoke blossomed, a series of ovals pushed in instantly by the wind and torn away. Then: *crack-crack-crack-crack-crack-crack*.

"That was no single-shot Remington," Ortiz said.

"That was a pistol," I said.

"Miguel did not have a pistol."

"Jubilo did."

"What does it mean?"

"One way to find out." I pointed the Deane-Adams at the sky and emptied the cylinder. The shots flopped around in the distance and expired.

In the silence that followed, the man atop the mesa stood

up the rest of the way, waving a rifle high over his head. Then he bent. Something fell from the rock. Fell and fell, turning in the air. A man. It struck the ground, bounced, and lay still. Again the man on top stood and waved the rifle.

A hundred feet in front of me, Francisco rose to his feet, tore off his sombrero, and slapped it at the sky. A shrill cry came from his throat, making all the hairs stand out from my body. In another moment the entire party of Mexican vaqueros and American cowboys was cheering.

"I liked Jubilo," I said.

Ortiz said, "If it was not he who killed your friend *Señor* Harper, he had a hand in it."

"He confessed to it. I can't help who I like."

"Frank Baronet has much to answer for."

We buried young Abbott where he fell, scratching a trench in the hard earth with what tools we had and covering him with rocks. Standing over the unmarked mound, John Whiteside removed his sombrero.

"Lord, we give you Jim Abbott, aged about twenty-two years. He pulled his own truck and sent home half his wages first of every month. Dick Lunghammer here says Jim told him his people made him study the piano, but none of us ever heard him play. I guess that's all about Jim."

Wedging the hat under the stump of his left arm, he extracted a small cylinder of oilcloth from inside the sweatband, jerked loose the tie with his teeth, and thumbed through a number of closely printed leaves folded inside. When he found the one he wanted he snapped it open and dropped the rest inside the crown. His harsh ramrod's voice rose as he read.

" 'If he smite him with an instrument of iron, so that he die, he is a murderer. The murderer shall surely be put to death.

"'And if he smite him with throwing a stone, wherewith he may die, and he die, he is a murderer. The murderer shall surely be put to death.

"'Or if he smite him with a hand weapon of wood, wherewith he may die, and he die, he is a murderer. The murderer shall surely be put to death.

"'The revenger of blood himself shall slay the murderer. When he meeteth him, he shall slay him.' Amen." He retrieved the oilcloth, returned it and the pages to the sweatband, and walked away, putting on the sombrero.

I watched Ortiz crossing himself. "I don't think that was your Testament."

"I am a good Christian, *señor,* or I was." He tugged on his slouch hat. "This does not mean I am blinded by my faith. The Holy Book is a gun with two calibers. One will suffice where the other falls short."

We mounted and rode. There were no further squabbles among our party.

The house stood nearly in the shadow of Chupader Mesa, a complicated arrangement of turrets, gables, and railed balconies, whitewashed blindingly in the relentless sun, a sharp contrast to the gray barn standing two hundred yards away with its slanted roof reaching almost to the ground. The sentry post Ortiz had described stretched a full story above the rest of the house and resembled nothing so much as a church tower minus its bell. There would be a rifleman crouching there to avoid silhouetting himself in the opening. There would be others as well, in the windows on the lower floors and in the loft of the barn. The grounds looked far too deserted for a working ranch in broad daylight. The shots from the mesa would have alerted the Baronets and their men long before the lookout had spotted us.

The loft opened up first, jets of flame spurting from the opening over the doors.

"Back!" Again Whiteside's bellow rang. The riders up front wheeled their mounts and galloped. A ragged volley answered from among our ranks, a delaying action while we regrouped. Whiteside passed me aboard his black, drew in, and stood up with the reins in his teeth, beckoning with his arm. The wagon jolted forward from away back.

"He does go forward until he has to back up, doesn't he?" I said to Ortiz.

"It is said that during your War Between the States he reported more casualties for every mile of ground gained than any other commander." The Mexican changed hands on his reins to adjust the bandolier over his left shoulder. "It is also said that he never lost a fight, though he was the only man left on his feet."

"I'm sure he put it just that way in his letters to the widows."

"If he could not lead he would not come. I think you suspected this when you sent me for him."

"I've never been one to stand in the way of a man who likes to ride up front," I said. "That's where the bullets are."

"Nor I, *señor*. And yet no man calls us coward, and you and I count four arms between us."

Whiteside intercepted the wagon and stepped out of leather to supervise the unloading of the dynamite crate. Moments later there was more shouting on his part. I cantered over.

"The fight's that way." I jerked a thumb over my shoulder.

The rancher was red-faced. "You tell him, jackass. I'm still deciding whether to send you home or tie you across a mule and point you toward that barn."

Wendigo, the mule skinner in charge of the wagon, stood with his hat in his hands. He had a beetled brow and black moustaches that folded like crow's wings over the entire lower half of his face. "Some caps got wet crossing the Pecos. You know the railroads won't ship that kind of freight. I had the box marked, but I forgot and taken it instead of one of the others."

"*Blasting* caps, goddamn it!" Whiteside waved one under my nose from the box standing open on the tailgate. It was green with mold and burst at the seam, leaking powder in damp clods. "We got a whole case, and not one of them fit to blow the pus out of a pimple. Dynamite's no good without them. You can set fire to it, Christ, *shoot* at it all day, and all you will get is a ringing in your ears. I wish to hell I could get just one of them to go off. I'd shove it up his ass and send him straight to China."

"There's a way," I said.

After he heard my proposition, Whiteside left me to it and busied himself deploying the men. Francisco translated his orders to the vaqueros. Ortiz, who had donated cartridges to the cause, watched me opening the ends of the sticks with my knife and poking the lead noses inside, leaving the brass primer ends exposed. The shooting from the barn had fallen off.

"You have done this before?"

"Couple of times. Someone is always going off and leaving the caps at home." I laid the finished sticks, dirty green and as long as Christmas candles but twice as big around, on the tailgate and selected a fresh one from the open end of the crate I was sitting on.

"It worked, *sí?*"

"Not even once."

"Mother of God." He crossed himself.

# CHAPTER 22

"**B**arn or house?" I was shoving the finished sticks into a burlap sack.

Ortiz said, "The barn. It is closer to us and commands the best view of the house. The man who takes it has carried the day."

"How is your throwing arm?"

"I have been known to hold my own at horseshoes. How is your marksmanship?"

"Better than my arm." I grasped his when he bent to pick up the sack. "Leave your horse behind. If we clean out the barn, whoever makes for it will have to move fast or get shot out of the saddle by that rifle in the tower. You're too fat."

His face looked tragic. "You are not a politician, *señor*." But he tethered his gray to a low piñon before lifting the sack.

Wendigo, eager to redeem himself for the incident of the blasting caps, climbed into the seat of the wagon and snicked the mules forward to provide cover. Ortiz rode sitting on the tailgate with the sack of dynamite cradled in his lap. I rode the claybank behind, dismounting as we drew within range of the barn and ground-hitching the horse. One of the repeaters in the loft splattered fire. Wendigo, unhitching the team, slapped both mules on the rump and sprinted for cover as they bolted. He didn't seem quite as ready to join his dead wife and children as White-side thought.

Ortiz hopped to the ground and together we lifted the back of the wagon and swung it sideways to the barn. A bullet splintered one of the top-bows near the Mexican's head.

"A man could get killed at this work," he said.

"Throw one in front of the doors." I rested the barrel of my Winchester across the seat. "On three."

Crouched on his heels, he selected a stick from the sack, counted, *"¡Uno, dos, tres!"* and sprang upright, bringing it over his head in a great loop. The stick spun end over end, catching the light on the brass butt of the .44 cartridge stuck in one end. When it landed and stopped rolling I sighted in on the brass. I tugged the trigger.

No explosion.

"Miss?" Ortíz, back in his crouch, stared at me.

"Let's hope." I levered in another shell and fired again. No explosion.

On the third try I swore I heard the bullet strike metal. The stick spun sideways and rolled to a stop at the base of the barn. I hung my head.

"The fourth time is lucky," Ortiz said. "It was as this when Serafina and I conceived Arturo."

I chambered and fired. The roar lifted the wagon's front wheels an inch off the ground, banging my elbow with the wooden seat. There was white light and a spray of smoke and dust and splinters. One of the big doors swept open and tore loose from its top hinge. It leaned drunkenly for a moment, then the bottom hinge gave and it fell headlong to the ground.

In the great ringing silence that followed, nothing happened. Then the repeater in the loft spoke. The wagon shuddered from the hits.

"Can you put one upstairs?" I asked Ortiz.

*"¡Uno, dos, tres!"*

I followed the stick's cartwheeling motion with the iron sights. Brass glinted just as it entered the square opening. I squeezed. Boards flew and the sky rained shingles. A cheer went up from the men surrounding the house and barn.

"Destroying buildings is much more fun than building them." Ortiz produced another stick. "Shall I throw this one in the same place?"

"Not just yet." There was movement inside the opening to the loft, which was no longer square now, canted left and beribboned with shreds of torn siding. A rifle barrel nosed its way out. I drew a bead.

"Hold your fire!" Whiteside.

I lowered the Winchester. A dirty white rag fluttered from the barrel in the barn.

"Throw it out!" called the rancher. "I have four dozen rifles trained on that hole, so mind what comes out with it."

The rifle emerged out of the shadows inside, attached to a hand and an arm in a pale sleeve. The sleeve was soaked clean through. Streaks of what had soaked it forked down the back of the hand and stained the weapon.

"Colt's revolving rifle," I said.

"Morgan Rood," corrected Ortiz. He was standing now with a fresh stick of dynamite in his hand, watching around the end of the wagon sheet. "I have not seen one in ten years, and with good reason. Perhaps he has shot his own hand."

The rifle dropped then, turning end over end before landing in the dust.

"How many are you?" Whiteside wanted to know.

The answer was barely audible.

"Three. One's in a bad way. I think Hatch is dead."

"Climb down and use the door. We're shooting at anything that moves fast."

This information was greeted with a feeble laugh.

Ortiz made a noise of revelation.

"I know this laughter," he said, when I looked at him. "It is changed, but still I know it."

Five minutes went by that could have passed for as many hours. At length something stirred inside the blasted-open doors at ground level. Another long space of time, and then all was motion.

It had to be one hell of an animal not to have bolted in the face of two explosions. Whatever had held it, it wasn't lack of spirit. The big American stud roan shot through the opening at full gallop, forcing its rider to duck his head to avoid the top of the door frame. In a flash I recognized the corduroy shooting jacket, the black plug hat with a feather in the band, the neat dark beard and big graceful handlebars, the brown jersey gloves with the fingers cut out; details noted in a lump and sorted out later. At the time there was no opportunity to sum them up, because the bloodstained hand that had surrendered the rifle now held a horse pistol and the muzzle was stuttering fire as fast as the hammer could be tipped back and released and tipped back again. He rode straight for the wagon, his mouth gaped in a rebel yell, his torso swiveling to right and left as he sprayed lead in every direction.

I centered my sights on the thickest part of his body, but by the time I fired my first shot, every rifle and carbine in Socorro County was barking. Dust flew off the corduroy jacket in spouts, each hit rocking him in the saddle, and still he came, pumping his trigger finger and directing his fire this way and that. At the end he was so close I heard his hammer snapping on empty shells, for he had spent the cylinder in less time than it took to count the shots. Then the roan threw up its head and turned back upon itself, breaking in half, and horse and rider wheeled over, struck the ground, and slid for several yards, dragging a plume of dust.

Again Whiteside called for a cease-fire.

The roan struggled to rise, snorting and blowing dust out of its nostrils. Its hindquarters, no longer connected to the rest of the animal except by meat and muscle, lay motionless.

*"¡Cuidado, señor!"* cried Ortiz. But I stepped around the end of the wagon and walked up to where the man lay trapped under his squirming horse. He had lost his hat. Rivulets of sweat had etched tributaries through the skin of dust on his face. He was bleeding in several places. A shard of bone, startlingly white and polished smooth, protruded from a tear below his left elbow. He was supporting himself on his right hand, which still held the empty revolver.

"Are you Ross Baronet?" I asked.

"Kill my horse, mister."

"Are you Ross Baronet?"

"Yes! Please, mister. His back's broken."

"Did you kill Dave and Vespa Spooner?"

"Who?" His face was a mask of pain. Sweat was stinging his eyes. He didn't know me from his raid on the Apache Princess. I was just something between him and the light.

I repeated the names. "In Lincoln County," I prompted.

"Yes."

"What?"

"Yes! I killed them both. Frank said—Please, mister! He's just a poor dumb animal."

"What did Frank say? Did he send you to kill them?"

His arm bent then and he turned his face into the crook of his elbow. He was breathing as heavily as the horse. Sobbing.

I exhaled, placed the muzzle of the Winchester against the hollow behind the roan's left ear, and fired. Its head dropped. Air shuddered out of its lungs.

Cradling the carbine along my forearm, I bent to take hold of Ross under the arms. He was pinned solidly. I straightened to call for assistance. Something thudded against the horse's carcass near the shoulder. The report, coming from the house, was deep and hoarse. I racked in a cartridge and returned fire, backing up as I worked the lever and trigger. Other rifles rattled from the circle around the house and barn and I sprinted back behind the wagon.

"That was no light repeater," Ortiz said.

"I was wondering what became of Ross's Springfield." I looked at Ross. He was lying as still as the expired roan.

"Dead, probably," said the Mexican, reading my thoughts. "He will remain in that condition this time, I think. I intend to miss him. A man is not responsible for his choice of brothers."

"Forget him. He was a woman-killer." I paused in the midst of reloading to meet his tragic gaze. "Sorry."

He shrugged. "*Está bien.* I shall meet up with him in hell and we shall relive the Battle of Chupader Mesa over tequila."

I finished reloading. "You can shoot at the house all day from this distance without hitting anyone inside. I'm going to try to make it to the loft. Can you reach the porch from here with that dynamite?"

"How close need one come, *señor?* It is dynamite."

"I'll require as much cover as you can lay down. Hitting a moving target with a long-range gun like the Springfield is tricky, and he'll have to reload between shots. Even so, he has the range."

"I have faith in your marksmanship."

It was a curious thing to say. As I was turning his way, he made two long strides, grasped the horn of my saddle, and mounted the claybank. He moved fast for a fat man. For any man. Gathering the reins and thrusting his Henry into the scabbard, he looked down at me. "My arm is tired from throwing, *señor.* It is your turn." And before I could respond he raked his spurs hard. The claybank whinnied and shot forward, grazing my shoulder as it passed the end of the wagon.

I recovered myself in time to send a stream of bullets

in the direction of the tower containing the man with the Springfield. The men of the Slash W and the Diamond Horn took my lead and stepped up their fire at the house. Ortiz, hunched low over the claybank's neck, bounded the horse over the corpse and carcass on the ground and galloped directly inside the barn without slowing. A volley came at him from windows on the first and second story of the house, but they were lighter arms than the Springfield and fell short. No shot came from the tower, which was beginning to look as if it had been out in the hail for a year. Pieces of siding hung down like tattered guidons and daylight showed through holes as big as a man's fist.

In less time than I would have thought possible for one of his bulk, Ortiz appeared in the opening to the loft, waving his Henry. Lowering himself to one knee and bracing an elbow against the shattered frame, he snugged the butt of the repeater into his shoulder and waited.

I leaned the Winchester against the wagon, selected a stick from the burlap sack at my feet, made sure the cartridge I'd inserted was secure, drew it back behind my head, and hurled it in the direction of the gingerbread porch, following through with my body. It pinwheeled in a long arc, steeper than I'd intended, and landed in the short feathergrass ten feet this side of the wooden steps.

The Mexican showed no disappointment. He took his time aiming. The Henry coughed. Dust spurted, the stick jerked and rolled a foot closer to the house. As soon as it stopped he fired a second time. It went up, taking a piece of the porch with it. I waited until debris stopped falling, then threw another. The trajectory this time was flatter and longer. It thumped on the boards and skidded to a stop against the threshold. When he hit the primer, on his third attempt, the porch flew apart in a cloud of shattered planks and amputated pillars. Again the men outside the house cheered.

The third stick came to rest near the foundation to the left of the ragged hole where the front door had been. Ortiz was sighting in on it when a shout came from inside.

"Don't shoot! We're coming out!"

Some fifty guns posted on that side of the house leveled on the opening. Inside, the first grasping fingers of flame clambered up the curtain to one of the windows and scratched at the casing.

One by one, obeying Whiteside's shouted instructions, seven men stepped down from the ruins of the porch, weaponless, hands high. Their faces and clothing were smeared with burnt powder. Two of them were limping, their trousers slicked with blood. Another two supported a third man between them with his chin on his chest, half his head apparently blown away.

There was someone missing, and with Ortiz in possession of the barn there was only one other place he could be. I checked the load in the Deane-Adams five-shot and contemplated the distance I had to cross to reach the house, burning steadily now and spilling gouts of black smoke out through the bullet-shattered panes.

## CHAPTER 23

I cast around for the pair of mules Wendigo had unhitched from the wagon. Mules are smarter than horses and rarely stray far from men and the comfort and security they represent. I spotted them, still joined by the double harness, grazing in the feathergrass a hundred yards upwind of the noise and smoke. I found a coil of rope in the wagon and strolled their way, taking my time to avoid spooking them. They were skittish, but not nearly as much as untrained horses would be under those circumstances, and the breeching prevented them from employing most of their best evasions. I threw the loop over the head of the near animal, jerked it tight before it could duck out, and set my heels. After the standard test of wills, and with strokes and whispered words I never used with any woman, I got them calm enough to let me walk them to the wagon.

The cowboys and vaqueros had meanwhile taken charge of the desperadoes from the house, inspected them for arms, and begun trussing them for transportation to Socorro City or a serviceable cottonwood, whichever was closest. All seemed peaceful, and I was wondering if I weren't being overcautious when the man with the Springfield opened fire once again from somewhere inside the burning house, scattering the men who had ventured too near in their eagerness to claim the prisoners and sparking a crackle of return fire from the posse. And now I knew beyond doubt the identity of the rifleman.

I pointed the mules at the house and straddled one. Grasping its collar and reaching across to grip the other, I slipped down between them. It was a close fit and they didn't want me there; their restless whickers rumbled like growls from their ribs to mine. But nervous was good. I raised my feet, filled my lungs, emptied them in a high-pitched yell, and sank my teeth into the neck of the animal to my right. I tasted salt and blood. The mule brayed and they bolted, jolting my arms nearly out of their sockets. Hoofs drummed, the wind lashed my face, cold then hot as we neared the flames. Smoke stung my eyes but I didn't dare close them. If I calculated wrong they could wire me back to Montana in a Western Union envelope.

Through the water I saw the ruins of the porch come up and the instant before the mules turned to avoid a collision I let go. Splinters of pain shot up from the soles of my feet when I struck down. My knees buckled and I nearly fell in

the terrified animals' path, but recovered myself on the
run and bounded up and over the shambles of broken lumber, drawing the Deane-Adams in midair and landing on
my chest and elbows inside what used to be the front door.

For a second I lay there, floor-burned and slightly
stunned, the revolver clamped in front of me between both
palms. Then I rolled to the side. It was a time-tested tac-
tic, but wasted. I was alone in the room.

It was a large parlor, and even through the blue haze I
could see that it was elegantly furnished, with a Brussels
carpet and overstuffed chairs and a massive old breakfront
in the corner, eight feet tall and filled with blue china.
Flames were snaffling at the printed wallpaper, blistering
and blackening and peeling it as I watched and pouncing
across the ceiling with a suckling roar. Orange coals the
size of acorns dropped to the carpet and burned black
holes on contact.

Ortiz had provided me with a description of the floor
plan, and climbing to my feet I started toward the center
of the house and the staircase leading to the tower. On the
way there I spotted a corner of the carpet turned back. In
the section of floor thus exposed I saw a square outline.

*With only a small trapdoor to defend, a man in that
dark hole might withstand a siege of many months.*

Crouching on my heels to avoid silhouetting myself in
the opening, I inserted my fingers in the crack between the
boards and lifted.

Something scuffed the carpet behind me. I turned with
the revolver. White light, brighter than any of the dynamite blasts, filled my skull. I felt myself tipping, threw out
a hand to brace myself, and touched space. Warm moist
blackness broke my fall.

A train was champing at the platform, maintaining a head
of steam.

The long hoarse chugs carried me back from wherever I'd been, to gray cold darkness and the beginning of an ache I knew from old experience would be with me for days and possibly weeks. Chiefly it was in my head, a living, breathing pain that bulged out of time with the uneven chugs and the smaller, sharper pains in my knees and elbows. The headache belonged to the blow that had taken me away from wherever I was now. I had acquired the others when I fell or was pushed to the hard smooth stony surface on which I lay. I placed a palm against it. Not stone; too even and, I sensed, not as hard. Not man-made, either; not even enough for that. Clay?

I turned onto my side. Through the murk I made out the faint gleam of light on glass, rows of curved glass objects stacked one on top of another, as on shelves. Jars? I began to know something.

Again I turned. I was on my back now, looking up at stripes of light some eight feet above me. I was disappointed in Ortiz. A good carpenter should be able to fit floorboards closer than that. As I was looking, a fall of glowing cinders showered down through the cracks and I threw a forearm across my eyes. The sparks stung my hand and face like hornets. The fire was still blazing. I couldn't have been out more than a few minutes.

The chugging continued, accompanied by a stream of dust and fresh cinders from above. Something blocked the light through several cracks. I remembered the big breakfront in the parlor then. Someone was dragging it across the floor in the direction of the trapdoor. I thought I knew who.

The pain in my head bulged when I sat up, blinding me for a second. I reached up, touched the sticky mass behind my right ear, and snatched my hand away when a fresh bolt shot straight to the top of my skull. I put the hand down to

push myself up and felt something I'd missed without even
knowing it was gone. The cool solid patient shape of the
Deane-Adams made me want to cry out. It must have
dropped from my hand through the opening before Baronet could catch it. It was the only thing that had gone
wrong with the trap he'd laid; but when a gambler's streak
turns bad it doesn't stop.

I curled my fingers around the butt, rose to my knees,
breathed, swallowed bile, and stood up. The basement did
a slow Virginia reel and rocked to a standstill. I was ready
to help move furniture.

A wooden ladder bolted to the stone wall led to the trapdoor. I holstered the pistol, climbed, and pushed with my
hand. It didn't give. I went up another rung and leaned
my shoulder against it. It was latched. I might have shot my
way through. I might have cupped my hands around my
mouth and shouted for freedom. Either way I would lose
my only advantage. I climbed back down.

The man struggling with the breakfront paused to
wheeze. I recognized Frank Baronet's voice. By now the
ground floor would be full of smoke. Soon the boards would
catch fire and collapse upon me, followed by the walls and
roof. The trap had felt warm against my palm.

I drew the five-shot and looked up, calculating. Before
my peacekeeping days I had spent a winter between round-
ups freighting iron stoves for a cartage company based in
St. Louis. My partner had a bad back and refused to pull
against a weight, explaining that pushing was easier and
not as likely to cause injury. His back wasn't nearly as bad
as the sheriff's, not having a bullet in it. I waited until the
breakfront began moving again, noting the angle by the
pattern of falling dust and the shadow between the boards,
and paced off the distance to the back. I pointed the revolver straight up and emptied the cylinder, spreading my

shots in a loose pattern. Smoky light poked down through the holes.

There was a short space of silence. Then something thudded the floor, hard enough to shake loose a pound of old dirt and dry rot.

I reloaded from the loops on my belt, stepped beneath the trapdoor, and placed all five bullets in a tight group in one corner. The result was a ragged, fist-size hole. Once again I shook out the empty shells and replaced them with fresh cartridges, the last in my possession. I scaled the ladder, inserted my fingers in the hole, and pushed hard with the heel of my hand. The door gave a little. I mounted the last rung, placed my shoulder against the door and one foot against the nearest joist, and heaved upward. A moment's resistance, then the agonized shriek of tearing wood, and suddenly I was breathing the hot smoky air of freedom.

The walls were totally engulfed. Part of the ceiling was gone, having fallen into a pile of flaming debris that blocked the exit. The carpet, which Baronet had rucked back in order to move the breakfront, was burning, and threads of flame were blistering the veneer on that massive piece. Coughing and covering my nose and mouth with one hand, I stepped behind the breakfront. A smear of blood stained the floor and dribbled out into the hall leading to the back of the house. I followed it, gun in hand.

The drops grew faint and hard to distinguish against the brown leaf pattern on the hall runner. Then I came across a gout of it on the bottom step of the central staircase, as if he had paused there, hemorrhaging and supporting himself on the newel post. The trail continued up the stairs.

I climbed the first flight, flattened against the banister with the revolver pointed up the well. At the top was a landing and a steep flight of naked wooden steps ending in another trapdoor. This one hung open, releasing a flood of sunlight down the narrow passage from the open sentry tower atop the house. The blood trail led squarely up the middle.

My head throbbed. It seemed to be saying, *Not again*.

A second-floor hallway ran north and south from the landing. I peered in both directions. Through the roiling smoke it seemed to me I saw a faint smear where someone had mopped a fresh spill from the oiled floor in front of the first door south of the staircase.

Keeping the Deane-Adams in front of me, I backed toward the steep flight of steps and climbed them backward. They creaked loudly.

The door in the hallway flew open. I took an instant to identify Frank Baronet lunging across the threshold, his big Remington rolling-block pistol trained up the stairs. I fired twice into the thickest part of him. He stumbled, faltered, raised the pistol again. I fired again. He retreated into the room. The door closed.

I descended the steps. In the hallway I spread-eagled against the wall and stretched a hand toward the doorknob. The latch hadn't caught. The door opened at a touch. When no shots came from inside I pivoted around and through the opening, clasping the revolver in front of me at arm's length.

It was a bedroom, paneled in dark grainy oak and containing a bed with a six-foot carved headboard, a marble washstand, and a dropleaf secretary and matching cherrywood chair. Baronet sat in the chair with his back to the desk and his long legs splayed out in front of him, one arm curled over the back of the chair to prevent him from sliding. He was in his vest and shirtsleeves, just as he was when he dealt faro at the Orient, but his collar and cravat were missing and his white shirt was crosshatched with soot. His right hand rested in his lap with the single-shot pistol in it. A .45-70 Springfield rifle leaned in the corner next to the bed. It looked like the same one Ross Baronet had carried into the Apache Princess the night of the robbery.

"'Satan's Sixgun.'" The sheriff laughed wheezily. "That piece doesn't even hold six."

His black hair, dank with sweat, hung in his eyes. His handlebars needed waxing. They drooped at the ends. The front of his person from the notch of his vest to the knees of his striped trousers was stained dark.

"Right now it's holding two," I said. "You should have shot me when you had the upper hand, instead of pistol-whipping me and dumping me into the cellar."

"We burn wife-stealers in this county."

It wasn't a subject for that part of the conversation. "You're all used up, Frank."

"I am not alone. There is no leaving this house now, for you or me. I designed it for dying in." A spasm shot through him, twisting his face into a rictus and tightening his grip on the back of the chair until his knuckles showed yellow. When it passed he was visibly weaker. Oxygen came hard. "I have got to ask why you carried it this far, Murdock. It wasn't because Ross tried to raid your place in San Sábado. Was it Colleen?"

"I didn't know about you and Colleen until a week ago."

"What, then? Did I use you so hard that day in Socorro City?"

"I've been used harder, and by worse than you," I said. "You should have let Dave and Vespa Spooner alone up in Lincoln. They made no difference to the war, and they got you killed."

He cast back. His brain was dying and thinking was a slow painful process. "That was months ago. What were the Spooners to you?"

"To me, nothing. Dave's father saved Judge Blackthorn's hide during the war with Mexico. The Judge asked me to come down here and pay his debt."

"I don't credit it. They were not worth all this bother. That's why I sent Ross to close their eyes."

That settled the point. I wondered why I felt no victory.

"Why did she shoot you?" I asked.

"The Spooner woman? She never. I don't believe I ever heard her speak."

"I mean Colleen Bower. Why did she shoot you?"

"What did she tell you?"

"She said you beat her up."

He smiled. It was as glassy-looking as his eyes. I doubted he could still see me. Seeing was becoming difficult for me as well. The air was thick with smoke and growing denser by the minute.

"Did you credit it?" he asked.

"I'm asking you."

The smile broadened. He raised the big pistol.

"Don't, Frank." I was still holding the Deane-Adams.

He tried to cock it. His thumb kept slipping off the hammer. He uncurled his other arm from the back of the chair to steady the gun while he tried again.

I cocked the revolver. "Don't."

He got the hammer back and locked. He raised the pistol. I shot him. He lost his brace and slid to the floor. Turned over on his side. I stepped forward and leaned down over him. "Why did she shoot you?"

"You still have a bullet." He pointed the Remington at me. I kicked it out of his grasp. The impact when it landed jarred loose the hammer. A bullet pierced the ceiling.

"Why did she shoot you, Frank?"

His lips were moving. I bent almost double, straining to hear the words. His mouth remained open when he stopped talking. His eyes did too.

When I failed to find a pulse anywhere on him I turned to the business of getting out. I got as far as the landing, where flames barred the stairs. I went back into the room, leaped over Baronet's body, pried at the window, found it painted shut, and kicked out the panes. Fire was chewing at the siding, but I climbed through the opening and stood on the sill, hanging on to the frame with one hand. I realized then I was still holding the Deane-Adams and jammed it into its holster. The drop was thirty feet to hard earth with nothing to slow me down. A pair of broken legs awaited me at the bottom, at the very least; a broken neck was more likely. Behind me the room was growing hot. I braced myself and pushed off.

Something swished past my ears and froze in front of my eyes, that familiar hang you looked for the instant before you leaned back with everything you had—but that was when you were on the other end. Instinctively I grabbed for it, but I wasn't fast enough and the loop closed under my arms and constricted my chest. My instinct then was to claw at the rope. Instead I hooked a foot inside the windowsill and turned to grasp the frame once again. As I did I looked up at the man on the other end of the rope. He was standing with his legs spread on the roof of the sentry tower, a thick silhouette against the sky in plain peasant dress without a hat.

"Miguel Axtaca?"

"This is my name," said the Aztec.

"How the hell did you get up there?"

"The same way we are going down." He fed me some slack for my descent and took another dally around the peak of the roof for his own.

# CHAPTER 24

The bell in the church tower was swinging, calling the faithful of San Sábado to Mass. I was scrubbed and shaved and my scrapes and bruises had been seen to, but I wasn't dressed for worship, having packed everything but my trail clothes. On my way down the main street I encountered Rosario Ortiz coming out the front door of the Mare's Nest, where he took sourdough and coffee every morning with Eille MacNutt in what was surely one of the most inexplicable friendships on record; what that pair had in common was anyone's guess. He had on his sombrero and his church suit, too tight in the chest and smelling of moth powder and cedar. He was one man who looked better in work clothes, be they stained overalls or cavalry kit and weapons. When he saw me he inclined his head.

"*Buenos días, Señor* Murdock. It is a fine morning to greet the Lord, is it not?"

"I suppose. I'll be glad enough to get up in the Bitterroots and greet some snow. I have had my fill of sunshine and adobe."

"You are leaving today?"

"I should have left last week, but I'm punishing Judge Blackthorne. His reply when I wired him about what happened at the Baronet ranch was less than polite."

"I think I see. He has guilt that the burden of justice fell to you, who had no personal stake in the matter, instead of to him."

"Maybe," I said. "If I live to be forty-one I'll never know what goes on under his hat."

"What do you intend to do with your interest in the Apache Princess?"

"That's what I'm on my way to discuss with Mrs. Bower." I stuck out my hand. "*Vaya con dios,* Marshal. I am coming away with that much Spanish at least."

He took it. For a moment he seemed on the edge of saying something. Then he ducked his head again and hastened across the street to join the crowd drifting toward the church. We were as ill at ease in each other's company as a man and woman who had become lovers for one night, only to awaken the next morning to find they had nothing in common but the passion of the moment. I never saw or heard from him again. If he's dead I hope he made it to heaven despite his convictions to the contrary.

At the alley I paused to raise my hat to a gaggle of widows hauling a train of dust with their black hems. They looked neither left nor right, turning the corner in a body on their way to church; identical in their weeds, anonymous behind their veils, and as formidable after their fashion as the combined and righteous might of the riders of the Diamond Horn and the Slash W, who had parted company upon delivering their prisoners to Lew Wallace in Santa Fe. By now they would have reverted to their old habits, rustling each other's cattle and trading shots across the oldest and bloodiest border in the western hemisphere. My last sight of Miguel Axtaca, after he had risked his life to save mine at the Baronet spread, had been of his broad unadorned back riding south between Francisco and Carlos at the head of Don Segundo's loyal band of vaqueros. His kind is gone now, if indeed it ever existed outside the early Spanish accounts of the Mexican conquest; even the dust of their bones has settled over the caves and deserts of Chihuahua and Sonora, indistinguishable from the sand. Don Segundo del Guerrero is no less dead now, his ranch divided, the lions he loved to hunt gone the way of the

Aztec and the Spanish grandee. We will not see their autocratic like.

John Whiteside died in Cuba. Against the advice of his friends, including Theodore Roosevelt, he had insisted at the age of seventy-four upon leading his own regiment of hand-picked cowboys into battle with the Spaniards, only to succumb to yellow fever in the stinking hold of a troopship in Havana Harbor without ever having set foot on the island. His body was brought back to New Mexico by some of his men for burial. You can't miss the monument. It's the tallest thing in Socorro County west of Chupader Mesa.

Judge Blackthorne, in forced retirement at the time and diverting his still-prodigious energies into articles for *Galaxy* and *Harper's Weekly,* wrote that the "Cuban debacle" may yet justify its expense by providing a dumping ground for "apoplectic grandfathers who have read Homer and taken him too much to heart." Then he, too, in excellent health and at the peak of his mental abilities, expired. A number of sanguinary accounts of his years on the bench were published in the years afterward, running about half for and half against. History hasn't yet decided what to make of him, and neither, by God, have I.

Colleen Bower answered the door at *Señora* Castillo's boardinghouse wearing a plain black dress cinched cruelly at the waist and covering everything from just below her chin to the shiny caps of her patent-leather shoes. Her hair was pinned up in back and she wore no paint, the first time I had seen her that way at that hour of the morning. She looked neither young nor old. *Timeless* was the word that came to mind. I removed my hat.

"I haven't much time, Page. I am late for church as it is."

"I won't keep you long. I just came to say good-bye. Where is the old witch?"

"She went on ahead. You're really leaving?" She closed the door behind me and led the way into the Victorian/

Porfiristan parlor. We remained standing, facing each other across the earthen floor.

I nodded. "I'm taking the short route by way of El Paso and catching the train from there. General Crook has Geronimo cornered in Arizona, so it should be safe."

"What about the Princess?"

"I'm selling out my third for what I paid. If you're interested, you can wire the money to Judge Blackthorne at the federal courthouse in Helena. It was his money to begin with. If you like you can advertise that for a little while you were partners with the Iron Jurist."

"I think I won't. It would only frighten away business. As it happens, however, I am interested. Eille MacNutt has asked to buy in. I was planning to discuss it with you, but I guess now I won't have to."

"So that's what you talked about during those long buggy rides," I said. "I wondered."

"He has a sound head for business, whatever else you may think of him. With the sheriff dead and county politics in a tangle, Wallace is considering a declaration of martial law. It will be an excellent time to acquire property, as the values are sure to be depressed. When the order is lifted and the immigrants start streaming in, the scramble will be on for every available acre. Eille has the capital. I am the draw. Are you sure you don't want to stay? There will be more than money enough for three."

"I'd just waste it on food and shelter." I reached inside my hat. "Eille now, is it?"

"You have a filthy mind, Page. Perhaps law work is best for you after all."

I gave her the slip of paper I'd removed from the sweatband. "That's the address of Junior Harper's mother in Chicago. I found it in his wallet. You can send his share of the profits to her."

"Does she know?"

"Yes. I wired her from Socorro City and made arrangements to ship his body north. I'm sure if you offer to buy
out his interest she'll go along. She is no saloonkeeper."

She folded the paper and tucked it inside her sleeve. "I'm
sorry about Junior, Page."

"Are you?"

"Of course. I liked Junior. If it were not for him—"

"If it weren't for him you'd still be married to Frank
Baronet and required by law to share your property with
him. As his widow you're free and clear, with the added
advantage of a little gentlemanly sympathy on the part of
the men who challenge your board. That's why you're
dressed in black. You wore the ring Baronet gave you
to keep them at arm's length. Now you wear mourning to
keep them off guard. And you owe it all to Junior."

"I told you he was drunk! He asked me to marry him,
and when he found out Frank was my husband he went
crazy. I tried to stop him."

"Did you tell him Frank beat you?"

"He wanted to know why I left. I told him the truth."

"You told him what you told me, that you shot Frank
out of fear and pain and ran away because you thought
you'd killed him. Junior was a romantic. The story made
him angry and filled his head with notions of chivalry. He
was drunk, but he sobered up on the trail. He'd have turned
back then if you hadn't mentioned that beating.

"But he was only part of it," I went on. "You knew Junior was no match for the sheriff and Jubilo both. You sent
him to his death, knowing I'd go after his killers. The beating story worked as well with me as it had with Junior,
putting just the right edge on it. Hell, you had an army on
your side. It was one hand you couldn't lose."

"You saw the scar."

"You got it in a fight with a jealous whore."

Her skin went transparent. I could see the network of

bones and muscles in her face. "Did Frank tell you that?" Her voice was metallic.

"Jubilo did. Frank told me why you shot him."

She said nothing.

"They were his very last words," I said. "'I don't go partners with anyone.' Quite an epitaph."

"It doesn't prove anything."

"There's nothing to prove. The only crime you committed was shooting a sheriff in the back, and he's dead by my hand. The only crime anyone can arrest you for in this life, that is. If I were you, I'd look out for Marshal Ortiz in the next. He thinks he's damned too, and all he did was put a bullet in his wife's brain when she begged him to."

"I was his draw."

I barely heard her. I asked her to repeat it.

She did. Her voice rose. "I drew his customers to the Orient. There are eleven saloons in Socorro City, and a faro table in each one. Why did they come there if not to play cards with a pretty woman? I herded them in, I fleeced them, and I sent them back out grinning to earn more wages so they could come back. I thought when I married Frank he would deal me in for half. That was my mistake; I should have made certain. He laughed when I asked him about it. Laughed in my face and showed me his back."

"Never a wise choice where you're concerned."

She tried to claw my face. I caught her wrists and forced them down to her sides. She struggled fiercely—there was pure sinew under the slender sheathing of her arms and legs, and she was filled with hate—then stopped. I watched her drawing composure from deep inside, like a glacier generating a fresh layer of ice to heal a scar. It would be the same way she handled a bad turn of cards. After a minute I let go. She smiled as she did when a player approached her table and turned toward the door.

"I wish you'd reconsider your decision to leave." She

lifted a small black felt hat from the ledge of the coatrack, an elaborate piece in carved mahogany complete with a built-in umbrella stand and a mirror framed in giltwood, standing next to the plain plank door. If *Señora* Castillo's theories on decorating ever caught on back East, there would be no stopping them. "How many years can a man have to wear the badge, and what does he have when he is through? You are already an old man in your work."

"I still prefer the odds."

She fixed the hat to her hair with a pin long enough to picket a horse and gathered up her reticule. The pocket pistol inside made it hang crooked when she slid the loop over her wrist. "It's a pity. I like you, Page. We could have enjoyed each other."

"You liked Junior."

She glared briefly at my reflection in the mirror. Then she lowered her veil over an expression of trackless purity and went out to join the other widows.

Read on for a preview of

# CAPE
# HELL

· LOREN D. ESTLEMAN ·

*Available from Tom Doherty Associates*
*in May 2016*

A FORGE BOOK

# CHAPTER ONE

**H**alfway back to civilization, Lefty Dugan began to smell.

It was my own fault, partly; I'd stopped on the north bank of the Milk River like some tenderheel fresh out of Boston instead of crossing and pitching camp on the other side. I was worn down to my ankles, and the sorry buckskin I was riding sprouted roots on the spot and refused to swim. The pack horse was game enough; either that, or it was too old to care if it was lugging a dead man or a month's worth of Arbuckle's. But it couldn't carry two, especially when one was as limp as a sack of stove-bolts and just as heavy. I was getting on myself and in no mood to argue, so I unpacked my bedroll.

A gully-washer square out of Genesis soaked my slicker clear through and swelled the river overnight. I rode three days upstream before I found a place to ford, by which time even the plucky pack horse was breathing through its mouth. In Chinook I hired a buckboard and put in to the mercantile for salt to pack the carcass, but the pirate who owned the store mistook me for Vanderbilt, and then the Swede who ran the livery refused to refund the deposit I'd made on the wagon. So I buried Lefty in the shadow of the Bearpaws and rode away from five hundred cartwheel dollars on a mount I should have shot and left to feed what the locals call Montana swallows: magpies, buzzards, and carrion crows.

The thing was, I'd liked Lefty. We'd ridden together

for Ford Harper before herding cattle lost its charm, and he was always good for the latest joke from the bawdy houses in St. Louis; back then he wasn't Lefty, just plain Tom. Then he took a part-time job in the off-season blasting a tunnel through the Bitterroots for the Northern Pacific, and incidentally two fingers off his right hand.

Drunk, he was a different man. He'd had a bellyful of Old Rocking Chair when he stuck up a mail train outside Butte and was still on the same extended drunk when he drew down on me not six miles away from the spot. I aimed low, but the fool fell on his face and took the slug through the top of his skull.

Making friends has seldom worked to my advantage. They always seem to wind up on the other side of my best interests.

It was a filthy shame. Judge Blackthorne had a rule against letting his deputies claim rewards—something about keeping the body count inside respectable limits—but made an exception in some cases in return for past loyalty and present reliability, and I was one. It served me right for not allowing for Lefty's unsteady condition when I tried for his kneecap instead of his hat rack. The money was the same, vertical or horizontal.

To cut my losses, I lopped off his mutilated right hand so I could at least claim the pittance the U.S. Marshal's office paid for delivering fugitives from federal justice. I packed it in my last half-pound of bacon, making do for breakfast with a scrawny prairie hen I shot east of Sulphur Springs. I picked gristle out of my teeth for fifty miles.

The money from Washington would almost cover what I'd spent to feed that bag of hay I was using for transportation. After I sold it back to the rancher I'd bought it from just outside Helena, I was a nickel to the good. I rode the pack horse in town until it rolled over and died. I wished I'd known the beast when it was a two-year-old, and that's as much good as I've ever had to say about anything with four legs that didn't bark and fetch birds.

I spent the nickel and a lot more in Chicago Joe's Saloon, picked a fight with the faro dealer—won that one—and another with the city marshal—lost that one—and would have slept out my time in peace if the Judge himself hadn't come down personally to spring me.

"You'd better still be alive," he greeted me from the other side of the bars. "This establishment doesn't give refunds for bailing out damaged goods."

I pushed back my hat to take him in. He had on his judicial robes, but the sober official black only heightened his resemblance to Lucifer in a children's book illustration. I think he tacked the tearsheet up beside his shaving mirror so he could get the chin-whiskers just right. His dentures were in place. They'd been carved from the keyboard of a piano abandoned along the Oregon Trail, and he wore the uncomfortable things only when required by the dignity of the office. It was unlike him to go anywhere straight from session without stopping to change, especially the hoosegow. I was in for either a promotion or the sack.

"How's Ed?" I asked. The city marshal's name was Edgar Whitsunday, but only part of his first name ever made it off the door of his office. He'd been named after a dead poet, but being illiterate he sloughed off the accusation whenever it arose. He was a Pentecostal, and amused his acquaintances with his imperfect memorization of Scripture as drilled into him by a spinster aunt: I think my favorite was "I am the excrement of the Lord."

"He's two teeth short of a full house," Blackthorne said. "I told his dentist to bill Grover Cleveland."

"That's extravagant. What did you do with the rest of the piano?"

He scowled. The Judge had a sense of his own humor,

but no one else's. "You realize I could declare court in session right here and find you in contempt."

"And what, put me in jail?" I looked at my swollen right hand. "At least I used my fists. Ed took the top off my head with the butt of his ten-gauge."

"You should be grateful he didn't use the other end." He sighed down to his belt buckle; it was fashioned from a medal of valor. Just what he'd done to earn it, I never knew. Even scraping forty years off his hide I couldn't picture him scaling a stockade or leading a charge up any but Capitol Hill. Probably he'd helped deliver the Democratic vote in Baltimore. "You cost me more trouble than half the men who ride for me. A wise man would let you rot."

"You make rotting sound bad." I slid my hat back down over my eyes. "Find somewhere else to distribute your largesse. This ticky cot is the closest thing I've had to a hotel bed since I rode out after Lefty."

"You can't refuse bail. Marshal Whitsunday needs this cell. The Montana Stock-Growers Association is in town, and you know as well as I those carpetbaggers will drink the place dry and shoot it to pieces."

"Good. I was getting lonesome."

"Shake a leg, Deputy. You're needed."

That made me sit up and push back my hat. He wouldn't admit needing a drink of water in the desert.

He said, "I'm short-handed. Jack Sweeney, your immediate superior, went over my head to Washington and commandeered all my best men to bring the rest of Sitting Bull's band back from Canada to face justice for Custer."

"They gave that bloody dandy justice at the Little Big Horn nine years ago. What's the rush?"

"Sweeney's contract runs out in September, and there's a Democrat in the White House." He held up a key ring the size of Tom Thumb's head and stuck one in the lock.

"Go back to your hotel, clean up, and report to my chambers at six sharp."

"Since when do you adjourn before dark?"

"I swung the gavel on the Bohannen Brothers at four. You've got forty-five minutes to clean up and shave. You look like the Wild Man of Borneo and smell like a pile of uncured hides."

"How'd you convict the Bohannens without my testimony? I brought them in."

"They tried to break jail and killed the captain of the guard. That bought them fifty feet of good North Carolina hemp without your help."

"Bill Greene's dead?"

"I'm sorry. I didn't know you were close."

"He owed me ten dollars on the Fitzgerald fight. I don't guess he mentioned me in his will."

His big silver watch popped open and snapped shut. "Forty-four minutes. If I catch so much as a whiff of stallion sweat in my chambers, I'll fine you twenty-five dollars for contempt of court."

"Collect it from the stallion."

"That's twenty-five dollars you owe the United States."

I swung my feet to the floor, stood, wrestled for balance, and found it with my fists around the bars. "What's so urgent? Did we declare war on Mexico again?"

He looked as grim as ever he had during damning evidence. "What have you heard?"